On Ravens & Riddles

From the Shelves

of the Noktern

Sean W. Bagan

On Ravens & Riddles
From the Shelves of the Noktern

This book is a work of fiction. While many landmarks have real-world equivalents, names, characters, places, and incidents are either the product of the author's imagination or are used fictitiously. Any resemblance to actual persons, events, or locales is coincidental.

ISBN: 979-8-9929084-0-4

First edition, May 2025

Cover art done by Alexandre P.
Manufactured in the United States of America

*Be proud of your courage to face shadows in
search of the light.*

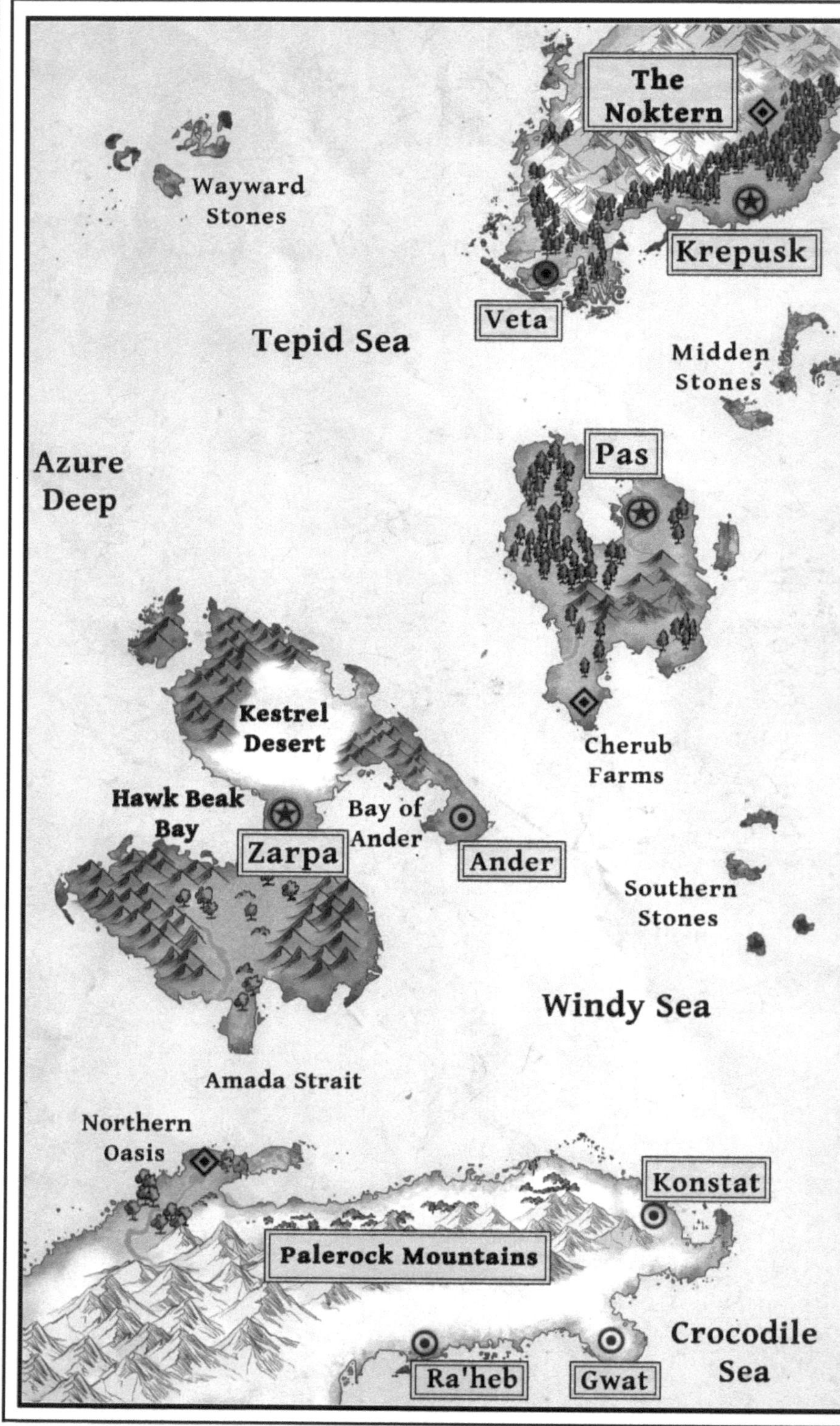

The Noktern
Krepusk
Veta
Wayward Stones
Tepid Sea
Midden Stones
Azure Deep
Pas
Kestrel Desert
Cherub Farms
Hawk Beak Bay
Bay of Ander
Zarpa
Ander
Southern Stones
Windy Sea
Amada Strait
Northern Oasis
Konstat
Palerock Mountains
Crocodile Sea
Ra'heb
Gwat

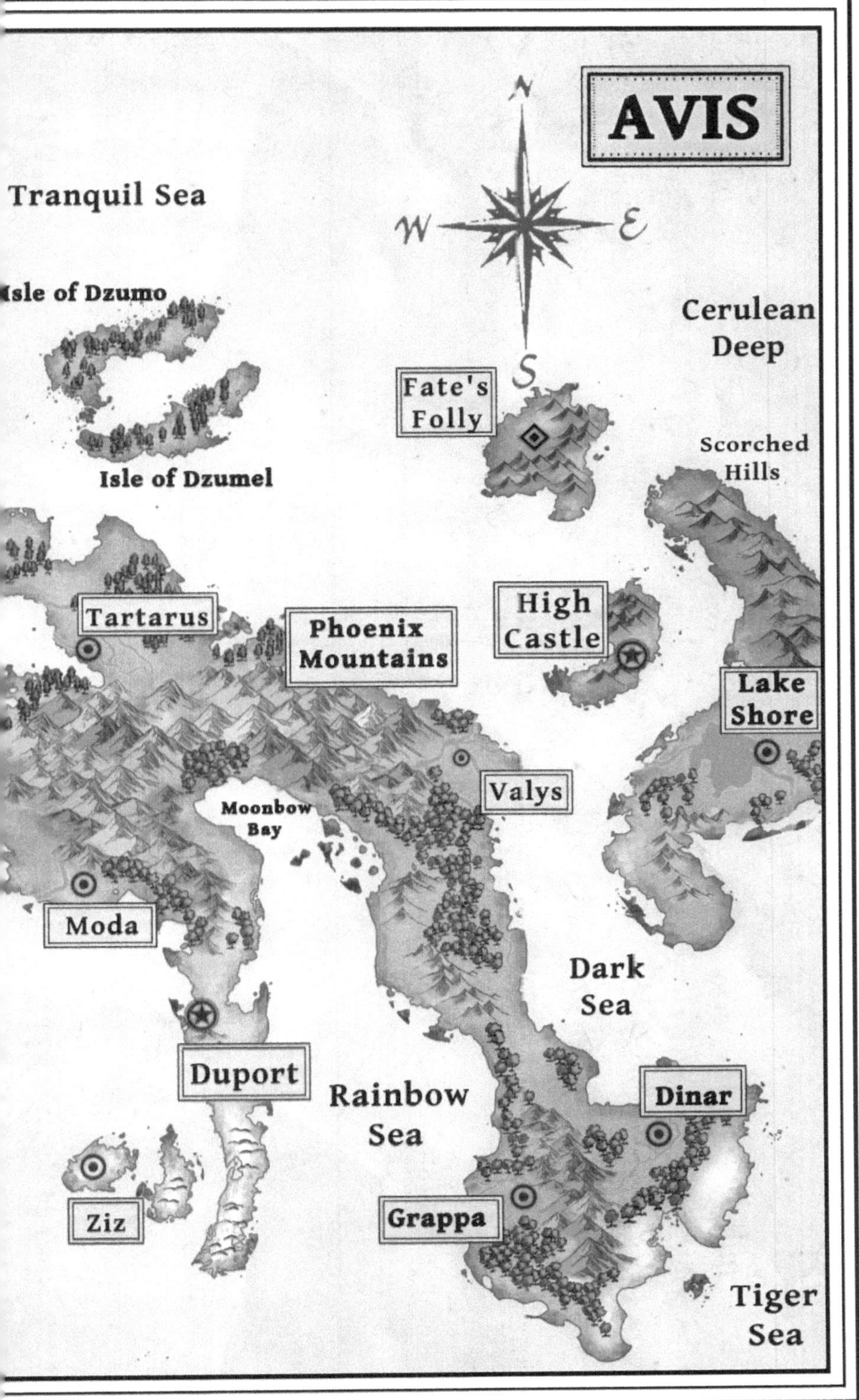

AVIS
Tranquil Sea
Cerulean Deep
Isle of Dzumo
Isle of Dzumel
Fate's Folly
Scorched Hills
Tartarus
Phoenix Mountains
High Castle
Lake Shore
Valys
Moonbow Bay
Moda
Dark Sea
Duport
Dinar
Rainbow Sea
Ziz
Grappa
Tiger Sea

Prologue

From: Tvanor@Noktern.no.org

Sent: 01 June 15:07

To: Admin@Noktern.no.org

Subject: Operation Innocence

Around 15:00, outposts on our western border picked up dozens of hypersonic missiles en route to major cities across the world. We knew the Lupine had been working on this technology, but our intel suggested that it couldn't be ready for another century. Traveling at Mach 22, the first will arrive here in roughly 30 minutes. We expect the other nations will retaliate, and all on the surface have prepared for the worst.

Primanor is still with us for now, though he had one of his bouts of hysteria. He has come down and is resting comfortably. I told him he should be at the Noktern, but he refused to listen. I was reading to him when the alarms sounded. It may have been the medications, but he seemed to be having one of his visions and he insisted this prophecy get to the Noktern. I took down whatever I could, and while it doesn't make much sense to me, maybe one of the scholars will be able to figure it out. I am attaching my notes to this email.

In these final moments, I'd like to thank all of you at the Noktern for the sacrifices that you have made these past few months. While I have not always seen eye to eye with the current administration, I do hope that the members of Parliament will consider my proposals for the new world. I trust that you will do what is best for the persistence and well-being of our kind.

While the launch of Operation Innocence has come much earlier than anticipated, I am confident that the Noktern is ready. This will be no small undertaking. I only ask that the scholars of the Noktern try to create a better world when everything we've built is gone. To my fellow patriots, I wish you the best of luck. Stay strong, and farewell.

With courage and honor,
Tvanor

Download Attachment

Chapter One
GIDEON

In the heart of Moda, where dull concrete streets stretched in every direction, a small patch of green clung to life. The trees of Jay Park seemed out of place in the urban sprawl, dwarfed by the high-rises that loomed on all sides. Morning light crept slowly over the city, the sun just beginning to rise over the distant Phoenix Mountains. When the city's granite clock tower tolled the hour, its deep chime echoed across the skyline. Nestled in his usual spot beneath one of the alders, Gideon flinched, his wings tensing at the sound. Every fifteen minutes it rang out; he'd heard it his entire life, but still, he never got used to it.

"Seven chimes." Lowering his book to his lap, Gideon watched as the sky erupted with vibrant hues. Waves of crimson, cyan, pale pink, and shimmering gold streaked across the morning air as the Finches took flight. Some wove through the alleys below, slipping between storefronts as shopkeepers unlocked their doors. Others soared toward the factories, massive edifices built to fuel the surging demand of Duport, the Finch capital.

Gideon hated the factories too, though not nearly as much as the clock tower. The wretched thing existed solely to remind the Finches of their duty to work. But the factories came close. The smoke that billowed from the stacks soaked into everything: the Finches' clothing, feathers, even the concrete walls and streets reeked of industry. It was inescapable.

Drawing in a deep breath, Gideon savored the smell of freshly-cut grass of the park, the only thing that could mask the stench of the city. Content, he settled onto his normal bench, its tired oak slats supported by intricate wrought iron legs. His wings draped across the back of the bench, the tips of his sapphire feathers barely grazing the ground. Absent-mindedly, he ran one hand through the clumps of red and yellow tulips beside him, the hum of insects tickling his ears over the sound of lapping water from the fountain that sat before him.

He had visited Fox Fountain almost daily since its inauguration. Salvaged from the depths of Moonbow Bay, it was the largest relic recovered from an ancient Sapien city submerged beneath the waves. Strange artifacts often washed ashore east of the city, prompting the Merchant Council to hire Croc divers to search the bay. They spent moons scouring the seabed, eventually uncovering ruins that stretched for miles. Most had crumbled with time, but a few treasures were recovered and now rest in museums across the Finch cities.

Lost in his own thoughts, Gideon heard the chime of the quarter hour and he put his hands to his ears. The only flaw he could ever find with this otherwise perfect spot was that there was little to drown out the ringing of the clock tower. Neither the fountain nor the bees came close to the deafening roar that the bells pounded out.

Once they subsided, Gideon exhaled, smoothing out the creases in his breeches and tunic. Satisfied, he laced his fingers around his book and returned to the story, a folktale from the ancient world about a puppet brought to life by his creator's wish. He had just reached the chapter where the wooden boy was tricked into burying his gold, believing it would sprout into a tree of riches.

"Happens here all the time," Gideon muffled, flipping the page. "The swindling, not the growing of magic trees," he added to no one in particular. The Finches were always chasing coin, and plenty were willing to do whatever it took to get ahead. Even his father had dabbled in shady dealings when the price was right.

As he read on, Gideon traced the illustration of the fox who had tricked the wooden boy. His gaze flicked between the book and the fountain ahead. At its center, a cluster of bronze figures stood, their surfaces corroded by age and the relentless saltwater. A fox sat among them, watching over two boys, one alive, one dead. Gideon had always seen the fox as a faithful companion to the living boy, but now, studying the lifeless figure at its feet, he wondered if there was something more cunning, more sinister behind its eyes.

His thoughts scattered as the half-hour bell rang. The sharp chime sent a jolt through him, each *ding* drilling deeper than the last. It grew louder every time, as did his distaste for the clock tower.

"One more bell before I've gotta go," he sighed. There was some relief in the thought, but also the daunting reality that he'd soon have to be at his father's shop. It was only a quick jaunt from the park, but his father strictly demanded that the shop be open exactly on the hour, one hour after the sunlight crested Mount Isadore.

"What a life," he huffed.

His brief moments in the park were his only snippets of peace. The shade of the trees, the hush of nature; this was where he belonged. Out beyond the grassy knoll, Moda churned his stomach. He couldn't help but feel that life had more to offer.

Ding dong. The third bell chimed.

"Of course," he sighed.

Packing the book away in his satchel, he rose and headed off toward the shop district. Turning back to the fountain, he spoke directly to the fox statue. "I'll see you tomorrow." His voice was warm with familiarity, though he was glad no one was around to hear him talking to a statue.

A skip in his stride, he thought he might actually be at the shop on time for once. He had no love for work, but avoiding another lecture from his father was motivation enough. His father always gave him a hard time if he was even a minute late. Unfortunately, *only* a minute late would have been a blessing by Gideon's standards.

"It's not my fault, really," Gideon mused. Some distraction or another always managed to monopolize his time. Sometimes he got lost in a chapter and couldn't bear to close his book. Other times, the scent of Wydah's bakery held him hostage, especially when she set her famous orange tarts out to cool on the window sill.

"To be fair..." he began aloud, only to catch the disapproving look of a passing orange-feathered Finch. He cleared his throat and dropped his voice to a whisper. "Wydah can only get fresh oranges from Zarpa every few weeks. So really, it'd be foolish not to stop." There was nothing quite like sitting by the café window, enveloped in the scent of citrus zest and freshly baked bread. In those moments, it was almost perfect.

On Ravens & Riddles

Craning his neck, Gideon caught sight of the face of the clocktower. "Two blocks and a few minutes to spare." He smiled wide with a gentle nod.

Then a booming voice rose from the sky above.

"Hey, Gid!"

"Oh no." It was a lighthearted, though half-pained murmur. He didn't even have to look up; there was only one person in Moda who would bother tracking him down.

Sighing, Gideon turned and looked up just in time to see Cas hurtling toward him. The sunlight caught the distinct crimson and chocolate-brown pattern of his feathers, making them gleam like rubies.

Cas's powerful wings carved through the air, each beat propelling him forward; Gideon braced himself. As expected, Cas barreled into him, almost knocking Gideon off his feet; he would have if Cas hadn't grasped him tightly enough to keep them both upright.

"How ya doin', buddy?"

"I've been better," Gideon wheezed, managing a laugh despite the vice-like grip around his ribs.

Cas had the energy of a Hawk and the strength to match. If it weren't for his red plumage, Gideon might have mistaken him for one outright. Everything about him screamed Hawk: the raw power, the barely restrained aggression, the way he turned even the simplest interactions into full-contact sports. His biceps alone were three times the size of Gideon's, and his legs were beastly. Gideon was sure that Cas could probably choke one of the giant horned goats native to the Phoenix Mountains using only his thighs.

"Cas!" Gideon gasped for air. "You're hurting me."

"Oops. Sorry, Gid." He let go and the air rushed back into Gideon's lungs. "The old man already giving you a hard time?"

"Well," he stammered, his breathing still somewhat haggard. "I should be on time, but I really have to get going. It was nice to see you, though." Gideon tried to set off, but no sooner had he taken a step, Cas threw his arm around his shoulder.

"Aw, c'mon Gid," Cas said in a playfully somber tone. "I was only foolin' around."

Ding dong. The hour chime tolled.

"Son of a-" Gideon exhaled, his shoulders sinking in defeat. For most Finches, a minute or two late was nothing. But for *him*? It was just another excuse for his father to complain. To him, a minute might as well have been an hour.

He could almost hear his father's words now.

Better three hours too soon, than a minute late.

At the last toll of the bells, Cas glanced down and caught the disappointment in Gideon's eyes. "Aw, sorry Gid." There was remorse in his voice. "I didn't make you late, did I?"

Gideon let out a short sigh. "It's alright Cas. I probably would have been late anyway." It wasn't true, but he didn't have the heart to be mad at Cas. His friend could be a bit of a brute, but he was never malicious.

The boys had met a few years ago at Moda's only school, *The Gouldian Establishment,* named after the city's founder, Poe P. Gouldian. Education in the Finchlands didn't come cheap, and only the fledglings of merchants could typically afford to attend. The curriculum was designed with one purpose: to mold them into the next generation of business owners. Avian history, mathematics, science, economics. Everything they needed to manage the wealth and trade that kept Moda thriving.

Prosperity was, after all, the city's life-blood.

Gideon, however, had never quite fit in. He kept to himself, avoiding the other Finches as best he could, preferring the quiet company of his books.

Cas, on the other hand, was a boisterous boy who wanted to be in everyone's business. On the school grounds, he would constantly be in the air doing somersaults and maneuvers to show off his skills, and loved to be the center of attention. Many of the other Finches found Cas obnoxious; they'd give him a few half-hearted laughs before moving on, never really taking him seriously. But that never seemed to bother Cas.

One day, during their allotted break time, Gideon had tucked himself away in a secluded corner of the courtyard, hidden behind an overgrown rosebush. He had just turned the page when Cas appeared out of nowhere, snatching the book from his hands.

"What's this?" Cas flipped the book open, squinting at the pages. "There's no pictures. And what are these scratch marks? Can you even read this?"

Gideon shot up, nose nearly touching Cas's as he reached for the book. "Give it back!"

Cas grinned, holding it high above his head, well out of reach. "It's in another language or something," he snorted. One of Cas's more astute observations.

Cas let out an exaggerated sigh before snapping the book shut and placing it gently into Gideon's outstretched hands. "Alright, Gid. But only 'cause you said please." He snickered as Gideon clutched the book to his chest and returned to his bench.

Lingering, Cas scratched the back of his neck and hummed a short tune to himself, but Gideon paid him little mind. "So, what are you reading exactly?"

Gideon's eyes shot up in frustration. "Why do you care?"

Cas folded his arms over his chest and rocked on his feet. "I dunno." He shrugged with a coy air. "Just wondering, I guess."

Still annoyed, Gideon couldn't shake the odd, fledgling-like quality to Cas's behavior. He was surprised that Cas was still there, let alone wanted to know anything about an ancient storybook. Part of him wanted to tell Cas to take off, but seeing him rocking back and forth that way had softened Gideon. Even today, he couldn't explain why, but he found himself explaining the epic. He told Cas of the Sapien fledglings who learned all sorts of magic and grew up to battle evil sorcerers. He spoke of the goblins, ghosts, trolls, and friendly giants. At some point during Gideon's retelling, Cas roosted on the bench next to him, balancing on the balls of his feet, the occasional flap of his wings to support himself.

Gideon tried to explain that magic wasn't real, even in the ancient times. Like the authors of Avis, the preavian species had also written grand works of fiction. Gideon spoke of the subject for the remainder of the break, Cas hanging on every word. Gideon had barely even noticed that the clock tower had rung the quarter hour twice while they spoke, making them both late.

On Ravens & Riddles

The unlikely pair had been best friends ever since.

As ever, Gideon still thought of Cas as a dope.

A dope with good intentions.

But at least he could say he had a friend. Looking back, Gideon realized that Cas was probably lonely too. There was a vibrancy to Cas that Gideon lacked. He channeled his energy in ways that made him endearing to some, disagreeable to others. But for all their differences, they had managed to find one another, and somehow, their friendship worked.

Cas's arm was still slung around Gideon's shoulder as the pair walked toward the shop. Gideon tried to match his stride, though at their pace, it had taken almost ten more minutes to reach the storefront. Along the way, Cas rambled about his mother's business. Something about employees not showing up—Gideon didn't catch all of it. Cas talked a lot, and his stories often bounced all over the place; Gideon only ever really half listened. Still, he didn't mind. It was good for Cas to have someone to talk to.

Arriving at the shop, Gideon drew in a deep breath, bracing himself for today's chastising. *Ding.* The quarter bell chime, a portent of his father's disappointment. *Dong.* Through the glass door, Gideon saw his father, Erasmus Finch behind the wooden counter. *Ding.* Trembling slightly, Gideon's hand hovered over the handle, but he hesitated. *Dong.* In that moment, Gideon realized that there was one thing in this city he hated more than the infernal clock tower. *Ding.* Having to face the constant disappointment of Moda's famous clockmaker. *Dong.*

Chapter Two

Socorra

Fluttering at the edge of the market square, Socorra's wings stirred up a hefty cloud of loose dirt. She made her way through the eerily quiet bazaar, an unusual stillness hanging in the air. Wooden stalls that should have been bustling with activity stood deserted, their wares gone and windows boarded shut. With the Litha Moon just weeks away, the streets should have been alive with Hawks preparing for the estival festivities, but today, only a handful of Avians drifted through the square. Undeterred, Socorra headed toward the blacksmith's tent.

"Socorra!" The smith's voice rang out before Socorra's hand found the linen flap, her voice sharp and clear above the rhythmic clash of her hammer against the anvil. "I've been expecting you."

"How'd you know it was me?" The tent flap fell behind her, blocking any breeze from reaching the boiling interior of the smithy.

"Heard you broke your spear." The smith raised an eyebrow, revealing deep creases in her forehead. "I figured you'd be coming round."

"The blade's come loose, that's all." Socorra shrugged.

Hepha let her hammer fall to the ground. "That's what happens with these old pieces." Grabbing a towel from a table off to the side, she rubbed the oil and grime from the dark skin of her hands and arms as she approached the hunter. Finished, she unfurled the towel and gently patted the sweat that pooled in droplets on her closely-shaven head. "I know you love this spear, but I wish you'd let me make you a new one."

"No thank you," she answered firmly.

"Alright, alright." The old Hawk shook her head. "Give it here."

Socorra relinquished the spear, hesitating to release her grip. She loathed giving it up, feeling naked without the weapon's weight in her hands. She trusted no one with it except for Hepha who was, by all accounts, the best and most renowned blacksmith in all of Avis and the major supplier of armaments for the Hawks.

Running a calloused hand over the blade, Hepha tested the integrity of the fasteners. "Tell you what, I've been doing some reading on adhesive techniques. Give me a couple of hours and hopefully you won't have this problem…*again*!" She accentuated the last word with a playful scowl, returning back to her anvil.

No matter how long Hepha needed, Socorra would wait; she wasn't going anywhere without it. Wrapping her wings loosely around one of the central beams, she leaned back against the sturdy wood, folding her arms tightly across her chest. Closing her eyes, she tried to meditate, but the heat stung at the exposed skin of her arms and neck, sweat pooling everywhere.

After a few restless minutes, Socorra couldn't stand to be in the oppressive heat any longer.

"I'll just be outside."

Hepha didn't respond, lost in her work.

Extricating herself from the sweltering tent, Socorra walked down the street and took a look at some of the vendors' wares, never venturing too far from Hepha's shop.

Finding an ornate hunting knife, she picked it up to examine it, running her fingers over the intricately carved bone handle.

"Please!" Socorra heard the despondent plea from the next tent over. "I'm looking for my brother. I've been all over Avis, but no one can tell me anything."

Leaning back, Socorra caught sight of muddied white wings, the otherwise pristine feathers coated with a layer of dirt. Travelers from the other tribes were rare in Zarpa, but their arrival often brought news of the goings-on in Avis. She listened intently to the exchange as a small crowd started to grow. They threw out rumors of disappearances, not just of the Dove's brother, but of several Finch businesses that had also been mysteriously abandoned, seemingly overnight. Closer to home, whispers had spread about a Hawk ambassador to the Crow Tribe who hadn't contacted the Elder Council in over two weeks. The air in Zarpa buzzed with speculation, each tale adding to the unease.

While Socorra found these tales unnerving, she tried to shake them off as nothing more than coincidence. She wasn't one to allow rumors of misgivings to stop her from doing what she loved most, hunting.

✻   ✻   ✻

Stretching her arms and wings, Socorra woke with a fervent yawn. The room was quiet; a quick glance-over told her that Kyte was already up. Not that it surprised her; she knew exactly where to find him. Throwing on a clean blue tunic and a previously worn pair of breeches, she descended from the second floor with a few flaps of her wings to soften the fall.

Throwing open the front door, she took in the beauty of the waning darkness, the scent of licorice sweeping over her, the anise fields lush in the late-spring air. The odor was pervasive, but Socorra loved it. The dew still clung to the white blossoms which gave the air a robustly sweet quality. She closed her eyes and inhaled deeply, feeling awake and rejuvenated.

With a few quick strides, Socorra launched herself into the sky. Somersaulting through the air, she stretched her limbs before gently landing on the red terracotta roof, folding her wings behind her as she nestled herself next to Kyte. He sat quietly, his gaze fixed on the horizon, waiting for her as always.

Laying her head on his shoulder, she let out a soft sigh of contentment. Kyte glanced down at her, the faintest smirk tugging at his angular jaw.

"Good morning," he whispered

She let her eyes lilt up, her cheek sinking further into the crook of his neck.

"Good morning," she murmured back, allowing her mind to wander in the peace of the moment.

Kyte nudged her with his shoulder. "What're you laughing about over there?"

Her smirk widened as she nuzzled his cheek with her nose. "I was thinking about the day I almost killed you," she teased, her voice playful. "Our first hunt together. Remember?"

"How could I forget?" He shook his head playfully. "Which part of that day were you thinking about exactly? When you put the spear to my throat?"

"You scared me half to death!" she interrupted, bursting into laughter as she gave him a gentle shrug.

"Or when you punched me in the face and gave me my crooked nose?" With a chuckle, Kyte grabbed her by the shoulders and pulled her into a tight hug.

"You deserved it, and you know it." She tried to wriggle free, laughing as he grasped her more tightly.

"I'll admit, it was a bad idea to try and kiss you after your first fox kill." He held her stare, his eyes full of mischief. He leaned in and pressed a quick, teasing kiss to her lips. "But breaking my nose? That was just uncalled for."

"I didn't even know you!" Socorra shot back, her giggling betraying any real sense of indignation.

"And look at us now." He laid his chin gently atop her head; the scratch of his stubble sent tingles running down her spine. "I guess sometimes you just know." He ducked in to give her another kiss, the rough skin of his hands rubbing gingerly at the nape of her neck. Letting his fingers linger a moment in her copper hair, he finally pulled back from her. "Are you ready to go?"

She met his gaze, her smile soft but certain. "I'm ready."

As the sun peeked over the horizon, Socorra and Kyte set out, their wings slicing through the crisp morning air in unison. They had done this countless times before, hundreds, perhaps thousands of hunts together. But after thirteen years, the exact number hardly seemed to matter.

Members of the Hawk Tribe rarely hunted alone, but partnerships seldom lasted more than a year or two. Hawks were not known for forming deep, enduring bonds, whether as hunters or as companions. Socorra and Kyte were the exception. Over the years, she had never met another Hawk who stirred her spirit like Kyte did, and she couldn't imagine hunting with anyone else.

Flying low over the brush, the grassland passed beneath them; neither said a single word. They had grown comfortable with their silence. There was no need to force idle chatter, but today, Socorra would have given anything for some conversation. What she'd heard in the market the day before rattled her. She was normally fearless and would revel at the thought of danger, but on this trip, the image of the Dove searching for his brother gnawed at the back of her mind. She couldn't quite explain why, but her hunter's instinct told her to be especially guarded. Still, she kept silent, not wanting to let her own fears disrupt their time together.

By early afternoon, the pair spotted a deer while flying over the expanse of the Great Plains. Large game was scarce these days near the Hawk capital. Circling high above, they tracked its movements, waiting patiently for the right moment to strike.

It was Kyte's turn to lead. With a subtle nod, he veered southward, angling for a prime position to attack. His spear gleamed in the sunlight as he dipped lower, signaling to Socorra that it was time to act. She tightened her grip on her own spear, her wings tucked tightly at her sides as she dove, angled to cut off the animal's retreat.

As Socorra began her descent, a sinking feeling gripped her. Her body tensed, the hair on her arms standing on end. She hesitated mid-dive, scanning the open plains below. There was a line of dark clouds on the horizon rolling ominously closer, but beside that, nothing seemed out of the ordinary.

She shook her head, brushing off the unease.

Refocusing on the hunt, Socorra dipped forward, picking up speed as the wind whistled in her ears. But as she raised her head to track Kyte's movements, her heart stopped.

There!

A faint blur in her peripheral vision, barely noticeable but unmistakably moving with violent intent. Fear clawed at her chest as she tried to call out to Kyte. The warning caught in her throat, drowned by the rush of wind.

She was too late.

The phantom struck with explosive force, knocking Kyte from the sky. He crashed to the ground, skidding across the dirt as his spear slipped from his grasp and dust rose in a choking cloud around him.

"Kyte!" Her voice broke as she jolted her wings to a stop. Hovering, she twisted in every direction, scanning the ground for any sign of his attacker. But there was nothing, no one. Her heart pounded in her chest as panic threatened to take hold. Redoubling her efforts, she pitched herself forward, cutting through the air in a desperate dive. The world around her went blurry, every thought consumed by the sight of Kyte crumpled on the ground.

Landing hard on the earth, she crashed and tumbled, but that didn't stop her. She picked herself up to her knees and glanced around at Kyte behind her. His chest rose in shallow breaths; Socorra was relieved, but not enough to chase away the dread that gripped her.

"Kyte," she whispered, her voice trembling. She stretched out her arms, ready to gather him up, to hold him, to protect him.

Only a hair's breadth between them, Socorra caught another flicker from the corner of her eye. She stopped short, but the specter was already upon her. Before she could react, it slammed into her, the sharp bite of steel cutting through the flesh of her arm. Her scream tore through the plains as it felled her to the ground.

Cupping her wound, she dropped her spear. Blood seeped from the gash, pain searing through her arm. She lifted her head and braced herself for another attack.

What is that thing?

Her mind raced.

Where did it come from? Where did it go?

Fear and fury surged through her. The pair had faced countless dangers over the years, but this felt different. There was no identifiable enemy, no beast nor Avian that she could pinpoint. This shadow, this specter that couldn't be tracked; how many of them even were there?

Rising to her knees, Socorra picked up her spear and cradled it between her arms, blood seeping down the shaft as she reapplied pressure. She scanned the surrounding area again, her eyes flicking between patches of trees and the empty expanse of grass, but aside from them, there was no sign that any creature had been there.

Still gripping her injury, Socorra crawled to Kyte's side, using her good elbow for leverage. Each movement sent a new wave of agony up her arm. The seconds dragged on, each stretching like an eternity.

Finally reaching where he had fallen, she rolled Kyte onto his back with an effusive grunt. The exertion sent radiating pain through her shoulder; she tamped down the pain. Her breath caught as she looked down at him, her heart hammering in her chest.

"Kyte?" No answer. "Kyte?!" She squawked louder. "Please say something!" He was still, as if in a deep sleep. She searched him over, but he didn't seem to have any serious wounds, just a few scrapes and bruises.

Lightning flashed to the north, the roar of thunder barreling over the countryside. A deep panic coursed through her. The elders hadn't predicted a storm, but she didn't dwell on the weather. All she could think of was how to get Kyte home, but she knew it was a futile effort. If she couldn't wake him, there was no way that she'd be able to carry him in her state. She thought to stay with him, but that would be deadly for them both. It would take her almost two hours to fly back to Zarpa.

Can I even make it?

She wasn't sure, but she had to try. After every close call the pair ever had, she wasn't about to give up. Hot tears streaked down her cheeks, the weight of her decision bearing down on her. She would fly back to Zarpa and request–

No, demand!

–that search parties be sent. She would plead her case to the Elder Council if she had to. The Hawks would find Kyte; she had no doubt. But an icy fear gnawed at her.

What if it comes back?

She couldn't leave him out in the open with some horror waiting in the lurch. She would have to hide him.

Her gaze darted across the landscape, searching desperately for any form of cover. He'd be too easily seen in the tall grass; whatever was hunting them would easily find him. Instead, she found a small outcropping of dried bushes and tangled weeds off to the right. It wasn't much, but at least it offered some cover.

She let go of her arm and slid her hand into Kyte's. Bracing her feet, she pulled with all her strength; he barely budged. Biting back a scream, pain tore through her, her muscles burning. With a few shallow breaths, she tried again, this time twisting at the collar of his tunic, but her hand slipped. She fell backward letting out a guttural wail, the agony unbearable. It was hopeless. The bushes were so close, only twenty feet away. But given her condition, they may as well have been on the other side of Avis.

"Please." Cradling his head, tears streamed down her face. "Please wake up."

Her voice cracked with each word, but he wouldn't answer. The stillness of his chest mocked her desperate pleas. Her grip loosened, and her spear slipped from her hand, landing softly beside him. She placed it carefully at his side. "May it protect you while I can't."

Leaning into him, she pressed her lips to his forehead. "I'll get you home," she whispered. "We'll be back to the hunt in no time."

Swallowing her sadness, she picked herself off the ground and steeled herself, wincing as the wound seared with a fresh wave of pain. She had no time to grieve, no time to falter. A few beats of her wings carried her into the air, leaving him alone in the brush.

She'd only made it a few miles before she was deep within the tempest, the wind howling louder the further she flew along. The storm's violent gusts battered her wings. Pockets of lightning illuminated the landscape; the roiling thunder shook her off balance, threatening to tear her out of the sky. Her feathers were heavy with rain and blood, dragging her down. Each beat of her wings took all her strength.

Her breath came in shallow gasps, and her vision blurred from exhaustion and pain. Every muscle in her body burned with effort. For a fleeting moment, she longed to give in, to fold in her wings and sink to the ground.

"Kyte…"

With a visceral cry, she surged forward, fighting through the agony.

In the distance, Socorra heard the faintest sound, like a heartbeat. She told herself she was hearing things, that delirium was setting in, but the sound only grew louder over the thunder. For half a second, she was hopeful that another Hawk had come to her rescue, but when she turned to look, a crippling dizziness overcame her. She could no longer keep her flight constant, struggling against the wind, until her body failed her. Her wings flailed and she pitched toward the ground.

Half-conscious, she couldn't regain altitude. To save herself, she unfurled her wings to their fullest span, letting the wind catch in her feathers to slow her descent. Impact imminent, she drew back her wings, forming a protective circle around her torso, enveloping herself in a sea of her own chestnut feathers.

Hitting the ground, the brunt sent her rolling; a deafening crack hit her ears. She tumbled across the sodden earth, the soaked grass and churned mud clinging to her body as she fought to spread her landing. But the shock of the impact rendered her numb to the pain.

She lay there in the Zarpan countryside, battered and bruised, with no one to comfort her. The rain pelted her face as if the sky itself wept for her. She felt nothing except the bitter taste of defeat and her own lamentations. She'd failed. She failed herself. In some way she couldn't help but feel that she had failed the Hawks; her proud people of hunters and warriors. But the worst pain of all was knowing that she'd failed Kyte. She abandoned him in the countryside, left him there to die alone. The Hawks didn't believe in an afterlife, but she knew that this failure would haunt her even into the void.

Looking up to the sky for what she was sure was the final time, the world around her spun. The storm howled around her, but all she could hear was the steady beat of wings as they approached.

She couldn't be sure what she was seeing. With a few hasty blinks to clear her eyes, the world came back into focus.

It was the specter descending from the clouds on top of her.

She couldn't make out its face, the creature nothing more than a silhouette against the storm-battered plains.

The only thing she saw was its enormous wings: black and feral, the feathers tattered and frayed. With a foul swoop, the creature did not attack, but landed firmly on two feet. It no longer needed to hide in the shadows, to attack as a blur; instead, it sauntered towards her, smugly, menacingly. It knew it had bested her.

It had won.

Chapter Three
GIDEON

Erasmus Thrush tinkered away at an obscenely large grandfather clock, the imported maple smooth and stained a beautiful chocolate brown. The black oil of the clock's machinery was splotched on the olive skin of his hands and face.

"Maybe your dad won't notice you're late," Cas suggested.

"And maybe you're an Owl." Gideon smirked. Cas's optimism was normally a welcome affair, but Gideon knew this suggestion was misguided. "But maybe if I can just slip in…" He gave the door a gentle push and the jingle of the doorbell announced his arrival. Freezing in the doorway, he cursed under his breath. "How could I forget the stupid bell?"

Paying little attention, Cas pressed forward, barreling straight into Gideon and they both fell forward. Cas tried to grab at Gideon's wings, but it was too late.

Gideon felt a sharp tug before he fell face-first on the oak floorboards with a thud. Letting out a groan, he lifted his head to glower back at Cas. The red-winged Finch stood frozen, his face flushed desperately trying to hide the clump of feathers he'd ripped out, but Gideon could see the blue poking out from behind Cas's back. With a dubious glare, Gideon moaned in frustration; Cas flashed him an apologetic grin. Dropping the fistful of feathers, he helped his friend to his feet.

"You're late, boy," Erasmus announced without turning to face them, pliers still in the guts of the clock.

"Yes, father." Gideon's tone was flat. "I'm sorry."

Erasmus turned to face the boys, but his hands never stopped working with the pliers. The arches of his wings puffed out behind him, his blue feathers a shade lighter than Gideon's, worn and faded with age.

Gideon stifled a laugh. His father's jeweler's glasses magnified his already bulging eyes, making him look like a bird—an ancient creature from before the Great End—with his hooked nose, oil-streaked hair fraying upward at the sides, and those comically monstrous eyes.

"Tardiness is not a laughing matter," his father spat, brandishing the pliers at him.

"Yes, father," he repeated with no emotion. He never meant it when he said it, but Gideon knew it was the simplest, easiest way through the verbal lashings he received almost daily. It was the response his father expected, and Gideon couldn't be bothered to draw out the process any longer than necessary.

Turning back to his work, Erasmus grabbed a gear off the counter and tightened it into place. "I don't understand why you can't keep your nose out of those damned books long enough to show up on time."

"Yes, father," Gideon had heard the speech so many times, he could probably recite it from memory.

"You're seventeen, Gideon." Erasmus let out a heavy sigh. "You're not a fledgling anymore, but you still act like one."

Gideon's cheeks burned.

"I'm really not asking for much, here. One day, everything I've built will be yours. How can I trust you with this business if I can't even trust you to be here on time?"

"Yes, father." Gideon shut his eyes; he'd learned after being chided for rolling them enough times. He resented his father's expectation that he would take over the family operation. Clocks were a status symbol among the Avian tribes. When his father started the business, the wealthy Finch merchants loved the idea of having clocks with intricate designs to impress their houseguests. Now, his father expanded to exporting his creations across Avis, even trying to spread into the market in Bengala, the Tiger continent to the east.

Gideon wanted nothing to do with it. He wasn't exactly sure *what* he wanted, but he knew he wouldn't find it in Moda, and certainly didn't want the responsibility of his father's business on his shoulders.

"Sorry, Mr. Thrush," Cas interrupted before Erasmus could continue. "It's my fault Gideon's late. Please don't be mad at him."

Erasmus visibly clenched his jaw, his tongue swirling about in his cheeks as he tried to find an even tone. Gideon's father couldn't stand Cas, a fact he never hid.

A waste of money on a hare-brained buffoon.

He'd said as such on various occasions, but never in front of Cas who was the son of one of the wealthier merchants of Moda. He didn't have to concern himself with being kind to Gideon, but Erasmus made it a point not to make enemies of powerful people.

"That's kind of you, boy, but you can't go around taking the blame for my son's contemptible habits."

"But, sir-"

Disregarding Cas's pleas, Erasmus turned back to Gideon.

"I can't keep covering this counter for you. I'm far too busy, and it shouldn't be my responsibility to make sure you're here to help customers."

"Yes, father." This time there was a sullen bite behind Gideon's response.

Erasmus took a breath as if to speak, but the bell above the entrance rang as the door swung open. Gideon let out a sigh of relief as he would have some respite from his father's lecture, but the feeling was short-lived. A wave of perfume hit him square in the nose, a wretched concoction of lavender and animal carcass. He didn't even have to look to know that none other than Altuna Goldfinch had walked through the door.

Sauntering into the shop, Goldfinch's unnaturally blonde hair was wrapped in a pristine bun high on her head, revealing small patches of gray at her roots. A violet cloth dress draped over her frame, cinched at the waist by an ornate golden bodice. Her canary-yellow wings had dulled over the years, their former brilliance now tinged with age. Gideon couldn't help but think she looked like a giant wasp who somehow managed to get trapped inside of a purple pansy.

"Late again, Gideon?" she asked in her usual condescending tone.

Gideon forced a wry smile. Altuna Goldfinch was a woman who, as far as he could tell, had nothing better to do than to walk around the city making other Finches miserable.

Erasmus, still fiddling with the innards of the grandfather clock, answered her. "He wouldn't be late if he kept his nose out of those books."

"You already said that," Gideon whispered to himself. He hadn't meant to say it aloud, but the words escaped his lips.

"Excuse me!?" Erasmus's feathers bristled, his wings trembling in anger.

"I said, I already apologized." His cheeks flushed.

"Apologies are only as good as the actions that follow, Gideon," Goldfinch chimed with a wag of her finger.

Biting his tongue, Gideon gave a gentle nod. He had a myriad of retorts that he wanted to spit at her, but he staved off for fear of his father's wrath. Altuna was one of, if not *the* richest and most powerful Avians in all the Finchlands. A widow, she inherited the business of her late husband, Alastair Goldfinch, one of the most prolific merchants of Duport. When it came to the up-and-coming Finch families, she loved to flaunt her riches and the power that she wielded to remind them of her station. Despite living in Duport, she managed to find a reason to visit his father's shop at least twice a moon.

"Erasmus," Altuna squawked, a layer of dismay in her voice. "I must say, I really thought you would have finished with that by now." She waved a weathered hand, gesturing at the grandfather clock.

"My apologies, Mrs. Goldfinch." Despite his own tired relationship with his father, Gideon hated that he called her, 'Mrs. Goldfinch' while she addressed him so casually. "We only received your custom order a few days ago. I've been hard at work putting it together myself given its complexity. Lamentably, I've been distracted." His gaze shifted to where his son stood; Gideon shuffled his feet and cast his eyes to the floor to avoid his father's glaring eyes. "I'll be sure to have it completed within the hour. I'd never dare to keep you waiting, Mrs. Goldfinch."

Erasmus chose his words carefully. Respected as he was in Moda, he knew better than to risk offending Altuna Goldfinch. A single misstep, and everything he'd built could crumble under the weight of her influence among the merchants. His answer left nothing to be desired, and yet, she was inscrutable. She ruffled her wings and smoothed the delicate sleeves of her dress, her expression impossible to gauge.

"See that you do, Erasmus." She placed her hands on her waist, the measured tap of her leather boot against the floor sent a quiet warning through the shop. "I'm hosting a group of Owl dignitaries a week from today and that clock shall be the focus piece of my dining room. I simply must have it ready in time for their arrival."

As laughable as he found her, Gideon couldn't help but be intrigued by this new tidbit of information. The Owls—the self-proclaimed *Keepers of Knowledge*, as they maintained the records of Avis's history—rarely left their secluded fortress in the northern tundra.

What business could they have in the Finchlands?

But prying information from Altuna Goldfinch would require tact. If he was subtle and played to her ego just right, perhaps she'd let something slip.

"Whoa!" Cas exclaimed. "Owls? What do you think they're coming here for?"

So much for tact.

Gideon squeezed his eyes shut in silent frustration, biting back a groan. He wished Cas hadn't spoken; now he might never get the information he wanted. Altuna wasn't the type to entertain crass outbursts, and Gideon braced himself for the inevitable huff of indignation. But to his surprise, Goldfinch's eyes lit up when her gaze landed on Cas.

"My, my! And who is this crimson devil?" Her eyes practically sparkled as she fluttered her lashes.

Well, that was…unexpected.

"Cassin Jay, ma'am." Ever oblivious, Cas folded his arms over his broad chest and grinned. "But you can call me Cas. Everybody does."

"Cassin?" Gideon whispered to himself. He'd known Cas for years. How did he not know Cas's full name? What else didn't he know about *Cassin Jay*. More importantly, why did Cas put up with such a bad friend?

Altuna visibly swooned. She was nearly three decades older than the boys, but she fawned over Cas like a schoolgirl.

Gideon blushed at the ridiculousness of it all. He might have been annoyed under any other circumstances, disgusted even, but his curiosity demanded information. If Cas's absurd charm could get it for him, so be it.

"Well, Master Cas," she winked.

Filthy.

"It's truly riveting. Sadly," she placed a solemn hand on her breast, "I'm not at liberty to divulge any information."

Damn.

The one time Gideon cared what she had to say and she wasn't going to share.

C'mon Cas. Get it out of her.

"I understand ma'am. It must be tough keeping a secret that important. Very noble of you to keep to your promises like that."

Gideon resisted the urge to roll his eyes. Cas was either laying it on really thick, or he *was* pretty thick.

Maybe both.

"Oh, you have no idea how hard it's been to keep their project a secret," she fawned. "They've asked me to help organize a space to meet their candidates. I've been making all these arrangements with the merchants of Duport without being able to divulge the *hows* and the *whys* of the situation. It's a wonder they haven't torn me apart for the details." With a few steps toward Cas, she placed a wrinkled hand on his shoulder. "And the Owls expect that I do all of this as a favor to them." Leaning in far too close for Gideon's comfort, she pressed her chest against him, ruffled her feathers, and put the back of her free hand to her forehead. "How gauche!"

Gideon's mind raced.

Candidates for what?

Every new piece of information only left more questions that needed answering, but he really commended Cas on getting this far.

"I normally don't do charity cases." She paused for a second. "But I'll gladly make an exception for the Owls." An ominous grin stretched across her face.

Gideon didn't even try to hide it this time; he rolled his eyes so far back that he was sure only the whites were visible. Fortunately, Altuna had been too busy ogling Cas to notice. What she'd meant to say was that she was going to spend whatever resources she had so that she could busybody her way into having Owl dignitaries as political allies.

"Candidates?" Cas raised an eyebrow to Gideon. "Candidates for what, Mrs. Goldfinch?"

Good job, Cas.

"Oh, I shouldn't. I've already said too much." She put her fingers to her lips, scanning the room as if anyone else were there to overhear the conversation.

Cas dropped to one knee, stroking the back of Goldfinch's hand. "Don't worry, I understand. Your secret's safe with me, I swear."

Altuna beamed; her face turned the same deep shade of scarlet as Cas's wings. "Oh, they would absolutely adore you!" she gushed, squeezing Cas's hand. "I'll make sure that you get an invitation to meet with them. You're just the cutest thing." Caressing his face, she ran her fingers down Cas's neck and down his bicep. "And so strong!"

I'm going to throw up.

"I bet they'd make you their champion at the first look of you."

Gideon's heart jumped into his throat.

Champion?

He still had so many questions.

"Would you like to come back to Duport with me to meet them? I'm sure we could arrange the trip with your parents. You won't be gone for hardly two weeks!"

Cas replied, "It's just me and my Ma. I'm sure she won't mind. She's always telling me to find fun things to do to keep me away from the shop. She says that the business stifles my creativity."

Gideon shifted his gaze away. It was effectively a subtle way of saying that Cas pretty much ruined anything he touched. He'd eventually inherit his mother's textile business, but Gideon was sure that Cas would never have anything to do with the daily operations.

"Erasmus!" Altuna's voice boomed, reverberating through the shop. Gideon's father startled at the sound. His magnifying glasses slipped from his nose, and the pliers he'd been holding flew from his hands and pierced the face of the cuckoo clock mounted on the wall behind him. "When you've finished with my grandfather clock, please have young Master Cas escort it to my carriage." Altuna's voice dripped with authority. She snapped her fingers and began to turn away, but Cas interrupted her fanfare.

"Gid can come too, right?" The question clung in the air. All three of them: Gideon, Erasmus, and Goldfinch turned to stare at Cas, stunned. The room was thick with pause, until finally, Gideon's father broke the silence.

"Absolutely not! My son will not go parading in the capital on some fanciful mission to try and impress a bunch of bloviating, puffed-up, know-it-alls when he can't even dedicate himself to the simplest task of arriving here on time!" He was panting by the end of his tirade, his face a gruesome shade of purple.

Gideon said nothing, but a lingering sense of shame, embarrassment, and frustration welled up inside of him. The sting of tears pooled at the corners of his eyes, but he refused to give his father or Altuna the satisfaction of seeing him break.

For once, Altuna appeared to be at a loss for words. Between her own inappropriate fascination with Cas,

Erasmus's outburst, and Cas's unexpected insistence on bringing Gideon along for the adventure of a lifetime, she simply stood there, momentarily overwhelmed.

"Please?" Letting go of Goldfinch's hand, Cas moved to stand beside Gideon, throwing an arm over his shoulder.

A tingle ran down to the tips of Gideon's wings, touched by Cas's sincerity. Ignoring Erasmus's still-flushed face of fury, Cas turned back to Altuna, speaking directly to her.

"It would mean a lot to have my friend with me." Cas's eyes widened.

Collecting herself, Goldfinch brushed the front of her violet frock as if the entire conversation had settled like dust on her bodice. "Come now, Erasmus," she said coolly. "Surely if Master Cas insists on bringing your son along, there must be some value to him."

The remark cut like a blade, but Gideon kept his mouth shut. He knew well enough that if Goldfinch insisted, his father would have little choice but to comply.

"Besides," she added, her tone light but laced with condescension, "maybe it will help to instill some small sense of responsibility in young Gideon." Her gaze flicked to him, the corner of her lips curling into a smirk. He met her stare, eyes like daggers, but he held his tongue. "I'll be sure to return him here to you in two weeks' time."

Swiveling back toward the door, she dipped her chin in Erasmus's direction, the hem of her dress twirling as she went. The bell above the eave chimed as she ripped open the entrance, the door banging against the wall.

"I'll have a carriage waiting outside the shop in one hour. Have these two carefully load my grandfather clock into the carriage, and they will ride with it to Duport. The journey should take them a few days, and they'll return on their own wings." She didn't wait for a response, slamming the door behind her, punctuating her egress.

Erasmus, Cas, and Gideon stood unmoving for a minute, the silence clinging in the air like a wet wool blanket. After a while, Gideon finally shifted his gaze to his father, an empty expression on his face.

"So…" It was Cas who broke the silence, a simple utterance, but the word made Gideon squirm. He felt like he'd been standing on a cliff overlooking the sea, and Cas pushed him right to the edge of the precipice. He waited for his father's response, barely breathing.

"You heard the infernal woman." Erasmus spoke in a rigid grumble, the words sliding out between gritted teeth. "Go home and pack. Be back here within the hour."

Almost gasping for air, Gideon let out a sigh of relief, his heart hammering in his chest.

I'm finally getting out of this city!

His mind burned with a thousand questions, his imagination running wild. He pictured the walled city fading behind them, the endless stretch of the Finchlands unfurling like a map in his mind.

He turned to Cas, watching as a wide grin spread across his friend's face. Without thinking, he lunged for the door, grabbing the handle.

"Gideon," Erasmus's voice cut through the moment.

Gideon froze in the open doorway, a cold prickle running down his spine. Slowly, he turned back. Erasmus's glare was sharp enough to pierce straight through him.

"Do. Not. Be. Late."

Each word landed like a hammer, slow and deliberate, thick with warning.

Gideon sprinted out the door, a smile plastered on his face. Cas followed behind, the pair running down the street until they reached the corner. Without thinking, Gideon threw his arms around Cas's shoulders, pulling him into a tight hug.

"I can't believe that worked!" he laughed, breathless. "You were amazing! She was eating right out of your hands!"

"Whatd'ya mean, Gid?" Cas pulled away and gave his friend a puzzled look.

"Oh c'mon, you know." He gave Cas a playful elbow to the ribs. "The compliments you gave her, when you grabbed her hand, the way she looked at you. All that! That was your plan, wasn't it?"

"Plan?" Cas scratched at his scalp, fingers catching in the knots. "No plan, I just really wanted to know about the Owls."

"So, you weren't trying to flirt with Goldfinch?"

He waved his hands out in front of him. "Ew, no way, Gid!"

Gideon raised his eyebrows. "Stop!" He chuckled, nudging Cas. "You didn't see her looking at you with her hungry eyes?"

"Hungry eyes?" He scratched the back of his head.

Gideon shook his head, trying to find the words to spell it out. "She was definitely interested in more than you being the Owls' champion…or whatever."

A look of horrified realization dawned in Cas's eyes. "Oh, disgusting!"

The boys burst into laughter, Cas folding over and bracing himself on his knees.

"Alright Gid. Gross as that is, I'm gonna head home and pack. I'll meet you back at the shop." Cas brought his finger up to Gideon's chest and, doing his best to imitate Erasmus. "Don't be late!"

With a final chuckle, he backed away, wings fanning out behind him. Then, with two powerful strokes, he was airborne, leaving Gideon grinning after him.

✳   ✳   ✳

Gideon made his way through the merchants' district, where the wealthier Finches could afford homes built for individual families. The houses, usually two or three stories tall, were lined in dull uniformity: gray stucco facades, gray stone streets, gray everything. There were no trees, no grass, nothing to soften the endless monochrome. Still, despite the bleakness of the district, he was grateful to live in a house. His wings were already tired from the short flight from the shop. He couldn't imagine living in the fourteen story high rises where the factory workers tended to reside.

"I'm tired just thinking about it," he muttered, still catching his breath.

That terrified him most about the trip. He had never flown such a long distance before and had no idea how he'd manage. Cas would probably be patient with him, but it would definitely slow them down. Maybe, just maybe, Cas could charm Altuna Goldfinch into offering them a carriage for the return trip. Then again, now that Cas was painfully aware of her…*interest*…Gideon doubted he'd be willing to cozy up to her again.

Or would he?

Before leaving to return to the shop, Gideon stopped in his mother's office. He opened the door and the smell of old parchment, a blend like dried grass and vanilla, washed over him.

In the corner was a roll-top desk piled high with stacks of paper. The right-hand wall was covered in maps of Avis, Bengala, and Aligaida, the southern Croc continent. They were worn and dotted with his mother's scribbles. To the left, shelves overflowed with her collection of preavian texts—two hundred or so books, gathered through years of travel and funded by his father's wealth.

When he was younger, Gideon had spent hours here, watching his mother pour over her research. She would stare at her maps as if expecting them to whisper their secrets. But no matter how consumed she was by her work, she had always made time for him.

Whenever he visited, she would pick a book from the shelves, carefully turning its brittle pages. She had taught herself to read the ancient scripts of the Sapiens, deciphering languages from every corner of Avis. And she had passed that knowledge to him. Thanks to her, Gideon could now read six languages with little hesitation.

His fingers drifted over the spines, his chest tightening. Those days felt so distant now.

It had been five years since his mother had set out on her last excursion, flying over the Tiger Sea to explore some ruins on the Bengal Peninsula.

She never returned.

His father had spent a small fortune on search parties, hiring Finch Guards and private mercenaries to scour the continents for her. But after a year, the searches were abandoned.

Swallowing hard, Gideon scanned the shelves, searching for something to bring with him. He knew Cas would do plenty of talking, but he'd need a distraction for the quieter moments. His eyes landed on the perfect book: the story of a girl who fell into another world, filled with dreadful queens, bizarre cats, and strange, impossible creatures. It had been his mother's favorite story to read to him when he was a fledgling. Carefully, he wrapped the worn tome in a spare tunic and tucked it into his pack.

Stepping into the hall, he shut the office door behind him and the distant clocktower boomed fifteen minutes before the hour.

"Perfect," he beamed. "I might actually be early for once."

Chapter Four

Socorra

From somewhere in the void, Socorra heard the pounding of wings, their rhythmic beat rising over the crash of thunder. A mist coiled through the emptiness; a figure emerged, standing stark against the darkness. An arm outstretched, he beckoned her.

Kyte!

She tried to call his name, but no sound escaped her lips. She willed her wings to move, but they remained frozen. Step after step, she ran toward him, her arms outstretched, her swarthy skin smooth and unmarred. He was so close now, she could feel his warmth against the frigid air. She reached for him, fingers brushing his arms.

She lost her footing; the ground beneath her gave way and she sank into the nothing below. Slipping further and further into the abyss, the void rushed into her lungs like water: choking, crushing, endless. She thrashed about, searching for Kyte; she hoped with every fiber that he would scoop her up and catch her, pull her in close. But he only stood above, watching solemnly as she sank.

He was swallowed by the dark, then there was nothing.

Socorra woke with a gasp, her body jerking against cold iron. Sweat trickled down her skin, her pulse hammering in her ears. The dream clung to her, the weight of the void still clawing at her chest. Then, stark reality cut through the haze.

She was dangling from the ceiling.

Suspended by her wrists, she was cuffed in shackles, the chains digging into her skin. Panic clawed at her and she struggled, every movement sending fire lancing through her limbs, a numbing trickle spreading from her shoulder. Fresh blood seeped through the gauze wrapped around her forearm.

The world around her spun into focus, the blur of stone walls gradually sharpening. The chamber was mostly barren aside from a handful of lanterns that hung from rusted hooks carved into the mossy stone bricks. Moisture clung in the air, heavy and stagnant, the chill biting her damp, exposed skin.

The room was circular, no more than twenty feet across. There were no windows, no exit save for the iron door which felt like a hastily added addition to the otherwise stark room.

Footsteps clacked from somewhere beyond the door, muted voices drifting through the stone. Their words blurred together, indistinct until they were just outside.

Then they stopped altogether.

A wooden slat in the door scraped open, golden light spilling into the chamber. "Ah, songbird, you're awake," a deep voice purred.

Before she could respond, the plank slammed shut. Keys jangled; the lock clicked and the door groaned open, the hinges whining under the weight of the iron.

With the intensified light from the hall, Socorra had to squint, her eyes adjusting as she took in the Avians. The smaller of the two stepped in first, her white wings giving her away as a Dove. She wore a simple gown that just skimmed her ankles, her hair tucked neatly beneath a wimple. Without a word, she stepped off to the side. Setting down her worn carpet bag, the leather weathered and fraying. She knelt beside it, rummaging through an assortment of bottles and compacts.

The man lingered in the doorway, his lean frame silhouetted against the torchlight. Then, with deliberate ease, he strode inside, tucking his wings carefully behind him to fit through the narrow entrance.

Socorra's lip curled. "Crow."

He let out a sharp, amused breath. "Is that the best insult you can muster?" His teeth glinted in a wicked grin. "I expected more from a Hawk. Your tribe certainly specializes in vulgarities."

As he closed the distance, Socorra noted the wiry strength beneath his lean build, the veins scrawling across his arms like spider webs.

"But you're mistaken, songbird," he chided, clicking his tongue. He dragged one hand through his long, pin-straight hair; the other remained neatly tucked at the small of his back. "I'm no Crow." He stopped just a few feet in front her. Then, with a slow, deliberate motion, he spread his massive wings to their fullest extent, their inky expanse brushing both walls of the chamber. "I'm a Raven," he declared, lifting his chin in a proud arc. "Stronger, faster, and more clever than any Crow could ever hope to be."

"There's no such thing." Socorra yanked at the chains that bound her, chasing away the icy fear that gnawed at her, heat flooding back into her limbs. "You're just a Crow with a few dirty tricks. Now let me down!" Her voice thundered around the room.

"Spirited," the Raven mused with a wicked sneer. "I knew you would be. Capturing you was a thrill. I'd been looking forward to getting at another Hawk. Your kind usually makes for good sport. That ambassador to the Crowlands certainly put up no fight. Fat, contented thing he was. It was…*disappointing*." The word was a venomous hiss. "But you made me work for it, gave me a challenge. I like that. It'll make it that much sweeter when we change you."

"Change me?" Socorra snarled, her face flushed with rage.

"All in due time, songbird," he crooned. "All in due time." The man inched closer until she could feel the warmth of his breath on her cheeks. "For now, I'm glad to see you've come out of that spell." Despite the menace in his tone, there was something disturbingly sincere, a thought that chilled Socorra to the core. "You've been knocked out for three days."

Three days!?

The realization tightened in her gut like a corkscrew. Her life had been torn apart days ago. And in the darkness of her nightmares, it felt like only moments.

"Fortunately, our Tama was able to keep you alive. Isn't that right Tama?" The woman stopped her rummaging, but did not respond. She simply dipped her head, her movement barely noticeable.

Socorra furrowed her brow. "Where am I?"

"Safe, for now."

"Safe?" she balked. "If I'm safe, then why do you have me in chains?"

He pursed his lips in a coy fashion, lifting his boots as he began a slow, deliberate prowl around the chamber's circumference. The rhythmic click of his steps echoed against the stone, his wings trailing just close enough for the tips of his feathers to graze her skirt.

The patter of his footsteps stopped, his voice slithering from behind her.

"For insurance purposes, songbird."

A shiver ran through Socorra as his breath swept the back of her neck.

"You don't think I'm going to let you just scamper away, do you? Not when I have the chance to corrupt another Hawk."

Another Hawk. The words scratched at the back of Socorra's mind.

"What did you do to him?" She hissed through clenched teeth.

"Who, my dear?" he asked with feigned irreverence.

"You know who!"

"You mean your little friend there?" His smirk widened. "The one that I killed?"

Rage surged hot through Socorra's veins.

"Ah, yes. I had nearly forgotten. What was his name again? Something with a *kuh*, wasn't it? Karith maybe?"

He was toying with her; Socorra could hardly breathe. "Don't."

"Kyne, perhaps?"

"Stop it," she spat.

He tapped a finger to his chin, rolling his eyes in mock recollection. "Ah, no. You screamed it after I knocked him from the sky…"

She gripped the chains, the iron biting her skin.

The Raven inhaled sharply, holding the breath as if savoring the memory. Then, with a triumphant snap of his fingers.

"Kyte!"

The name echoed through the chamber, shattering the last of Socorra's restraint. A primal, visceral roar tore from her throat, the kind only a wounded animal could make. The agony she'd felt moments before vanished, replaced by unfiltered fury. She lurched forward, wings flailing, shackles rattling as her legs kicked wildly. But the chains held fast. After a minute, her strength ebbed, and the pain came flooding back, fresh blood seeping from her reopened wound. Defeated, she slumped in the irons, her breath ragged.

Across the room, the Dove woman had shrunk against the entrance, her trembling hands clutching at the doorframe, but the Raven didn't stir. He stood there, unshaken, his yellow eyes smoldering in the dim light, a wicked smile carved into his face.

"Tsk, tsk, tsk." He clicked his tongue in mock disappointment. "We can't have that, now can we, songbird?"

With deliberate delay, he pulled his hidden hand from behind his back.

Socorra's breath caught in her throat.

Talons?

The grotesque claws extended from his fingertips, each at least six inches in length. The keratin was thick, black as polished obsidian, the edges serrated. Beneath them, his hands had transformed—his skin roughened into leathery patches, grotesque and unnatural, as if hardened into scales.

A sickness twisted in her stomach.

Gingerly, he slid one of the claws beneath her bandage. With a flick of his wrist, the fabric fell away, exposing the torn gash beneath. Blood welled at the wound's lips, running in crimson rivulets down her arm.

Socorra barely had time to react before his claw gripped the edges of her face. She gasped, the needle-like points pressing against her skin, teasing her temples down to her cheeks. Her chest heaved, terror boiling inside her.

"If you continue to misbehave," he murmured, his voice feigned sweetness, "that will never heal."

"What are you?" The words were a strangled whisper.

Craven's face remained impassive. "I simply am as my Master made me, my dear."

He released her with a flourish of his talons, grazing the skin, and swiveled on his heel. He swung his wings outward; they slammed against her, sending her chains swaying violently. Pain lanced through her, but she gritted her teeth, swallowing the cry that threatened to escape.

His hand found the door handle, but he paused. "I suggest you learn to mind yourself while you're here," he warned, his back still to her. "My hospitality has its limits, and I won't tolerate any more outbursts."

His gaze flicked to Tama who had since crawled back to her carpet bag. "Get her cleaned up," he squawked before striding into the hallway. Just before vanishing, he clicked his heels, wings blocking the last of the hallway's light.

"Once you're fit to travel," his voice carried through the chamber, "I will bring you to Raven Rock, where the Master will decide what to do with you. Until then, do try to contain yourself."

Then he was gone, his mirthless cackle echoing back through the hallway until all was silent.

A hollowness swelled in Socorra's chest; she inhaled, but the air felt empty, lifeless, as if breathing no longer tethered her to the world.

A faint *clink* broke the silence as Tama rose, two vials tapping together in her trembling hands.

"Where am I, Tama?" Socorra rasped.

The woman remained silent. She set the vials at Socorra's feet, then went back to rummaging through her bag. Finally, she pulled free a bottle, uncorking it with a soft pop. A pungent, bitter odor filled the air. Pouring the contents onto a linen cloth, the Dove met Socorra's gaze, hesitation flickering across her face. There was a fleeting softness as if she were weighing her decision.

With a heavy sigh, she returned to Socorra and pressed the cloth firmly over the Hawk's mouth and nose. Socorra jerked back, holding her breath in defiance, but Tama had surprised her. The vapors clung to her throat, forcing their way in.

Up close, Socorra could see the age in Tama's face; the wrinkles creased deep, the years weighing heavy on her.

The Dove lifted the rag from her mouth and sniffed it herself before letting it drop to the floor.

As the Dove worked to redress the wound, Socorra could feel nothing, a strange numbness settling over her.

Watching Tama work in the dim light, Socorra took in the contrast between the Dove's softness and the harsh cruelty of the chamber. Tama refused to look at her, but Socorra caught glimpses of kindness in her expression.

"What do they want with me?" She slurred her words, her tongue thick and heavy.

Tama didn't answer.

Unable to support herself, Socorra's head lolled to the side. "You don't belong here, do you, Tama?"

Again, silence, but a single tear slipped down the Dove's cheek, a faint sob escaping her cracked lips.

Socorra swallowed hard as the world blurred, the lanterns swirling in dizzying rings of red. She closed her eyes, but before the darkness took her again, she made herself a promise.

I will escape this prison and wipe the grin from that monster's face.

Chapter Five
GIDEON

Perched atop a hill, Gideon stared across the rolling valley, a blanket of mist in the twilight. The first slivers of sunlight crested over the horizon, a heavy wind rustling the boughs of the fir that towered above him. The gust swept through the valley, peeling away the haze to reveal the Finch countryside, a rolling sea of evergreens rippling over the hills below.

"It's beautiful," he whispered to himself, his lips quivering. "I never want to go back."

There was a twinge of sadness in his voice. Soon, their journey would end when they reached Duport and would have to return to Moda, the city's familiar chaos waiting for them. He lingered a few minutes longer, then rose, brushing dirt from his backside, damp from sitting in the sodden grass.

Back at the carriage, Manni, their gray-feathered driver, was already breaking down camp. Gideon offered to help, but Manni merely shook his head and shooed him away.

Cas, meanwhile, was still sprawled out, snoring, somehow able to sleep through his own racket of grunts and wheezes.

"Get up, you lazy bum," Gideon snapped playfully. He tapped the tip of his boot against Cas's arm, but the boy barely moved, swatting him away.

Scratching at the stubble of his chin, a wicked idea tickled Gideon. Stretching his wings behind him, the Finch brought them down with as powerful a stroke as he could muster. The gust scattered the loose dirt and gravel, peppering Cas with tiny stones.

Cas jolted upright, coughing and spitting dust.

"That's more like it," Gideon laughed with a light air.

Springing to his feet, Cas shock the red dust from his bare chest and breeches. "Oh, you're gonna pay for that, Gid!"

With a grin—his teeth speckled with splotches of rust-colored dust—he lunged, but Gideon was already running, his wings snapping open to propel him up the hill. Cas gave chase, but instead of running, he took to the sky. Laughter echoed from above as Cas closed the distance. With a playful tackle, he knocked Gideon off his feet, sending them both tumbling down the grassy knoll.

Gideon had never felt so alive.

"Come, gentlemen," Manni called out in a sterile voice. Everything packed, the boys climbed into the carriage for the fifth and final day of their journey. Though the cab was luxurious in size, it mattered little when they were squeezed in next to the enormous grandfather clock. Still, for short stretches, it was manageable.

Drawing back the velvet curtain, Gideon looked out over the rolling expanse as they approached the apex of a hill. Before him, a few miles to the east, the Windy Sea shimmered with sunlight, dotted by the scattered silhouettes of iron ships. To the south, the skyline of Duport rose into view, the tops of its marble buildings peeking above the immense white wall. He guessed they were still about five miles away.

"It's a little weird, don't ya think?" Cas asked from his seat, eyes staring out his own window. "Y'know, that they spent all that time building a giant wall when Avians can fly over?"

Gideon nodded. "It may seem silly when you think about it that way, but Duport didn't always have walls. They were only built about a hundred and fifty years ago to regulate people coming in and out."

Cas let go of the curtain and shifted his gaze back to Gideon. "That doesn't really explain anything."

Turning his full attention to Cas, Gideon let the drape fall, casting the cab in a rich violet light. "Sorry, not people like you and me…people like the Sapiens. The city built the walls to control their way in and out."

Cas tilted his head with curiosity. "But don't the Sapiens live in the Desertlands?"

"Yes," Gideon replied, his excitement building. He loved talking about history, Sapien history in particular. "But they didn't always live there." He leaned forward, eager to share what his mother had once told him. "Several hundred, maybe even thousands of years ago, most of the ancient Sapiens perished in an event known as the Great End."

Cas's ears perked up at the mystery in Gideon's voice.

"Some of the survivors roamed the remaining lands without a home to go to. Others were less fortunate and became food for the Crocs and Bengalans."

Cas leaned forward with an exaggerated grimace. "That's disgusting! Why would they wanna eat humans?"

Gideon flinched at the word. "Cas, don't call them that. They're Sapiens, not humans." The term stung; too many Avians used it as an insult. It made Gideon shudder with anger. That's how his father always referred to them.

Filthy humans, hairy, greedy, good for nothing!

Gideon felt ashamed that he never spoke up against his father. He'd never been strong enough, but he was sure Cas would understand.

"Sorry Gid." Cas's eyes dropped to the floor. "I didn't mean it that way, honest." He stretched back against the side of the cab, resting his hands behind his head. "Don't stop, though. What happened next?"

Gideon picked up where he left off, explaining how the Sapiens who had survived the Great End wandered what remained of the world, searching for refuge. Eventually, this journey brought them to Duport.

"As time passed, the number of Sapiens in the city and surrounding areas became unmanageable."

Cas furrowed his brow. "Ok, so they built the wall to be able to control the flow of Sapiens?"

"That's what they say," Gideon flicked his head to the side. "If you ask me, it's more likely the wall was built to keep Sapiens out altogether. You see, Duport was still pretty small back then. The city couldn't support both the Avian and Sapien populations because of massive overcrowding."

Cas turned his gaze forward, clearly distracted. "Yeah, sure. Who doesn't hate overcrowding?" He yawned, a sign that his attention was elsewhere. Gideon knew Cas didn't care much for history. Much of what Gideon said went in one ear and out the other, but Cas never stopped him when he talked about it. He seemed to like when Gideon got excited about anything.

"As a more permanent solution," Gideon continued, "the Finch Council ceded the hostile Desertlands to the Sapiens."

"Ah, makes sense." Cas's eyes fluttered shut as he sank back in his seat.

"So, after that, the council had all of the Sapiens in the city and surrounding areas rounded up and brought to the harbors."

"Mhmm…" Cas's breathing slowed.

"They loaded them up on the boats and shipped them off to the Desertlands." Gideon let out a frustrated huff. "I mean, I still can't believe that. I understand that the council had to do something, but those poor people." He pulled his knees to his chest, resting the soles of his boots on the bench cushion. Wrapping himself in his wings, he curled into a ball, nuzzling his chin through his feathers. "It must've been terrible for them. Tired, frightened, not knowing what was going to happen to them. They had already risked so much getting to Duport. Then they were herded onto boats and sent away."

Gideon wanted to continue the conversation, but Cas had fallen asleep during his rambling. Laying his own head on one of the cushions, he stole a final look at Cas's napping figure, gentle snores rumbling through the cab. Gideon yawned, his eyes growing heavy in the purple twilight. He knew they'd be in the city soon, but sleep called to him.

His mind drifted to Cas. How lucky he'd been to find a friend who understood him despite their differences.

Then he thought of his father. He could already hear the scolding he'd receive when he returned home, the guilt and disappointment in his father's voice, despite having agreed to the trip.

As he sank deeper into his drowsy haze, his thoughts wandered to his mother. He had still been a fledgling when she disappeared; he wondered where she was now, if she were even still alive. From somewhere in the corners of his memory, he heard her voice, soft and comforting, reading to him, *"...the March Hare and the Hatter were having tea at it: a Dormouse was sitting between them..."* She would always make the characters sound so funny, and it would make him laugh until his sides ached.

A bittersweet smile tugged at his lips, but then, the sorrow hit him like a wave. He'd never hear her voice again. All he had left of her were the memories.

"No, that's not all," Gideon whispered, trying to comfort himself in the silence of the warm afternoon. "I have her stories."

*　　　*　　　*

A sudden jolt startled the boys awake, followed by the heavy crash of metal, the iron gate of Duport slamming shut behind their carriage with a sound like the maw of a great beast.

"Hey, Gid!" Cas rubbed the sleep from his eye, already brimming with excitement. "Let's pull over and explore a bit!"

Gideon was reticent, but there was something fledgling-like about Cas's excitement. With a sigh, Gideon tapped the roof of the carriage, signaling Manni to stop.

As the carriage slowed, Cas leapt to the door, eager to jump out and onto the stone streets. But as he opened it, an acrid odor rushed in, assaulting Gideon's senses. The fresh scent of pine and olive trees that had lingered in the Finchland countryside was replaced by the rancid stench of rot and decay. It made Gideon long for the aroma of the billowing smoke of Moda, which he previously thought vile.

Bolting from his seat, Gideon yanked the handle away from Cas and slammed the latch shut.

"What're you doin', Gid?" Cas protested. "I wanna check this place out!"

"Uhh..." Gideon fumbled for a response. He had imagined Duport would be just as grim as Moda, and the smell only confirmed his suspicions. He had gotten to explore the Finch countryside as it were, and now his sole focus was meeting the Owl delegation. "I think we should just get the clock to Goldfinch before we start wandering around the city." It wasn't exactly a lie, but Gideon felt guilty being deceptive.

Disappointment spread across Cas's face, his lips pursed to one side, his eyes drifting downward; he twisted a finger through a knot of his feathers.

"Alright, Gid. You're right." Cas sighed, pounding his fist against the back of his seat before shouting for Manni to keep going. He threw his hand up to steady the clock as the carriage jolted forward.

A few minutes passed and Cas continued to sulk in silence. Hoping to avoid the awkwardness, Gideon dug the book from his pouch and flipped open to the page he'd marked. Just as he started reading, Cas broke the silence between them.

"I can't wait to find out what they want–" he cleared his throat. "–with this champion, that is."

Gideon looked up, still holding the book open. "You mean what they want with *you*."

"Pshaw." Cas waved a dismissive hand, but a glint of wonder caught in his eye. "You think I could really be the champion the Owls are looking for?"

"Well." Gideon snapped the book closed again. "Altuna certainly seems to think so. And why shouldn't you be? You've got all of the qualities of a champion. You're strong, brave..." He trailed off as he caught Cas staring intently at him, his lips curling in a grin. "But, yeah–" Gideon stammered, his cheeks flushing. "I'm curious to learn more about the Owls' gambit as well."

They'd spent hours speculating during the journey, each offering their best guesses. Eventually, they'd agreed it probably had something to do with the rumors of disappearances. The day before they had left, Gideon had heard two merchant wives discussing the subject in Cardinal Park. One of the women had heard of a friend of a friend whose husband had gone missing from a ship sailing the Windy Sea.

Despite their lively conversations on the road, Gideon was content to spend the final hour in near silence. Finishing his chapter, he tucked the book neatly into his pack and joined Cas in watching the city pass by the carriage windows.

The buildings of Duport were all marble and white concrete, their starkness blending seamlessly with the city's walls. Some incorporated spruce into their support beams, but there was little color to break the monotony aside from the thousands of Finch wings fluttering by. The city stood like a pillar of white against the calm sea and the rolling greenery beyond. Gideon watched Cas's excitement grow with every new section they passed, his wide-eyed wonder reminding Gideon of a fledgling seeing candy for the first time. But for Gideon, Duport felt like any other city, exactly the same as Moda—a place that offered nothing new.

"Except that vile stench," he muttered under his breath.

"What's that, Gid?" Cas asked, barely looking away from the sights.

"Nothing." Gideon lied resignedly. Cas was too caught up in exploring the city to notice, and Gideon didn't want to spoil it for him.

By the time they arrived at their destination, the sun clung low in the sky, dangling on the horizon above the sea. Cas threw open the carriage door; Gideon braced for the grotesque stench to overtake his senses. He flinched, but was pleasantly surprised to find that the air smelled fresh. It seemed the pungent odors were confined to the city's outskirts, where the poor had to endure them.

A fresh ocean breeze blew in from the harbors, and he breathed in the salty air. Despite having lived in a city on the same sea his entire life, he'd never once smelled the robust brine of the water over the noxious smog in Moda. He thought of Wydah's bakery and her delicious, sweet-smelling orange tarts. For a fleeting moment, he longed for home, to sit on his bench and listen to his mother read aloud from one of her books.

What did she smell like?

He tried to find any memory of her scent, but he couldn't quite remember.

Over the wind, a shrill voice rang out. "Boys, don't dawdle! Get my grandfather clock up here, and be quick about it!"

The prodigious house stood atop a steep hill; at its zenith stood Altuna Goldfinch. Her dress was the color of daffodils, gleaming against the sterile marble of the colonnades that supported a heavy awning. Gideon took in a final deep breath, contemplating whether being Altuna's guest, even for a short while, was truly worth meeting the Owl delegation. He knew the answer was yes, but the circumstances certainly didn't thrill him.

He glanced at Cas, whose jaw nearly scraped the cobblestones. "Cas," Gideon said with a grin, tapping his friend's chin lightly, "close your mouth before a locust lays eggs in it."

Chapter Six
GIDEON

Gideon let out a sigh of exasperation. The screw that held the pendulum in place fell to the floor for the third time, landing silently in the thick, wine-colored carpet.

The clock wasn't particularly difficult to set up, but he had no patience for the tiny bits and pieces and the delicate processes that it demanded. Silence might have helped, but the constant movement in the dining room made it impossible to focus. Servants bustled past, setting the grand table with an overwhelming array of place settings, their chatter blending into the clinking of fine china.

Cas, of course, had abandoned him long ago to explore, leaving Gideon alone with the tedious task.

As he secured the final counterbalances, the scent of citrus wafted under his nose, his stomach gurgling from hunger. After days of surviving on dried fruit and salted meat, the aroma was tantalizing, almost taunting him. He snapped the glass door of the clock shut and pushed himself up from the floor, his body aching from the tedious work.

The scent pulled him forward, guiding him through the double doors at the end of the dining hall. Distracted and not watching his step, he tripped, stumbling headfirst into the kitchen.

"Woah!" someone squawked.

Gideon flailed, barely managing to steady himself before hitting the floor. Heat crept up his neck as embarrassment settled in.

"You alright dere?" the voice asked.

Lifting his head, he took in the sight of an Avian wearing a well-worn apron splattered with stains. But what truly caught his attention were her jet-black wings.

"You're a Crow," he gasped without thinking.

"Very observant of you." She raised an eyebrow, visibly annoyed, though she never stopped flitting about the kitchen.

Sorry, I didn't mean—"

"Gatya," the Crow snapped.

"I'm sorry?" He shook his head.

"My name…" Bouncing to another worn-brick oven, she dipped her finger into a pot of what Gideon guessed was soup, and took a taste. ". .is Gatya. And you are?"

"Gideon," he stammered, venturing further into the small alcove.

"Y'ungry, Gideon?" She bade him sit at a small counter, brushing aside bits of carrot and potato. Gideon didn't answer, but took a seat as commanded. Without another word, she disappeared into a side room. Returning moments later with a plate in hand, she set it down before him with a fork.

It was the most beautiful tart he had ever seen; a honey glaze dripped down the perfectly crimped sides, fresh fruit and candied lemon zest layered on top like a work of art. Without stopping to think, he devoured it greedily, savoring the smooth custard and sharp lemon. The pastry crumbled under his fork and melted in his mouth.

"You're an incredible chef," he managed, still chewing the last bite. The only thing that might have made it better was if it had been orange-flavored, but Gideon took what he could get.

"Tank you." Whisking away the plate, she dropped it in a stone basin and returned to her work. Gideon watched silently as she twisted about the row of hearths that lined the wall. The dim glow of the flames caught the burnt copper undertones of her feathers as she worked, her hands never still, each motion deliberate.

Gideon didn't want to interrupt her work, but he had never met a Crow before. Knowing little of their culture, his curiosity begged him to ask questions.

"What part of the Crowlands are you from?"

"Dinar." She answered tersely, never looking up from the vegetables she was cutting.

"Do all Crows speak the same way you do?" Gideon hoped that his question wasn't rude because he loved her accent. All Avian tribes spoke the same language, but her deep voice carried a rich trill on her 'r's unlike any he'd heard before.

"All Crows in Dinar, yes." She carefully lifted the lid from a simmering pot, steam curling into the air. Ladling stew into a wooden bowl, she set it on the table before taking the seat across from him.

"Oh, I'm sorry." A stone settled in his stomach and he rose from his seat. "I didn't mean to distract you–"

"Is fine," she interrupted. "Everyone 'ere alvays 'as qvestions for de Crow." She brandished her spoon at him in a way that was half invitation, half command. Gideon faltered, then sat back down. "Some farmers in Lakeshore also speak like dis. But oder Crows, dey are artists and artisans. Dey swallow deir 'r' and dat veird 'tuh-huh' ting dat you do."

"You mean '*thhhh*'?" He drew the sound out.

"Yeah dat. Is veird."

"Fascinating," he said with genuine enthusiasm. "How did you wind up here?"

"I love cooking since I vas fledgling. I grew up on farm and my papa and mama, dey save up for a long time to send me 'ere to learn 'ow to be chef. De old chef 'ere, 'e kick de bucket and I take de job. Goldfinch, she vas blown avay by my cooking, and I am 'ere ever since."

Slurping down her remaining stew, Gatya tossed the bowl into the basin; a column of water and soap shot halfway to the ceiling.

"Okay, bluebell, your time almost up. Y'ave one last qvestion before I go back to vork. Goldfinch vould tvist my vings if she caught me chitter-chattering."

Gideon thought for a moment, running his hands along his breeches. "Are all Crows really as bad as they're made out to be?"

As soon as the question left his mouth, Gideon was filled with regret. He clenched his hands, his cheeks burning with guilt.

"I'm sorry," he stammered. "I didn't mean–"

Gatya cast her gaze to the floor, then threw up both hands to stop him. "Is ok," she sighed. Lifting her head, she met Gideon with a hard, but kind stare. "De Crows of Dinar, ve are a varm people…in Lakeshore too." Her voice was firm, but gentle as if speaking to a fledgling. "But de Crows in 'Igh Castle, dey…pfft." She paused, searching the room as if looking for the right words. "Dey are prickly.

Cold even. Dey stick der noses in de air and keep to demselves. For dat reason, de oder tribes treat us all de same."

Laying her elbow on the table, she raised a single finger. "But now I ask you, are all Finches as greedy as de Crows believe? Are all Doves as pious, and all 'Awks as reckless, too?"

The question hit him square in the chest. He had no answer.

Rising from his stool, Gideon hung his head and turned to leave. Before pressing past the swinging doors, Gideon stole one last look at Gatya. She had already returned to chopping vegetables but, sensing his gaze, she looked up and flashed him a forgiving smile, and Gideon left the kitchen.

Returning to the foyer, Gideon paused in the open doorway that led to the dining room. The Goldfinch Estate buzzed with activity; servants dusted every nook and cranny while others swept and mopped sections of the granite floor. High above the open atrium, others beat dust from the heavy tapestries lining the walls. One Finch, amusingly resourceful, wiped down trinkets while using the tips of her wings to brush away cobwebs in the corner behind her.

Amid this chaos, Altuna Goldfinch fluttered about the entire operation squawking orders.

A small Finch pushed past Gideon in the hall. "M'lady," he panted, his hands and legs trembling. "I know you specifically requested that the gold-plated utensils be used tonight, but a few of the settings seem to be missing."

Altuna threw her hands in the air and shrieked. "How can we be short on my gilded utensils? I had plenty shipped from the humans last moon."

There it was again—*the humans.* Gideon bit his tongue, shame welling inside at his own cowardice.

"Use one of the silver-plated sets." She dismissed the Finch with a tempered flourish of her hand. "But don't think for a second that those missing pieces won't be coming out of your pay, Arius."

The Finch scurried back down the hall toward the dining room, his face contorted with fear and disgust as he muttered obscenities under his breath.

Altuna closed her eyes and rubbed her temples. "Why is good help so hard to find these days?"

Gideon tried to retreat, but he stumbled into another Finch behind him, her squeal enough to draw Goldfinch's attention.

"Ah, young Gideon," she said, her eyes gleaming with a strange intensity. Her voice oozed feigned excitement, tinged with a condescending edge. "I trust my grandfather clock is all set, then? Or did you dawdle like your father?"

"Mhmm." Gideon bit back his disdain, pursing his lips, though he was sure he looked ridiculous. Altuna's sneer did nothing to convince him that he'd been successful in hiding his irritation. Still, he couldn't be outwardly snide; he was, after all, her guest.

"Excellent." Fanning her wings, her feathers rustled behind her. "I'm glad to see you proving your worth around here."

She clapped twice. "Arius," she boomed before the Finch could disappear into the folds of the mansion. "Before you return to your duties, please show Gideon where he and that luscious Master Cassin, ooh–" she cooed. "–I mean, Master Cas will be spending the night."

"Yes m'lady." Arius's tone carried a note of reluctance, but he stepped toward Gideon, muttering curses under his breath. "This way," he grumbled.

Unfurling his wings, Arius lifted gracefully off the tiles and fluttered up to the balcony. He slipped through a gap in the balustrades that led to the second floor. Happy to escape Goldfinch's presence, Gideon followed.

✻　　　✻　　　✻

Flopping onto the canopy bed, Gideon reveled in its luxury: satin sheets, silk blankets, and cotton pillows. It was so large, he could nearly spread his wings without touching the sides, a tremendous upgrade from his own bed where his wings drooped onto the floor while he slept.

With a contented sigh, he slid off his boots, and reached for his knapsack on the bureau, fishing out his book. He flipped through the pages to find his place—the March Hare and Mad Hatter's tea party. They were his favorite characters, their whimsy and absurdity absolutely enchanting. Creations of a runaway imagination, they were like nothing he'd ever known. He could still hear his mother's voice, the ridiculous and exaggerated tone she used to bring them to life. It was like she was there beside him.

"Why is a Raven like a writing desk?"

The voice shot through Gideon like an arrow; he sprang up from the bed, the book flying from his hands to the floor behind him.

An Owl stood in the doorway, dipping in a slight bow, the sleeves of his robes brushing the floor. "I'm sorry, I didn't mean to startle you." His face was stoic, but not unkind.

Without waiting for an invitation, he stepped inside and closed the door behind him. His silvery wings nearly blended in with the marble walls, streaks of white threading throughout his feathers, the tips brown as if his wings had been sprinkled with rich cacao.

"I'm Pelanor."

"Gideon." Still flustered, the Finch extended a hand, but the Owl didn't seem to notice. His stark gray eyes bore deeply into Gideon as if he could see directly into his soul.

"Yes, I know." Pelanor's voice was smooth, if not a little distant. "Madame Golfinch informed me I might find you up here. I wasn't sure when nobody answered my knock."

"Sorry about that," he stammered. "I was just reading. I guess I didn't hear you."

"I didn't realize reading was such a loud activity." Pelanor's lips twitched in what Gideon thought might be amusement, but it was slight. He couldn't be sure.

"Can I help you with something?" The question was more brusque than Gideon intended.

"Perhaps." There was a nonchalance in the Owl's demeanor, but the word held a certain curiosity. "I was actually looking for Master Cassin. Would you happen to know where he is?" With a few crisp strides, Pelanor skirted around the bed, plucking Gideon's book off the floor. He turned it over in his hands, skimming through the pages seemingly disinterested in his own question.

Gideon hesitated, his mind racing with questions of his own. "Cas should be back soon, I think. He wanted to explore the city…it's our first time here."

"And yet, you chose to stay here, reading a Sapien's storybook." With the Owl's inflection, Gideon couldn't tell if it was a question or a statement.

"Yeah," he stammered, a flicker of embarrassment in his voice. "It was my mother's."

"She must be someone important to have acquired something so rare." Despite the Owl's compliment, he spoke as if stating an obvious fact. "I assumed only the Noktern possessed copies of this type of work. What's more, I thought we were the only ones who could read the ancient languages."

He extended the book back to Gideon, his gaze sharp and searching. Something in the Owl's intensity made Gideon pause. Sensing his hesitation, Pelanor let out a sigh and relaxed his arm.

"So, did you ever figure out why a Raven is like a writing desk?" he asked as Gideon finally took the book.

"You've read it then?" Gideon's eyes widened, flipping through the pages until he found the tea party scene.

"Several times. It's quite popular with the Owl scholars."

"Really?" Gideon's voice piqued with surprise. "Forgive me, I just thought that a Sapien storybook would be beneath the scholars of the Noktern."

"And why is that?" For the first time, there seemed to be genuine intrigue in the Owl's tone.

"You're the Keepers of Knowledge." Gideon shrugged. "I just didn't think–"

"Knowledge can be found in many forms," Pelanor interrupted. Wrapping his hand along one of the bedposts, he pulled himself closer to Gideon, his eyes watching intently as Gideon flipped page after page. "Sometimes in the places where we least expect."

Gideon took a step back, suddenly aware of the Owl's closeness. Pelanor mirrored, recognizing the Finch's discomfort.

"It's funny you should ask." Gideon cleared his throat. "I was actually just getting to the part with the Hatter's riddle when you came in."

With a final turn of the page, he found what he'd been searching for—an illustration of Alice, the Hatter, and the March Hare sitting down to tea. Amid the print, the Hatter's riddle was circled in ink, the pressure of the pen having left a deep imprint on the next page. The margins contained a hastily scribbled note; the ink had faded quite a bit with age, but it was still legible enough.

Because it can produce a few notes, though they are very flat; and it is nevar put with the wrong end in front.

Looking up from the page, Gideon thought he saw a glimmer in the Owl's eyes, but it vanished as soon as it had appeared.

"What a strange answer." Pelanor's tone was cool and measured. "I'm certain it would intrigue the other Owls. I'll have to tell them myself."

Without another word, Pelanor pirouetted and strode to the door.

"Should I let Cas know you were looking for him?"

"No need." The Owl flicked his wrist in a dismissive wave before throwing open the door, never glancing back. "I'm sure we'll see him at dinner. I'm sorry to have intruded. Until this evening."

Before Gideon could press any further, the Owl was gone, the door slammed behind him

Gideon stood motionless on the far side of the bed.

What just happened?

He mouthed the words, but no sound came out.

Waking from his reverie, the Finch sank back onto the bed. He tried to focus on reading, to lose himself in the page, but the words, even familiar, all blurred together. His thoughts kept circling the cryptic conversation.

Before he could make sense of it, the door burst open. Cas stood in the doorway, breathless, his hands trembling with excitement. His mouth opened and closed once before he finally blurted, "Gideon, you'll never guess who I just ran into!"

"Pelanor?"

"Who?" Cas scratched his head.

"One of the Owls."

Cas blinked, then his face lit up. "Oh, yeah! How'd ya know?"

Gideon quickly recounted his strange encounter with Pelanor, watching as Cas's eyes grew wider with each detail.

"That's so weird!" Cas exclaimed when Gideon finished. What do you think it was all about?"

"I'm not really sure." Gideon frowned. "But he didn't stop to talk? He said he'd been looking for you."

Cas shook his head.

"Strange." Gideon furrowed his brow. "I bet we'll find out more at dinner, but I don't want to wait until then!"

"Oh! I was s'posed to tell you!"

Gideon leaned in, hoping for any tidbits that might help him to unravel the mystery.

"Goldfinch says we should start getting washed up for dinner."

Gideon sighed, his wings sagging back onto the bed. "Of course she does."

The boys washed up in the luxurious bathroom; a central basin of hot water and soap had been provided. Cas chattered away about his adventure in the city, but Gideon barely heard him, lost in his own pensive thoughts. He imagined the hundreds of scenarios that might unfold at dinner.

Once they finished, the boys retired to their separate rooms. Laid out on the bed, Gideon found a suit that must have been left by Goldfinch's servants. He eyed the oversized white shirt, the tweed coat, and the plain gray slacks with growing dread. Sighing, he pulled them on, feeling utterly ridiculous.

His shame only worsened when Cas arrived to fetch him. Dressed in a sleek black suit, Cas practically glowed in the chandelier's candlelight. His typically unruly mane of chestnut hair was slicked back with some kind of grease, giving him an unfamiliar air of refinement.

"You look good, Gid." Cas beamed.

Gideon's cheeks burned like wild fire. "I look frumpy," he sighed. "But you look…"

Cas scratched at the back of his neck, his eyes expectant as he waited for Gideon to find the words.

Gideon stammered, "...very good."

Cas's grin widened, but before Gideon could say anything else, his stomach grumbled audibly.

"Ugh, me too!" Cas snorted. "I'm starving! Let's get food!"

Grasping Gideon by the arm, Cas dragged him out of the bedroom and down the hallway, only letting go when they'd reached the balcony of the foyer.

Settling at the dinner table, Cas and Gideon sat across from each other. The Owl delegates occupied one end, while Goldfinch and a group of ten merchants filled the opposite side. Gideon recognized most of them from when they'd visited his father's shop. To Goldfinch's left sat Thur Gould, a retired Finch Guard captain who had bought several iron mines in his retirement, his wife beside him. On her right was the entrepreneur Lonchura Lilac, a florist to the merchants who reminded Gideon of Altuna in every way. Both were condescending older women who lived off the wealth of their late husbands. It made sense that they would keep each other company.

Gideon had met all the merchants except one, a Crow seated next to Cocco Thrastus, the renowned perfumer.

"What're you doing here?" Gideon asked aloud, keeping his voice a dull whisper so as not to draw attention to himself. There was a glimmer of regret as he thought about his conversation with Gatya, but the Crow was sorely out of place at the table of Finch merchants, especially given the way Crows were spoken of in the Finchlands. "Must be some up-and-coming artist from High Rock," he shrugged.

"Did you say something, Master Gideon?" Pelanor took the seat to Gideon's right.

The Finch shifted uncomfortably in his seat. "No, sorry. Just thinking out loud I guess."

The first courses were served and idle chatter filled the space. Over the din, the grandfather clock ticked away in time with the crackling of the twin fireplaces on either side of the room.

A piercing *clink* rang through the room as a knife struck a glass. After the initial shock, the room settled.

"Thank you all for being here this evening." Rising from his chair, Captain Gould donned the monocle that hung from his decorated war vest. "My dearest Altuna, I hope you won't mind if I should take the honor of toasting our guests."

Batting her eyelashes, Goldfinch's face turned a bright scarlet. "Of course, my dear, of course. Do go on!" She laced her fingers up and down the captain's sleeve.

Cas and Gideon exchanged an understanding look.

Clearing his throat, Captain Gould raised his glass. He welcomed the delegation and spoke at length about the age of prosperity that might come from their collaboration, expressing his excitement about the potential for the two tribes to work together in the Finch capital. Everyone at the table raised their glasses in a cheer, all except for the Crow woman, who sat with her arms crossed, her expression unreadable.

As the commotion died down, Gould resumed his seat. "Now," he addressed the Owls directly. "I think this is a good time to get down to brass tax. We would all like to hear from you about your business here in Duport."

Whispers rippled through the merchants, their eyes fixed on the Owls, waiting for a response. Gideon glanced at Cas, who was practically bouncing in his chair, his silverware dancing across the table in front of him. The tension in the air was thick, palpable.

One by one, the Owls turned to the foot of the table where their elder sat. He surveyed the crowd of merchants, his gaze scanning each face before it finally landed on Gideon.

"The Owls would first like to thank our gracious host, Madame Goldfinch, for her hospitality and generosity in welcoming our delegation," he began, his voice calm but firm. Removing his flat cap, he dabbed at his thinning silver hair with his napkin before sitting back in his chair, tossing the napkin casually onto the table. With a deliberate motion, he folded his hands into the sleeves of his robes, the gilded silk of his cuffs forming a neat ring around his arms. "As I'm sure you're all aware, there have been strange happenings throughout Avis."

"The disappearances." Gideon blurted the words before he could stop himself. Horror and disdain rippled across the merchants' faces, but the Crow woman at the end of the table merely smirked.

The Owl nodded in Gideon's direction. "Indeed, my boy. The Scholars of the Noktern believe that these disappearances are more than coincidence, and are the portents of dark times. In response, the Noktern has sent delegations throughout Avis looking for a champion to save us from whatever evil lying in wait, those who would seek to destroy all that we have built since the Great End."

"Evil?" Lonchura balked. "Surely the Owls aren't afraid of something so trivial."

"Hear, hear!" shouted Captain Gould. "This seems preposterous. Talk of evil and dark times, I thought we were here to talk business."

The elder Owl raised his head, his bushy white brow lifting to reveal wizened eyes. "Believe what you will, but the Owl scholars have long anticipated the arrival of these wicked events."

A ruckus erupted, Finches squawking across the table and pointing derogatory fingers. Goldfinch swooned. Even Cas went wide-eyed, his face teeming with worry. The only one who did not stir was the Crow; she sat in her chair with little concern, seemingly detached from the conversation.

Raising his voice above the din, the elder continued with little regard for the Finches' squabbling. "It was The First Owl himself who prophesied these times would come, and that a champion would save us from the impending darkness."

Adrenaline pulsed through Gideon. "The First Owl?" he asked, unable to contain his excitement. "As in the first of your tribe?"

"As in the very first Avian," the Owl replied. "While each tribe had a first of their people, Primanor was the very first of our kind to walk among the Sapiens in the ancient times. A great seer, among other things, he warned of the coming troubles before he died.

The Crow chimed in with an eerie calm. "And what, pray tell, does the prophecy say will befall Avis in the darkest of her days?"

"You'll beg my pardon, dear lady." A deep breath rattled in the elder's chest. "But that information will be shared with the Owls' champion, and them alone…should they be present among us, that is."

There were rumblings of discontent among the Finches before the elder Owl continued.

"What we *will* share is that we believe a small group is behind these disappearances, kidnapping Avians from all of the tribes, and that the prophecy foretells of black wings."

The sharp squeal of chairs echoed through the room as several Finches hastily scooted away from the Crow woman, their faces contorted in distrust. This time, it was Goldfinch who stood.

"Fear not, everyone!" Her voice was full of a songlike cheeriness. "I assure you that Zokya is of no harm to anyone here. Crow may she be, but she has been invited here as my guest."

"Thank you, Madame Goldfinch." Still seated, the Crow bowed at the waist. "You're too kind, and I'm grateful for your hospitality."

Gideon's gaze lingered on Zokya, catching a brief flicker in her eyes. There was something almost otherworldly about them, an undulation of purple. He blinked a few times, unsure, but the color seemed to dissipate; he brushed it off as the dancing of the flames in the fireplace.

Pushing himself up from the table, the Owl rose slowly, his ancient knees cracking. "We have no reason yet to believe that the Crow Tribe is to blame."

Her expression impassive, Zokya dipped her head acknowledging a level of gratitude.

"However," the Owl continued, "the fact remains that the kidnappings have involved beings with black wings. Several witnesses have come forward confirming this suspicion. But fear not, for we are confident that our champion, once chosen, will triumph over whatever evil lurks in the shadows of our continent."

The Finches exchanged curious glances, but the whispers that had once rolled through the room now fell silent, the stillness hanging in the air. Digging his nails into the armrests, Gideon sat on the edge of his seat as the Owl spoke.

"These disappearances have been an enigma to us at the Noktern."

"One might say it's been quite the riddle." Pelanor smirked, taking a long sip of water. Glancing around the table, Gideon noticed the stares of the other Owls, twinges of annoyance in their eyes.

"Indeed, Master Pelanor." There was a growl in the head Owl's voice.

"You've made your point, Valanor." The wood creaked as many shifted in their seats, turning to face Goldfinch, who had once again risen from her chair, her palms spread across the head of the table. "We can all agree to disagree on the severity of the disturbances. A few missing Doves and Finches aren't enough to scare the merchants of Duport. But we are here to entertain the summons of the Owl Parliament. So please, if we can be on with it, I have every confidence that your champion sits among us. Why don't we skip the pleasantries, and you can name him."

"It's funny you should say so, Altuna."

Goldfinch pursed her lips at the informality, but said nothing.

"This very evening, our young Master Pelanor, believes that he has discovered the identity of our champion."

Gideon shot Cas a look of admiration, but his gaze went unnoticed. Instead, Cas turned to Goldfinch, who beamed back at him. A sharp twinge of pain hit Gideon's chest, but he forced it down as he shifted his gaze to Pelanor. To his surprise, the Owl's eyes were fixed on him, an intense stare that seemed to pierce straight through him.

"It is believed that the champion, who was long ago foretold, shall be the answer to our plight," the elder Owl continued. "In turn, the champion shall be the one who possesses the answer to a riddle lost to time itself."

Gideon's ears perked. "A riddle?" The word slipped from his lips in a barely audible whisper, a numbing tingle running through his arms down to the tips of his fingers.

"As representatives of the Owl Tribe, we now ask that the champion answer our riddle."

The five other Owls present rose from their chairs, speaking in unison.

On Ravens & Riddles

"Why is a Raven like a writing desk?"

Time seemed to stand still; breathing felt like a chore, a weight pressing down on Gideon's chest. He could feel the eyes of the entire Owl delegation staring at him, waiting for him to answer.

"Is this some kind of joke?" Lonchura's shrill voice filled the hall, followed by a chorus of murmurs from the other Finches, their dissent ringing in the air.

Gideon turned toward Pelanor who leaned in closer and placed a cold hand on Gideon's forearm. The Finch boy shot up from his seat, his chair clattering to the floor behind him. A dull thud echoed through the room as the wood hit the carpet.

"Excuse me." The words scratched at Gideon's throat; he looked longingly at his water, but the thought of sitting back down in the sea of expectant faces made his heart race. "I...I don't feel well." His legs wobbled beneath him as he stumbled toward the open doorway, his wings brushing against the wall.

Pelanor stood and righted the Finch's chair. "Perhaps you should sit back down, Master Gideon."

"No," Gideon blustered. "Thank you, but no." He fought to quell the panic rising in his chest, but his legs trembled beneath him, barely able to support his weight. "I think I'll just head to my room, if that's alright."

"Yes, yes." Goldfinch dismissed him with a wave of her hand, paying him little mind as she returned her attention to the Owls. "Now, on with this champion..."

Goldfinch's voice faded as Gideon bolted down the hall, practically throwing himself onto the balcony with two strokes of his wings.

Reaching his chamber, he threw open the door and slammed it behind him. With a panicked leap to the bureau, Gideon rifled through his bag and wrenched the book from his leather sack, flipping through it viciously.

There it was, in black and white, the riddle that Pelanor had recited to him earlier, that the entire delegation repeated as if they had rehearsed it.

"This doesn't make any sense!" Thoughts flurried through his mind so quickly that Gideon couldn't follow them, broken fragments of ideas and questions blurring together into nonsense. Head in his hands, Gideon slid down the post of the bed to the floor, folding himself in his wings. He took a few shallow, frantic breaths, feeling the air slowly return to his lungs until he finally managed to steady himself.

"You're being silly," he chided himself. The slurry of thoughts slowed, a thin veil of calm wisping through him. "This is just a misunderstanding." The words offered a fragile sense of comfort. "That's it, Gideon, you just misunderstood. Go back downstairs and ask the Owls–"

He froze mid-thought, the flicker of doubt slicing through him. "No, don't ask the Owls anything. Just go back down, act like nothing happened. You and Cas will laugh about this tomorrow."

Albeit still a bit shaky, Gideon settled in his resolve. Grasping at the bedpost, he lifted himself off the floor and brushed the dust from his backside.

Then, a piercing shriek shattered the silence.

Plates crashed, followed by the sickening thud of bodies hitting the floor. Gideon froze, the blood draining from his face. Cold dread crept through him like ice.

A savage roar rang through the mansion, the guttural bay of some kind of wild animal. Then came footsteps, heavy boots thudding down the hall, the paintings on the wall jostling as it drew closer.

Gideon's heart pounded. Slowly, he retreated, moving as quietly as possible, his hand pressed against the bedframe to steady himself. The tension in the air was suffocating. Whatever was happening downstairs, it wasn't just a misunderstanding.

A gust of chilled air swept through the room as the window flew open, the wooden frame slamming into the wall as it swung in on its hinges. Falling to the ground, Gideon looked up to find himself face to face with a Hawk. Ducking his head and tucking his wings, the stranger stepped in through the window and strode over to the Finch boy. Bending on one knee, his face was steely, but not unkind.

Violent banging erupted from behind the door, the wood visibly bowing with every thunderous *bang*. The stranger laid one strong hand on Gideon's shoulder, drawing the Finch's attention.

Amid the chaos, the Hawk's voice was unusually calm, resonating with confidence.

"You're gonna want to come with me."

Chapter Seven
GIDEON

Gideon's head spun trying to make sense of what was happening. He needed time to think, but he didn't have that luxury. The door was seconds from bursting off its hinges. Decisions had to be made.

"Cas!" he gasped. "I have to go help him."

"There's no time for that." The Hawk's voice was steady, but his lips curled in a snarl as the doorframe groaned under the pressure. "It's now or never." He thrust out his hand. "Are you coming?"

Nodding sheepishly, Gideon took the Hawk's arm and pulled himself upright. The stranger released him and climbed back on the sill.

"Wait!" Gideon darted to the bureau, yanking open his satchel. His fingers brushed against the worn leather of his mother's book, sending a wave of comfort through him. Tying off the knapsack, he slung it over his shoulder and hurried to the window.

Before he was able to climb up on the sill, the door exploded; splinters pelted the nape of his neck.

"Gotcha!" The voice was guttural, thick with phlegm.

Gideon went to turn around, but the Hawk's powerful hand yanked him backward by the collar of his loose undershirt. Before he could resist, he was pulled out the window, free-falling toward the sloping street below.

Gideon flared his wings, the night air rushing beneath his feathers as he caught the wind, gliding down to the cobblestone alley behind the estate.

Realizing that he had miscalculated his landing, panic crept in. He flapped hard, trying to gain altitude, but too late. He plowed straight into the hedgerows lining the estate's perimeter.

He hit the ground with a thud, knocking the breath from his lungs. Dazed, he pushed himself up just as the thunderous sound of wings descended upon him.

Without thinking, Gideon dove headfirst into the hedge, wriggling to escape out into the street beyond. wigs snapped, leaves tore, and barbs snagged his tweed sleeve, tightening their grip the harder he struggled. His outstretched fingers skimmed open air on the other side, but no matter how much he pushed, he was stuck fast.

There was a sudden squeeze on his palm before he was yanked through the topiary with brutal force. Branches clawed at his face, shredding what was left of Goldfinch's dinner jacket as he was ripped free. He tumbled out onto the cobblestones, spitting a mouthful of leaves and picking twigs from his amber hair.

"Let's go."

Before Gideon could catch his breath, the Hawk pulled him down the street by the arm, dragging him west toward the sea.

"Would you hold on a second!" Gideon shouted, twisting his arm against the Hawk's vice-like grip, but he wouldn't relent.

From above, wings pounded against the wind, sound growing impossibly loud. Gideon's eyes snapped upward just in time to see a silhouette that blotted out the stars, the creature plummeting toward them like a meteor.

Upon impact, the street exploded in a shower of cobblestone and dust, the shockwave rattling Gideon's bones.

There's no way it survived that landing…right?

But the Hawk didn't stop running.

To Gideon's horror, the creature rose from the debris, shaking off the rubble as if it were nothing.

Terror surged through Gideon as he stumbled, struggling to keep pace. The Hawk pulled him along, weaving through courtyards and alleyways, twisting through the labyrinthine streets in a desperate attempt to lose the beast.

Finding a covered passage, the Hawk pulled Gideon into the tight recess, the walls barely wide enough for Gideon's wings.

"What kind of champion are you?" The Hawk furrowed his brow, speaking between heavy breaths. "You're no fledgling, but not quite a man either. Not particularly bold by the likes of it, and you don't seem that strong."

Wrenching his arm from the Hawk's grip, Gideon doubled over, hands on his knees. "I…am not…a champion," he panted between gasps.

"Ah, good." Throwing his hands in the air, the Hawk turned back down the alleyway. "Then I shouldn't waste my time saving you, I guess." His rich tenor was tinged with dry amusement, but that didn't detract from his serious undertone. "Why don't you waltz back up the road and tell whatever-the-hell-that-thing-is chasing us that you're not the Owls' champion. I'm sure he'll take your word for it."

Biting his lip, Gideon peered down the alley, still able to hear the creature's pounding footsteps.

"Please," he begged, his voice raw." I don't know what's happening, but I just want to get out of here. Will you help me?"

"I'm sorry." The Hawk casually leaned his shoulder against the marble wall. "But I'm only here to help the Owls' champion. That's not you…you said so yourself."

Panic-stricken, Gideon glanced between the stranger and the main road, weighing his options. "If I were the champion…" He hesitated. "And I'm not saying I am…why would you want to help me?"

Feigning contemplation, the Hawk turned back to him, twisting a finger through his goatee. "Maybe it's because there's a two-ton lunatic barreling down the street trying to kill the one person the Owls believe can save all of Avis." Despite the sarcasm in his words, his delivery was deadpan. Then, flashing a knowing smile, he shrugged. "But that's just my working theory."

The Hawk extended his arm. "So, are you the champion, or not?"

Gideon's heart skipped a beat. Every instinct screamed at him to run, to dive into one of the barrels that pocked the alley and wait for sunrise. But his legs wouldn't move.

A low, grating sound rumbled behind him. He turned just in time to see the creature forcing its way through the narrow passage, stone walls crumbling against its sheer size.

A sharp gasp tore from Gideon's throat. Without thinking, he seized the Hawk's arm.

"I'm the champion!" he squealed. "Now let's go!"

The Hawk took off running, Gideon scrambling to keep up. The path twisted and turned like the coils of a serpent, each alleyway leading into another. Right, then left; they barreled through the maze of buildings, stumbling over barrels and wooden crates in the dark.

At last, the passage widened, but their relief was short-lived. A towering wall loomed before them.

"Nowhere to go but up." Releasing Gideon's arm, the Hawk unfurled his wings and prepared to take off.

"Wait! Gideon threw his hands up. "He'll see us go up and then he'll catch us in no time. I mean, did you even see how big his wings are?"

The stranger paused, considering. "You're right. You stay here, and I'll go up."

"Excuse me?" Gideon balked. "You're not leaving me alone." Gideon brought a finger up to his chest. "Champion here, remember?"

The Hawk pressed two fingers to his forehead in a mock salute. "Yes, your excellency."

Gideon was already beginning to hate the Hawk's stoic sarcasm.

"Look," the Hawk continued, his tone sharpening. "I'm going to fly up, make some noise, and keep him distracted. You stay put until it's clear. Got it?"

Gideon felt a bite of remorse for snapping at him. "And then what?"

Gripping the Finch's shoulders, the Hawk leaned in close, his breath thick with the stench of salted fish. "Get down to the south harbor and board the *Pimpinella*. If anyone gives you a hard time, tell them you're with Rune."

"Rune?"

The Hawk raised an eyebrow. "You have a problem with my name?"

Gideon cast his eyes to the floor, slouching his shoulders to make himself seem smaller. "Nope, no…just making sure I heard you."

Rune shot him a sideways glance before launching into the sky. Dust and grit whipped up in his wake, forcing Gideon to shield his eyes.

"I'll give you the signal," Rune called down, his voice nearly lost in the wind. "Then get to the harbor. Fly low to the roofs and I'll try and keep him busy for as long as I can."

"What about you?"

"I'll be fine. Just wait for my signal and get to the ship."

Wait!" Gideon yelled after him. "What's the signal?"

But the Hawk disappeared beyond the rooftops.

All alone, the sheer walls of the alley were suffocating. Gideon paced in tight circles, one hand yanking at tufts of his hair while he gnawed fingernails on the other. The gravity of his situation felt so much more real.

His mind was flooded with what-ifs.

What if Rune couldn't get the beast's attention?

What if I can't figure out the signal?

What if—

"Shit!" His thoughts screeched to a halt. "What was the name of the ship?" He panicked, trying to remember. "The Citronella? The Pumpernickel?" He smacked his forehead with his palm. "I'm going to die because I can't remember the name of a stupid boat!" His voice cracked, pitch rising. "At least I'm not talking to myself in a dark alley like a lunatic." A quiet wail caught in his throat. He buried his face in his hands, taking slow, deep breaths.

Anticipation coiled tight in Gideon's chest. He couldn't just sit and wait any longer. Slowly, he fluttered up to the nearest rooftop, pressing himself flat against the slick marble. He craned his neck, scanning the sky for any sign of Rune or their pursuer.

"I think the coast is clear."

Backing away from the ledge, he rose cautiously, steadying himself before taking a running leap. His wings unfurled, the blue of his feathers popping out against the alabaster rooftops as he soared.

One rooftop. Then another.

Ahead, Gideon could make out the twin harbors of Duport, like stolid soldiers guarding the waters of the walled city.

Flying low, Gideon skimmed the rooftops, undulating his flight to match as they rose and fell beneath him. The white stone made for an easy path in the dim night, lit only by the waxing moon and scattered oil lamps below. The south harbor couldn't have been more than a thousand yards away.

Coming over a steep peak, a sudden force slammed into him, ripping the air out of his lungs. He fell to the roof with a thud, crashing into the polished stone. His body rolled, the momentum carrying him to the edge of the rooftop.

On Ravens & Riddles

Tipping over the eave, Gideon braced himself when a firm hand clamped around his leg.

Gasping, Gideon twisted his neck, his heart hammering.

"I thought I told you to wait for the signal!" In the dim light, Rune's rugged features came into focus, rubbing his forehead with his free hand.

Still dazed from the collision, Gideon couldn't find the words to answer. He scrambled for anything to grab onto, to pull himself back up onto the roof.

"Calm down." There was an urgency in the command. "We need to move fast. When I let go, get back in the air and make a beeline to the ship. Ready?"

Swallowing hard, Gideon nodded, hoping Rune could see. The Hawk released his leg and Gideon fell over the side. Using the momentum, he spread his wings, feeling the rush of the night air between his feathers. With some maneuvering, he gained altitude and steered himself in the direction of the harbor.

Behind him, a crash erupted on the rooftop where he had been only seconds before, a cloud of dust billowing off the gable. He thought to look back, but it wouldn't do any good. Either Rune was gone and it was too late for Gideon to be of help, or the Hawk was fine. If he turned back now, he'd only make things worse.

Gideon landed on the dock with a soft thud, the wooden planks creaking under his boots. He jogged down the row of barges, muttering to himself as he read the names aloud. "*Sea Serpent*? No. *Pastoral*? Maybe…doesn't sound right. I'll keep looking."

On Ravens & Riddles

At the end of the dock, Gideon could see the pale moonlight shimmer over the Windy Sea; there were no boats left.

His stomach sank, a numbness stinging his chest.

"What do I do now?"

Just as he was about to give up hope, he caught sight of a silhouette in the darkness, an oblong shape gliding out to the open ocean.

"That's got to be it!"

Gideon could already feel a burning in the muscles of his wings; he'd never flown this much or as hard in his lifetime. The ship had to be the right one. If not, he wasn't sure what he'd do.

With no time to lose, he took off again, pushing himself over the abyss.

Despite his aching muscles, Gideon found himself closing the distance to the shadowy ship faster than he'd expected, covering a mile in a few minutes. Duport faded away into the night as he progressed toward the vessel, the tension in his back and wings growing with every stroke. He felt ashamed to struggle this way; other Avians could fly for hours without needing a rest, yet here he was ready to give up only after a few minutes of flight.

In the quiet of his struggle, he made a silent vow: if he made it out of this, he'd train harder, push himself further.

The vessel loomed beneath him when he couldn't push any longer. His wings began to droop, and he glided toward the deck, where the figures of Avians could be seen moving, gathering at the sight of him. They rallied together as they spotted him, ready to deal with an unwelcome arrival.

Gideon's landing was less than graceful. He barreled into a pile of crates and rope laid out against the side of the deck. Several crew members approached him, some with concern in their eyes, others looked ready to throw him overboard.

"What do ya think yer doin', boy?" A hand grabbed his collar, yanking him upright. Gideon's mind raced, but only a jumbled mess of words came out.

"Yer not welcome aboard." The sailor lifted him off the ground, ropes tangled around his legs.

"Throw 'im overboard, Angus!" A chorus of agreement rose up from the Finch crew.

"Please, wait!" Gideon pleaded. "I'm with Rune!" Several of the sailors exchanged hazardous glances. "Is this the…" Gideon racked his mind, scrambling for the name. "The *Pomperetta*?"

"*Pimpinella*." The crewmate, Angus, released Gideon's collar with a sharp shake of his head.

"Yeah, that sounds right." Gideon crossed his arms over his aching stomach, trying to ease the sharp discomfort.

"Where's Rune?" A burly, pink-plumed Finch called out from the group, his wings unnaturally small for his stature. "He better have the money to honor our arrangement, otherwise, you're out of here."

"He should be here soon," Gideon mumbled, though doubt gnawed at him. Still, he had to hope that Rune was alright. If the crew planned to toss him overboard, there was no way he'd make it back. He wasn't sure he could muster the flight back, and he couldn't swim.

With a slow, heavy step, he made his way to the stern, gripping the cool metal railing. His eyes scanned the night sky, searching for any sign of Rune or the titan that had been chasing them. The minutes ticked by, and the city of Duport became nothing more than a faint line on the horizon.

As the cruiser cut through the water, waves slapped against the hull and the crew bustled, preparing for the journey ahead. Gideon turned away from the sea, bracing himself for whatever fate awaited him at the hands of the crew.

Over the din, Gideon thought he heard the beating of wings.

Hope fluttered in his chest as he whipped around, his eyes darting to the sky. Two shadows flitted through the sky, barreling and rolling, their silhouettes darting amid the stars.

Gideon watched them intently, elated to know that Rune was even still alive. But the terror of it all clawed at him, knowing that they were exposed, in the open, with the creature still hunting them. Out on the open sea, there was nowhere left to hide.

Gideon tried to come up with anything that might help, but he was too spent to act.

Rune was on his own.

Not twenty feet from the cruiser, he could almost make out the Hawk's rugged features. The Hawk climbed into the sky, the beast close behind. Higher and higher they rose, until both figures disappeared into the black expanse of the night.

"Look, there!" One of the sailors squawked, pointing toward the sky with a gnarled finger. Even from so far below, the two figures stood out, falling like blazing comets from the heavens.

"He's going to dive into the water." The words rattled in Gideon's chest. None of the tribes boasted any great ability to swim; the water weighed down their feathers, making flight nearly impossible. He watched in horror as Rune, seemingly making the ultimate sacrifice, dove toward the sea.

If this was Rune's plan, it was a desperate one. He would have to swim back to shore, or worse, sink into the depths. Gideon's breath caught in his throat as he watched the two figures plummet toward the water.

Rune struck the water first, his figure serene. The beast was not far behind, realizing only too late what Rune had planned. Struggling against his own momentum, the creature went hurling into the sea behind the Hawk, sending a cascade of foam into the air behind him.

And then silence filled the night.

Gideon couldn't move, trapped by the weight of the sacrifice that a perfect stranger had made for him. The chase was over. He was safe thanks to Rune.

A hand fell on Gideon's shoulder. He turned around, ready to face the crew, to be turned away, forcibly removed from the ship.

"Rune!"

Gideon's mouth fell open, a toothy grin spreading across his cheeks. His legs trembled, hardly able to believe it, but there he was.

"How did you–"

Rune threw a firm hand over Gideon's mouth, silencing him. His grip was firm but not unkind, his calloused palm pressing gently against Gideon's lips. The Finch froze, wide-eyed, as the Hawk's sharp gaze swept over the crew. Water dripped from his soaked clothes, pooling at his feet, yet his wings remained impossibly dry.

"Not here," Rune murmured, his voice barely above a whisper. "I promise to answer all of your questions another time." His tone left no room for argument.

Gideon swallowed hard and nodded. Rune released him, stepping back just as the crew began to gather, their expressions ranging from wary to impatient.

"Toulouse." At his call, the squat, pink-winged Finch made his way through the crowd of sailors. "Can you show Gideon his accommodations please?"

"Be happy to." The Finch sneered and spat on the deck. "Once we get our payment." He held out his hand and rubbed his thumb over two fingers as if rubbing a coin.

"Ah," Rune exclaimed heartily. "I forget myself when it comes to the language of the Finches. There's a sack behind the barrels of eel in the galley. You'll find some golden utensils and other trinkets. Melt it down or sell it, I don't care which."

Gideon raised an eyebrow. "Goldfinch's missing utensils?"

Rune winked.

Toulouse grunted and motioned for Gideon to follow. He led him across the deck to a set of stairs descending into the lower levels. Before stepping down, Gideon glanced back at Rune, who had moved to the guardrail.

"Can you at least tell me where we're going?"

Rune didn't turn around. "Tomorrow."

Gideon exhaled and trudged down the steps, letting his wings sag behind him. "What about you, Toulouse? Where's this ship headed?"

The sailor didn't break stride. "You heard Rune."

"Yeah, yeah," Gideon muttered. "Tomorrow."

Chapter Eight

Socorra

The chamber door creaked open, Tama struggling under the weight of the iron. Instead of forcing it wider, she slipped her frail frame through the narrow gap. Like clockwork, she came twice a day, her carpet bag filled with medicinal herbs, potions, and a small offering of food. Today, it was a piece of dry toast and an apple.

Lying face-down on a filthy bed of straw, Socorra's chains were still intact, though she was no longer suspended from the ceiling. Now, her ankles were shackled, the chains bolted to the wall, allowing only minimal movement.

"Good morning." Tama's voice was feeble, but kind. "Will you eat something today?" The Dove placed the food on the floor near where Socorra's hand dangled over the edge of the bed.

It had been three days since Socorra had eaten; she'd refused each time Tama brought her a new plate, but hunger gnawed at her resolve. Slowly, she pushed herself up with her good arm, careful not to jostle her broken wing. Swinging her legs over the makeshift bed, she flinched as her bare feet met the icy stone floor. Without hesitation, she snatched the plate and devoured the toast. It was stale and cold, but the apple, sweet and crisp, washed away the dryness in her throat.

"I wasn't sure you'd ever snap out of it." Tama chirped as she rummaged through her bag.

Dropping the apple core back onto the plate, Socorra let out a huff. "I guess being locked in a dungeon really does something to your mood." She pulled her feet up onto the mattress, wrapping her arms around her legs.

The sound of Tama's rummaging stilled, leaving only silence between them. Finally, she let out a long breath. "I'm sorry. I know this can't be easy for you."

Socorra snorted. "That's an understatement."

Tama lowered her gaze, exhaling through her nose before raising her hands. "Turn around. Let's have a look at you."

Socorra hesitated but eventually shifted, allowing Tama to adjust the cloth sling. Her fingers pressed gently along the sinew where the Hawk's wing met the muscles in her back. A sharp sting shot through her shoulder, and she winced.

"It's coming along," Tama's voice was detached, professional. "Another three days of rest, and you should be ready to travel. It won't be fully healed, but Craven shouldn't do more damage when he flies you to Raven Rock."

Socorra's ears perked. "Craven? Is that the bastard's name?"

Tama gave a small, reluctant nod as she adjusted the sling. Heat flared in Socorra's blood. "And what exactly does this Craven have planned for me at Raven Rock?"

"I don't know." Tama pulled her hands away, her voice unsteady.

Turning, Socorra caught her picking at her cuticles, tiny beads of blood welling beneath her nails.

"Ama Tama, what's wrong?"

The Dove lifted her head, her eyes glistening with surprise. Her lips parted slightly, as if grasping for something just out of reach. "What did you call me?"

"Ama," the Hawk said softly. "It's an honorific for our female elders."

"Oh." With a sigh, the Dove cast her eyes to the floor. "That's what my son used to call me when he was a fledgling." She spoke in a whisper, sorrow dripping in every breath and crack of her voice. "It took him a long time before he could say 'mama' correctly." A wistful smile crossed her lips. "He's a bit younger than you, I suppose, but not by much. Now, he calls me *mother*, and not often with kindness." A single tear slipped down her cheek, landing on the wrinkled skin of her hands.

Socorra let her wings and shoulders relax, softening her stance to be more welcoming. "Why are you here, Ama?"

The Dove furrowed her brow, lifting her eyes. She wiped her eyes and fussed with her wimple. "If I tell you, you have to promise that you will never tell Craven that we spoke." Her fingers ran along the fabric of her white frock, pressing out the sweat from her palms as she rocked lightly on her toes.

Socorra skirted to the side of the bed, making room on the crooked frame for the Dove to sit. Tama accepted the invitation, carefully gathering the folds of her maroon frock in her hands, as if keeping them still would quiet her trembling. "I'm here for him," she murmured. "For my son…my Rocque."

"They have your son?" The Hawk was heartbroken for her, but relieved; she had wondered how gentle Tama became entangled with the likes of Craven.

"Yes." Tama choked on the word. "When I found out he'd been taken, I begged Craven to release him." She placed a trembling hand against her chest, her breath coming in short, uneven bursts. "He refused."

"How did you find out?" Socorra rested a hand on the Dove's shoulder.

"It was an accident, really." Tama fussed with the hem of her skirt but didn't pull away from Socorra's touch. "You see, a few years ago, Rocque told my husband and me that he had fallen in love. We were thrilled and told him that we wanted to meet her, and that's when things changed. Rocque told us that he hadn't fallen in love with a girl…but with another man."

"Oh." Socorra was unsure of how to respond. For Hawks, this was perfectly normal. True love was a rarity. If two souls were willing to dedicate themselves to one another, no one stood in their way. But the Doves were different. They were steadfast in their religious beliefs, and many were unwilling to accept this type of behavior.

"That's exactly what I said when he told me…*oh*." Tama folded her arms and rose from the bed. "I'll never forget the hurt on his face when I said it." She grimaced and paced slowly across the room. "I was in shock, but my husband had the worst of it. The man was a stark-eyed lunatic! He told Rocque that he would not besmirch our family with his filth, and that he had no son." She pressed a hand to her breast as if the memory caused her great strain.

"When Rocque left the house, I ran after him into the street. It didn't matter to me who or what he was. A mother's love is unconditional. I wouldn't let my son be sent away. He hugged me, and in that moment, I felt like everything was going to be ok…like we could be a normal family. When I invited him back inside, he said that he couldn't."

Her lip quivered, dropping her head into her hands to hide her tears. "He told me he wouldn't live in a home where he wasn't accepted. And I–" her breath hitched. "I got so angry that I cursed him. I told him he was tearing our family apart." A sob wracked her shoulders. "Do you know what he did then?" She let out a broken, bitter laugh. "He hugged me. He held me and said he understood that I was angry. Can you imagine what it feels like? To curse your own fledgling, only for him to turn around and try to comfort you?"

She wiped at her eyes, staring down at her lap. "He finally let me go and told me not to worry about him, that his partner…" she paused, the word lingering in her mouth. "He told me that his partner had a home for them in Tartarus where he'd be accepted."

Socorra had heard of Tartarus—a small encampment of huts and make-shift houses. It was a place for Doves who felt like they didn't belong with the rest of the tribe, a refuge from religious persecution.

"I wanted to be able to meet him somewhere just so I could see him," Tama continued. "But I wouldn't go out to Tartarus. Thinking about the way they all live out there…in their sin…I couldn't see my boy like that."

She turned to Socorra, pleading for understanding, but the Hawk remained silent. While she pitied Tama's grief, she couldn't bring herself to agree with how the Dove had handled things. She hoped to become a parent one day and have fledglings to nurture all her own. She couldn't imagine hating any part of them, no matter who they were or whom they chose to love.

"I told him to meet me the day of the full moon, near Cherub farm on the south shore. We've met there once a moon ever since." Tama's voice softened. "There's a beautiful oak tree at the crest of a hill where we'd sit and eat our picnics. We didn't talk much after the first few times…I suppose it was painful for him whenever I'd mention his father, and he knew it hurt me when he'd mention his…" She let the sentence trail off. "It was nice just to be in each other's company."

The Dove's expression darkened, her eyes glistening with a renewed sadness. "Then, about a moon ago now, Rocque didn't show up. At first, I thought maybe he was running late, but as the sun started to fall, I knew something was wrong. I went to check the farmhouse. It had been abandoned for decades, but I didn't know what else to do. It wasn't like Rocque not to show up.

"When I got to the barn, Craven was coming out." The echo of her footsteps on the stone faltered. "I called out to him from across the field, asking if he'd seen my son. And then–" she took a stifled breath. "I'm still not sure how he did it, but within a second, he had me by the collar, those horrible nails to my throat."

She fell to her knees, her wails piercing the chamber like jagged glass. "He threatened to kill me, but I begged, and begged." Her voice cracked into sobs.

Socorra pushed off the bed to comfort her but barely made it a few steps before the chain on her ankle yanked her back. Frustration flared in her chest. She exhaled sharply, then sank to the floor, closing the distance as much as she could. "Shhh," she soothed, offering soft coos.

Tama sniffled, lifting her tear-streaked face. Slowly, she crawled the last few feet and grasped Socorra's hand in her own, her grip desperate. She opened her mouth to speak, but before she could, Socorra interrupted.

"You don't have to keep going," Socorra gently squeezed the Dove's hand. "I understand."

"No, it's ok. It feels good to talk about it…to let it go." With a sniffle, Tama wiped away her fresh trail of tears from her eyes.

Socorra bowed her head and firmed her grip in Tama's hand, letting the Dove know she was listening.

"Besides, being with you here, it's almost like being with him." Tama swallowed hard, choking on her words. "I didn't get to see him before they took him. It was like a knife to my heart, each day waiting for them to bring him back."

Tama forgot herself, her voice rising until she was almost yelling. "When you didn't eat and lay there so sullen, so alone, it hurt so much. My poor Rocque!" She screamed his name, the echo bouncing around the chamber, her cries raw and unrestrained.

On Ravens & Riddles

Patting her shoulders, Socorra pulled the frail Dove into her arms.

Minutes passed before Tama could collect herself. With a shuddering breath, the Dove pulled away, tucking stray strands of hair back into her wimple. She wiped at her face, smoothing the wrinkles in her frock with shaking hands. "I'm sorry," she murmured, regaining composure. "Where was I?"

Socorra swallowed against the lump in her throat. Despite her best efforts, Tama's grief was getting to her. She exhaled sharply, forcing herself to stay steady. "Craven threatened to kill you."

Tama nodded, as if she had found her place in a book. "He set me down and told me he was taking my son to Raven Rock. Said that if I stayed and served him, maybe I'd see Rocque again."

"Did he tell you why he took your son to Raven Rock?" Socorra pressed.

"No." Tama shook her head, her voice calm with a level of resolve. "The only thing he said was that Rocque would be a changed man if I saw him again. That was weeks ago and I still haven't seen him."

"Have you asked Craven about him?"

"Once, and only once." Tama's eyes widened. He told me that if I asked again, he'd kill my boy."

Socorra's heart ached for the Dove. "No more tears." With a gentle touch, she took the Dove's hand in hers, her voice soft, but resolute. "I'm sorry I ever asked, I didn't mean for you to have to relive that."

Tama went to speak when the iron door slammed against the stone wall, startling the pair. Tossing away the

Hawk's hand, Tama jumped to her feet, leaving Socorra alone on the floor.

Carrying a lifeless figure in his arms, Craven strode into the chamber, followed closely by someone else, another Raven, Socorra presumed.

"Leave us, Tama." Craven didn't even so much as glance at Socorra.

Without a word, Tama snatched up her carpet bag. She turned back for the plate she had brought, but would not meet Socorra's eyes. As she hurried toward the exit, her hands trembled, and rounding the corner, the plate slipped from her grasp. The ceramic shattered into splinters against the stone floor.

"Tama!"

Socorra lunged forward, but the chain on her ankle jerked her back. She collapsed, landing hard on her side. A sharp pain shot through her arm, but a quick check revealed the gauze still held. She let out a pained groan, pressing her palm into the floor to push herself up.

"Don't you worry yourself, songbird." Craven smirked. "It's just a family reunion." With careless ease, he hoisted the unconscious boy toward the chains hanging from the ceiling. His companion stepped in, securing the cuffs around the boy's wrists.

"Let him down, Craven!"

From where she sat, Socorra couldn't see the boy's face, but the state of him was enough. His suit jacket was torn, stained with blood, and his ruby-red feathers were ragged, plucked in patches.

He must have put up one hell of struggle.

Ignoring her outburst, Craven crossed the chamber and grabbed the bucket of Socorra's drinking water and tossed the murky liquid on the Finch.

The boy woke with a violent start, chains rattling as he thrashed. His wings flared, his body jerking against the restraints in pure frustration. Socorra swallowed hard, a twinge of shame hitting her. She must have looked just as pitiful when she had been in his place.

"That's enough of that."

With deft hands, Craven's razor-sharp talons flashed to the Finch's throat. The boy froze, his heaving breaths the only sound in the room. Then, with a satisfied smirk, he reeled back and spat in Craven's face.

Craven didn't flinch. He stood there, a wretched smirk stretching across his lips as the ooze dripped down his cheek.

"You *will* regret that."

"Just try it," the boy balked.

Despite the talons at his throat, he kicked out, landing a solid hit to Craven's stomach. Snarling, Craven retaliated with a swift slash across the boy's cheek, just below his eye.

"Let me out of these cuffs, coward! I'll show you!"

He's either incredibly brave, or really stupid.

Socorra couldn't decide which.

"All in good time." Craven stepped back, shaking the blood from his claws. "But first, you're going to answer a few questions."

"Like hell I will!"

Craven let out a low, amused chuckle. "My boy…" He spread his hands in an invitation, his face twisting in a vile grin. "You seem to think you have a choice." His eyes flicked to his companion. "Zokya. Trance him."

Socorra cocked her head, her feathers bristling.

Zokya was much smaller than Craven, her frame lithe and compact. Her dark hair was swept to one side, revealing a shaved patch where a tattoo of a purple eye stood stark against her bronze skin. She moved soundlessly, the only disturbance the crisp rustle of her suit jacket.

Stopping in front of the boy, she held his gaze, her posture relaxed yet unwavering. Without a word, her eyes flashed a vibrant purple that pulsed in the dim light.

Socorra felt a shiver coil down her spine, an eerie mist rolling in at the edge of her vision. A numbness crawled up her legs, spreading like ice beneath her skin. Squeezing her eyes shut, she wrenched her head away from the Raven's stare. The moment their connection broke, sensation flooded back into her extremities.

"What's your name?" the Raven asked.

Something about her voice unsettled Socorra. It had a soothing, hypnotic quality, the way a snake lulls its prey into a false sense of security just before it strikes.

"Cassin Jay, but you can call me Cas. Everyone does." His tone was neutral, stripped of the anger and defiance that had been there moments before.

"Well, Cas..." Zokya coyly ran a finger up the boy's arm. "What can you tell me about the Owl's prophecy?"

Cas answered without hesitation. "The First Owl foretold of a great darkness that would come, and that a Champion who possessed the answer to the riddle would save Avis."

"Yes, yes." There was a touch of annoyance in Zokya's voice. "I was at the dinner. What else can you tell me?"

"That's all I know."

Craven stepped forward, eyes narrowing. "He's lying."

"He *can't* be lying," Zokya snapped. "He's tranced. I'm not surprised he doesn't know anything. The idiot never answered their riddle. That lummox, Rocque, came barreling in before the Owls told him anything."

Socorra listened intently, trying to piece together their conversation. The details swirled around her, elusive yet intriguing. But one thing was clear, the Ravens believed Cas was at the center of some kind of prophecy.

"I never had the answer to the riddle." Cas lifted his head.

Zokya's calm demeanor quickly devolved into frustration. "Goldfinch was so certain, that hag." She clenched her fists and brought her face to Cas's. "If you don't have the answer, then who does?"

Cas was silent.

The Raven's fists trembled with anger, the muscles in her neck straining. "Who?" Her voice boomed, reverberating through the chamber.

"Gideon."

Socorra thought she heard an air of remorse as the name left the boy's lips.

"The blue-winged brat you let get away?" Craven exploded.

In two swift strides, he was on her, his clawed hand rearing back, ready to strike. But just as he swung, his arm jerked to a stop, frozen mid-air, hovering inches from Zokya's face. She flicked her head and with a sharp twist of his wrist, Craven pressed the talons to his own throat. His anger flickered into panic, gasps hissing through his teeth.

"Craven." Zokya sneered, her voice eerily serene; it gave Socorra shivers. "You should know better than to tussle with me. You act tough, but underneath it all, I know who you truly are…a scared, whimpering nothing who couldn't cut it as a Hawk."

Socorra shook her head.

Craven, a Hawk?

Zokya tilted her head, watching Craven squirm. "If you *ever* raise that deranged claw at me again, I will make you shred yourself to ribbons." Her voice dropped to a whisper. "Do you understand?"

Craven swallowed hard. "Yes."

Zokya looked away, and Craven's arm dropped from his neck as if someone had cut the puppet's string. Without sparing him another glance, she turned to Cas.

"Sleep."

Another flash of purple and the boy went limp, his body slack in the chains.

Socorra's heart beat wildly.

Craven was already a formidable foe, but this witch was something else entirely.

How the hell am I going to fight against that?

Zokya turned, her gaze dismissive. "What a waste." Her footsteps made no sound as she strode toward the door.

Without turning back, she paused in the doorframe. "Get him down and take him to Raven Rock. Even if he isn't this champion, I'm sure the Master will want him for her collection." A cruel smile etched on her lips. "I'll see what I can find of the other boy." She didn't wait for a response, she turned down the hall and was gone.

With a guttural roar, Craven swung his arm, slicing through the Finch's chains. The metal split with a sharp *crack*, and the boy crumpled to the floor. Before Socorra could react, Craven hauled him up, throwing the unconscious Finch over his shoulder like a sack of grain. His limp body dangled between the Raven's wings.

Craven turned, grinning over his shoulder. "I'll be back for you soon, songbird. Tama says you'll be ready in a few days. Then you'll join this one at Raven Rock."

The door slammed shut, the tumblers clicking in the lock.

Socorra sat still, ice creeping through her veins.
I have to get out of here, but how?

*   *   *

It felt like an eternity before Tama returned to the cell. Socorra had begun to worry that she might never see the Dove again.

"Ama Tama," Socorra beamed through the gloom, relief washing over her. "I'm glad you're alright. I was worried."

Tama said nothing, setting down the plate of toast.

"Ama, are you okay?" Socorra asked, her concern deepening. She sat up on the straw bed, Tama taking a place beside her, still silent. "When you screamed, Craven said that you'd seen Rocque. I wasn't sure what to think."

Tama turned her head slowly, her eyes locking onto Socorra's with a deep, unsettling gaze. "That creature wasn't my son." Her voice was hollow, devoid of the warmth and kindness Socorra had come to know. "It may have had his face...but it wasn't my Rocque."

"What do you mean?"

"They did something to him at Raven Rock. His body was misshapen…huge like he could tear a house down with his bare hands. He looked at me like he didn't even know me anymore, such hatred in his eyes."

Socorra's mouth fell open. "I'm so sorry, Ama."

"It would've been better if Rocque had died." She turned back to the plate she had set down, handing it to Socorra with a stiff, deliberate motion. "Eat," she insisted. "I'm sorry I didn't bring you anything last night, but I–"

"There's no need to apologize," Socorra interrupted softly. "You needed time to grieve, I understand."

"No," Tama snapped, her voice sharp. "I will not grieve. No more tears."

Setting the plate on the floor, she rose from the bed and stood in the center of the room. "I won't cry for my son anymore. I want Craven to pay for what he's done." The Dove took a deep breath in through her nose, letting out a controlled exhale. "I spent all night coming up with a plan to make that happen."

Socorra's heart twisted with sympathy for Tama, but a new sense of awe washed over her. The fragile woman she had seen before had vanished. In her place stood someone unshaken, resolute, a woman with a renewed sense of purpose.

"What do you need me to do?"

Chapter Nine
GIDEON

The dining hall of the Goldfinch Estate was empty, its furniture cleared away. Cas stood at the far end, his back to a roaring fire in the marble hearth. He faced Gideon, horror glistening in his eyes.

The fire crackled behind him, exploding into purple flames, a villainous light against the pallid stone. Cas threw his arms out, pleading, but Gideon couldn't move. No matter how hard he tried, his body remained frozen. The fire surged, pouring from the hearth like a feral creature, its arms grasping for him, embers licking his skin.

Cas let out a horrific, ear-piercing wail as the fire consumed him whole.

Gideon jolted awake, slamming his forehead against a metal pipe that stretched overhead. He hissed, rubbing the sore spot as he caught his breath. Sweat misted his brow, the dream clinging to him like a phantom weight on his chest.

Drawing a deep breath into his lungs, the Finch swung his legs over the edge of his net hammock and climbed down. The cabin was stifling, its cramped walls crisscrossed with ducts and hoses. Wiping the sweat from his legs and torso, he threw on a clean tunic and a fresh pair of breeches. His boots and knapsack sat in the corner. He hesitated for a moment before grabbing the bag. He doubted he'd need it, but leaving his things unattended didn't seem like a wise choice.

Opening the bulkhead, Gideon was assaulted by the stench of burning coal. The metal floor seared his bare feet, forcing him to hop back and slip his boots on. His eyes darted up and down the dimly lit corridor; he tried to remember which direction he had come from the night before.

"Whatever," he shrugged. "I'll figure it out."

He turned left, following the lanterns that swayed from the low ceiling. The only thing he heard was the steady hiss of steam through the pipes and the rhythmic thud of his own footsteps. The corridors twisted like a labyrinth; every turn looked the same as the last, until finally, he stumbled upon the staircase that led to the deck.

Sunlight streamed down through the open archway, forcing him to squint. The moment he stepped onto the deck, the salty breeze hit his lungs, reviving him after a night of restless sleep.

Rolling back his shoulders and stretching his wings, Gideon sauntered to the stern. He slung his arms over the railing, resting his head on his forearms as he gazed at the endless expanse; the sea and sky met in a seamless horizon, blue everywhere he looked. For a brief moment, he felt at peace.

Then the gravity of his situation crashed down on him, heavy and inescapable.

"I hope Cas is safe."

There was also the question of where Rune was taking him, and what his plans were once they arrived.

Questions buzzed in his head, each demanding an answer. All Gideon knew was that the Hawk owed him explanations.

His stomach grumbled.

"Food first." Turning back to the bridge, Gideon set off on the hunt for the galley. "Then answers."

Trotting up the deck, doubt started to creep in.

What am I even doing on this ship?

Why did I follow Rune?

Things had happened so fast, it was all a blur.

"Too late to worry about it now."

Reaching the accommodation, Gideon paused before the doorway. Not far, Rune soared above the water, his ruddy wings cutting effortless through the air.

Gideon watched in awe as the Hawk tilted forward, skimming the waves with his wingtips before plunging his arms into the sea. In one swift motion, Rune shot upward, a fish clutched in his grasp, its silvery scales glimmering in the sunlight.

Gideon exhaled, both impressed and envious. "What I'd give to be able to do that."

With three powerful strokes, Rune flew back to the ship, landing with ease at Gideon's side. "Good morning." He shook the seawater from his arms. "How'd you sleep?"

"Fine," Gideon stammered.

"You're lying." Rune cast him a sideways glance. "I can see it in your eyes."

"I had a bad dream," he snapped, more irritably than intended. "That's all."

Gideon's wings tensed as the Hawk studied him. Fortunately, a well-timed groan from his stomach seemed to break Rune's scrutinous concentration.

"Let's get you something to eat." Rune slung the arm-length fish over his shoulder by the tail and started toward the door. "I know you've got questions. I'll do my best to answer them over breakfast."

The Hawk pushed open the swinging door to the galley, motioning for Gideon to follow. The instant the Finch stepped inside, the smell of fish and hot grease hit him like a wall. Folding over himself, he gagged.

Rune clapped him on the shoulder. "On second thought, why don't I grab you a plate?"

Gideon nodded vigorously and bolted back through the door, gulping in the fresh sea air. Spotting a pile of wooden crates near the front of the ship, he fluttered up onto them and sat down, overlooking the endless blue. The way the waves shifted and shimmered under the sunlight was mesmerizing. He didn't want to look away.

Minutes later, Rune flopped down beside him, handing over a plate heaped with food. Gideon's stomach ached with hunger, but when he looked down, the fried cod's glassy eye stared right back at him. Grimacing, he tore off a piece of bread and placed it over the fish's eye.

Much better.

Now that he didn't feel watched, he dug into the rest of his meal: eggs, bread, and even some of the fish.

"So, what would you like to know?" Rune tore into the plate, using a slice of bread and his hands as utensils.

Gideon swallowed his mouthful of food. "Where did you learn to fish like that?"

The Hawk raised an eyebrow. "With everything that you've been through the past day, that's what you want to talk about?"

Gideon shrugged. "I was just curious."

"Huh," Rune grunted, unreadable. He took another bite before finally answering. "My father was an osprey."

Gideon cocked his head.

As if sensing the Finch's confusion, Rune continued. "That's what we call our specialized fishermen in Zarpa. He used to take me out to Hawk Head Bay as a fledgling…taught me everything he knew."

"I wish I could fly like you."

Rune paused mid-bite, a line of fish grease trailing down his chin. "What do you mean?"

"Oh, come on, like you don't know?"

Rune arched a stern brow, and Gideon immediately regretted his tone. He shifted, clearing his throat.

"I just mean…the way you fly. The loops, the twirls…you make it look effortless! I could barely make it to the harbor last night, and that was just a straight line." He gnawed the inside of his cheek. "It was exhausting."

Rune wiped his chin with the back of his hand. "Have you ever tried?"

Gideon thought for a moment. "Not really."

"Then how do you know you can't?"

Gideon had no response. He knew Rune was right, but admitting it was another thing entirely.

Rune let the silence hang for a moment. "Any other questions?"

That small push made Gideon feel uneasy. There were too many things he needed to ask, but the right words refused to come. His head felt like it might split open with the pressure. And then, suddenly, the questions poured out.

"Who are you, and what were you doing at my window last night?" He set the plate down, his appetite forgotten. "Where are you taking me? Is Cas alright? What happened to everyone downstairs? Who was that monster chasing us?"

He ran out of breath.

With a quick draw of air, he continued.

"Why do you and the Owls think I'm some kind of champion?"

Turning his head, Gideon tried to meet Rune's gaze, but the Hawk kept his eyes fixed straight ahead. "Any particular order you want those answered?" His voice betrayed no sign of emotion.

Gideon's shoulders sank. He turned his attention to the sea, hoping for comfort, but the cresting waves offered none.

"Can you just tell me what's going on?" Desperation cloyed in his tone. He picked up his plate again, more to fidget with the food than to eat it. His stomach still grumbled, but his appetite had soured under the weight of uncertainty.

Rune huffed. "I was hired by one of the Owls at the dinner party. They asked me to act as an independent agent, to help out if anything went wrong. Beyond that, I didn't know the details of the job."

Gideon frowned. "How did you know something had gone wrong? How did you end up at my window?" He tore off a piece of bread, nibbling as he waited.

Gideon narrowed his eyes. "I got to the Goldfinch estate a few hours before you did."

"Is that when you stole Altuna's gold utensils?"

"It was." Rune smirked and the tension between them eased. "I had some time to canvas the town and take care of a few errands. After getting the layout, I spent most of the evening listening at windows."

Even though Gideon was finally getting answers, more questions crowded his mind, but he forced himself to remain quiet as Rune continued.

"Once the Owls revealed that you were their champion, my job became keeping you safe no matter what."

"Wait," Gideon blurted. "So, you definitely think that, *me*, I'm the Owls' champion?" Gideon could taste the fish coming back up. "How do you know?"

Rune shot him a sideways glance. "Getting a look at you, I'll admit…I'm just as surprised as you are."

The words stung more than Gideon expected, but he swallowed his bitterness.

"But sure enough," Rune continued, "he was certain that you were the one who would save Avis."

"He?" Gideon raised an eyebrow.

"All in due time."

"Really, Rune?" Gideon whined, his voice riddled with frustration.

"I have very specific orders," Rune said flatly. You'll get your answer, but not here."

Gideon shot him an inquisitive stare, but the Hawk didn't budge.

"Fine," Gideon spat. "He's wrong though, I'm no champion."

Rune remained silent, keeping his gaze fixed ahead.

Gideon let out a *huff*. "Did you at least see what happened to my friend Cas last night?"

The Hawk's demeanor didn't change, but something in his voice softened. "No, I'm sorry."

A sinking feeling weighed in Gideon's stomach. Everything he ate churned as if a storm hit the sea, torrents sloshing about in his gut.

"I was outside the window of the dining room when the Owls asked their riddle," Rune explained. "Then a chair fell. I peered in to make sure everything was alright, but you'd already bolted from the table. I figured you'd head back to your room, so I went to your window just in case things went wrong. I never saw what happened to the others."

Gideon fought back tears. He wanted to believe Cas was alright. Maybe he'd escaped the dinner party and was safe back home in Moda. Maybe he was even out searching for Gideon now. But the bitter edge of doubt gnawed at him, relentless and sharp. He feared the worst.

He turned away from Rune, frustration pressing against his composure, though he doubted he was hiding it well.

"As far as the giant," Rune continued, "I don't know anything about him. I can only assume he's part of this darkness that the Owls mentioned."

Gideon wiped his eyes and turned back to the sea, barely looking at Rune. He took a slow, steady breath, forcing the emotions down before asking, "So, what is your plan for me when we get to the Desertlands?"

Rune cocked his head, a slight flinch in his brown-speckled wings. "Who said we're going to the Desertlands?"

"The sun's behind the ship, which means we're still heading west from Duport," Gideon said evenly.

Rune dipped his head slightly, but said nothing.

"Even if that weren't the case," Gideon continued, "we've been sailing for nine, maybe ten hours by my best estimate. If you were taking me back to Moda, we'd see the Finchlands by now."

The Hawk leaned back, resting his palms on the crate behind him. "You've been sailing before, have you?"

"No." Gideon shrugged. "It's basic geography."

"Well, aren't you a scholar?" Rune nodded in approval. "We should arrive in Konstat this evening before the sun sets."

"And from there we'll sail back to Moda." It was a statement, not a question.

The contentment on Rune's face faded, replaced by his normal stoicism. "From there we'll travel north. You're wanted at the Noktern."

Gideon tensed. The Noktern—the Owls' great sanctuary, where scholars safeguarded the world's history before the Great End. Their knowledge and influence stretched across the continent, revered by all tribes. A flicker of curiosity tugged at him, the part of him that longed for answers.

What could they possibly want from me?

"I want to go home." His voice was quiet but firm.

Gideon had no great love for Moda, but he longed for the simplicity of his old life. He wanted to read by the fountain, to walk to Wydah's bakery for an orange tart. Even with all his resentment toward his father and the rigid world of the Finches, there was security there. No monsters in the dark. No two-ton Avians chasing him.

Rune made no sign that he had even heard Gideon. The two sat in silence for what felt like forever. Around them, the crew bustled about the ship, squawking orders at one another. The sun beat down on Gideon's neck, but the heat was nothing compared to the growing weight in his chest.

Finally, Rune stood, gathering both plates in his hands. His wings stretched out slightly behind him as he turned. "If that's what you truly want, Gideon, I'll see you home."

Gideon searched for any trace of emotion in the Hawk's face, but as always, Rune gave nothing away. Without another word, he strode toward the galley, leaving Gideon alone with his thoughts.

Unsure of what to do next, Gideon leaned against the railing, staring out at the water. He thought Rune's promise to take him home would be a relief, but all he felt was hollow disappointment. A flush of embarrassment burned his face, like he'd somehow let the Hawk down.

"What do I care? I don't even know him." He tried to convince himself, but the thought did little to ease his frustration.

Gideon spent the next several hours lying on top of the bridge, trying his best to stay out of the sailors' way. At the peak of the ship, Gideon could see for miles around him, nothing but sea, the breeze tugging at his hair and feathers. He had fetched the blanket from his cabin and laid it out to keep from burning on the hot iron.

By mid-afternoon, he had nearly finished his book. When he finally glanced up from the pages, the jagged peaks of the Palerock Mountains pierced the horizon like the teeth of a great beast. Gideon lay on his belly, arching his wings to block the glare of the sun before turning back to his story.

Oh, I've had such a curious dream!

The line struck him; his own journey felt no more real than a traipse through Wonderland.

"I'll wake up soon," he murmured to himself. "Just like Alice." He turned the final page, carefully tucking the book away in his knapsack. "Hopefully, this is the final chapter in my journey, too."

The heat pressed down on him, making his limbs heavy. As his eyelids drooped, a wanton loneliness crept in.

"I hope Cas is ok."

With that, he drifted off to sleep.

*   *   *

Gideon wasn't sure what to do. The ship was ready to dock at Konstat; he had searched the entire vessel, but he couldn't find Rune anywhere. With a resigned sigh, he gave up and settled himself amid a cluster of crates in a corner near the bow, keeping a tight grip on his knapsack.

"Just sit right here." A passing sailor eyed him strangely. Gideon lowered his voice to a whisper. "Rune will come find you."

"Drop anchor!"

A chorus of voices echoed the command. The ship shuddered as chains rattled against the hull, and the anchor plunged into the sea, sending up a burst of white mist over the railing.

Just ahead, two Finches unhooked the chains securing the railing, clearing a path for the gangway. Below, another team of dockworkers maneuvered the grated iron plate into place. The harbor buzzed with movement: crates hoisted onto shoulders, voices calling orders, the steady rhythm of boots against the deck.

Gideon watched for twenty minutes. Still no sign of Rune.

With a reluctant sigh, he pushed himself up, deciding to check below deck one last time. He had barely taken a few steps when a gruff voice called out behind him.

"Where do you think you're off to, boy?"

Gideon turned sharply. Toulouse.

The burly Finch squared his shoulders and puffed out his chest.

"I'm just–" he stammered. "I'm looking for Rune."

Toulouse's expression darkened. "I don't think so." He flicked his wings in irritation and jabbed a thick finger toward the gangway. "Get off my ship!"

"Of course, I just have to…"

His voice trailed off as Toulouse stomped toward him. Though Gideon stood a head taller, he had no doubts the stocky Finch could snap him like a twig.

"Off!" Toulouse squawked, his breath hot and furious.

Gideon didn't wait for another warning. Heart hammering, he ducked around the crates and bolted for the gangway, dodging crew members who sneered and jeered as he passed. His feet hit the dock, and he kept running, weaving through the crowded shipyard, pushing past merchants, sailors, and traders.

Only when his lungs burned did he finally stop.

"What do I do now?" he muttered between ragged breaths. His chest ached with anxiety, his pulse thrumming in his ears. He stood in the heart of the shipyard, surrounded by strangers too busy with their own business to notice the distressed Finch in their midst.

"Think, Gideon," he told himself, forcing his mind to steady. "What's the next move?"

Chapter Ten

CAS

Writhing against the cuffs that bound him to the steel slab, the tattered leather dug into Cas's wrists. Every jerk sent fresh agony lancing through him as iron chains pierced his wings, shredding flesh with each desperate pull. Blood pooled beneath him, matting his feathers in thick, sticky clots. Still, he struggled, biting down on the cloth gag stifling his cries, his body convulsing with every shock of pain.

The light was unbearable, an unnatural radiance searing through his closed eyelids, leaving him blind and vulnerable. Stripped of sight, he forced himself to focus on his other senses. Footsteps, sharp and deliberate, clicked against the floor, drawing closer. He thrashed harder, the chains rattling, his breathing ragged as the sound circled him, slow and menacing.

A muffled scream tore from his throat as something cold and sharp pressed against his forehead. His body seized with renewed fury, his thoughts awash with raw, unfiltered rage. He wanted to tear free. To rip. To make them pay for treating him like some caged beast.

A soft shush slithered into his ear, a breath brushing against his skin.

"Enough of that now," a woman cooed. Her voice was low and laced with amusement, like she was soothing a crying fledgling. She traced whatever sharp implement in a deliberate path across his forehead, one side then the other, before retracting it. The pressure released and a sharp jab hit the tip of his nose like the sting of a wasp.

"Craven, dear," the woman murmured, her tone dripping with tenderness. "Do be sweet and dim the lights so our poor Cas can see."

The sharp glare receded. Cas blinked through the lingering pain, his vision adjusting. The world came into focus, alien shapes, machines unlike anything he'd ever seen. His eyes darted about the room, hunting for the voice.

The woman stood to his right, her eyes studying him. As he caught her stare, Cas felt his fear and anger melting away. There was something about her that reached deep and filled him with a quiet euphoria. The gray tiles behind her turned to mist, the sterile room fading until only she remained against a hazy backdrop.

He had been ensnared by Zokya's trance before, but this was different. There were no invisible strings pulling at his will, no compulsion worming its way into his mind. He simply felt at ease, weightless, as though he were drifting on the Azure Deep.

She placed a hand on his shoulder, her touch like silk against his skin. "I'll take the gag out of your mouth," her thin lips curved, "but you have to promise me you'll behave. Can you do that for me?"

Cas nodded effusively.

Slipping the cloth from his mouth, she let it fall away. "You may call me Cecilia." Her voice dripped like honey.

"Cecilia." His own voice sounded strange, distant.

She was older than he had first thought; he guessed she was about his mother's age, but time had barely touched her. Golden tendrils framed her delicate features, but streaks of silver wove through her hair, betraying her otherwise youthful appearance.

Turning away, Cecilia moved with an effortless grace, her linen gown trailing behind her like wisps of smoke. Her wings unfurled ever so slightly, dark as a storm against the night, streaked with veins of aquamarine that shimmered like cracks of lightning. For a moment, Cas simply watched them, mesmerized.

With a flick of her wrist, the vapor tugging at his vision undulated, partially revealing the room, at least, the items around her. She reached for a metal case mounted on the wall, the hinges shrieking in protest as she opened it. The heavy lid slammed against the wall, exposing a panel of buttons and levers.

Cecilia's fingers danced over the controls before settling on one. A sharp *click*. The low grind of gears.

He tensed as the steel platform tilted forward, slow and deliberate, dragging him upright. The weight of his body pulled at him, the iron chains in his wings rattling as gravity took hold. But the restraints held firm.

Cecilia returned to where Cas hung; her presence felt effortless. A fresh wave of panic surged in his chest, but it faded just as quickly as it had come. From this new angle, he could finally see what she had dragged across his skin. Her left hand bore jagged, onyx talons—the same grotesque claws as Craven. But her right hand remained unblemished, smooth and delicate.

Cas's breath hitched, his mind urging him to recoil, to resist. And yet, as she tilted her head, watching him with that knowing smile, his fear melted away. Bliss washed over him, drowning out the alarm screaming in some distant corner of his mind. Even the sight of her monstrous claws barely registered.

"Such a strong young man," Cecilia purred, her voice wrapping around him like a warm breeze. Cas flushed at the compliment. "And handsome, too. Don't you think, Craven?" She glanced over her shoulder, though from where Cas stood, there was no one there.

"I suppose…if you're into brainless fledglings."

The mist behind Cecilia shifted, swirling in slow, almost rhythmic eddies. A figure began to take shape, Craven, just barely visible through the fog. Cas knew he should be angry; he should snap back at the insult. Something deep within him twisted and thrashed, clawing its way toward the surface.

His lips parted, but no sound came.

"Ah, Craven." Cecilia let out a soft, musical laugh. "Ever the bleak naysayer." She moved with an effortless grace, reaching behind her. A moment later, a metal cart emerged from the haze, its surface gleaming with an array of sharp, glinting instruments. "You were much less depressing before the change."

"I don't care to remember it."

"I know, dear." She pouted, her lips curling in mock sympathy. "It must have been difficult, a Crow boy growing up in the Hawklands."

"I was never a Crow." The words came out as a choked snarl, raw and venomous.

"No," Cecilia sighed, her voice thick with amusement. "I suppose you weren't. You did have those brown wings before I changed you. But those hazel eyes, pale skin and hooked nose?" She tilted her head, studying him. "Dead giveaways of your ancestry."

"Don't."

The single word was sharp, but Cas caught the tremor in Craven's voice. Up until now, the man had been a monster, cruel and remorseless. Yet here, in the presence of the Master, he was reduced to a sniveling fledgling.

"Oh, come now, Craven." Cecilia waved a dismissive hand, as if batting away his discomfort. "There's no shame in having had a Crow father."

"Leave him out of this!" Craven exploded, his rough figure heaving with anger. "He was a good man, and those bastards–" His voice faltered, His silhouette wavered before retreating deeper into the mist.

"I know, my love," she entreated, her eyes softening. "No need to be upset. What's done is done; there's no sense in dwelling on the past."

A breath of silence. Then, from somewhere in the fog–

"No," Craven muttered. "We can only seek revenge."

Cecilia's lips curled. "Is that why you remain in my service, Craven?" she asked, her tone teasing. "For revenge?"

There was a short pause before he answered, his tone hushed. "You've given me the power to take it." He swallowed hard before continuing. "I serve you to show my gratitude."

"Whatever drives you, my sweet. Now, be off and ready the recovery chamber."

"Yes, Master," Craven answered, his voice barely above a whisper. Though Cas couldn't see him through the mist, he heard the rustling of feathers. A sudden gust of air swept through the chamber as Craven took flight, lifting the loose ends of Cecilia's golden locks. With a single talon, she tucked them neatly behind her ears.

Even in his hazy, blissful state, Cas found the silence unsettling. The way she toyed with the instruments on the cart, the quiet clinking of metal; it gnawed at him. He wanted to hear her voice, that angelic lilt that sent warmth through his veins. "Cecilia, I–"

She silenced him with a single motion, pressing the sharp edge of her talon to his lips. There was a sting as it grazed the skin, a warm trickle of blood pooling on his tongue. Shushing him softly, she withdrew her claw, returning her attention to the tray as if he were no more than a fledgling who had spoken out of turn.

From the cart, she plucked a small vial, tilting it between her fingers. A thick, black liquid clung to the glass, sluggish and ominous. Cas squinted at the label, but the script was foreign to him.

"I bet Gideon could read that," he mused aloud, his mind still swimming. "He's so smart."

Cecilia stilled; a flicker of annoyance crossed her face. When she turned her head, her gaze was sharp. "Then it's a shame your friend isn't here to tell you what it is." The sweetness in her voice had curdled.

A pang of regret struck Cas, though he wasn't sure why. He knew he had upset her; he didn't want that. "I'm sorry," he offered, but the words felt hollow. Something inside him writhed, anger and confusion. It built in his chest, crawling through his limbs like a foreign invader. The restraints rattled as his muscles tensed involuntarily.

Cecilia arched a delicate brow, more intrigued than concerned. "Stronger than Craven led me to believe," she mused, watching as his body fought against her spell. "Impressive."

Her voice coiled inside his mind, wrapping around his thoughts like a serpent. His limbs fell slack. He was weightless, trapped in the vast nothingness of her control. His mind, however, still reeled. He wanted to scream, to curse, to demand answers, but his lips refused to move.

"Not that strong, I guess." Her lips curled in an arrogant sneer. "It won't matter. Once you change, you'll have no choice but to comply."

Comply? This woman is nuts!

Cecilia plucked a syringe from the tray. Tipping the vial, she stabbed the needle into the rubber cap, drawing the thick liquid into the barrel. Holding it up to the light, she flicked the glass with a sharp tap, sending a tremor through the black fluid.

Cas's breathing became labored. He wanted to run. To fight. To do anything. But his body was no longer his own.

Cecilia leaned in, her breath warm against his cheek. "Don't worry, it'll be over soon, and then you'll be mine."

The needle plunged into his neck.

A firestorm ignited in his veins. Cecilia's trance shattered as agony consumed him, his screams tearing through the sterile chamber. The black liquid surged through his bloodstream, spreading like a disease. His arms convulsed, fingers clawing against the steel restraints. His skin burned, his bones ached, but nothing compared to the searing torment in his wings.

From the corner of his vision, he saw it happening. The crimson bled from his feathers, the color draining away like ink in water. For a fleeting, horrifying moment, he thought they were burning. His once vibrant wings darkened, black as the abyss.

Through the haze of pain, he saw her—Cecilia. But she wasn't Cecilia anymore. The kindness in her eyes had vanished. What remained was something hollow, something cruel. Her delicate features twisted, her lips curling into a grin as she watched him, relishing in his torment.

✳   ✳   ✳

Pain lanced through Cas's body as he stirred, the cold stone floor biting into his skin. He had no sense of how much time had passed, but it felt like only seconds; the memory of the slab was vivid, seared into him as if he were still bound to it.

He pushed himself up, slow and unsteady, when something slipped from his fingers. A crumpled piece of paper fluttered to the ground. Bending to retrieve it, he squinted into the darkness, but the words were lost in the shadows. His gaze flicked around the chamber. A thin shaft of natural light filtered through a grate in the ceiling.

He tried to hover, wings twitching, but they were leaden, lifeless. The effort sent a dull ache rippling through his back. Gritting his teeth, he angled the note in the light.

Behold what you've become.

His pulse stuttered. He flipped the paper over, searching for more. An explanation, a name, anything. Nothing. With a frustrated breath, he crumpled the note and let it fall.

The chamber was bare. No doors, no windows, just a pile of mildewed straw in the corner. The only other object was a full-length mirror, precariously hanging from a rusted nail. His reflection caught his eye, and he froze.

A stranger stared back at him.

His body was bulked with unnatural muscle, veins bulging beneath his skin. His wings were black, the color of matte charcoal, save for the tips, where thin lines of crimson remained. His breath quickened. He scrubbed at his feathers, desperate to rid them of whatever filth stained them. Pain shot through his arms, but he kept rubbing.

Nothing changed.

A fire burned in his chest, rising in his throat. Before he knew what he was doing, he lunged at the mirror. It exploded, splintering into thousands of shards. He hit the ground hard, pain flaring where jagged edges bit into his shoulder. Blood pooled warm against his skin, but he barely felt it.

All he saw were the broken fragments around him, dozens of fractured reflections.

Each one stared back at him with the same glowing, infernal red eyes.

Not his eyes. He'd become a monster.

Chapter Eleven
GIDEON

Screams rained down from the ships, the voices of Finches foaming in a cacophonous mess. Gideon swallowed hard, a lump forming in his throat as bodies jostled past him, shoving without a second thought. Trembling, he clutched his knapsack, wishing that the chaos would pause long enough for him to think.

"Hey, mister," A rough voice cut through the din. Gideon barely registered it before the speaker coughed, softening her tone. "You alright?"

The world snapped back into focus. Blinking, Gideon lifted his head, still feeling untethered in the frenzied shipyard. Compared to this, Moda felt like a quiet backstreet. He tried to center himself, focusing on the girl before him. She couldn't have been older than twelve, draped head to toe in a flowing black robe.

"I'm fine," he stammered. "Just a little lost, I guess."

"Silly," the girl giggled, a bright, tinkling sound. "How can you be lost when you just got here?"

Gideon found himself chuckling despite the tension in his chest; her laughter was infectious.

"I'm Fatima." She gathered the fabric of her robe and attempted a clumsy curtsy.

"Gideon."

"Where are you trying to go, Gideon?" Her persistent giggling rang like a bell. "Maybe I can help you find your way."

On Ravens & Riddles

Leery to trust another stranger after being abandoned, Gideon hesitated before responding. "I'm trying to get back home to Moda."

Fatima tilted her head, giving him a curious look. A few strands of dark, wavy hair slipped out from beneath her headscarf. "Do you have a lot of cargo or something?" She raised an eyebrow. "Why don't you just fly?"

"Oh, uh," Gideon sputtered. "I'd rather take a ship is all."

"If you say so." She shrugged, then leaned in and grabbed his hand. "Come on, I'll take you to where they sell tickets."

Before Gideon could say anything, she spun around and started pulling him up the dock. They passed several Finches who were busy loading and unloading ships.

"Why are there no Sapiens working the dock?" Gideon shouted above the noise despite how close she was. "It's all Finches."

Fatima stopped short, and Gideon almost barreled into her.

"You don't see any Sapiens at all?" There was a hint of amusement in her voice

Gideon scanned the bustling dock, then looked back at her. Of the dozens of people they'd passed, all of them had wings. "No, I…" He blinked, his thoughts catching up. "You're a Sapien!"

His voice shook with disbelief; he couldn't believe he hadn't noticed that Fatima had no wings.

"Yes, I am."

Gideon's cheeks reddened. "I'm sorry, I didn't even realize."

Hand to her mouth, Fatima chuckled.

"You like to laugh a lot," Gideon remarked, studying her quizzically.

"It's good to laugh, isn't it?"

"If you say so," he answered, though something about it felt off. He couldn't put his finger on why, but it unsettled him.

Gideon couldn't help but stare at her; he had never seen a Sapien before. He had only read about them in stories or overheard other Finches gossiping. As he looked at the exposed skin on Fatima's forearm, he noticed the short hairs there. It wasn't what he had expected. He had always imagined Sapiens to be furrier, but Fatima looked every bit like a Finch, except for her lack of wings.

Maybe she's too young. She hasn't grown into her coat yet.

"Or maybe the stories Finches tell are just wrong." He whispered to himself without realizing it.

"Did you say something?"

"Nope," he stammered.

They reached the end of the harbor and climbed a set of stairs carved into the low cliff overlooking the sea. At the top, a limestone street stretched out before them, flanked by squat mudbrick buildings that seemed to rise directly from the ground. As they walked through the street, Gideon marveled at the dozens of Sapiens milling about. He was in awe. Even the adults looked just like Fatima. Most of the women were covered from head to toe, leaving only their faces exposed, but the men were far less hairy than Gideon had imagined. Apart from their inability to fly, they truly resembled Avians in every other way.

"Fatima," Gideon began. "If you don't mind me asking, what's all over the robes people are wearing? They almost look like pearls."

"It's called plastic," Fatima explained without breaking her stride.

"Oh, I've heard of that. Sometimes it washes up on the beaches in the Finchlands. Some larger pieces end up in museums, but I don't know what happens to the rest of it."

"Your Merchant Council has it shipped here, and we repurpose it." She pointed out some of the decorations on the storefronts, noting that they were reused plastics. "Our ancestors used to make things with it. Now we use them for decoration. We sew them into our clothes, make furniture, and in our art. We use them however we can."

Despite being so close to the sea, Gideon noticed that the salty air was giving way to the dry scent of earth. As they walked, he kicked up loose dirt and dust from the tan brick path.

Stopping abruptly, Fatima turned and pulled Gideon into a hug. "Well, Gideon." She gripped him tighter. "It's been a pleasure meeting you. The tickets are sold three stands down." She giggled lightly. "I hope you get back to Moda safe and sound."

Gideon tensed in the embrace, unsure how to respond. "Thank you," he said awkwardly, giving her a gentle pat on the shoulder. "You too." His face flushed a deep red.

You too!?

He was mortified, but Fatima said nothing about it.

After what felt like an eternity, he finally managed, "Fatima, can I go now?" He didn't want to seem rude in case a long embrace was part of a local custom, but he couldn't take it any longer.

"Oh, of course." Without letting go, Fatima spun them both around, as though they were waltzing. Gideon quickly scanned the area to see if anyone was watching. Of course, they were. A group of Sapien men at one of the stands were shaking their heads in disbelief.

Pulling away abruptly, she placed her hands behind her, stepping back slowly. "It's been lovely. Good luck." With a quick twist, she turned and hurried down the street.

"What the heck just happened?" Gideon muttered, scratching his head. He glanced back at the group of men, who were still eyeing him with pity. Trying to avoid their disapproving gazes, he made his way to the ticket vendor, where a surly-looking woman was working behind the counter.

"Good morning." Gideon cleared his throat.

"Eh, what's so good about it?" The woman spat; her breath reeked. Despite his best efforts, Gideon winced at the smell. "Hey, you got a problem, Finch?"

"Who, me?"

"Yeah, you. You birds are always coming in here looking down on us Sapiens. Why don't you tell me what you want so I can stop looking at ya."

Gideon felt his cheeks flush with heat. "Just a boat ticket to Moda, please."

"Sure, whatever." Muttering under her breath, she pulled a small card from beneath the desk and scribbled a few notes on it. She slammed a stamp down with force, sliding it across the counter, her thumb still pressing on it. "Ship leaves in three days."

"Three days?" Gideon exclaimed. "I can't stay here for three days."

"Listen, kid. I don't make the schedule. The ship leaves in three days. Take it or leave it."

"Fine," he grumbled. "Better than nothing I guess." As he reached for the stub, the woman slammed her fist down on the counter, sending a cloud of dust into the air.

"Something wrong with ya, kid?" Lifting her fist, Gideon thought she was about to strike him. "That's fifty gold. I thought you were supposed to be high-society folk. Apparently they don't teach ya nothin' in the Finchlands."

Wanting to leave, Gideon fumbled to find the leather cord of his knapsack, but it wasn't there.

"My bag!" Someone had cut it from the cord and taken everything. His eyes darted around, the weight of the loss settling in. "Fatima!"

He turned and looked down the street, where dozens of Sapiens milled around the stalls. A few Finches were scattered among them, and off to the side, an Aligaidan Croc haggled over a slab of meat. Under normal circumstances, Gideon would've been intrigued by the Croc, but now, he had more important things to worry about; he needed the gold to get home.

"And she has my mother's book!"

Gideon bolted down the street, the worn soles of his boots slipping on the smooth stone beneath him. He dodged and weaved through the crowd, ignoring the angry shouts of Sapiens as he scanned the adobe structures, hoping to catch sight of Fatima. He was already well past the harbor when the thought struck him: "What am I doing?"

On Ravens & Riddles

With a frustrated grunt, Gideon leapt high into the air, unfurling his wings. A hot breeze ruffled his feathers as he climbed above the maze of alleys. Konstat sprawled out beneath him, far larger than he had imagined. It was a sprawling hub of Sapien life, its stone buildings stretching for miles in a grid from the harbor to the mountain foothills. Though the buildings were smaller than those in Moda, they reminded Gideon of home.

From above, he scanned the twisting alleys, searching for any sign of Fatima. The minutes dragged on like hours, and the heat of the sun began to drain his hope. He had many of his mother's books, but that one was different. The memories attached to it were irreplaceable: his mother's funny voices as she taught him to read, the joy of learning ancient languages on her lap. He couldn't lose it. Not like he'd lost her.

Out of the corner of his eye, Gideon spotted a flash, a fledgling running through the streets. He cut his flight short, twisting in midair to hover. "

There!" he shouted triumphantly. Fatima was running west, already more than halfway to the city's edge. A surge of fire ignited in his gut, burning away his earlier frustration. His wings beat fiercely behind him, propelling him toward her. Within minutes, he closed the distance, his shadow falling across her path.

He tried to pull back, but she'd already spotted him. Without hesitation, she bolted down a narrow side street, her footsteps echoing off the tight buildings. The alley was cramped, the structures so close together that only a sliver of the street was visible below. Gideon followed, matching her pace as best he could.

She turned onto another major street, darting through the crowds. Gideon dove, his wings skimming the heads of pedestrians, clipping their headdresses as they cursed him, but he ignored their shouts.

There was a flash of metal in the girl's hand; she was carrying a knife. She veered to the side, slashing it across a stack of wooden casks, cutting the ropes binding them. The barrels bounced free, rolling toward Gideon.

Screaming, the Sapiens ducked into store fronts, the barrels careening down the street straight. Gideon tried to gain altitude, but they were already on top of him. One by one, he shoved them aside, using his hands and feet to push over them, his wings helping him surge forward. With one final heave, he cleared the last barrel, ascending swiftly into the air.

Ahead, the edge of the city loomed. Fatima had nowhere to go but into the open desert. Confident that she was out of options, Gideon dove, closing in on her with only a few feet between them. But just as he thought he had her, she darted around a corner.

He adjusted his course, angling down the street, narrowly missing a wall. As he rounded the corner, he slammed into something solid—an enormous, grotesque creature. Its teeth were large and Avian-like, its fur matted and filthy. It rose on its hind legs with a startled cry.

Gideon tried to pull up, but his wings couldn't catch enough air in time. He fell backward onto the pavement, scrambling to recover. The creature charged, its front legs like sticks but with deadly power. Gideon threw his arms over his face, bracing for the impact of its cleft hoof, but it missed him by mere inches. The beast let out a frustrated growl before running off into the desert.

Gideon rose to his feet, brushing dust from his tunic and coughing from the dirt he'd inhaled. His eyes darted around, searching for the creature, but it had already crossed into the desert, Fatima perched on its back. His wings tensed, ready to take flight, but before he could even stretch them, a sharp voice cut through the air.

"I would strongly rethink what you're about to do."

His boots scraping the pavement, Gideon whipped around to find Rune standing atop one of the mudbrick buildings nearby, arms crossed and shaking his head.

"Nice of you to finally show up!" A lump rose in Gideon's throat. "Have you been watching me this whole time? You couldn't even help?"

"You looked like you had things under control." Rune rested an arm on the raised edge of the rooftop as he vaulted over the side. Spreading his wings, he hovered effortlessly to the ground, landing just a few feet from Gideon. "That was some impressive flying."

"What are you talking about?" Gideon snapped, caught off guard.

"C'mon, don't pretend like you don't know." The Hawk's lips curved into a half smile.

Despite his frustration, Gideon paused. The words sank in. He had just flown across the whole city. While a twinge ran through his wings, the exhaustion and pain he'd felt during his escape from Duport hadn't returned—not even with the aerial maneuvers he'd just pulled off. Maybe he wasn't as helpless as he thought.

"So, you ready to head home?" The Hawk cocked his head, his expression slipping back into stoic calm.

Snapping himself out of his daydream, Gideon shook his head. "What are you talking about? I have no money, and there's no ship leaving for three days." His face flushed with heat, frustration simmering beneath his cheeks. "What are you even doing here? You abandoned me on that ship and now you just want to come waltzing up to take me home? This wouldn't have happened if you hadn't left."

Gideon stormed up to Rune, standing on his toes, almost nose-to-nose with the Hawk. "Now, if you'll excuse me, I'm going to go get my stuff back." He turned on his heel, striding toward the desert.

"If you go after her like this, you'll die."

Gideon heard, but his frustration burned too hot to stop. He kept walking, determined not to give the Hawk the satisfaction of a response.

"Gideon, it's noon. The desert is sweltering. Even if you caught up to her dromedary, you'll be stranded out there with no food or water. If you survive long enough for nightfall, then you'll freeze to death."

Gideon halted, his feet sinking slightly into the soft sand. He gritted his teeth, barely suppressing his irritation. "So, what am I supposed to do?"

"A ship is leaving for Moda in about two hours."

"That's not what the ticket vendor said." Gideon turned, his jaw clenched.

A smirk tugged at Rune's lips. "Well, there wasn't supposed to be a ship leaving Duport's harbor either. But one did." He winked.

Gideon's mind spun. This was his chance to finally leave the Desertlands behind and get back home, but a heavy hesitation rooted him in place. He could part with most of what little he had brought with him, even the gold, which, though it would anger his father, wasn't worth dwelling on. But the weight of losing his mother's book lingered, suffocating him.

"I can't go home yet."

"Glad to hear you've had a change of heart." Rune's voice was calm, but his expression remained unreadable.

Gideon's fists clenched, resolve flooding his veins. "I have to get that book. I'll track her through Gwat and Ra'heb if I have to."

"I don't think you'll need to track her that way." Rune's eyes narrowed, his tone calculating. "It looked like she was heading north."

"But, there's nothing north…"

"Not entirely true. When your people gave these lands to the humans–"

"Sapiens," Gideon interrupted sharply, wincing at the word.

"Right, sorry…Sapiens."

Gideon welcomed the Hawk's apology, feeling the sharp edge of his tension soften as a surprising levity crept in.

"When they settled here," Rune continued, "they focused on the southern ports. A few years ago, the Hawks took over the northern peninsula and built a settlement there."

"How do I get to her if I can't chase her through the mountains?"

"*We…*" Rune drew out the word, "…get there with the supplies I've got for our trip."

"Trip?" Gideon sniped. "You planned for this?"

"If you remember, before I promised to take you home, my plan was to take you through Zarpa and up to the Noktern. So, yes. I planned for a trip through the desert."

The Finch gave him an incredulous look.

"Gideon, if it means that much to you, I promise we'll get your book back."

Sighing, Gideon knew that he'd need Rune's help to catch Fatima. But there was still something gnawing at him.

"Before I trust you again, I need to know why you left me on that boat."

"I was trying to ensure your passage back to Moda."

"You couldn't have told me?" Gideon snapped, his voice a mixture of disbelief and anger.

"I should have." Rune gave a curt nod. "I'm sorry."

It was hard for Gideon to gauge the sincerity behind Rune's words. He didn't exactly wear his emotions on his sleeve, but for some reason, Gideon believed him.

"Fine," the Finch huffed. "What's the plan?"

Chapter Twelve
GIDEON

Gideon hated to admit it, but Rune was right; he'd never have been able to catch Fatima on his own. Chasing her through the mountains would've been disastrous. The desert's heat was unforgiving, and the wind stung with sand that felt like glass against his skin as they flew.

After hours of grueling travel, the sun dipped below the sea, and Rune descended with Gideon trailing behind. When they reached the beach, Gideon immediately shed the heavy pack of supplies Rune had provided and collapsed onto the damp sand, letting the saltwater cool his arms. His wings ached, and the soreness in his muscles made him feel like he might collapse.

"Head over to the brush and gather some dry wood for a fire," Rune ordered. "I'll set up camp for the night."

"Camp? A fire?" Gideon scoffed. "If it's cooler at night, why don't we just keep going to the oasis? I won't be able to sleep knowing she's still out there with my mother's book."

"Just wait." Rune shot back. "It'll be freezing soon. We wouldn't want icicles in your feathers."

Rolling his eyes, Gideon trudged up the beach toward the dense line of brush at the foot of the mountains. As he walked, he couldn't help but admire the immense Palerocks. He'd only read about them; he never expected to see them firsthand. Now, standing at the foot of the towering peaks, he tilted his head back, marveling at the jagged cliffs stretching toward the evening sky.

With the light fading fast, he ducked through the tangled underbrush to gather dry twigs. Reaching down to grab a branch, he froze.

Footsteps.

Gideon's eyes darted to the side; silhouettes of half-a-dozen Sapiens crept through the brush, only twenty yards away, heading toward the beach.

He crouched, trying to obscure himself in the dense thicket, his heart thundering in his chest. He held his breath, praying they wouldn't hear him. When the group of Sapiens finally moved far enough away, Gideon exhaled, feeling a brief sense of relief. But then his gaze snapped to the beach, and his stomach dropped. Rune was alone, exposed.

Carefully, Gideon made his way back through the brush. Branches snapped underfoot, and he flinched, terrified the Sapiens had heard him. But when he peered out from behind a thick clump of leaves, the figures were still moving, oblivious to his presence. His eyes locked onto Rune, still unaware of the danger approaching.

Suddenly, the air seemed to ripple with a sharp, deafening explosion. The sound was followed by a scream, and Rune crumpled to the sand. The Sapiens emerged from the shadows, their figures taking shape in the dim light, heading straight for the small camp Rune had been setting up. One man approached Rune, pointing a long, cylindrical object at him. The others began rummaging through their supplies.

What is that thing?

Gideon racked his memory, the image of a boy in one of his old stories flashing before him. The character had once seen something similar the Sapiens had called:

A Rifle.

Terrified for both Rune and himself, Gideon froze, rooted in place.

What am I supposed to do?

He thought of flying for help, but Konstat was too far, and there was no one for miles. Even if he did try, he wouldn't make it into the air unnoticed, and the Sapiens would likely shoot him down.

Fighting is out...I'm not strong enough to face one of them, let alone six.

"Unless..." His mind racing, Gideon cobbled together a rough plan. It would require a bit of luck, but he had to do something. He slipped back into the brush, flattening his wings against his back as he crouched low. Crawling through the loose dirt, his palms scraped against the ground, searching. His fingers brushed over a stone, but it wasn't right. He needed something harder.

Minutes stretched into what felt like hours as he scoured the earth, frustration building. Just as he was about to give up, a glint caught his eye. A rough white stone, nearly buried in the sand. His pulse quickened, unable to believe he'd actually found what he was looking for.

The next part of the plan would be delicate. The sound of scraping stone would give him away for sure, but he didn't have a choice. On the far side of the bushes, he lay flat against the ground, his heart hammering in his chest. Through the dense branches, he could just make out the legs of the Sapiens, moving about the camp, rummaging through their packs.

Gideon unsheathed a knife from his boot. Rune had given it to him as a precaution, its steel edge catching the faint moonlight. He began shaving the stone. The sound sent a chill crawling up his spine.

As he worked, he thought of the story of a Sapien boy lost in the woods with nothing more than an ax. He had survived in part because he was able to create fire. Gideon would have to replace the ax with his steel knife, but the idea should be the same.

After a minute of working the stone, a flurry of yellow sparks erupted from the edge of his knife, the embers catching a pile of dried leaves. He grabbed a stick, and let the flames lick it into a makeshift torch.

Crawling as far from the Sapiens as possible, Gideon hurled the torch into the heart of the brush, then scrambled to put as much distance between himself and the flames as he could. The dry brush erupted in a blaze, crackling and spreading rapidly. The beach was soon consumed by a roaring inferno.

Screams rang out from the men, their orders lost in the chaos. They scrambled to grab what they could, panic setting in as they rushed eastward. Gideon kept low, moving swiftly to a safe distance. He peered back just in time to see the last man turn, raise his weapon, and fire several shots into the air. Sand erupted around him in clouds before the man finally ran off to join the others.

Gideon's breath came in shallow gasps. "I can't believe that worked."

On Ravens & Riddles

Once he felt safe enough to leave his position, Gideon bolted to the beach where the Hawk lay, blood gushing from his shoulder.

"Gideon..." Rune's voice was strained, his eyes heavy. "What happened?"

Gideon knelt beside him, hands trembling. "A bunch of Sapiens attacked you with–"

Rune grunted and shook his head sharply to interrupt. "I got that part," he said, panting. "Skip ahead to the fire."

"I started it," Gideon stammered.

"You?" Rune shot him a curious eye, wincing as he applied pressure to his shoulder. "But how?"

"Well, I read about something like it in one of my books where a fledgling is flying, but he doesn't have wings. He crashes in the wilderness but..."

"Gah!" Rune let out an emphatic groan. "Never mind, kid. You can tell me later. We've gotta go."

"Rune, you can't go anywhere like this!" Gideon's voice trembled with concern.

"I'll be fine." The Hawk spat. "Get whatever you can from the packs. I'll wrap myself up and then we're out of here. There's likely more of them and we're prey sitting in the middle of a bonfire."

Swallowing his fear, Gideon dashed to the scattered supplies. The beach was a mess of chaos; he couldn't tell what had been taken, but he stuffed everything he could find back into his bag, the urgency in Rune's words ringing in his mind.

"Kid!" Rune's voice cracked through the noise, a hint of panic now creeping in. "Tell me they didn't take the coats!"

Gideon scanned the area quickly, spotting a few dark shapes in the growing shadows. "Looks like they're still here!"

"Then thank whatever gods you Finches pray to. We'd be dead without 'em. It's going to be a cold flight."

*   *   *

The final leg of their journey had been grueling. Gideon checked on Rune every few minutes, but the Hawk continuously brushed him off. When they finally landed, Gideon's legs felt like jelly, dizzy from exertion. His eyes begged for sleep. He collapsed beside a palm tree, the weight of exhaustion dragging him down. Pulling the fur jacket tighter around him, he nestled his head into the fox tail draped around the collar, feeling the warmth seep into his bones.

Rune knelt beside him, dipping cupped hands into the oasis pond for a drink. "I'll give you five minutes, but then we have to go." His voice was flat. "You can sleep in a bit, but we can't stay in the cold."

"I'm dying..." Gideon grumbled, his eyelids wavering.

"You're not the one with a metal ball in your shoulder." Rune's voice was dry, a hint of sarcasm barely covering his concern.

Gideon was too tired to argue. He had barely shut his eyes before Rune shook him awake. In spite of his fatigue, the Finch pushed himself up off the ground.

"Here." Rune extended his arm to Gideon, a red nut about the size of an acorn between his fingers. "Chew this."

"What is it?" Gideon blinked groggily.

"It's a kola nut. They're native to Aligaida, but Hawks have managed to grow them here in the oasis. We use them to keep us alert on long hunts. It'll help wake you up."

Gideon hesitated, but took the nut all the same. Fiddling with the tough exterior, he finally managed to reveal the white flesh and popped it into his mouth. He squinted hard and puckered his lips as the bitter flavor sat on his tongue. "That's awful."

Unwinding the bandages on his shoulder, the Hawk paid Gideon no mind, his focus fixed on his scabbed wound. With a practiced motion, he withdrew a hunting knife from his boot, its edge scraping against a flat stone that lay at the edge of the oasis pond.

"You're not about to cut that thing out of you, are you?" Gideon's stomach roiled at the thought.

"Do you have any better ideas?" Rune's gaze never left the blade. Gideon could only shake his head, the grimace on his face betraying his unease. Rune sighed, the sound a mix of frustration and resignation. "If you can't watch, then head to the inn. Start asking around about Fatima. Sapiens aren't common in these parts. If she's around, someone's bound to have noticed."

Without waiting for Gideon to answer, the Hawk pressed the blade to his shoulder. The sound of it cutting through flesh made Gideon wince, and without a second thought, he scrambled to his feet, racing toward town.

"Wait," Rune called after him. "If you see a dromedary along the way, it's probably hers."

The grunt that followed was sharp, almost a growl, and Gideon's imagination spiraled at the thought of Rune's self-inflicted pain. His heart thudded in his chest as he sprinted away, unwilling to look back.

The kola nut's effects were already taking hold, his legs buzzing with energy as the streets of the town unfolded before him. Every step felt charged, his pulse quickening with the rush of the bitter stimulant coursing through his veins. The air felt heavier as he walked, each breath sharp and forced, the adrenaline blending with the desert heat.

The town seemed abandoned, its buildings sagging under the weight of years. Clay shards and broken tiles littered the ground, the faded stucco walls, stained yellow by time, added to the impression of neglect. There wasn't a soul in sight, save for one Hawk tending to a scrappy garden of weeds. Gideon considered asking her about Fatima, but the woman's surly air and bloodshot eyes left the Finch with a bitter taste in his mouth.

Maybe that's just the Kola nut.

Either way, he pressed on without inquiring.

Reaching the center of town, a lump formed in Gideon's throat. Dangling precariously at an angle, one of the signs read, *Inn,* the paint chipping away. Questions gnawed at the back of his mind.

If I catch her, will she just give me my stuff back?
Am I going to have to fight the fledgling?
What if she isn't even here?

He shook his head, chasing the thoughts away.

Pushing past the saloon doors, Gideon winced at the loud creak of the hinges. The main room was only lightly furnished. A counter in one corner stood unattended and a narrow hallway lined with doors to his right. Sparse tables and mismatched chairs dotted the space, only one of them occupied.

"Gideon." The voice came as a low murmur, soft yet commanding. The Owl sat perched near the window, his silvery wings curving gracefully around him as he sipped from a delicate teacup.

"Pelanor." The name left Gideon's lips with a numbing tingle.

He gestured toward the chair across from him, an invitation that seemed both casual and unnerving. "Won't you join me?"

As if whisked by some invisible force, Gideon meandered between the tables, the weight of his supply pack dragging at his back, before it slid unceremoniously to the floor. Without thinking, he took the seat opposite the Owl, his gaze fixed on the older Avian.

"Tea?"

"No thank you." Gideon stared deeply at the Owl, his thoughts stymied.

"I'm glad you found me." The Owl took another sip, his eyes focused somewhere behind Gideon, never meeting his gaze directly. "You and Rune certainly took your time getting here."

"You knew I was with Rune?"

"In a way. Afterall, I did ask him to deliver you safely from the Goldfinch Estate."

"So, *you* planned all of this?" The bite in Gideon's voice was sharp.

"If by 'all of this' you mean orchestrating your arrival to the oasis, then certainly. Whatever happened in between was..." Pelanor's eyes flickered, but he didn't seem troubled, "...circumstantial."

"Circumstantial?" Gideon's pulse quickened, the blood boiling beneath his skin. "We were attacked by a monster, my best friend is missing, and Rune got shot! That's all circumstantial to you?"

The Owl exhaled through his nose, a soft sigh that seemed to dismiss the weight of Gideon's words. "There's no need to get irate." He set the empty teacup back on the saucer with a *clink*. "My job was to keep you safe, and in spite of everything you've been through, here you are. Safe and...mostly sound."

The air caught in Gideon's chest. He wanted to scream, but nothing came out.

"Is Rune alright?" The question was more of a merchant checking in on his assets rather than an expression of genuine concern.

"He's busy digging shrapnel out of his shoulder," Gideon spat.

Pelanor cocked his head. "Did you say shrapnel? As in...from a gun?"

Gideon nodded his head sharply.

"Guns haven't been used in Avis since before the Great End." The Owl's glance seemed distant, a brief flash of concern in his stare. "Who shot him?"

"Some rogue Sapiens. They came out of the mountains and tried to rob us on the way here."

Pelanor scratched at his goatee. "They must have found a cache that survived the fallout then. There's no way they could have made those weapons on their own. They don't have the technology to do so. I'm surprised they still worked."

"Yes, fascinating." Gideon's legs bounced violently, jostling the table. "Tell me what happened at the dinner party. Where's Cas?"

Pelanor was silent, his face inscrutable. Folding his hands into the sleeves of his robe, he closed his eyes.

"After you left the dining room, your friend got up to follow you." Guilt churned in Gideon's stomach. "He barely made it to the hall when the doors to the kitchen exploded behind Lady Goldfinch. The same beast that chased you and Rune came barreling in, and chaos erupted. Everyone tried to flee, but Goldfinch–" He paused, his wings tensing behind him. "She grabbed a steak knife and started gutting the Finches. Like she was possessed."

Gideon's breath hitched.

"The only one in the room who seemed unbothered was the Crow woman…Zokya, I believe her name was." Pelanor's voice dipped lower. "She sat there, laughing. It was…disturbing to say the least."

Pelanor spoke calmly, but Gideon could see the Owl's eye twitch as he spoke—a flicker of unease that felt wrong coming from the Owl.

"What happened to Cas?"

Pelanor swallowed hard. "Your friend jumped in to help, but what became of him, I'm not sure." The table lurched as Gideon jerked upright, knocking the remnants of Pelanor's tea across the table. The Owl remained unfazed, simply watching the trace amount of liquid seep into the grain. "I tried to get out of there as quickly as I could. The only thing that mattered was making sure that you were safe."

"What about the other Owls? Were they involved in your plan?"

Pelanor cast his gaze to the floor, lost in reverie. "No," he answered quietly, his voice laced with resolve. "The other Owls were slain by Goldfinch and the beast. Only I managed to escape. Valanor–" the Owl choked. "Goldfinch drove a knife into the elder's heart. It's the last thing I saw before getting away."

A sullen hollowness crept into Gideon, despair gnawing at his every fiber. The image of Goldfinch butchering the Owls disgusted him, but he couldn't bring himself to believe Cas was gone.

He wouldn't.

The saloon doors slammed against the walls as Rune strode in. "So, have you told him everything?"

"Almost." Pelanor picked up the fallen cup and set it back on the saucer, dabbing at the spilled tea with a cloth, though it did little to help.

"Almost?" Gideon raised an eyebrow, his constitution waning at the thought of more to be revealed.

"There's still the matter of the champion."

Gideon's stomach sank. "Pelanor, I don't know what makes you think I'm qualified for this, but I'm no champion."

Crossing the room, Rune leaned on the counter. He said nothing, but made a point of watching, his presence a silent weight in the conversation.

Pelanor's gaze didn't waver. "Gideon, you heard Valanor at dinner. The champion is the one who possesses the answer to the Hatter's riddle. Like it or not, that's you." His voice was calm, but there was no mistaking the purpose in his tone. "Too many things have aligned for this to be a coincidence. You own a copy of *Alice's Adventures in Wonderland*. Not just any copy, but one with the answer written inside. An answer that was lost to the world save for us at the Noktern."

He leaned forward. "And you can read the damn thing!" Pelanor's lips curled in a half-smile. "Not many Avians can read ancient scripts, not even some of our own scholars. But you...a Finch, born to a merchant family...you *can*. That's no accident."

From the folds of his robe, Pelanor withdrew a book and let it drop onto the table with a heavy *thud*.

"You, Gideon Thrush, are the champion that the First Owl foresaw."

Gideon flinched. "My mother's book? How did you–"

Before he could finish, the soft patter of footsteps echoed from the hallway. He turned just as a familiar voice cut through the tension.

"Hello, Gideon."

Fatima stood sheepishly in the doorway, guilt glimmering in her eyes.

Gideon's gaze flicked between the three of them, the weight in the air pressing against his ribs. "Does anyone want to tell me what the hell is going on?"

Chapter Thirteen

Tama

Brushing away the clumps of straw, Tama lifted a trapdoor leading into the barn's cellar. The stone steps were smooth and slick with lichen. She descended carefully, easing the door shut behind her, mindful not to alert the Ravens that she was visiting Socorra earlier than usual.

Still clutching her bag, she moved deeper into the tunnels, following the flickering torchlight toward Socorra's cell. At the end of the corridor, she fished inside her satchel, fingers trembling as they closed around the brass key. Anxiety coiled tight in her chest.

She drew in a slow breath, letting the air sweep through her lungs. Everything in her screamed to run–to cower in a corner or to return to her husband back in Pas and live out the rest of her days in blissful ignorance. But the lock clicked, the weight of finality settling over her. There was no going back. Shaking off the lure of banality, she pressed forward, pushing open the door as its rusty hinges groaned in protest.

Though she was clearly awake, Socorra lay on the bed, deep bags under her eyes. Tama felt a pang of sympathy; neither of them had slept well.

"Good morning." Tama shut the door behind her.

"Good morning, Ama," the Hawk echoed, her voice thin and unsteady. She was more nervous than Tama had expected.

"I'm sorry. I didn't bring you anything to eat, but you'll be better off without anything in your stomach if this is going to work."

Setting down her bag in the center of the room, Tama knelt on the cold stone and flicked open the latch. From its depths, she withdrew an array of vials, a mortar and pestle, a mixing bowl—each item carefully placed before her.

Rising from the bed, the chains that bound Socorra clattered along the floor. "Ama, I don't know that I can go through with this." She hesitated. "I can't leave you here alone with these monsters."

Lifting her head, Tama met the Hawk's gaze. "This is the only way." She spoke with resolution in her voice, her mind made up. "Craven will be back soon. If you don't get out of here, he'll drag you to Raven Rock and do to you what he did to Rocque."

She pressed a hand to her chest, the memory of her son a raw wound, though she remained steady.

"If I leave you here, he will kill you."

The Dove stood, taking Socorra's hands in hers. "But if you don't go, it'll kill me to know what you've become."

Socorra winced as the words settled over her like a weight. "But what about your revenge? If anything happens to you, then where's your justice?"

A wanton smile crossed Tama's face, tears welling behind her eyes, though she shed none. "Your people believe that death is final, so this may not make sense to you. But I have never, and will never, believe that." She squeezed Socorra's hands "If today should be my last on this earth, then I promise that I'll be looking down on you when you win your victory over these hell-beasts."

"No Ama…" Socorra gave the Dove a reassuring look, but Tama could see the pain in her eyes. "…our victory."

The words struck deep. For nearly two years, Tama had tried to make amends with Rocque, but in her heart, she wasn't sure he had ever forgiven her. She couldn't blame him. Her sins, where he was concerned, were innumerable. Given the chance, there were many things she would have done differently, but it was too late.

All she could do now was press forward. Do right by Socorra. It wouldn't bring her son back, wouldn't undo the past, but perhaps, in freeing the Hawk, she could find a sliver of solace.

"Well, then, let's get started."

Tama returned to her carpet bag, knelt down, and withdrew the last of the ingredients.

Socorra watched intently as the Dove worked: mashing, grinding, mixing—pouring the final concoctions into three separate vials.

Scooting toward the bed, she slid the first vial to the Hawk, who lifted it hesitantly.

"That smells awful." Socorra coughed, pinching her nose. "It's like rotting flesh."

"That's the point." Tama scooped out a handful of the sticky substance. "It's a mixture of pulverized wood ear, oak sap, and dragon lily. This'll mimic the smell of a nasty infection. It should be enough to keep Craven from inspecting you too closely."

She peeled away Socorra's bandage, dabbing the foul-smelling paste onto the scab. It oozed like pus.

Satisfied, she wrapped the wound again, pressing the cloth firmly into place.

The second vial contained a thick, inky liquid.

"I hope this one won't smell as bad." Socorra forced a lighthearted chuckle.

"Mildly floral, but don't let that fool you…our entire plan hinges on this." Tama looked deeply at the Hawk, her face the portrait of urgency. "It's nightshade and azalea. Vile stuff, deadly to Sapiens. This one you'll drink as you hear Craven's boots on the stone in the hallway. Finish the vial and hide it in the mattress. You'll have to feign ill for a moment, and then the draught should take full effect."

"But it won't kill me, right?" Socorra's voice shook.

"No, dear." They had gone through the steps before, but Tama didn't blame the Hawk for being wary. "Your body will go slack, your heart rate will drop, and parts of you will go cold as the blood pulls closer to your heart. I've seen other healers use this concoction to perform surgeries, and the likeness of death is chilling. So long as he doesn't examine you too closely, Craven will think you're dead."

Socorra took a deep breath, steadying herself. "How long before I wake up?"

Tama pursed her lips. "Therin lies the worry." Unease edged her voice. "Given the dose, I'd say about half an hour, give or take. You're going to have a terrible headache though."

Sifting through her bag, Tama pulled out a gnarled tuber. "Here," she offered. "Hide this somewhere safe and chew on it when you wake up. It'll help."

Socorra took the stubby root and tucked it carefully at her waist. "What is it?"

"Wild ginger. I picked it this morning."

"And what's the last one?" Socorra pursed her lips at the final mixture, a leather pouch that held a green paste.

Tama's shoulders sagged. "You don't have to worry about that one. That one is for me."

Socorra opened her mouth, but Tama raised a hand, cutting her off with a small shake of her head. The Hawk didn't press further, but her brow furrowed.

Silence settled between them, thick and heavy. Tama fidgeted with the fabric of her frock, searching for the right words. It was time to say goodbye, but they wouldn't come. Before she could force them out, Socorra pulled her into a tight hug.

"Thank you." The Hawk's voice wavered, barely above a whisper. "I'll come back for you. I promise."

"I appreciate that, dear." Tama ran her fingers through Socorra's cropped auburn hair. "But you should never make promises you know you can't keep."

Socorra's tears were silent, but they streamed down her cheeks. She clung to Tama for a lingering moment before stepping back.

"Goodbye, Ama Tama."

"Goodbye, Socorra."

✶   ✶   ✶

The door slammed against the stone wall as Craven tore it open. Tama flinched, her breath catching as she peered past him. Socorra lay sprawled on the mattress, drool glistening down her chin, her body wracked with convulsions. Fear twisted in Tama's gut. Had she miscalculated? Had she condemned the girl to a true death?

With a single leap, Craven was on her, gripping Socorra's shoulders and shaking her violently. "Don't just stand there…help her!" he bellowed.

Tama rushed forward, pressing her hands against the Hawk's head. "Lay her down." Her voice was firm, leaving no room for argument.

To her surprise, Craven obeyed without resistance, lowering Socorra onto the cold stone. He backed away, hovering, his breath ragged as he watched Tama fumble through her carpet bag. She made a show of her efforts, wiping the girl's brow with her sleeve, tilting her head, administering rosewater that she knew would do nothing.

Then, the convulsions stopped. Socorra's body went eerily still.

Tama exhaled through pursed lips, her fingers trembling as she pressed them to the Hawk's throat. Nothing. For a split second, icy fear gripped her.

There.

The faintest flutter beneath her fingertips. Relief surged through her, but she swallowed it down, making sure Craven saw only despair in her eyes.

"She's gone." Letting her voice waver just enough, Tama turned away, balancing on the razor's edge between feigned indifference and grief.

A blood-curdling scream echoed through the chamber. With shocking speed, Craven swiped at the mattress, his talons raking through the fabric and splintering the frame with a sickening crack. Tama recoiled, heart racing, fear tightening in her chest. She half expected him to turn on her next.

The Raven strode to Socorra's side, his eyes narrowing as he yanked back the bandage on her arm. A grimace twisted his features, but he didn't speak. Instead, he let the bandage fall back over her skin.

"How did this happen?" His voice was unnervingly calm, as if the storm brewing beneath it were barely contained. "You said she'd be ready for today. And now look at her."

Tama's voice caught in her throat as she stammered, "I thought she would be. But after you left, the infection...it grew worse. There was nothing I could do."

Craven didn't answer, only pressed his fingers against Socorra's throat. Time dragged on in agonizing silence, and Tama's stomach churned with dread. When he finally pulled away, she braced herself for the discovery of her deception.

"I'll deal with this." Craven's tone remained cold. He retrieved a key from his waist and unlocked the shackles that bound Socorra to the bed. "When I return, you and I will have a conversation. Since I'll need to explain to the Master why his subject hasn't arrived, you'll answer for her death. Maybe I'll let your precious boy have a few lashes for you."

Tama's eyes fell to the floor, her lips pressed tight. Still kneeling, she watched as Craven lifted Socorra effortlessly, the Hawk's body limp in his arms. With a final sneer at Tama, he carried her through the door and down the hall, his footsteps fading until they were swallowed by the silence.

On Ravens & Riddles

Tama exhaled, the tension in her chest easing. Reaching into her apron, she pulled out the leather pouch and tilted it to her lips. The green paste was bitter, coating her tongue with a foul taste. She swallowed, the thick goop sliding down her throat.

She dropped the pouch on the floor; a sense of calm washed over her.

Tama made her way through the hall and up to the cellar door, stepping out of the barn without bothering to close it behind her. Sliding off her shoes, she felt the warm grass beneath her soles, a faint smile tugging at her lips as she rubbed her toes in the dirt. She stretched her wings wide, the wind catching in her feathers, and with a gentle push from the ground, she soared into the air, teetering briefly before gaining stability. She flew past the untended fields, a small patch of forest in the distance.

She landed lightly at the foot of a hill, then climbed to the summit where a solitary oak stood, its roots exposed. Tama curled into a hollow at the base, watching mayflies dart through the long hay. The heat of Litha wrapped around her as the soft sound of waves lapping against the distant shore reached her ears. It felt like a lifetime ago that she'd sat here with Rocque, sharing the small details of their lives. She hadn't returned to this place since the day she found out he'd been taken.

Now, she had nothing left to do. Socorra was on her own, and she could only pray she hadn't doomed the girl. But even if she had, nothing could be worse than the mutilation she'd witnessed on Rocque. All that remained was for her to pray; she prayed for Socorra's safety and for Craven's demise; she prayed that her son's soul might find peace, and she prayed that, one day, Rocque could forgive her for all the wrong she'd done him.

The Dove could feel the mash of yew leaves sapping her strength. Unable to keep herself propped up any longer, she slumped to the ground, her chest tightening. It wasn't a pleasant way to go, but it was better than giving Craven the satisfaction of putting his talons to her throat.

"Speak of the devil."

Wings sliced through the air, followed by a heavy gust of wind that whipped the wimple from her head, strands of gray hair falling across her face. He landed just a few feet away, his footsteps heavy as he approached.

Tama refused to face him with fear in her eyes; she had spent too long cowering before the beast.

No more.

A part of her longed for him to realize that he was too late, that she and Socorra had outwitted him. She wanted him to know, even if only for a fleeting moment, that frail, old Tama had beaten him. That she had won.

"Go to Hell." Tama choked out the words with the last of her strength.

She was finally free.

Chapter Fourteen

A sharp tingle rushed through Socorra's cheeks as consciousness crept back in. The pounding of wings echoed in her skull, the wind tugging at her feathers. She felt weightless, as if she were floating.

Her eyes fluttered open and her stomach lurched. Cradled in Craven's arms, she was soaring through the sky.

Minutes dragged on as they cut through the air. Terror ignited in her chest, burning hotter as blood surged back into her limbs. Her skin prickled as if dragged through nettles, each nerve coming alive with painful awareness. Then the wind shifted, changing direction as Craven slowed.

He knows.

The Hawk fought with all of her strength to move, to fight, but her body remained paralyzed, still locked under the potion's effects. She couldn't even turn her head. The Raven hovered midair, holding her limp form like a discarded thing. Socorra shut her eyes, forcing herself to accept whatever was coming next.

Then she dropped.

Rolling from the Raven's arms, the moment ripped the air from her lungs. Tumbling toward the sea below, her wings flared instinctively, the sinewy tissues straining against the fall. But her body refused to obey. She spiraled, helpless, the wind roaring past her ears.

She surrendered to it.

On Ravens & Riddles

If these were her final moments, she wanted to think of Kyte. What were his final thoughts before he was taken? Had he known? Had he been afraid?

The sea rushed up to meet her.

She struck the water like an insect against stone. The impact slammed through her, a brutal, crushing force that sent pain exploding through every inch of her body. A muffled cry tore from her throat, swallowed instantly by seawater.

The pain rippled through her, igniting her body. She thrashed, limbs sluggish but desperate, clawing toward the surface. Her wings, heavy with water, dragged at her, making each stroke an agonizing battle. Pain lanced through her body with every movement.

Breaking the surface, she gasped, choking on salt air. Waves crashed over her, threatening to pull her back under, but she fought to stay afloat. Spitting seawater from her mouth, she forced herself to focus, twisting around in search of land.

The coastline lay a half-mile away.

Like most Avians, Socorra wasn't a strong swimmer, but Kyte had taken her to Hawk Beak Bay a few times to practice. She was grateful for those lessons now, and even more grateful that the sea was calm, each stroke cutting smoothly through the water.

But it was exhausting. After only a few minutes, her muscles ached for rest. She couldn't afford to stop. The longer she took, the harder it would be to stay afloat.

What I wouldn't give for some preening oil.

Hawk fishermen used the salve to keep their wings from becoming waterlogged. It was rare in Zarpa; supplies were always limited, but Kyte's father had made sure they had a small stash while he was alive. He was an osprey, always insisting they bring some on hunts. They never listened. Now, she wished they had.

But there was no time for regrets.

Gritting her teeth, she pushed forward, arms sweeping through the water in a steady breaststroke, legs kicking in rhythm. It was grueling work, every movement a battle, but the shoreline inched closer. For now, survival was the only thought she allowed herself. She had come too far; she would not let a stretch of water defeat her.

The sea floor revealed itself as she neared the coast, the murky depths giving way to clearer waters. A few more yards. She pushed through, lungs burning, limbs trembling.

Then her foot brushed sand.

The moment her feet touched solid ground, a wave of relief crashed over her. The loose sand clung to her skin as she crawled out of the surf, dragging herself onto the beach. She collapsed onto her back, chest heaving, the warmth of the Litha sun pressing against her skin. For the first time in what felt like hours, she let herself breathe.

The ache in her muscles dulled, but a sharper pain flared along her hip. Wincing, she tugged down her breeches just enough to inspect the damage. A deep purple welt, swollen and tender from the impact. She grimaced, pulling them back up. It could have been worse.

Pushing herself upright, she trudged across the beach and up a short mound of dirt, the dry earth sticking to her damp skin. She didn't stop to brush it off. If Craven happened to circle back, she couldn't risk being seen. The farm couldn't be far.

On Ravens & Riddles

At the tree line, she slumped against a sturdy oak, its rough bark grounding her as her head throbbed. She patted her tunic, searching for the ginger Tama had given her, and popped the root into her mouth. The salt from the sea clung to it, but beneath that was a sharp, peppery bite.

As she chewed, she murmured a silent prayer for the Dove.

A sudden gust tore through the forest. Socorra's feathers bristled, a crackling energy prickling her skin as if a storm were brewing.

Crack.

A bolt of lightning struck the sea.

She sprang to her feet, instinct driving her deeper into the trees. But something felt wrong. The shift had been too sudden, the rise of the storm unnatural. Crouched in the underbrush, she kept her eyes locked on the sky.

Black wings stretched against the swirling gray as Craven shot to the southeast.

As abruptly as it had begun, the gusts died down. The clouds peeled away, trailing after the Raven as if drawn to him.

Socorra remained frozen, her breath shallow. A knot tightened in her gut. If she was going to take the Ravens down, she needed a plan. But their powers: Craven's speed, Zokya's hypnotism, and whatever monstrosity Rocque had become, seemed insurmountable. Even if she managed to bring one of them down, the others would be waiting.

Her fears aside, Socorra wouldn't waver in her mission. Under the cover of darkness, she'd fly for Zarpa. It was a hundred miles to Ander from this part of the island of Pas. She could make it in a few hours. Then home.

On Ravens & Riddles

Home.

The thought lingered in her mind, tethered her. Memories of Kyte washed over her: perched on the roof at dawn, sharing silent sunrises, tracking prey through the brush. She would never see him again, never hear his laughter, never hunt at his side. The grief threatened to swallow her whole, but she shoved it down.

She had work to do.

When she reached Zarpa, she would go to the place where Kyte fell. His remains deserved a proper burial. But more than that, she needed her spear.

Her fingers curled into a fist.

"I'll plunge it right into Craven's heart."

Chapter Fifteen

Fatima

"I thought you were paying me in gold?" Fatima's voice was tinged with playful sarcasm.

"There's gold in there," Rune answered evenly.

"Yeah…gold utensils." She thrust a hand into the cloth sack, pulling out a gilded fork and brandishing its tines at him. "And a bunch of other junk."

Rune only shrugged. "I promised to pay you. You should have been more specific about your terms."

"Fair enough." With a sigh, she tossed the fork back into the sack and cinched the drawstring tight. She bent to hoist it over her shoulder but faltered under its weight.

"Need a hand?" The Hawk offered.

"Nope." She grunted, dragging the bag along the ground. "All I can say is this better be worth its weight in gold."

"It should be," Rune said flatly.

"It's a joke. Are all you Hawks so lively?"

A smirk crossed Rune's lips. "Travel safe, little one."

Fatima rolled her eyes but didn't argue. Making her way behind the building, she found Jamal, her dromedary, resting with his legs folded beneath him, lazily chewing on whatever grass his long neck could reach. She hefted the sack to his side, securing it to the saddle with a leather cord before wiping the sweat from her brow with the edge of her headscarf. The sun was already blistering, and the journey back to Konstat would be brutal, but she wasn't about to linger.

On Ravens & Riddles

Grabbing Jamal's reins, she led him toward the oasis at the edge of town for one last drink before they faced the desert again. As he drank, she made her final checks, ensuring they had enough supplies for the trek ahead.

"Ready to go, Jamal?" Fatima scratched the dromedary's wide haunch.

Jamal, still submerged in the water, let out a disgruntled huff.

"I know, it's not ideal. But we need to get back soon. Omar and Nadia are waiting for us."

The dromedary raised his head and flapped his leathery jowls, water spraying everywhere.

She sighed, planting her hands on her hips. "Fine! Ten minutes, and then we go."

Chuckling to herself, she shook her head. Her father used to say the same thing to the stubborn animal. As Jamal dipped his head back into the pond, Fatima made her way to the nearest tree, settling against its trunk. The grass felt cool even through her robe, and the palm's shade was a welcome relief.

"I think what we earned today should last us a while," she mused, her thoughts drifting to home and the expenses waiting for her. Food was the first priority, but Nadia needed new shoes, hers were practically falling apart.

"Maybe I could even use some of it to pay a master for an apprenticeship." She tilted her head, considering. "What do you think, Jamal? Could I become a blacksmith?"

Jamal remained silent, still lapping at the water.

"No, you're probably right." She smirked. "What about a mason?"

Jamal didn't so much as flick an ear.

Fatima huffed. "You're not very helpful, you know."

She sat up, pressing her back against the tree trunk, fidgeting with a blade of grass between her fingers. She twirled it absently, letting her thoughts spin just as wildly.

"What if being a thief is the only thing I'm cut out to do?"

The words barely left her lips when Jamal let out a high-pitched wail, making her jump.

"I know, I know," she muttered, more to reassure herself than the dromedary. "I promised I wouldn't let it come to that, but look how much he paid me! And I didn't even really steal anything! I, mean…I gave the stupid book back. Maybe this is how we scrape by."

Jamal responded with a loud snort. He craned his neck, fixing her with one large, glossy eye.

"Fine," she sighed. "You're right."

Silence settled between them, heavy and uncomfortable. Guilt pressed against her ribs.

"Do you think Gideon hates me for what I did? Do you think he'll forgive me?"

Jamal dunked his head back into the water, then shifted his hind legs, turning his back to her.

"Rude." She scowled.

Another snort.

"Oh, so what if he doesn't?" she scoffed, folding her arms. The scene at the inn played in her mind, and her scowl deepened. "Jamal, you should've heard him whining.

First about the book, then about some champion nonsense. He sounded like a snotty child." She sneered, slinking lower against the tree.

The more she thought about it, the more it gnawed at her. Gideon had treated her like a common criminal, like she was nothing. But if he knew why she took the book, why she accepted Rune's job…would he still have been so angry?

None of my business.

She got what she came for. In less than a day, she'd be home, with enough money to keep her family afloat.

So why did she feel so ashamed?

"Ugh!" Fatima tore at the grass beneath her palms before pushing herself up. She dusted the sand off her backside, frustration burning in her chest as she stomped back toward the village. "Don't move from that spot," she snapped, jabbing a finger at Jamal. "I'll be right back."

The dromedary lifted his head just enough to let out a deep, guttural snort.

She reached the inn within minutes, slipping through the narrow streets with practiced ease. Just as she went to shove past the saloon doors, muffled voices from inside made her pause.

"You promised you'd help me get Socorra back," one voice seethed. "And all I've done is play escort."

Fatima frowned. *Rune?* She pressed closer, careful not to be seen.

"Kyte." She recognized Pelanor's voice, not as firm, but steadier. "You need to calm down.

Who the hell is Kyte?

"Calm down?" Rune—Kyte—squawked.

On Ravens & Riddles

Fatima risked a glance around the corner, spotting only Rune and the Owl inside. "I told you from the start, Socorra is my priority, Pelanor. I–"

"I told you we would get her back, Kyte." The Owl cut him off; his voice remained measured "And we will."

"When?" Kyte–

Rune?

Fatima wasn't sure anymore.

–whomever bellowed.

"Soon," Pelanor assured him. "I don't have all the details yet, but I'm confident Socorra will be found before we reach the Noktern. Everything is going according to plan."

"According to plan?" The Hawk's voice cracked with disbelief. "Socorra is still missing, your little dinner party was ambushed by…whatever the hell that thing was…and I got shot! You call that according to plan?"

"Please stop yelling," Pelanor's voice was still maddeningly calm. "Gideon might overhear, and we can't have that."

"And why's that?" Kyte scoffed. "I busted my ass to get this boy here and now you're going to keep him in the dark too?"

Fatima strained her ears as Pelanor lowered his voice.

"You worry too much," the Owl dismissed. "Gideon will come around without us having to convince him."

"You're not serious," Kyte snapped. "The boy wants nothing to do with this, and after this stunt, I doubt he'll trust either of us."

"I specifically said that it won't be *us* convincing him." There was a pause. "You'll understand shortly."

Kyte scoffed, about to argue, but his voice cut off abruptly. Straining to hear, Fatima pushed herself off the wall and peeked over the saloon doors, both Avians already training their eyes in her direction.

Well, shit.

She snapped back to the wall hoping to retreat, but it was too late.

"It's fine, fledgling," Pelanor called, his tone oddly inviting. "Come in."

Everything inside of her screamed to turn and run, to get back to Jamal and leave whatever mess this was behind. But something came over her…fear…guilt? She wasn't sure.

Taking a slow breath, she pushed past the swinging doors, the hinges groaning. Ky—whatever the hell the Hawk's name was, rose from his seat, his brow furrowed, but Pelanor remained seated, his back to her.

"What're you doing back here?" The Hawk's voice was a low grumble.

"I–" she hesitated, then jabbed a finger at him. "I thought your name was Rune."

"It is," he shot back defensively.

"Don't bother," Pelanor interjected smoothly. "She heard everything."

Fatima folded her arms. "No, I haven't."

Pelanor gave her a sidelong glance, lip curling with amusement. "Gideon's in the third room on your left." Lifting his teacup, he waved a dismissive hand. "Just down there."

Her eyes darted between the hallway and the exit. Against her better judgement, she turned and proceeded down the hall, catching the hushed voices behind her.

"What if she tells Gideon?" The Hawk muttered.

"She won't," Pelanor answered tersely.

"But…"

She couldn't make out the rest.

Reaching the door, she held out her hand to knock, faltering before gently rapping her knuckles on the olive wood.

"Gideon?"

There was no answer.

A part of her felt relieved, the other disappointed. She turned back toward the hall. Pelanor was still watching her, his gaze heavy, expectant. It was as if he willed her to enter.

She turned back to the door and, without breaking eye contact with the Owl, twisted the knob. Silently, she slipped inside, pressing the door shut behind her with a soft *click*.

The room was dim, the air dry and heavy with the scent of musty wood.

"Gideon?" Fatima called softly from the doorway.

The Finch lay curled in a hammock on the far side of the room, his back to her, wings draped around himself like a cocoon. At first glance, he seemed asleep.

"I know you're awake," she murmured. "I can hear it in your breathing."

She'd spent years sharing a room with her siblings, learning the rhythm of sleep, the way breaths changed when true rest took hold. Gideon's breath still wavered, too controlled.

And yet, he didn't answer.

The wooden floor groaned beneath as she tip-toed lithely to the center of the room. Adjusting her robe, she lowered herself to the floor.

"I'm sure I'm the last person you want to talk to right now," she swallowed. "So, I'll say my piece and leave."

She wasn't quite sure how to begin.

"I'm sorry for deceiving you." She sucked her teeth. "I didn't want to. But I didn't have a choice."

There was a small tremor in Gideon's exhale.

"Well, that's all I wanted to say." She pushed herself to her feet, turning toward the door.

"Why didn't you have a choice?"

She stopped, fingers hovering over the knob.

"I lost my parents a few moons back." Her tone was even. "My father was killed. My mother…taken. In the middle of the night."

A sharp inhale. The hammock creaked as Gideon shifted, turning toward her. His chin rested on his folded arms, wings trailing over the sides, half-open. His amber eyes met hers, searching.

"I'm sorry," he said.

Fatima pressed her lips together, running her tongue over her teeth. "Don't be."

The Finch blinked, his head tilting slightly, eyes widening at her response.

"Sapiens don't waste time dwelling on the terrible things that happen to us," she continued, rolling her shoulders back. "If we did, we'd all lose our minds. Our ancestors waged war, caused a global extinction, and nearly destroyed the planet in the Great End." She flashed him a wry, hollow smile. "Given our history, we've learned to move on quickly. So don't be sorry."

Gideon shifted, struggling to sit up as the hammock swayed beneath him. "Sorry," he muttered, then winced. "I mean…not for that. For saying it like–" Fatima rolled her eyes as he stumbled over his words, rambling through a second wave of apologies. "So, if you don't mind…what happened to them?"

"You're nosy," she snorted. "And I do mind."

The red in his cheeks deepened. "That's fair. But that still doesn't explain why you didn't have a choice."

She cast her gaze to the floor, exhaling sharply. When she spoke again, her voice had softened.

"Ever since I lost my parents, it's been just me and my younger brother and sister." A mix of warmth and longing flickered through her as she thought of Omar and Nadia. It had only been a day since she'd seen them, but it already felt too long.

"I take care of them. Make sure they're fed, have clothes, that they're happy…you know." She shrugged. "Bare-minimum parenting."

She gave a short, bitter laugh. "I've tried getting honest work, but most shop owners won't even consider hiring a girl my age. They take one look at me and decide I'm useless."

"And stealing my things for Rune was useful?" Gideon asked, his voice teetering between curiosity and frustration.

On Ravens & Riddles

The Hawk's name hit her ears and Fatima paused. She considered telling Gideon what she'd overheard, but no. He had enough to deal with. She was here to make amends, not stir up more trouble.

"To be fair–" she held up a finger, "you have your book back, so I didn't really steal it." She paused, searching for the right words. "I…temporarily liberated it from you." Flashing a toothy grin, she waited for a reaction.

Gideon just stared at her, utterly unphased.

"Geez." She scoffed. "You and Rune must get along great with that sense of humor."

At that, Gideon snorted.

Mildly encouraged, Fatima continued, "Yesterday morning, I was out near the docks, trying to get the ticket lady to give me a job. Figured maybe a woman would be more understanding of my situation, but she had about as much sympathy as a Bengalan with a thorn in its paw." She huffed. "After she turned me away, I ran down to the docks, just looking for a place to be alone. That's when I met Rune.

"When he found me, he asked if I was interested in making some gold. Honestly? I thought it was a scam. But then he pulled out a purse, and…well." She let out a small, humorless laugh. "I changed my mind."

Her voice cracked on the last words. She shook her head, trying to clear the heavy feeling creeping in. Dark waves of hair spilled out from under her headscarf. "Now, at least, we won't go hungry for a while."

The Finch's nose scrunched as his gaze wandered. "Can I ask you a weird question?"

Fatima, caught off guard, tried not to show it. "Will you forgive me?"

Gideon narrowed his eyes. "Sure," he said tersely. "If you answer my question first."

She shrugged. "What do you want to know?"

He fidgeted, fumbling his thumbs. "Pelanor and Rune want me to be some kind of hero, a champion." The word landed like a pinprick. "But that's just not me."

Fatima raised an eyebrow. "Don't you think that's something you'd rather talk about with a friend?"

There was a flicker of sadness in the Finch's eyes.

"Well, I just meant…" she backpedaled, stumbling over her own words. "It's just…kind of strange that you'd want to talk to me about something like that."

"The last few days have been…a lot." Gideon sighed, rubbing a hand over his face. "I have too much on my mind, and I can't talk to Rune about it." He let out a sharp breath. "I mean, he hired you to steal–"

"Temporarily liberate," she interrupted.

He exhaled a short laugh, but his expression quickly turned serious. "He hired you so I would come here instead of going home." His voice was flat, but the weight behind the final word was impossible to miss.

"That's fair. So, what's your question, exactly?"

Fatima listened intently as Gideon spoke. At no point did she hear a question, but she found herself drawn in by his story. At times, he would start to ramble, especially when he talked about his friend, Cas. From time to time, she found herself reining him in, just as she did with Jamal.

As his story continued, Fatima could feel a disquiet settle in her stomach. At first, she thought he might be embellishing, but the Owls' warning struck a chord with her. The memory of black wings flashed through her mind, tugging at something buried deep within her.

"Fatima?"

She blinked, realizing Gideon had moved closer, kneeling beside her. His brow furrowed. "Are you alright? You had this look of terror on your face."

"I'm fine," she said quickly.

"Are you—"

She didn't let him finish. "I said I'm fine!" The words came out sharper than she intended.

Gideon flinched. A tense silence hung between them. He waited, giving her space.

Fatima exhaled, pressing her palms to her face. "I'm sorry, I didn't mean…" She trailed off, shaking her head. "Just…go ahead."

He studied her for a moment. "That's it, really…So, what do you think I should do?"

Fatima sighed. "Gideon, I don't know what you want me to tell you." She shrugged. "When I lost my parents, my siblings needed me to take care of them. And yeah, I'm still a kid myself, but sometimes responsibility is what it is." Her voice was firm, carrying the weight of someone far older than her years. "Truth be told, you don't look like much of a champion to me."

Gideon's face fell. His shoulders slumped, eyes cast toward the floor.

"But," she continued, a flicker of warmth entering her voice, "think about what you've already done. You crossed the desert and you managed to save Rune, from what I heard." Her lips curled. "That's got to count for something. Gid—do you mind if I call you Gid?

The Finch flustered, mouth opening as if to protest, but she pressed on, not waiting for an answer.

"Gid, what you did out there was amazing. Those men had guns! I thought those were just a myth—a bedtime story parents tell to scare kids into doing their chores. But somehow, you defeated them." She dipped her head in reverence. "That's pretty champion-like if you ask me." She winked.

Gideon shifted, his wings ruffling as his face flushed.

"Look, Gid, I don't know if you're supposed to be the Owls' champion or not..." Her voice held a note of playful skepticism. Pulling her legs to her chest, Fatima curled herself into a ball. "I guess I don't really have an answer for you. But..." She paused, her fingers tightening around her knees. "I've seen the black wings." Her tone lost its lightness. "I know how awful they are."

She noticed Gideon relaxing, his shoulders unwinding, wings drooping low to the floor. He looked like he was settling in, the same way her siblings did before bed, waiting for a story.

"It was really late," she began. "We woke up to the sound of thunder...rain pelted the roof. We knew something was wrong and it terrified us.

Gideon tilted his head. "Why were you afraid of the rain?"

"We live in a desert, dingbat." She huffed, playfully. "It only rains here in the wet season, never in the dry."

"Oh. Right." Gideon's cheeks flushed.

"We heard the front door slam open, and then my mother screamed like someone had died. I thought it was just some ragtag bandits. I told my brother and sister to hide and ran to help my parents." She drew a sharp breath, steadying herself before continuing. "Before I could even open the door, I heard these loud bangs…then my mother went silent."

Gideon swallowed. "What happened then?"

"I'm getting there. I swear, you're worse than Nadia." She shook her head.

"When I opened the door, everything was dark. There was a flash of lightning, and I finally saw him." Fear crept into her chest, tightening around her lungs. She forced in a deep breath, trying to break its hold.

"I saw his wings first. I've never met one of your Crow people before, but I doubt they all have wings as big as that." Her voice wavered, but she pushed forward. "When he started to take off, I got a good look at him. Tall. Lanky. Honestly? He looked sickly." She pressed her lips together. "But he threw my mother over his shoulder like she weighed nothing. And then he was gone."

She exhaled sharply. "I tried to chase him. Like that would do any good." A dry laugh escaped her, humorless. "Didn't even make it a few feet before I tripped on something. And I–I remember being so mad, thinking Omar had left one of his toys in the middle of the room again."

She stopped there, letting the details she didn't want to relive slip away, swallowed by the dark corners of her mind. Some things, Gideon didn't need to know. Some things, she'd give anything to forget.

Fatima shook her head, forcing the past away.

"It was my father," she choked. "The Crow cut his throat before he kidnapped my mother."

Gideon inhaled sharply. "Fatima, I–I'm so sorry."

"Don't be sorry!" she snapped, her voice hard as stone. Before he could flinch away, she seized his wrists. "I didn't share that with you because I wanted your pity. I need you to understand that bad things are happening."

"Fatima, what happened to you is awful." Gideon gently pulled away from her grip. "But I don't know how to help you." He turned away, crossing the room to the window and fidgeted with the shutter. "How am I supposed to help anyone? "I'm just the son of a clockmaker…and a pretty poor one at that if you ask my father." His wings ruffled, a feather floating to the floor. "So I solved some dumb riddle…what does that even have to do with anything?" He let out a bitter laugh. "The Owls are wrong about me…I'm no champion."

Fatima clenched her hands into fists. "Do you hear yourself?" She shot up from the floor. "My father is dead. My mother is gone." Her voice rose, anger sharpening every syllable. "And I'm not the only Sapien in the Desertlands who has lost someone to that monster."

In two strides, she crossed the room, grabbing Gideon's shoulder and spinning him to face her. Rising onto her toes, she pressed her face close to his, dark eyes blazing.

"You don't even know what the Owls want and you're already giving up." She jabbed a finger into his chest. "I didn't ask for what happened to my parents, but here I am…I don't get to walk away. My brother and sister are counting on me, and whether I like it or not, I have to be strong for them." There was a tremor in her voice, but her resolve was steadfast.

"I don't know why the Owls chose you, but they did." She took a step back, eyes burning. "People are disappearing. Families are suffering. The least you can do is hear the Owls out. If you can't even do that, then you're right…you're no champion of anything."

Without waiting for a response, she turned on her heel and stormed out of the room.

*   *   *

Pressing deeper into the pass, Fatima clung tightly to Jamal's neck, her fingers tangled in his coarse fur. They kept to the shade as much as possible, seeking relief from the desert heat. The mountains rose sharply on either side of the pass, their jagged peaks cutting off any glimpse of the horizon.

Coming to a bend, Jamal buckled beneath her, kicking up a cloud of dust beneath his hooves.

The unmistakable boom of thunder rumbled in the distance.

"That's not possible."

Her eyes darted upward to the sliver of sky between the peaks, clear, cloudless, impossibly blue. But as they pressed forward and the mountains parted, she saw them.

Storm clouds barreled in from the northeast. Relentless, they devoured the sky.

A shudder ran through her. "It's him."

Her grip tightened around the reins, panic creeping into her voice. She flicked them hard, nudging Jamal forward.

The dromedary didn't move.

"Jamal, please."

She stroked his neck with a trembling hand, feeling the wiry bristles beneath her fingertips.

"We have to go."

Chapter Sixteen
GIDEON

Perched on the sill overlooking the small oasis village, the night air felt cool on Gideon's face. It was a peculiar window—nothing more than a square hole carved into the cement with unfinished palm shutters. There was no glass, no wooden grilles, just an empty hole.

Beneath him, the lobby was still, bathed in the soft orange glow of a single candle. The flame flickered as a breeze rolled in, shadows dancing along the edges of the book in his lap.

The rabbit-hole went straight on like a tunnel for some way, and then dipped suddenly down, so suddenly that Alice had not a moment to think about stopping herself...

The faint light made it difficult to make out some of the words, but Gideon didn't need to see. He more or less knew the story by heart, able to fill in the gaps without effort. Really, he just needed something to keep himself occupied, anything to keep his mind from circling the same thoughts. Lying in the hammock had become unbearable. The woven palm fronds scratched his skin, and Fatima's words weighed heavily on his mind.

Either the well was very deep, or she fell very slowly, for she had plenty of time as she went down to look about her, and to wonder what was going to happen next.

Gideon's eyes were heavy. He blinked several times, trying to restore some moisture. A thin sheen of wetness coated them, the words on the page blurring together.

Down, down, down. Would the fall never come to an end!

Clapping the book shut, he placed it on the concrete beneath the arch of his legs. He rubbed at his eyes, trying to chase away the tiredness, but all he managed to do was chafe the skin.

"Down, down, down," he whispered. A yawn overtook him, his head lilting back against the window frame "Now I know how you feel, Alice." The book seemed to be mocking him.

"Couldn't sleep?"

The Finch whipped his head around to find Pelanor standing in the hallway.

"I didn't mean to startle you," the Owl added.

Before he spoke, Gideon stole a final glance out the window. Pink clouds streaked the horizon as dawn approached. With a quiet exhale, he grabbed the book and slid from his perch, wings spreading slightly as he fluttered to the floor. "It's fine." The Finch shrugged, his bare feet grazing the smooth wooden planks.

Sweeping through the lobby, Pelanor's robes flowed elegantly with each poised step; even at this hour, the Owl was impeccably composed. He knelt at the hearth, poking at the coals until flames licked back to life, feeding hungrily on the fresh logs he placed.

Gideon took the opportunity to rake his fingers through his unruly hair and smooth the wrinkles from his tunic, tucking it into his breeches to look more presentable.

"Please sit." The Owl motioned to the table with an open palm.

Worry crawled up the Finch's spine. He'd wanted to speak to the Owl today, but had hoped to approach the conversation on his terms; he felt ambushed.

"I'll make some tea."

As the Owl flitted about the room, Gideon took a seat away from the fire to escape the heat. Placing the kettle in the hearth, Pelanor returned and took the chair opposite him. Silence settled between them, the tension building. Gideon's leg bounced under the table again. He wished Pelanor would just say whatever he needed to say so they could get this over with. Maybe then his mind could settle.

"How are you feeling, Gideon?"

The pressure in Gideon's chest unclenched for a moment. "I'm...fine." His voice faltered.

"I'm glad to hear it." The words felt rushed and disingenuous. "I've been meaning to ask you–"

Gideon was sure the Owl could hear the tapping of his heel. He pressed a hand against his thigh, trying to quell his nervous tick.

"Where did your mother get a copy of this book?" He laid a delicate finger on the leather binding.

Gideon exhaled, some of the tension easing from his shoulders.

"It's well preserved," Pelanor continued, turning the book slightly. "The pages are crisp but not brittle, and the ink is immaculate."

"She–" Gideon stammered, his mind suddenly sluggish. Closing his eyes, he tried to chase away the fog. "She found it on an excursion to the Wayward Stones, I think."

"And what was your mother like?"

Gideon's mouth fell open slightly, his head tilting to the side. He said nothing at first, his mind racing to decipher Pelanor's motives. Paranoia curled around his nerves, tightening its grip.

"Is everything alright, Gideon?"

The Finch snapped his eyes to Pelanor, the Owl's face inscrutable.

"I guess…" His stomach churned. "I don't know. I guess I expected you to ask about something else."

Shifting in his seat, Pelanor crossed one leg over the other, folding his hands on the table. "I just thought I'd make conversation." His tone was light, seemingly genuine, but the uneasy feeling gnawed at Gideon.

Then, with a slight smirk, Pelanor raised an eyebrow. "But since you mentioned it…what, in particular, did you wish to discuss?"

"I…" Gideon trailed off. Heat creeped up his neck and flushed his cheeks; he felt like he'd played right into the Owl's hand.

Leaning in, Pelanor rested his elbows on the edge of the table, waiting.

"I've thought about it," he exhaled sharply. Lacing his fingers together, Gideon pressed his hands between his knees to keep them from shaking. "What exactly do you want from me?"

On Ravens & Riddles

Pelanor's gaze penetrated deep, but it was not unkind. "I assume you're referring to the responsibilities of the champion?"

Gideon's stomach lurched. "Yeah, that."

He flinched as the Owl rose, an inexplicable tension prickling down his spine. Pelanor wasn't physically imposing, but there was something about his cool, unreadable demeanor that unsettled him.

Digging a hand into his sleeve, Pelanor withdrew what Gideon thought were two sticks.

The Finch cocked his head. "What are those?"

"Read them," the Owl said, handing them over. "Then you'll know about as much as I do."

"Read them?" Befuddled, Gideon hesitated before taking them. The objects were lighter than he expected, and as he examined them more closely, he realized they were scrolls made of birch bark.

Carefully, he unrolled one. The delicate wood crackled under his fingers, releasing a fine sprinkle of black dust. Charcoal etchings lined the surface, Sapien script. The same language as *Alice's Adventures in Wonderland*.

The first strip read:

Dark wings will rise and pluck the kin of men. The sun will set beyond the dark sea, and the land shall be cast in ebony and the echo of the ancients will sound.

But a champion will rise to clip the wings of fate. Power bound through the ages, the champion's strength is shared only by the source, for there are no others left beyond our walls to share in their knowing.

In the dim, the sword prevails, piercing the heart twisted in darkness. The shield saves, but is lost when the light flickers out.

Before innocence is undone, seek the one who possesses the answer to the Hatter's riddle.

"The tea should be ready in a few minutes." Pelanor's voice cut through the Finch's thoughts "The leaves just need to steep."

Gideon didn't acknowledge him, hastily unfurling the second scroll.

If the champion does not succeed at first light, the earth will run red and the pillars of Avis will fall. Innocence will be forfeit, but a crimson dawn shall make way for blue skies across Avis.

Gideon scanned the scrolls, the words tumbling through his mind like leaves caught in the wind.

"What is this?" he asked, though deep down, he already knew the answer.

Across the room, the clink of china echoed as Pelanor poured tea. "Don't you know?" the Owl mused. "I thought you'd have figured that part out on your own."

"The prophecy?" Gideon turned to him.

Leaning against the hearth, Pelanor gave a slight nod.

"So, what does it mean?"

Pelanor met his gaze. "What do *you* think it means?"

Excitement flooded Gideon, not enough to dispel the fear that broiled in his stomach, but enough to consume his interest.

"The 'ebony' is pretty clearly the darkness your elder mentioned, the Avians who attacked us at dinner."

"Very straightforward, yes." As Pelanor stood, Gideon thought he caught a glimmer of sadness in the Owl's eyes, but it vanished just as quickly. "But a good catch."

Gideon frowned at the next line. "I don't understand how the sun can set beyond the dark sea. The sun sets in the west over Zarpa, not the Crowlands."

Pelanor snapped his fingers. "An astute observation. What else?"

Gideon pondered a moment. "The next line about the champion clipping wings is also pretty obvious."

"Yes," the Owl started. "Clearly in reference to you stopping the darkness."

The word *you* struck Gideon square in the chest. It felt too personal, too final, like Pelanor had driven a stake through his heart.

"Right," he muttered, unsure of what else to say.

Pelanor let the silence settle for a moment before speaking again. "Go on," he urged.

"Well, I'm not sure about the third line." Gideon rubbed his eyes, drawing in a sharp breath before continuing. "But 'red earth and blue skies'—I'm guessing that refers to a battle before this can be over."

"Another excellent conclusion." Pelanor offered a brief, approving smile. "Though it would seem that only happens if you can't stop it in time, what I assume 'first light' refers to."

Gideon didn't respond, an overwhelming pressure settling in his chest.

"And you obviously know the answer to the Hatter's riddle."

"But what does it mean?" Gideon stammered. "I've never understood the answer."

Pelanor shrugged. "If I'm being honest, I don't think anyone fully understands what it means. The riddle itself was written as nonsense…why shouldn't the answer be as well?"

"But then, why does me having the answer to this riddle mean anything to you?"

"Because it's part of the prophecy, Gideon." Pelanor spoke calmly, matter-of-fact. "And not just that, but it's the answer that has been handed down to us for generations from the First Owl himself. What do you think would happen if we asked this question to every random Avian? Don't you think someone might come up with an answer that sounded clever?"

"I guess," Gideon answered hesitantly. "But that doesn't really explain it."

On Ravens & Riddles

"Gideon," Pelanor's voice softened. "I know you want everything to have an explanation, but sometimes life doesn't come with that luxury. I can't tell you what the answer to the riddle means. I have my guesses, but they're just as good as yours. The only thing that I can say for certain is that this is the answer that would reveal the champion. I have faith that the First Owl knew what he was doing, and that all will be revealed in time."

Gideon paused, digesting the Owl's words. "If you say so," he shrugged. Shaking his head, Gideon returned his focus to the scrolls. "Why are there two separate ones though?"

Silence.

"Pelanor?" The Finch pressed, his fingers tracing the delicate etchings in the birchbark. When the Owl didn't respond, his patience frayed. "Pelanor!"

Tearing his eyes away in frustration, Gideon finally looked up only to find the Owl standing motionless. There was an eerie opaqueness in his stare, his eyes hollow, mouth slightly agape. Gideon couldn't tell how long the two of them sat there, the Owl's trance uninterrupted. Two minutes, two hours? Gideon had no way of knowing.

Summoning his courage, he cleared his throat, a small, deliberate sound in the oppressive quiet. "P-Pelanor?"

With a jolt, the Owl sprang back to life. "Sorry," he said with a quick shake of his head. "What were we discussing?"

Gideon's brow furrowed. "Are you…okay?"

"Never better." Pelanor's response was smooth, immediate, as if nothing had happened. "Ah, yes, the scrolls. You asked why it's in two pieces." He gestured at them dismissively. Unfortunately, it tore in transit."

Gideon stared blankly. "So, we're not going to talk about what just happened?"

Pelanor blinked. "Talk about what, Gideon? Are *you* feeling alright?"

Gideon couldn't tell if Pelanor was being serious or mocking him. Either way, pressing the Owl for answers felt like a losing battle. With a quiet sigh, he turned his attention back to the scrolls, flipping the birchbark over to examine them more closely.

Looking over both sides carefully, something didn't sit right. The edges were too neat, too precise for a tear. Running his fingers along the grain, he noticed an inconsistency

"Pelanor, the patterns of this bark don't line up..." He wanted to continue, but the Owl interrupted.

"The tea's ready."

Gideon cast his eyes to the side, his gaze burning into Pelanor through his peripheral vision. "That's nice..." His voice was laden with sarcasm. "But I think there's a piece missing from between these scrolls." Doubt crept into Gideon. "Either that or they weren't one piece to begin with."

"Do you want anything in your tea? Lemon, sugar?"

Gideon clenched his jaw. "No, thank you." His patience waned. "But the scrolls–"

A startling noise split through the inn, cutting him off. It sounded like a foghorn, but its tremble carried something deeper, something that gnawed at the base of

Gideon's spine. A pained, guttural groan followed, echoing from somewhere in the village.

Pelanor had gone still, the clinking of china silenced.

Gideon swallowed hard. "That's not good."

Tearing himself from the chair, Gideon rushed through the saloon doors, Pelanor trailing behind at a more leisurely pace. Sprinting down the dirt road, a trail of dust formed a cloud in the air as the dromedary trampled the path.

Gideon's stomach churned.

"What's going on?" Rune called from inside the inn.

"It's Jamal," Gideon called back.

"Oh, come," Pelanor dismissed. "It could be any beast."

Despite the Owl's protestations, Rune was already pushing past them.

He strode forward, reaching for the animal's reins with his good arm. The dromedary reared onto its hind legs, hooves slashing at the air. But Rune held firm, murmuring low, steady words as he pulled the creature back down. The struggle lasted a breath longer before the beast finally stilled, shuddering beneath Rune's touch as he rubbed its neck and scratched gently under its chin.

"Is it definitely the girl's?" Pelanor called out from Gideon's side.

Rune didn't answer right away. He kept one hand tight on the reins, the other rifling through the packs strapped to the animal's back. The dromedary was still trembling, breath coming in frantic bursts, its cloven hooves shifting anxiously against the dirt.

"He's definitely Fatima's." Gideon's heart sank.

Where could she be?

She had spoken so much about responsibility and needing to get home to her siblings; he couldn't imagine her abandoning the dromedary and her belongings in the desert.

"Shame." Pelanor spoke under his breath, his voice nonchalant. "We'll have to see if anyone will take in the poor beast."

Gideon whipped his head around so quickly it made him dizzy. "What do you mean?" he asked pointedly.

"Well," Pelanor began, his voice touched with condescension. "Usually when an animal is abandoned, either intentionally or circumstantially, they require a new home."

"He doesn't need a new home," Gideon spat. "We need to get him back to Fatima. She could be hurt."

"Or she could already be dead." Pelanor didn't bother to turn, his tone as indifferent as ever. "We need to get you to the Noktern as quickly as possible, and prepare you for what needs to be done to save Avis. We don't have time to waste on rescuing a thief."

"She wasn't a–"

"Gideon," Rune's voice cut through his protest. He approached, Jamal's reins firm in his grip. "I know you don't want to hear it, but Pelanor's right." Rune's voice was gruff and distant as always. But unlike the Owl, Gideon heard the care with which Rune spoke. "The more time we waste here, the worse things will be for the rest of Avis. It's best to forget about this."

Gideon shook his head. "But what about Omar and Nadia?"

Rune and Pelanor exchanged glances.

Gideon let out an exasperated breath. "Fatima's brother and sister," he explained, recounting what Fatima had told him about her family. He left out the major details of what happened to her parents.

Pelanor sighed. "That's very sad, Gideon," he said, sounding more annoyed than moved. "But we have bigger concerns than one ill-begotten family of Sapiens."

Gideon turned to Rune, hoping for support, but the Hawk's expression remained unreadable, his silence a quiet betrayal.

Standing there defeated, Gideon struggled to comprehend the heartlessness of the men who stood before him. His mind raced, piecing together a plan to get Jamal back to Konstat, alone if he had to.

Finally, Rune spoke. "I'll bring him back to Konstat and look for Fatima along the way." He rubbed Jamal's neck to comfort the beast.

A jolt of hope coursed through Gideon. "I'll go grab the packs and we'll head out."

"No." Rune's voice was firm. "I'll search. You'll go with Pelanor to Zarpa."

Gideon opened his mouth to argue, but the Hawk's stony glare silenced him. There was no point in fighting it. As long as someone was looking after Jamal and the three Sapien fledglings, he could live with it. Turning back to Pelanor, he braced himself for an argument, but the Owl only twisted his lip in agitation. He didn't like it, but he didn't object either.

After an uncomfortable silence, Gideon finally spoke. "I thought we were supposed to be going to the Noktern, so why Zarpa?"

Pelanor cleared his throat, the irritation receding from his face. "We have to make a stop before continuing on."

Gideon waited, but the Owl offered nothing more. "I gathered that much," he shot back sharply, his voice ripe with annoyance. "But why?"

"We'll be outfitting you with a sword and shield." Pelanor answered blankly, as if that explanation should suffice.

Gideon blinked. "I'm sorry, we need to get me *what*?"

Rune snorted. "A sword and shield, Gideon." His gruff voice took on a teasing edge. "A shiny, pointy stick and a flat piece of metal. You might've read about them in your storybooks."

"Bu–but–" Gideon held the back of his neck, heat prickling his skin. "It's a prophecy. Doesn't that feel just a bit…on the nose?"

"I concur," Pelanor huffed. "But Rune insisted."

The Hawk shrugged. "Better safe than sorry. Besides, if you get into trouble, you'll want more than just words to defend yourself."

Part of Gideon wanted to push back, to remind them that he never agreed to any of this. But deep down, he knew he couldn't walk away. His eyes flicked to Jamal's empty saddle, and Fatima's words echoed in his mind.

You can't run from your responsibility.

"Fine. Let's go, I guess." The words sat on Gideon's tongue, acrid and bitter.

As he turned toward the inn, Rune's large hand clamped down on his shoulder.

"I'll meet you both at the Noktern in a few days. Travel safe." The Hawk wore his usual deadpan expression, but there was something in his eyes that Gideon couldn't quite place. A silent *thank you*, maybe.

Strangely, a sense of calm settled over the Finch. After a moment, Rune released his grip, and Gideon turned toward the inn to pack. He still had dozens of questions, but he figured he would have the time to ask along the way.

✻   ✻   ✻

The Amada Strait stretched seventy miles from the edge of the oasis to the island of Zarpa; for Gideon, it might as well have been a thousand. Pelanor led their flight in silence, his wings cutting steadily through the gusting air. Though the sun shone brilliantly, the Windy Sea lived up to its name, battering them with relentless currents from the west. The turbulence tugged at their feathers, but they pushed forward, unwavering.

Reaching the Zarpan coast, Gideon felt at ease again. Unclenching his jaw, he relaxed his shoulders, the knot in his stomach unwinding. Before him stretched the Great Plains cradled between craggy hills to the east and west.

Time seemed meaningless in the repetitive landscape, the hours slipping away as his mind wandered. He imagined the swirling steam of Wydah's bakery, the scent of fresh bread curling through the streets of home. His father would be furious if he arrived any later than expected. Then, his mind shifted to Fatima, lying motionless on the desert sand. He could only hope Rune would find her in time. Finally, Cas.

Lost in memory, Gideon barely noticed Pelanor descending until the Owl was already halfway to the ground. He banked instinctively to follow, but the wind caught his wing at an awkward angle. He faltered, wings snapping open as he hovered to regain control.

It was then that he saw her—a Hawk, moving below in the plains, her sharp gaze scanning the ground as if searching for something.

Gideon's eyes flicked back to Pelanor as he rapidly approached the earth below.

"What is this Owl up to?"

Chapter Seventeen

Socorra

Lacing her fingers around the first stone she could find, Socorra crouched waist-deep in the grass, waiting. The intruder approached from behind, their shadow growing longer in the late afternoon sun. Dry weeds crunched under their soles.

She held her breath.

The moment they were close enough, she sprang.

Launching skyward, Socorra twisted midair, her wings steering her sharp pivot as she swung the jagged shale forward, ready to strike–

An Owl.

A shockwave of realization shattered through her. She yanked her arm back in alarm, the abrupt motion knocking her off balance. Her wings dragged her backward, sending her tumbling through the grass.

Frustration flared.

"What's the matter with you?"

With a sharp huff, Socorra shot to her feet and hurled the rock into the open field. She twisted toward the Owl, arms flung wide in exasperation.

"I thought an Owl would be smarter than to sneak up on a hunter unannounced!"

The Owl remained infuriatingly unshaken. "My apologies."

Socorra brushed loose dirt from her tunic, her glare smoldering, but movement beyond him caught her eye. Another Avian landed a few feet away, a mousy Finch, smaller, quieter, jogging over to the Owl's side.

"I'm Pelanor, and this is Gideon."

The Finch said nothing, but gave a sheepish wave.

She pressed her tongue to her cheek. "Socorra." Her voice softened slightly, the sharp edge fading.

"What are you doing out here, Socorra?"

She narrowed her eyes, hand resting on her hip. "I might ask you two the same question." She shielded her eyes from the blistering sun behind them, her gaze flicking from the Owl to the Finch.

A thin smirk tugged at Pelanor's lips; Socorra bristled. "We saw you out here searching for something. I thought we might lend a hand."

The Finch cocked his head, a quiet dissonance between them.

"Well...Pelanor, was it?" She gave a graceful sneer. "Thank you for your concern, but I'm on a hunt." She lied, folding her arms over her chest. "And I manage just fine without your help."

"Of course. I simply meant that you seem to be out here all alone. That's pretty uncommon for a Hawk hunter, is it not?" He arched an eyebrow, the subtle challenge hanging in the air.

Socorra ground her teeth. She hadn't expected him to see through her lie; she should've known better than to deceive an Owl, what's more, a scholar.

"Unless, of course..." The Owl's words were staccato, each chosen carefully. "You've lost your hunting partner."

Her chest tightened, and a surge of frustration bubbled in her throat. She fought to keep her expression neutral, biting down on the bitter retort that almost slipped free.

"If you must know," she muttered, her voice tight. "I'm looking for my spear. I lost it on my last hunt, and I want it back."

The Owl stood there, his expression quizzical, as though he were weighing his options in the uncomfortable silence. Socorra could almost hear the gears turning in his mind.

"Fair enough," he said finally. "We're on our way to Zarpa ourselves."

Socorra squinted, raising an eyebrow. Something about his words didn't sit right. Most travelers came to the island via Ander, the northern route. It was the closest point to the mainland, making it the most logical path if other tribes were planning to visit Zarpa. So, what were they doing this far south?

"What for?" she asked, suspicion creeping into her tone.

Pelanor opened his mouth to speak, but Gideon beat him to it. "I need a sword." He rolled his eyes, an undertone of sarcasm in his voice.

A smile tugged at Socorra's lips, and she caught the subtle flash of aggravation in Pelanor's eyes. The Finch had clearly spoken out of turn, and it made Socorra wonder whether that was information the Owl intended to keep from her.

"So," Socorra began, her tone laced with amusement. "I gather you'll be going to see Hepha then?"

"Indeed." Pelanor answered through clenched teeth, his composure cracking slightly. "It's well known that she makes the finest quality steel. And as you've undoubtedly heard, Master Gideon needs a sword."

Socorra shook her head. "I wish you luck." There was a touch of mirth in her voice, but it was underlined by a knowing skepticism. While the Hawk and Owl tribes maintained mutual respect, there was little love lost between them. The Hawks were bold and brash warriors, while the Owls were more calculating, valuing knowledge above all else. Many Hawks simply couldn't see past those differences.

"Hepha doesn't normally help outsiders," Socorra continued, her words tinged with irony. "Not even for the revered Owls." She drew out the word 'revered' with a touch of sarcasm, clearly enjoying the rare moment of getting under the Owl's skin.

"Is that so?" Pelanor sucked his teeth.

"Hepha's a good friend." Socorra answered with conviction. "I know she won't help an Owl."

"If you say so." Pelanor shrugged. "But I don't think we'll have any issues."

"What makes you so sure?" She asked coolly, though the Owl's certainty piqued her curiosity.

"Why don't you come with us so you can see for yourself?"

Socorra couldn't decide if the Owl displayed confidence or arrogance—maybe a bit of both. Still, as irksome as he was, Socorra couldn't deny a begrudging respect for the way he carried himself.

"I'm sure you could get a new spear." His tone was casual, as if offering a suggestion. "You look tired from searching. Maybe it's time to move on."

The Owl's words felt like a stab in the heart. She stood frozen, unable to mask the desperation on her face.

"Or don't," the Owl added, his voice suddenly softer. "Whatever you choose, I wish you well in your mission."

Socorra's heart skipped a beat. "I'm sorry…" The shock in her voice betrayed her otherwise calm exterior. "My what?"

"Your mission," the Owl repeated, never breaking her gaze.

She hadn't misheard him.

Her mission.

The same words she'd used since Tama helped her escape Cherub Farm. Was it a coincidence? Or had the Owl caught onto something more than he was letting on?

"And what mission would that be?" There was an edge of suspicion in her voice.

The Owl's demeanor shifted from unreadable to strangely jovial. "To find your spear, of course." An unnerving smirk stretched across his face, his voice slipping back into an enigmatic tenor. "That is, unless you had something else in mind."

Socorra drifted from sadness to anger, though both quickly faded as an apprehension settled in her stomach. She glanced at the Finch, who seemed just as lost as she felt, his expression unreadable.

Something was off. The Owl's words, his timing; he was trying to say something, or perhaps steer her in some direction. She couldn't help but feel like a fledgling for her idle speculation, but she had a gut feeling that the Owl's words went deeper than the surface.

"No," she blurted, brushing the thoughts away with a shake of her head. "Sorry. Safe travels to Zarpa."

Pretending to return to her search, Socorra took a few steps away, but her mind remained on edge, wary of the Avians and the strange weight their presence seemed to carry.

"As you wish," Pelanor responded smoothly. "Come along, Gideon."

Their footsteps crunched against the dry earth, fading into the distance. But then–

"Socorra."

Her pulse quickened. She didn't answer.

"I have a feeling that our paths will cross again."

Then came the rush of wings, the gust of their departure, and finally, silence. Their shadows stretched briefly across the plains before vanishing northward.

A shiver ran through her.

Maybe it was just a coincidence, but something about the Owl's words unsettled her. It wasn't just what he said, it was *how* he said it, like each word had been chosen carefully…catered just for her.

Shaking off the feeling, she turned back to her search. Another hour passed. Still nothing. The sun had dropped lower in the sky, its golden light stretching long over the plains.

She was sure this was the right place, but out here, everything looked the same. Her stomach twisted with hunger, her knees wobbled from exhaustion, yet the thought of stopping made her sick with guilt.

She wanted to believe she could find Kyte.

But what if the Owl was right about moving on, even if that wasn't what he meant?

No, I won't give up.

She just needed time to regroup.

With a heavy sigh, Socorra dropped to the ground, absently pulling at the blades of grass between her fingers, willing herself to think.

Make a list.

One: stop at the house and eat.

Two: go see Hepha. Maybe she's heard something about Kyte. By now, she'll have chased off the Owl and the Finch.

Three: get a good night's rest Come back in the morning with a clearer head.

She took a deep breath, settling into the plan.

Rolling forward, she sprang to her feet; a wave of dizziness slammed into her, forcing her to pause. She wavered, then steadied.

One last look over the plains.

The golden grass rippled in the wind, the sun catching each blade in shimmering light. Sorrow coiled around her chest, guilt anchoring her feet to the earth. But the moment passed, brief as a breath.

Then, a memory surfaced, Kyte sitting beside her on the roof of their home. Their final morning together. The stillness had been warm, comfortable. And then, at last, he broke the silence.

"Are you ready to go?"

The ghost of his voice lingered as the vision faded.

Sniffling, Socorra dipped her head to the empty grasslands.

"I'm ready," she whispered. "But I'll be back for you.

*　　　　　　*　　　　　　*

Landing at the end of the street, Socorra wove her way past the tightly packed stalls. The familiar scents of sizzling meat and sun-dried spices filled the air, Hawks buzzing about the shopfronts, but she barely noticed any of it.

Arriving at the smithy, the deafening *clang* of Hepha's hammer reverberated through the street. The sheer familiarity of the sound nearly made her legs buckle. It felt like a lifetime since she had stood here.

She tore open the tent flap, naturally finding the smith hunched over her anvil, sweat glistening on her dark skin as she shaped a chunk of red-hot steel.

Hepha turned, her eyes locking onto Socorra. The hammer in her grip slipped from her fingers, falling to the dirt floor with a thud. She took one staggering step forward. Then another, her calloused hands clenched at her sides.

"Socorra?" The smith's voice was hoarse, almost strangled.

Socorra beamed. "It's good to see you, Ama Hepha."

Hepha lunged forward, crushing Socorra against her chest. Her arms wrapped around her like a vice, one hand cradling the back of her head, the other gripping her shoulders so tightly it hurt.

"You're alive," Hepha rasped. "I don't believe it." Her voice cracked, and Socorra felt the tremor in her arms.

The moment of joy was suddenly over as Hepha pulled back, her hands gripping Socorra's arms, eyes raking over her. Then, her gaze landed on the healing wound on Socorra's arm.

Her nostrils flared.

"What the hell happened to you?" Before Socorra could answer, Hepha's rough fingers brushed over the scar. Socorra winced, but Hepha didn't let go. Her touch wasn't gentle, Hepha never was, but there was a desperate reverence in the way she traced the jagged edges of the wound.

"It's a long story, Ama." Socorra leaned in, pressing her forehead to Hepha's. The familiar scent of smoke filled her nostrils, grounding her. Hepha's closely shaven hair prickled against her skin, but she didn't care. She was just grateful to be here, in the smith's presence again.

"I thought you were dead," Hepha grumbled, voice rough with something unspoken. With a firm shove to Socorra's shoulders, she broke their embrace. Socorra staggered back slightly, catching the trail of soot smeared across her tanned skin where Hepha had touched her.

"We all did," Hepha went on, crossing her arms. "The whole city's been up in arms since you and Kyte disappeared."

"Disappeared?" Socorra echoed, her stomach sinking. Her gaze dropped to the ground. "So, no one has seen…"

A voice from the entrance cut her off.

"That'd explain the weird looks you were getting in the market."

Socorra's head snapped up, her brow furrowing. Pelanor.

Hepha's expression hardened as she turned toward the Owl. "Socorra, you know these people?"

"In a way," Socorra muttered, irritation creeping into her voice. "But no. I met them earlier, and now it seems they're following me."

"Tut-tut," Pelanor chided, his smirk infuriatingly smug. "*Following* is a strong word. I did tell you our paths would cross again. Besides, I specifically mentioned we were coming here. So maybe it's you who's following us."

"You two better turn around and leave." Hepha rolled up the sleeves of her woolen tunic, stomping toward them. "Or I'll–"

Socorra swiftly lifted an arm, blocking Hepha's advance. "Don't worry, Ama." She exhaled, exhausted. "I'll handle this."

"Hmph." Hepha snorted but didn't move. Her sharp eyes flicked between the two strangers before settling on Pelanor with undisguised suspicion. "The little one looks easy enough, but I don't trust Owls. Prolly has a knife tucked away in those robes."

"Charming," Pelanor sniffed.

With a final sneer, Hepha turned back to her anvil, yanking another hunk of metal from the forge. She retrieved her hammer from the dirt and brought it down hard, each strike sending sharp, rhythmic clangs through the smithy.

A wave of nausea rolled through Socorra. The Owl's presence was unnerving, yet she couldn't shake the feeling that something tethered them together. Her fingers twitched at her sides.

"What do you want?" she demanded, fixing Pelanor with a fierce glare as he lingered at the entry-flap.

He met her stare with a curt nod. "I told you before, Master Gideon needs a sword."

Hepha let out a barking laugh, the sound cutting through the steady clang of her hammer. "That's rich. I assume you told them, right, Socorra?"

"Told us what?" Gideon asked timidly.

"That there's no way I'm helping you." Hepha gave him a sharp nod, her tone flat and final. "I only smith for Hawks."

Socorra barely registered the exchange. Her focus stayed locked on Pelanor, her patience wearing thin. "You know what I mean," she said, her voice low and edged. "I specifically came here after you should have been gone. You left the plains…there's no reason you should be here now."

She clenched her jaw, tired of the Owl's games.

"Ah, I see," Pelanor said with a wave of his hand. "Impeccable timing, really. As soon as we arrived in Zarpa, Master Gideon mentioned he was hungry." He clapped a hand on the Finch's shoulder. "The boy has a weakness for orange tarts. And as you're well aware, oranges only grow in Zarpa. We couldn't pass up the opportunity to have a tart made with fruit picked straight from the tree."

Socorra arched an eyebrow at Gideon, whose face promptly turned the shade of the forge's flames.

"We searched for a while," Pelanor continued, his voice smooth, practiced, "and ended up just a few stalls over when I happened to spot you coming down the street."

He offered an innocent smile, but Socorra wasn't fooled. His story was probably technically true, but she had no doubt he'd orchestrated the whole thing.

"It seems fate would have us meet again."

Socorra pursed her lips, rolling her eyes before spinning on her heel.

If he's going to be an arrogant ass, I won't even bother.

Ignoring him, she made her way back toward the anvil, ready to resume her conversation with Hepha. But as she neared, something caught her eye—the charred tips of the smith's feathers.

"Ama," she frowned, "have you been busy?"

Hepha always had a few scorched patches. They were an expected hazard in a cramped forge, but this was worse than Socorra had ever seen.

"You bet your sweet buns I have." Hepha straightened from the anvil, her back cracking as she stretched. "Those old goons on the council have me working day and night, cranking out weapons."

"What for?" Pelanor's voice cut in from behind, his tone almost accusatory.

"Wouldn't you like to know, Owl boy?" Hepha cackled, hammering away at the red-hot ore. Sparks flew wildly, lighting up the smithy in bursts of orange. Socorra watched as a molten ribbon of metal landed on Hepha's umber skin, but the blacksmith didn't even flinch.

"Are you always this surly?" Pelanor asked, stepping forward into the cascade of embers. "This should change your mind about helping us."

The hammer froze mid-swing. Hepha's sharp eyes flicked to the Owl as he produced something from his sleeve–a tightly rolled scroll, bound with twine.

"What's this?" she scoffed, lowering the hammer to her side.

"Read it and find out," Pelanor instructed with a bite.

Sucking her teeth, Hepha set the hammer aside, yanked off her ashened gloves, and snatched the scroll from his grasp. As she unrolled it, her sneer deepened, muttering under her breath as her eyes scanned the parchment.

"Socorra."

The voice arose from behind.

She turned sharply, finding two boys standing at the smithy's entrance. They couldn't have been past their first spring of adulthood, yet they carried themselves with rigid authority. Blood-red leather armor marked them as members of the Hawk Guard, spears in hand, short swords at their waists.

"Can I help you, officers?" Socorra folded her arms.

Behind her, Hepha let out a sharp gasp. Socorra stole a glance back; Hepha's wrinkled hand was pressed to her chest.

"The Elder Council requests your immediate presence." The guard tried to use a voice of authority despite the fledgling-like quality in his tone.

Socorra sighed. She had anticipated as much, but she'd hoped to be out of Zarpa by the time the council received word of her return.

"For what purpose?"

"For, um–" The guard stammered, looking to his partner. Both shared a blank stare.

"Neither of you know…" Her voice was tinged with frustration. "Do you?"

"No ma'am."

Ma'am? Socorra felt a twinge in her chest.

"We've been instructed to bring you before the council," the other guard added stiffly. "So please, if you'll come with us."

They stepped forward, hesitant.

Over her shoulder, Socorra caught Hepha's stricken expression, her mouth slightly ajar. She wanted to say something, but the guards grasped her by the forearm, one on each side.

"I can see myself out, thank you."

She cast one last glance around the smithy. Hepha could handle herself; she always had. But then her eyes landed on Gideon. The Finch stood stiff and uncertain, like a frightened animal separated from its pack.

A twinge of pity stirred in her chest.

With a slight nod of farewell, she turned and stepped through the exit, the guards falling into step behind her.

Chapter Eighteen

The austere walls of Accipiter Manor loomed over Zarpa, perched atop the escarpment at the heart of the city. Socorra ascended the grand hallway, flanked on either side by Hawk Guards. At the far end, a massive set of oak doors awaited, their iron bands etched with the sigil of the Hawks. Overhead, the domed ceiling stretched high, supported by ancient steel beams, salvaged remnants of the ancient city that had become the Hawks' stronghold.

Her boots clicked against the cobblestone, each step pounding in time with her heart. As they neared the elders' chamber, flashes of Craven flickered through her mind, flooding her memory.

"Socorra Buteo!"

The call rang out as a guard heaved the heavy doors open, the hinges groaning in protest.

Gasps rippled through the chamber. Several elders rose from their seats, their eyes wide with disbelief. The tension was suffocating. Despite it, Socorra lifted her chin, refusing to let them see her unease.

The chamber itself was modest in size but lavish in its display of power. Oil-filled sconces cast a golden glow over antlers and trophy heads mounted along the walls. Pelts softened the stone floors, their presence unsettling. She avoided stepping on them as she strode toward the solitary chair at the center of the room.

The thirteen elders sat behind long, imposing tables arranged in a U-shape, their expressions unreadable. Hawk

Guards lingered at the doors, sealing off her escape. She was surrounded, trapped like an animal in a cage.

Reaching the chair, she did not sit. Instead, she stood at attention, legs squared, hands clasped behind her back.

An interminable silence stretched between her and the elders until, at last, one deigned to speak up.

"Welcome home, huntress."

A smattering of applause followed, scattered voices murmuring their approval. A few called out, *hear, hear.*

But most remained silent; they kept their gaze fixed on her, wary.

Thank you for receiving me." Socorra swallowed hard as the din settled around her. "To what great pleasure do I owe an invitation before the Elder Council?"

"Drop the formalities, girl," a sharp voice cut through the chamber.

Socorra recognized the speaker before she even turned to him. Elder Brutus. She had never met this council before, but his reputation preceded him. He rocked in his seat, then heaved himself to his feet with a groan, his squat frame barely clearing the table.

"You're here—" he growled, jabbing a thick finger in her direction, "so we can learn what in the void is happening to our people."

"Mind yourself, Brutus."

The sharp rebuke came from across the chamber. Socorra's gaze flicked to the speaker, Cassia, she guessed, based on the elder's more youthful appearance in the group. A former osprey, fierce and lean, she lounged in her chair on the left wall, watching Brutus with open amusement.

"Maybe you should sit down before you have a coronary," she added dryly.

Laughter rippled through the room.

Brutus squawked, his face twisting in fury. "How dare you?" he boomed, his jowls quivering. "So help me, Cassia, I'll–"

"You'll what, Brutus?" Cassia cut in. "Waddle over here and teach me a lesson? You'd have to catch me first."

This time, the laughter boomed. Most of the elders exploded in a fit of hysteria; even Mirabel had to cover her mouth with a delicate hand to hide her giggling.

The only one who didn't laugh was Brutus.

The rotund Hawk's face darkened to an alarming shade of purple. His jaw clenched, he flopped back into his chair, the wood groaning beneath him.

A knot of unease twisted in Socorra's chest. She had expected the council to be austere—a group that conducted themselves with decorum. But the boorish behavior before her was deplorable, if not downright shocking.

"Brother Brutus speaks the truth!"

Another of the elders slammed his fists against the table, his voice ringing through the chamber. Socorra turned her attention to him, an unfamiliar man with a hooked nose and a permanent scowl.

"Six members of our tribe are missing," he seethed. "And only she has returned." His glare burned into her, his finger an accusatory dagger aimed straight at her heart.

"Vexus, do calm down," another elder groaned.

That was all it took.

The chamber devolved into absolute chaos.

Elders jeered, hollered, barked over one another, spittle flying as they slammed hands against the tables, their voices rising in a cacophony of insults and demands. Some screamed directly into their neighbors' faces, others bellowed across the room like battle cries.

Socorra stood frozen in the center of the storm, watching in disbelief.

No wonder Hepha always refused to join the council.

Amid the chaos, only one elder remained calm.

Socorra's eyes landed on Elder Mirabel, seated at the center of the main table. The ancient Hawk was motionless, her palm pressed to her forehead, a deep crease of frustration etched into her brow. Her wings, once a rich brown, had faded to a dull gray, blending with her shoulder-length hair. Though the council chamber roared around her, she made no move to stop it, perhaps waiting for the room to settle itself.

But as the bickering continued to swell, Mirabel abandoned her patience.

Her fists slammed onto the table with the force of a hammer striking an anvil.

Then she rose.

Her wings flared wide, nearly brushing the ceiling.

"Enough!"

With a mighty sweep of her wings, she brought them down, sending a violent squall rippling through the chamber. The whistle of the wind drowned out the elders' voices, the flames of the hanging candelabras flickering wildly as the gust ripped through the room. Socorra barely had time to shield her face before food and dinnerware went flying. Metal clanged and glass shattered against the floor, a sharp cacophony that marked the abrupt end of the chaos.

When the air settled, there was only silence.

Lowering her arms, Socorra took in the disarray. Wine and ale stained the cobblestone floor, food was strewn across the chamber, and elders stood stunned; some smoothed their wind-blown hair, others wiped stew from their robes. Even the chair meant for her had been thrown across the room, now lying in splinters against the doors.

Socorra tingled with awe.

"Socorra." Mirabel's voice, though tender, carried a strict authority. She leaned forward over the table, pinning Socorra with a gaze both apologetic and firm. "You have my sincerest apologies for the behavior of my colleagues."

Then, sharper: "*Spizae!*"

The young Hawk Guard flinched as his name rang out. His legs wobbled slightly as he stepped forward.

"Fetch the speak-spear," Mirabel commanded.

A disgruntled murmur rippled through the council. Some elders shifted uncomfortably; others cast disapproving glances at Mirabel, but none dared challenge her outright.

Spizae hurried to a small dresser in the corner, fumbling with the drawer before retrieving something. He rushed back to Mirabel, his hands shaking as he passed the object to her before retreating quickly to his post.

Raising the item high, Mirabel declared, "As you all know, only the council member holding the speak-spear may talk."

The flat spearhead gleamed in the dim light, and Socorra stared at it, stunned.

Her eyes darted to the other elders. Some shook their heads, clearly displeased, but no one spoke against Mirabel's ruling.

"I'm sorry to resort to this *again*," Mirabel continued, her voice measured, "but it is obviously a necessary evil if we cannot even make it to the first question."

Again?

Her eyes widening, Socorra barely managed to keep her composure.

The Elder Council, leaders of the Hawk Tribe, wielders of immense influence, needed a *speak-spear* just to maintain order?

She was beside herself.

"Would you like another chair, Socorra?" Mirabel asked politely.

Socorra snapped out of her thoughts. "No..." The word came out slowly, lingering in her mouth. "Thank you."

"Very well." Mirabel settled back into her seat. "We were hoping you could explain what happened. As Brother Vexus pointed out, several members of our tribe have gone missing." Though her voice remained composed, there was an undeniable sadness beneath it. "As you undoubtedly recall, all communication with our ambassador to the Crowlands ceased not long before you and Kyte disappeared. Since then, three more of our hunters have vanished. You are the only one who has returned."

A knot of grief formed in Socorra's stomach. She rocked her legs languidly from side to side, as if trying to shake off the weight of Mirabel's words, but it was no use. The pain of losing Kyte crept in and nestled in her chest once again, its grip as relentless as ever.

"Socorra," Mirabel pressed gently, "when you're ready, we need to know everything."

Socorra took a deep breath, blinking away the tears that lingered in the corners of her eyes. She willed herself to keep her chin high despite the weight of so many stares.

She recounted it all: the attack in the Great Plains, her imprisonment, her escape. By the time she finished, her hands were trembling. She tried to steady herself, to mask the storm raging inside her, but her breaths had grown uneven, betraying her.

"So," Brutus spat, "those damnable Crows are behind this!"

Several elders slammed their palms against the table in agreement.

"I never said–" Socorra began, but Mirabel cut her off.

"Brutus!" Her voice cracked like a whip. "I will not remind you again…unless you have the speak-spear, you do *not* speak!"

Brutus scoffed. "Then give it here, woman!" He thrust out a plump hand.

Mirabel's lips curled into a devious smile. Holding the rusted spearhead between her fingers, she leaned back slightly, fire flickering in her eyes. No one moved to stop her.

"You want it so badly, Brutus?" She reared her arm back. "Take it!"

With a deft swing of her arm, she let the spearhead loose toward Brutus' head.

Socorra gasped, hands flying to her mouth as the spearhead whistled through the air, striking Brutus' chair with a dull *thunk*. It jutted from the wood just above his balding scalp.

For a long moment, Brutus sat frozen, his lips curled in furious panic.

Socorra glanced around the room, expecting shock, but the other elders barely reacted. Some rolled their eyes. A few looked outright bored.

"That was incredible," Socorra breathed, her mouth agape.

Mirabel let out a sharp laugh. "Don't flatter an old woman, dear," she teased. "Especially when she *misses* her mark." She winked.

Brutus twisted the spearhead loose, grumbling, "One day, Mirabel…you're going to put someone's eye out with this thing."

"And *that* will be the day I retire from this wretched council," she quipped. "Until then, follow the rules, and it won't be an issue."

Brutus scowled but didn't argue. Instead, he smirked, holding the spearhead aloft. "Tut-tut! I have the speak-spear! Who's breaking their own *stupid* rule now?"

Mirabel merely extended a palm toward him, granting him the floor with a sweeping gesture.

Brutus straightened in his chair, his voice swelling with self-importance. "You all know where I have stood since we lost contact with our ambassador. And now, based on what this girl tells you–"

"Socorra," the hunter interrupted.

Brutus' eye twitched. "Excuse me?"

"My name," she said firmly, "is *Socorra.*"

Silence settled over the chamber. Some elders remained indifferent, but others nodded in approval.

Mirabel, however, was absolutely beaming, a delighted grin spreading across her face.

"Based on what *Socorra...*" Brutus let her name hang in the air, laden with disdain, "...has told us, I hope you can now see that the Crows must be stopped before they continue to pillage–"

"It's not that simple," Socorra interjected.

All eyes snapped to her.

She hesitated, but Mirabel dipped her chin, encouraging Socorra to continue.

"I understand that black wings make the Crows seem like the obvious villains in all of this, but they're not the ones to blame. The people responsible call themselves Ravens."

A fresh wave of murmurs rippled through the chamber.

"I can't explain exactly what they are," she continued, choosing her words carefully. "But they seem to be members of other tribes who...*change* themselves somehow. Tama's son was working for Craven, and he was a Dove."

Brutus' voice exploded through the room.

"One defecting Dove does *not* exonerate a group that clearly works for the Crows! They abducted our ambassador. That alone was an act of war! And now, more of our people are taken, and still, this council refuses to see what is plainly before our eyes?"

Before Socorra could respond, Vexus reached across another elder and ripped the spearhead from Brutus' grasp.

"By her own admission," he bellowed, thrusting the dull tip toward Socorra, "these devils are taking our people to Raven Rock, in the Crowlands!" His voice swelled with fury. "I agree with Brother Brutus! The Crows must be stopped!"

Socorra's pulse thundered as tension ignited the room.

Elders flanked Vexus, some trying to wrest the spear from his grasp, others shouting in agreement.

Lifting the spearhead above his head, Vexus roared, "The time has come for war against the Crows!"

Chaos erupted.

Chairs scraped against stone as elders leapt to their feet, voices colliding in an earsplitting frenzy. Some fought for control of the speak-spear, while others abandoned it entirely, screaming at the top of their lungs.

Even Mirabel joined the fray, jabbing a furious finger at Brutus, though Socorra couldn't make out her words over the din.

Disgust churned in Socorra's stomach. This was *her* Elder Council? The so-called wisest among the Hawks, behaving like fledglings in a squabble?

And war, *real war*, in Avis? It had been centuries since the Hawks and Finches reclaimed the Desertlands from Aligaidan invaders. The idea of tribes turning against one another now was almost unthinkable.

Then, from behind her, the slow groaning of hinges echoed through the chamber.

The room went silent; Brutus' face twisted in fury.

"What do you think you're doing here, Owl?" he bellowed. "This is a closed-door meeting."

"Pelanor," Socorra growled. As much as she despised Brutus, she found herself echoing his sentiment.

Pelanor's voice was smooth, self-assured. "Since I've opened the doors, it seems this has become an open-door meeting."

The Hawk Guard tensed, edging closer with their spears drawn; Spizae's legs wobbled beneath him, the tip of his weapon bobbing like a fishing lure.

"Lower your weapons," Mirabel commanded. Pelanor flashed the guards a smug grin as they reluctantly returned to their places near the entrance.

"I remember you, young Owl." Mirabel's voice was almost wistful. "Pelanor, wasn't it?"

"Indeed, Elder Mirabel," Pelanor replied with a bow. "I'm honored that my name still graces your memory."

Disgusting.

Mirabel blushed slightly. "You came to arrange the Owl delegation, seeking some kind of hero."

"Our champion, yes," Pelanor replied smoothly.

"Bah!" Brutus scoffed loudly. "Enough of the pleasantries. Mirabel, tell this Owl to get lost before I show him the way out."

"Control yourself, Brutus," Mirabel snapped firmly.

"You're squawking mad to think I'll control myself," Brutus shot back, his face red with fury. "He doesn't belong in this chamber."

"Vexus, hand me the speak-spear," Mirabel demanded, her gaze never leaving Brutus.

With a look of reluctant compliance, Vexus passed the spearhead down the line to where Mirabel sat. She seized it, then pointed the spear straight at Brutus.

"Brutus," Mirabel said sharply. "We both know this rusty scrap of metal is more powerful in my hands than any freshly sharpened sword in yours. Contain yourself, or I'll come over there and do it myself."

Brutus grumbled and slouched down in his chair.

"Pelanor." Mirabel spoke his name evenly before turning to face the Owl. "Why have you returned before our council?"

Socorra stared at him, her frustration growing.

What right does he have to be here?

"You'll forgive me for eavesdropping…" Pelanor's words were calm, but a low roar of discontent rumbled through the chamber. "Or maybe you won't. Either way, I couldn't help but overhear several of you blatantly ignoring Socorra's suggestion that the Crows cannot be blamed for everything that is happening to your people."

His eyes shifted to Socorra, meeting her gaze.

"I am here to tell you that she speaks the truth."

Socorra stared blankly at the Owl.

What is he playing at now?

"The threat to Avis may come on black wings, but you cannot lay the blame solely at the Crows' feet. All the tribes, including the Crows, are suffering losses at the hands of this group. To declare war on them would spill innocent blood and ignore the greater problem at hand."

Brutus shifted in his seat, ready to argue, but Mirabel shot him a fierce look that froze him in place.

"Pelanor," Mirabel said, her voice steady but with a hint of frustration. "While I understand that other tribes are suffering as well, this council was designed to protect the Hawk people. Certainly, we must do that, but the threat is closer to home. We cannot ignore these disappearances, and there is a growing call for action among our citizens. So, tell us…who do you propose is responsible for these disappearances?"

"The delegation we sent should have explained this already," Pelanor replied dismissively. "A small group of black-winged Avians are responsible for the kidnappings. We don't yet know their full goal, but I believe Socorra's insights could be invaluable in helping the Owl scholars continue their search for answers."

Socorra stood in stunned silence.

Why did he wait until now to bring this up?

"My boy," Mirabel shook her head. "While your first delegation did explain much of what you've just mentioned–"

"I'm sorry," a subtle expression of unease passed over Pelanor's face, "first delegation?"

For all his calm and collected demeanor, the way he stared blankly at the Elder Council unnerved Socorra.

"Yes." Mirabel replied firmly, straightening her posture. "Your first delegation came in search of someone who could answer a riddle. They explained, just as you and Socorra have, that our fears were misplaced and no action should be taken at the time. But after several days and three missing Hawks, a second delegation arrived."

Socorra watched Pelanor closely. Despite his usual mastery of expression, his shock was plain now.

"It was their considered opinion that we could no longer rule out the Crows' involvement in the disappearances of our people." Mirabel leaned back in her chair, fingers pressed together in front of her chest. "So Pelanor, where exactly do the Owls stand on this issue?"

Pelanor remained silent for a long moment. "I'll have to get back to you on that," he muttered, his tone distant and dejected.

"See that you do," Mirabel replied with a trace of disappointment. "In the meantime, I think the council has taken up enough of your time." She turned her attention to Socorra with a softer expression. "You are dismissed, Socorra. Again, welcome home. The council will contact you should we need anything further."

With a quick flick of her chin, the Hawk Guards moved in, guiding both Pelanor and Socorra out of the chamber.

The doors slammed behind them, the echo resonating through the vast hall. Pelanor walked with purpose, his robes swishing as he moved, leaving Socorra trailing behind. She quickened her pace until she reached a light trot to keep up.

"Would you wait?" She called out. "You knew about all of this? Why didn't you say something sooner?"

Stopping abruptly in the middle of the hall, Pelanor turned on his heels, his expression hardening. "Why would

I have?" His voice returned to its arrogant tone. "I didn't know what happened to you until just moments ago."

"I'm not stupid enough to believe that," she retorted, her voice calm but firm. "You knew who I was out in the Great Plains, didn't you?"

Pelanor paused, scanning the hall as if weighing his words. "Not exactly."

"What does that even mean?" Socorra demanded, narrowing her eyes.

"It's complicated."

Socorra fixed him with a steely glare. "Then you better start explaining."

His gaze met hers, unyielding and intense. "Fine," he muttered after a beat. "But not here. Meet us at sundown, at the southern tip of the Kestrel Desert. I have a feeling that we can help each other."

Chapter Nineteen
GIDEON

"So," Gideon began, his voice nearly drowned by the last flaps of Pelanor's wings. "What–"

"Nope," Hepha squawked before he could finish. "I told the Owl I'd help you, but I didn't say I'd talk to you." The Hawk rummaged through a disorganized assortment of weapons scattered across a long table: battleaxes, warhammers, swords, daggers, and various other cruel instruments of war. "Plop down somewhere where you're not gonna be in my way." She picked up a smaller sword from the pile, nodding to herself in apparent satisfaction. "I'll tell you when I'm ready for you."

The acrid stench of smoke tugged at Gideon's memories of Moda, burning his eyes and scratching at the back of his throat. He moved toward the open entrance of the stall, seeking some air, and leaned his back against the leather tarp that made up the walls of the tent. The material creaked under his weight. He let one arm fall across his pack, twirling at the weeds creeping along the perimeter of the tent. Gripped by boredom, he dug through his knapsack and pulled out the two scrolls of birch wood that Pelanor had given him. He unfurled them, scanning through the lines of prophecy, hoping for something to make more sense. No matter how many times he read it, his eyes always fell on the same line.

Power bound through the ages, the Champion's strength is shared only by the source.

The words drew him in, taunting him.

Power. Strength.

He whispered the words under his breath, barely audible even to himself. "Power? Strength?" His fingers tightened around the edges of the scroll.

I don't have either of those.

If Cas had been named champion, the line would have made more sense.

"No." He shook his head and shoved the scrolls back into his satchel. He was too far down the rabbit hole now. Thoughts like that wouldn't do him any good.

"Just keep going, and this will work out in the end." Even if he didn't believe it, saying it aloud made it feel real, if only for a moment. But he didn't want to think anymore. He was tired of being alone with his thoughts.

What would Cas do right now?

His gaze drifted to Hepha, who sat at the grindstone, running the reflective steel of the sword against the wheel. The machine screeched, a sharp hiss rising from the metal. Gideon winced. He hadn't noticed the sound before, but now it clawed at his eardrums.

He'd probably tell Hepha to knock off the racket.

A small smile played on his lips. "Probably best if they never meet," he muttered. "And I really need to stop talking to myself."

Without thinking, his hand plunged into his pack. His fingers brushed against his book, and before he could stop himself, he pulled it free, flipping to his page.

I must be getting somewhere near the centre of the earth. Let me see: that would be four thousand miles down

I think–' (for, you see, Alice had learnt several things of this sort...)

"All right, Grendl," Hepha blurted, a note of disinterest in her voice.

"It's Gideon." He slid a dry blade of grass between the pages of his book, snapping it shut as he turned his attention to her, eager to get started.

"Did I ask?"

His shoulders sank. Sighing, he pushed himself up against the supple wall, dusting off his breeches with the tips of his wings.

"Any day now." Hepha tapped her foot impatiently, arms crossed, the hilt of a sword nestled in her armpit.

Not wanting to test her patience, Gideon hurried over to the anvil.

"Here."

She thrust her arm out, catching him square in the chest with the flat of her fist. Pain flared through his shoulders as he doubled over, gasping.

"Don't be such a fledgling," she scoffed, rolling her eyes. "I barely touched you."

"Yeah," he wheezed, forcing air back into his lungs. His gaze flicked to the sword still clutched in her gnarled fingers.

"What're you waiting for?" Hepha growled, baring her rust-colored teeth. "Take the damn thing already."

Trembling, Gideon reached for the sword. Impatient, Hepha shoved the hilt into his unsteady grip.

The leather binding was rough against his palm, but as he lifted the weapon, disappointment settled in his chest.

It was much lighter than he'd expected; there was no overwhelming sense of reverence, no sudden weight of responsibility. It dangled uselessly from his limp wrist.

"Well?" Hepha grumbled. "Don't just stand there gawking. Give her a swing. See how she feels."

Embarrassed, but unwilling to argue, Gideon pitched the tip of the blade forward, his arm swinging stiffly from side to side.

"Boy," she screeched. "You're swinging a sword, not whacking weeds! Do you even know what you're doing?"

Gideon poked the tip of the sword into the dirt and shook his head.

Hepha let out a long, suffering moan, shuffling toward him and muttering under her breath. "Ain't no way you're leaving here just to embarrass me and my steel."

Without warning, she grabbed his arms, positioning one tightly at his side, the sword held aloft, the other pressed flush against the small of his back. She adjusted his grip, shaking his wrist to loosen it, then delivered a light but firm kick to his ankle, forcing him into a stance—feet shoulder-width apart, left foot forward.

"Now, let's go over the bare bones." She backed out of his striking range, arms crossed.

At her instruction, Gideon brought the sword down in an arc, letting it come to rest just below his chest.

"Follow through," she bellowed. "Don't stop short cuz your opponent sure won't."

They drilled through the most basic cuts and stances. With every correction, every barked command, Gideon felt frustration creeping in, but he bit his tongue, channeling it into each swing.

For half an hour, she kept at him, ruthlessly adjusting his footwork, aggressively guiding him through every movement. The smithy was like a furnace, heat pressing down on him, sweat dripping from his brow. His arms ached, his breaths came heavier, but he pushed through.

Then, in a flurry of cuts, he stepped too close to one of the wooden columns supporting the thatched roof.

Thud.

The sword lodged deep into the beam, a shockwave rippling up his arm. He gasped, instinctively releasing the hilt to clutch his shoulder. The impact faded quickly, but the soreness lingered, his muscles burning from overuse.

"Not bad, Gollum." There was a rare touch of approval in Hepha's voice. "Could use work on your form, but you're not as bad as I thought you'd be."

Gideon blinked, the general kindness—or at least absence of cruelty—shocking him.

"What're you gonna name her?"

"Oh." He hesitated. Ripping the sword free from the beam, he held it parallel to the ground, inspecting it as if a name might leap from the steel itself.

He'd read about so many legendary swords: *Vorpal, Sting, Hrunting, Orcrist, Brisingr.* But none of those seemed to fit. The swords in stories were grand, decorated, imposing. This one was simple. No embellishments, no intricate carvings, just steel and purpose.

Before he could answer, Hepha raised a warning finger.

"One thing," she said. "If you even *think* about

naming it Excalibur or something stupid like that, I'm taking it back."

Another literary reference?

He hadn't pegged Hepha as someone well-versed in Sapien literature. Before he could ask about it, he was interrupted.

"He'll have to settle on a name later, I'm afraid."

Gideon whipped his head around to find Pelanor striding toward the anvil, his usual elegance replaced by an uncharacteristically heavy gait, his brow furrowed.

At his approach, Hepha stiffened, squaring her shoulders. The sneer returned to her lips. "Did you tell her?"

Gideon cocked his head, waiting for the Owl's answer, though he stayed silent. Before Pelanor left for the Elder Council, Hepha had forcibly insisted that he share the contents of some letter with Socorra.

"It didn't come up," Pelanor waved dismissively.

"You're disgusting." Hepha spat the word like bile. "She has every right to know."

"And she will," Pelanor assured her, his tone infuriatingly cool. "Feel free to tell her the next time you see her."

"You can be sure I will, Owl."

Pelanor ignored the venom in her voice, already shifting the conversation. "Is everything set?"

Hepha exhaled sharply through her nose. "Your boy has a sword." She pointed a crooked finger toward a rack on the opposite side of the smithy, her glare still laced with ire. "He just needs to grab a shield."

Without ceremony, Pelanor swooped over to the

rack and grabbed the first shield he saw, shoving the polished steel into Gideon's arms. Then, as if suddenly remembering something, he brushed past them to another stockpile of weapons, yanking a spear from the pile. Several weapons toppled with a loud *clang*.

Gideon braced himself, expecting an eruption from Hepha, but to his surprise, she said nothing. Her jaw, however, was visibly clenched.

"Perfect!" Tucking the spear beneath his arm, Pelanor strode toward the exit without looking back. "Let's be off, Gideon."

"Hold up." Hepha rolled her eyes. "You're forgetting something."

"Am I?" Pelanor feigned innocence, though his smirk gave him away. "Ah, of course." Fishing through his sleeve, he rummaged for something.

Gideon blinked. "How much stuff do you keep in there?" He was half joking, but he also really wanted to know.

Pelanor ignored him, pulling out a small parcel wrapped in twine and extending it toward Hepha.

"What's this?" She snatched it from his hand with the grace of a striking viper.

"Open it."

Tearing at the twine, she peeled back a section of the parchment, her eyes widening.

"Where did you get this?"

Curious, Gideon craned his neck just enough to catch a glimpse of a worn leather book cover. The title was embossed in gold-leaf scrollwork, though the words were too faded for him to read.

"Will that take care of the cost?" Pelanor asked smoothly.

"Pfft." Hepha's face twisted in annoyance, but as her eyes scanned the book's cover, her fingers unconsciously traced the worn spine. With a huff, she crumpled the parchment back in place and cradled the package in her arms.

"Good enough. Whatever it takes to get you out of here."

Pelanor scooped up the pack of supplies and brushed past Gideon without another word, launching into the evening sky.

Gideon cast Hepha a quick nod before following, flapping after the Owl's shadow. "What did you give her?"

Pelanor didn't answer.

"Will you at least tell me where we're going?"

For twenty minutes, they flew in silence, the land below shifting from scrubland to endless, rolling dunes.

Gideon groaned under his breath. "Not another desert."

The Finch swooped after Pelanor, angling toward the edge of a scraggy plain where a small campfire flickered against the darkening sky.

"You came."

Socorra rose from tending the fire as they touched down, the parched grass crunching beneath their boots. Her voice lacked its usual sharpness; there was something hollow in it, something distant.

"You thought we wouldn't?" Pelanor's tone was almost accusatory.

"I didn't know what to think."

Gideon studied her face in the firelight; her posture was stiff, her gaze unfocused.

"Here."

Pelanor lifted the spear from Hepha's forge, letting it hang at his chest for a moment before tossing it toward her feet. Socorra made no effort to catch it. The weapon landed with a dull *thud* in the sand, but she didn't even flinch. Her eyes remained locked on some unseen point beyond them, as if she were staring straight through them.

Gideon and Pelanor exchanged a wary glance.

"Are you alright, Socorra?" Gideon asked, his voice careful.

"Fine."

The emptiness in her tone made his skin prickle.

Slowly, she bent at the knees, reaching for the spear with a deliberate, almost mechanical movement. Gideon swallowed hard, his heartbeat hammering in his throat.

The moment her fingers curled around the wooden shaft, something inside her snapped. Her expression twisted with rage, her eyes wild and alight with something savage.

With a few rapid beats of her wings, she lunged.

Gideon barely had time to react before she was upon him. The spear sliced through the air, inches from his chest. He stumbled back, the weight of the shield hanging uselessly from his arm, but his body refused to move beyond that. He was frozen.

His breath caught.

I'm going to die.

Squeezing his eyes shut, he braced for the pain–

It never came.

"Am I dead?"

He forced his eyes open to find Pelanor standing between them, the spearhead caught in the fabric of his sleeve.

With a sharp yank, the Owl wrenched his arm free, dragging the spear away from Gideon. The motion tore the cloth, sending an assortment of trinkets and small objects spilling onto the ground.

Socorra didn't pause. She twisted the weapon free, whipping the spear around in a deadly arc.

"Stand still," she snarled, "and I'll make this quick."

Pelanor's hand darted toward his sleeve, but before he could retrieve anything, Socorra lunged again. The spear scraped against his shoulder as he twisted away.

He drew a hunting knife, parrying her next strike with the practiced ease of someone who had done this before.

They moved in a vicious, fluid rhythm: dodge, strike, counter, swivel. Socorra's aggression pushed Pelanor back, his precise footwork keeping him just out of reach.

Gideon clutched the shield to his chest, watching the clash unfold.

He willed himself to move, to help, to fight, to *be* the champion he was supposed to be.

But his feet wouldn't budge.

Driving the spear forward, Socorra managed to land a blow. "Once you're dead, I'll remove the champion. And to top it all off, I'll be sure to see that Craven is punished for letting this little songbird get away." Digging the spear further into the Owl's bicep, she cackled, the strange echo of her laughter tickling at Gideon's ears from somewhere behind him.

Looking over his shoulder, Gideon peered out into the desert, his eyes scanning the stone monoliths that pockmarked the sand. Among the shadows were two violet orbs.

"Gideon!" The Owl let out a pained squeal, the blade of the spear scraping along his thigh. "It's Zokya. She's controlling Socorra. Whatever you do, don't look her in the eyes."

"Zokya?" Gideon racked his brain. "The Crow woman from Goldfinch's dinner?" He pictured her across the table—her dark skin, an eyeball tattoo inked into the undercut of her thick, wavy hair.

"I'm a little busy here!" Pelanor squawked. "Figure something out." Unfurling his wings, the Owl took to the air, dodging another strike. "And hurry! I can't keep her off me all night."

"How do you fight someone you can't look in the eyes?" Gideon muttered, scrambling for a plan. "I could try sneaking up on her, but that's a gamble." He shrugged, firelight glinting off his shield. Then, an idea took hold, creeping across his lips in a grin.

"Medusa..."

Slipping away from the campfire, he trotted to a nearby outcropping of stones. Ducking and weaving between pillars, he arced around to where Zokya was hiding. Turning away from her, he raised the shield like a mirror and walked backward, each step agonizingly slow over loose sand and jagged stone.

Almost there. Just a few more feet...

A thought hit him like a punch to the gut.

Am I going to kill her?

A flash of silver flickered across the shield; Pelanor dove, Socorra in ruthless pursuit.

I have to save them. Don't think, just do it.

A few more steps. Any closer was too great a risk.

Gideon sucked in a breath, strapped the shield onto his arm, and gripped his sword the way Hepha had taught him. Eyes shut, heart hammering, he turned toward where she should be.

He lunged.

With an explosion of force, Gideon's blade sliced through air. He took another step and swung, metal biting into earth. Wicked laughter erupted from every direction.

Gideon spun, slashing wildly, the momentum nearly knocking him off his feet. The laughter swelled, crawling under his skin. He clenched his lids tighter.

Tearing the shield straps free, he lifted it like a looking glass and cracked his eyes open, panning the shield in every direction.

There!

Her amethyst eyes gleamed on the surface of the shield. She barreled through the air, dagger in hand, poised to strike. Gideon's heart pounded wildly, the thrum echoing in his ears.

Just a little closer.

With a violent twist, Gideon with the shield around, catching the edge of her jaw. A sickening *crack* erupted through the night. Zokya shrieked, her body hurtling backward, slamming into one of the rockface monoliths.

Gideon lunged to finish her, but she rolled, sand kicking up in her wake. His sword screeched against stone, sparks flying in every direction.

Scurrying on hands and knees, Zokya seized his ankles. With a flourish of her wings, she hoisted herself off the ground and yanked Gideon off his feet. Crashing onto his back, the shield was flung from his grasp. He tried to recover, but she was already on top of him, pinning his arms and wings to the ground with her knees.

Zokya leaned in, her voice a venomous whisper.

"Open your eyes, boy. Then be mine."

With an exasperated gasp, Gideon clenched his eyes shut, squirming beneath Zokya, her breath hot against his skin.

Even through his eyelids, violet light burned, searing into him. Something deep inside urged him to look, a siren song drawing him in. Seconds stretched. The urge to fight faded. A strange euphoria slithered through him, cold and numbing.

He opened his eyes.

"That's better."

Zokya's voice trickled like a stream, soothing and endless. Over the lapping waters in his mind, a strange whirring sound surfaced, distant but growing. It wasn't just in his head; Zokya heard it too. She turned toward the sound.

The witch screamed and fine mist washed over Gideon, warm and sticky. The haze evaporated, her spell shattered.

Zokya staggered, clutching at the spear buried in her shoulder. Her grip on him loosened. Seizing the moment, Gideon tightened his fingers around his sword and lashed out, the hilt smashing into her eye. She shrieked, wrenching the spear free, tearing flesh in her panic. Hands flying to her face, she writhed, blinded by pain.

Gideon shoved her off, scrambling to his feet, breath ragged as he backed away.

Wings thundered through the air as Socorra barreled toward them.

Don't let her get away!" Socorra thundered.

Gideon turned just in time to see Zokya stagger upright. Bloodied but defiant, she spread her wings and launched into the sky. He started to give chase, but Socorra's voice cut through the wind.

"I've got her. Go check on Pelanor."

She shot past, her wings sending up a gust that rustled his hair and feathers. Gideon hesitated only a second before shaking off the last echoes of Zokya's spell, his head throbbing. He bent down, scooped up his shield, then turned back toward the campfire.

Pelanor was on his knees.

Alarm shot through Gideon. Worried that Pelanor might be hurt, he quickened his pace, only to realize that the Owl was frantically gathering an odd assortment of scattered items, spilled from where Socorra had torn his sleeve.

Gideon bent down to help, collecting several items that had been flung to the fringe of the small camp.

"No, don't!" Pelanor called, but it was too late.

Straightening, Gideon turned over a thin strip of birch bark in his fingers. Unfurling the ribbon, his jaw clenched, the carvings familiar.

There was more to the prophecy.

Barely visible in the flickering firelight, Gideon stared wide-eyed at the dull charcoal etchings.

Before all is undone, the champion's blood must spill.

Chapter Twenty

GIDEON

It's a prophecy.

Tossing and turning, the words rolled around Gideon's head.

It could mean anything.

Pelanor had said it so matter-of-factly—no emotion, no sense of worry or empathy. The prophecies in stories were often misleading, that much Gideon knew, but this wasn't one of his stories. This was his life.

"Maybe I'll just be wounded." Gideon shrugged, a tendril of hope swirling in his mind.

Even if I don't die, how much is that going to hurt?

"Ugh!" Gideon rubbed the exhaustion from his eyes as the first slivers of sunlight crept over the horizon. His back and wings ached from a sleepless night on the stony ground. He rolled his shoulders, trying to shake off the discomfort.

The champion's blood must spill.

The vision of his lifeless body churned his stomach.

"Nope! I'm done." The words snapped him out of his spiraling thoughts. "I'm done with this stupid quest that's only going to get me killed." Frustration burned in his chest, hot behind his eyes. He needed a new plan.

"If I fly straight from Ander, I can reach the Southern Stones in a few hours. Rest up there, then head back to Moda. Maybe even grab an orange tart at Wydah's before she closes for the evening. Then I'll go home…back to my boring life in my father's shop."

His father's scolding tone already menaced his ears, but that seemed like a small price to pay to keep himself safe.

Gideon stood, arching his back and stretching his wings toward the murky sky. A ripple of satisfaction washed over him as his joints cracked. He pulled a worn tunic from his knapsack, shaking off the morning chill before stamping out the dying coals of the fire.

"Going somewhere?"

Gideon jumped, whirling around to find Socorra leaning against a tree a few yards away. She watched him with an inscrutable expression.

"How long have you been standing there?"

"Long enough to hear you have a conversation with yourself." Her tone was light, almost amused. A soft smile played on her lips, but heat still crept up Gideon's neck. "Pelanor asked me to come and collect you. We're supposed to be heading to the Owlands."

"You're coming too?"

She raised an eyebrow. "Pelanor didn't tell you?"

"He doesn't tell me anything, apparently." His words dripped with acrimony.

Socorra sighed. "I'll fill you in on the way."

"I'm not going."

He turned back to the coals, grinding them into dust beneath his heel, frustration crackling through every movement.

"If you say so." Her voice impassive, she turned on her heels.

"That's it?" Gideon asked, caught off guard by her lack of argument.

"Mostly." She stopped a few feet away, her back still turned. "But before I go, I wanted to thank you."

Gideon cocked his head. "For what?"

"For saving me." She cast a cursory glance over her shoulder. "And Pelanor for that matter."

His brow furrowed. "What do you mean?"

Turning to face him, Socorra hung her head with a certain reverence. "I don't know how, but you broke me from that witch's spell." When she raised her eyes, her stare bored into him. "I was there for all of it…every jab, every cut. It was like watching everything from behind foggy glass. I could see what I was doing, but I couldn't stop it."

Gideon shuddered, an icy chill running down his spine as he recalled his own brush with Zokya's power. "Her hold on you must've broken when I attacked her with my shield."

"I see." Socorra turned away again. "Well, thank you."

"Hold on!" Gideon blurted before she could leave. "If you don't mind me asking…what happened to your arm?"

She ran a hand up her fresh scar, something heavy settling in her eyes.

"My mate and I were out hunting when we were attacked."

Lowering herself onto the ground, she gestured for Gideon to join her. He folded his legs beneath him as she began to speak.

She told him about Craven's ambush, about the fight that had nearly taken her life, about the long and painful journey that had led her here. Gideon listened, taking mental notes of the questions that burned at the back of his mind. He'd learned from Fatima that interrupting wasn't always welcome. He imagined Socorra wouldn't be as patient with him as the fledgling.

"So, there you have it," she said finally. "You're all caught up."

"I'm sorry that happened to you." The words felt inadequate, but he didn't know what else to say. A beat passed before he added, "I lost someone too." He paused, unsure if he should continue, but he'd already started. "It's nothing like what you've lost," he admitted, "but…Zokya took my best friend."

Socorra's lips curled slightly, though her eyes shone misty. "Kyte may have been my mate, but he was also my best friend." She held his gaze. "So, it's not as different as you think. And it certainly doesn't make the pain of losing Cas any less real."

Something twisted in Gideon's chest. He choked.

"Wait." His voice came out hoarse. "How do you know about Cas? I never told you his name."

"Pelanor filled me in last night." Her lips pressed into a solemn line. "I also happened to meet him back at Cherub Farm," she added.

Gideon's world tilted, his mind reeling.

"Gideon," Socorra said gently, "I think there's a good chance Cas is still alive."

"Really!?" The sheer hope in his voice cracked. Euphoria surged through him, vibrant and dizzying.

"Craven took him to Raven Rock only about a week ago." She shrugged. "I can't promise anything…but Rocque made it back from Raven Rock alive."

"Wait," Gideon snapped. "Didn't you say that Rocque was transformed somehow? That his own mother called him a monster?"

The Hawk nodded sharply.

"No!" The word burst from him, making Socorra flinch. "Sorry, I just–" He couldn't think straight; his thoughts felt like they'd been shoved into a meat grinder.

If Rocque was in fact the creature that had chased him and Rune through Duport, would Cas be twisted like the Dove?

"If there's a chance that he's alive, I have to help him right?"

"Gideon, I–" Socorra shook her head.

"But Pelanor still lied, and there's the prophecy. What if I really do have to die?"

Socorra said nothing, but her eyes widened slightly. Without a word, she pushed herself off the ground and strode to a fallen log at the edge of Gideon's makeshift campsite. Settling onto the hollow but sturdy trunk, she picked up a flat stone and began sharpening her spearhead, allowing Gideon to continue his monologue uninterrupted.

"Cas needs my help." The urgency clawed at him, his wings twitching at his sides. "But I *can't* go back to Pelanor…not after everything…" His fists clenched. "I'll just go to Raven Rock myself."

Socorra shook her head vigorously.

"No?" He frowned. "You're right. That would be a failure of epic proportion."

Socorra dipped her head in approval.

There was a stretch of silence before Gideon asked, "Would you come to Raven Rock with me?"

"Or…" Socorra rose from the log, letting the word linger between them. "You could talk to Pelanor and work past this nonsense between you two."

Gideon exhaled sharply. "He told you what happened then?" He rubbed the back of his neck. "That's…surprising. Pretty out of character for him, actually."

Shaking her head, Socorra rolled her eyes. "Once you two are sorted, we can go to the Owlands and find out what their plan is. Then, and only then, are we going to be able to save Cas."

Something about her struck Gideon. She was good-hearted, less rough than Rune, and definitely not the bully Pelanor was.

I wonder if she pities me because she lost Kyte.

"I think that's the safest option for both you and Cas," she added.

Gideon paced the campsite, raking his fingers through his hair.

I can't trust Pelanor, and by extension, the Owls. Socorra is right though; this is the only practical course of action. But what about the prophecy? If worse came to worst, am I really prepared to make that sacrifice?

"Cas is worth it," he whispered.

"I'm sorry?" Socorra interrupted his thoughts. "I didn't catch that."

Gideon let out a sigh. "Never mind. It's nothing. Let's just get this over with."

They packed up his meager belongings, idle chatter between them. But as they took flight, the sinking feeling in Gideon's gut only deepened. With every beat of his wings, bile churned in his stomach, roiling higher until they finally landed.

"That took longer than expected." Pelanor's voice was edged with impatience.

Gideon's cheeks flushed, but he kept his tone steady. "You should've told me."

Pelanor exhaled heavily, his voice rising. "Gideon, as I've already explained–"

"It's only a prophecy, I know." Gideon clenched his jaw, keeping his expression calm but firm. "It doesn't necessarily mean I have to die. I get it. But still…you should have told me."

Pelanor sighed, his shoulders relaxing. "Gideon…if I had shown you that part of the prophecy back in the Desertlands, would you have ever agreed to come with me?"

Absolutely not!

"How would you know if you never gave me the chance?" The Finch responded.

Pelanor chewed on the inside of his cheek. "Maybe you're right."

Gideon's eyes widened. He tried to mask his surprise, but his fidgeting betrayed him.

"But what's done is done," Pelanor continued. "I can't take back my actions, and all we can do now is move forward. You know the truth now, though you probably don't know any more than I do." His voice took on an authoritative edge. "I don't know what your fate is, Gideon, but I trust you'll do the right thing."

Biting his tongue, Gideon let the Owl's words sink in, somehow embroiled with rage and guilt at the same time.

Why do you let him get to you so easily?

"So, Gideon," Pelanor said, his gaze sharp, "are we off to the Noktern? Or will you abandon Avis and go home?"

Don't give him the satisfaction.

Gideon stared him down, unwavering, hoping his silence might unnerve the Owl even a little.

"I'm going with you."

"Excellent–"

"But…" Gideon interjected before Pelanor could continue. "I want you to understand something." He folded his arms tightly across his chest. "I'm not going for you. I'm not even going for Avis." His voice remained steady, unwavering. "If I happen to save Avis along the way, then great. But I'm only coming because I have a chance to save Cas. Is that clear?"

Pelanor halted mid-step, barely turning his head to glance back. A smirk ghosted his lips.

"You'll have to remind me to thank young Cassin Jay the next we meet, then."

Chapter Twenty-One

Zokya

How long have I been out?

The last thing Zokya remembered was flying over the barren wasteland of Raven Rock, the ancient turrets of Fate's Folly rising over the horizon. But after that? Nothing.

A sharp, acrid stench filled her nostrils, triggering a pounding headache. She'd only smelled it once before; the Master called it *bleach.* She tried to open her eyes, but the one the Finch boy had slammed shut remained plastered closed, the other blinded by a searing light.

Her nausea subsiding, Zokya flicked her good eye open, only for panic to seize her. Where the sterile tiles of the Master's laboratory should have been, there was only purple fog.

"Don't struggle," Cecilia cooed. "You'll only make it worse."

As she spoke, the haze thickened, constricting around Zokya's torso like a vice. The weight of it pressed against her ribs, each breath a labored struggle. Tendrils of smoke slithered toward the wound in her shoulder, curling around the torn flesh like grasping fingers. A sharp, needling pain shot down her arm, from her shoulder to her fingertips. She winced. The pain grew like hundreds of invisible needles burrowing deeper into her skin.

"There, now," Cecilia whispered in her ear. "That wasn't so bad, was it?"

The haze coiled higher, brushing over Zokya's lips and up her nose, the pressure against her swollen eye growing unbearable. She gasped for air, but the pain in her bruised skin stole her breath. Desperation surged through her, but no matter how hard she tried to lash out, to just move, but Cecilia's trance held her fast.

"Not much to be done here, I'm afraid."

The Master's voice rang with cold annoyance. "I imagine you'll lose all sight in that eye." A long sigh. "Better not lose the other one. Otherwise, you'll be useless to me."

A different kind of pain settled in Zokya's chest. She had been nothing but dedicated to the Master's cause, her loyalty unwavering. Yet she had long known that Cecilia was nothing if not pragmatic. Still, it didn't dull the sting of just how conditional the Master's love for her was.

Now," Cecilia murmured, the fog thickening. "Let's see what's happened to you."

Zokya tried to scream, the word *wait* trailed on her lips, but no sound emerged.

Thunder rumbled through the mist, the haze erupting into a tempest; the world spun as the wind tore at her limbs.

As suddenly as it had come on, the storm ceased. Darkness swallowed everything.

Zokya hung, suspended in nothingness. She turned her head in every direction, searching, until something caught her eye.

A Crow fledgling in a white dress.

The lace sleeves stood out stark against her brown skin. She sat on the endless slate of void, focused on something before her. Zokya couldn't quite make out what.

On Ravens & Riddles

Cautiously, she stepped closer. Only a few feet away, the details sharpened—jet-black hair, dark wings spreading behind her like ink spilled across the abyss.

That's me.

Zokya's breath caught in her throat. She was a spectator now, trapped as the Master sifted through her memories. She had walked through the minds of others before, but she had never known the violation of being the one exposed.

"You have no business being in here!"

Her voice echoed into the abyss, but no answer came.

A canvas tarp was sprawled out in front of the younger version of herself, a healthy splattering of paint spread before her, though considerably less than what covered her arms, legs, and wings. Yellow, aqua, magenta: vibrant colors against the void.

A door creaked open behind her.

Zokya didn't need to turn; she knew what came next.

Her father's sharp gasp filled the space. His shadow crossed the fledgling's vision, but Zokya couldn't watch. She turned away, staring into the nothing as if she could disappear into it.

A harrowing squeal rang through the abyss.

A tear slipped down Zokya's cheek, burning as it trailed over the distended skin around her wounded eye.

"Move along, Zokya," the Master's voice coiled through the vacuum, impassive and cold. "Show me what I want to see."

On Ravens & Riddles

Glad to escape the shrill cries, Zokya pressed forward into the darkness, her steps slow with apprehension. She knew these memories couldn't harm her, but that didn't stop the gnawing dread of what she might see next.

Most of her memories from before the change were sad and pathetic. She had been a meek, impish fledgling, the unwanted fledgling of a neglectful mother and an abusive father, self-proclaimed artists who fancied themselves vanguards of the abstract.

No one else ever saw them that way.

She wandered a seemingly directionless path, but memories flickered to life around her like ghosts unwilling to stay buried. She had spent years trying to forget these moments, shoving them down, burying them deep inside herself. And yet, faced with them now, how could she resist a passing glance?

To her left stood the house of her fledglinghood. A carcass of crumbling stone, its walls were riddled with holes. Zokya shivered at the memory of those brutal winter nights, when her father refused to light a fire to save a few gold pieces. She could almost feel the biting cold creeping beneath her feathers, her fledgling down offering little protection as she huddled in vain against the chill.

To her right, another scene unfolded: the lavish salon of Florensia Corva, a magnanimous socialite of High Rock, the Crow capital. Her mother stood among a gathering of well-dressed women, their laughter airy, their words meaningless. Gossip and empty pleasantries spilled from their painted lips.

Young Zokya was nowhere to be seen.

The Raven's eyes darted to the table; behind the embroidered cloth, she caught the fledgling's silhouette. She'd spent many an evening there, hiding from the other fledglings who mocked her drab clothes and parroted the cruel things their parents whispered about her family.

Zokya had no idea how deep the hallways of her mind might go. Her pace quickened, each memory dragging up more sadness. More hatred. More rage. Her fists clenched, her shoulders tightened, and before she knew it, she was running, desperate to find the memory the Master sought, racing to end this nightmare.

A muffled sob drifted through the void, soft and broken.

She skidded to a stop, knowing the scene all too well.

Her eighteenth birthday. The day she ran away.

She watched as the younger version of herself stepped through the door of that miserable home, the first rays of dawn slipping over the walls of High Castle. The sunlight caught in her puffy, tear-swollen eyes, a faint glimmer of hope behind the deadness in her stare.

That girl had no idea how drastically her life was about to change.

"Oh, how touching," Cecilia's voice slithered through the darkness, thick with mockery. "But I don't have time for sentiment. Show me what happened!"

The world lurched. Zokya barely had time to scream before she was yanked forward, the emptiness swallowing her whole. She twisted midair, catching a fleeting glimpse of the hooded figure stepping toward her past self—the guise the Master had worn that night. Then it was gone, swallowed by a storm of memories blurring too fast for her to grasp.

The impact sent her sprawling face-first against an invisible floor, the breath knocked from her lungs. Zokya groaned, pushing herself up with her good arm, but before she could steady herself, the scene flickered into place.

The miserable Finch boy, the hilt of his sword, the blinding pain as it smashed into her eye.

She saw herself stumble back, saw her own wings flare in panic before she fled. But something was wrong. There was a sound, muffled at first like the crinkle of leaves, but it grew into a crackle.

Fire? That wasn't part of this memory.

The noise swelled, from a whisper to a roar. Heat licked at the back of her neck. Zokya spun around, a wall of fire surging around her. It devoured the darkness, closing in fast. She flared her wings, trying to launch herself into the air, the muscles in her back straining, but her wings refused to obey.

"Master!" Zokya shouted, her voice barely cutting through the inferno's howl. "Please, I can explain!"

"*Explain?*" Cecilia's voice roared from the void, her fury shaking the space around them. "I watched your failure with my own eyes."

A knot coiled tight in Zokya's stomach, panic rising as the flames edged closer, their heat suffocating. Smoke billowed thick around her, stinging her eyes, tears carving hot tracks down her cheeks.

"Your job was simple. Find the Owls' champion and bring him here."

The words slithered closer, a whisper curling at Zokya's ear. A flash of lightning split the dark, and then, suddenly, Cecilia stood before her, materialized from nothing, regal as ever. Chin high, eyes glinting, her metallic gown catching the flickering firelight, reflecting it so seamlessly she seemed made of the inferno itself.

"But instead," she continued, her voice like silk over steel, "the Hawk girl—who was supposedly dead, mind you—nearly skewered him. And then you let them all escape without so much as a scratch!"

She threw her arms wide in exasperation. "And now, thanks to you, he's surely on his way to those filthy, despicable, derelict Owls." She spat the word like venom.

"Master," she forced out, summoning whatever courage she had left. "I know I failed you. But please–" She dropped to her knees. "Let me make this right."

For a moment, Cecilia was silent, her lips pursed in thought. A flicker of hope sparked in Zokya's chest.

"No."

The Master snapped her fingers, and the flames lurched forward, ensnaring Zokya. It seared through flesh and bone with merciless hunger. She screamed, a raw, guttural sound as agony consumed her. Seconds stretched into eternity; she crumpled to the ground, writhing, trapped in a torment with no end. Her feathers curled and blackened, liquefying into thick, tar-like sludge that fused to her blistering skin. The rancid stench of burning hair and charred flesh clogged her throat, suffocating. Then, blessedly, numbness crept in. Her vision blurred, darkened. The fire shrank to embers, then to nothing. Weightless, she plummeted into the abyss, spiraling deeper.

Deeper.

Zokya slammed awake. Air flooded her lungs like foreign poison, her body spasming as the acrid scent of bleach burned her nostrils. A blinding light seared through her skull, pain blooming behind her bruised eye. She tried to shield herself, but her arms wouldn't move, held fast by thick leather straps.

Panic roiled through her, bracing her for a fresh wave of torment. Through the narrow slit of her good eye, she glimpsed the Master. Cecilia leaned over, methodically undoing one of the restraints, her sleek hair brushing against Zokya's arm. The Crow held her breath, waiting for rage, for punishment. But Cecilia's face was unreadable, cold, detached like she was fastening the clasp on a shoe rather than unshackling a prisoner.

"Head down to the holding cells," Cecilia commanded, standing upright. The second clasp fell from her clawed fingers, clattering against the slab. She strode toward a nearby control panel, throwing several levers. The overhead lights flickered and dimmed, the room plunging into a pale-yellow haze.

"Fetch the boy." Her voice was flat, disinterested. One hand on the door, she continued, "He'll escort me to that disastrous little farmhouse to collect the other two idiots. Cherub Farm, wasn't it?" She scoffed, then sighed, as if the whole ordeal were a tedious inconvenience. "Then we'll head to the Owlands to clean up this mess *you* made."

The door slammed against the wall as she wrenched it open.

"But first, Craven will learn his lesson."

"Yes, Master." Zokya's voice barely registered in her own ears, her mind still reeling. "I'll get him and we can be off."

Cecilia paused mid-step, arching a brow. "We…? No," the Master said simply, her tone almost amused. "You've done enough damage for one day."

Zokya's blood ran cold.

"You'll stay here and oversee the experiments in my absence."

"What?" she squawked. "Master, I can help—"

"Enough!" The lab quaked with Cecilia's rage.

Slowly, the Master smoothed her dress, readjusting a stray curl in her hair. The outburst vanished from her expression as quickly as it had come on.

"You'll stay here and do as you're told." Her voice returned to a cool indifference. "If you can handle *that*, perhaps I'll reconsider your worth around here."

She turned to leave but paused just before stepping through the threshold. "Oh. And keep a close eye on the Sapien girl."

Zokya stiffened.

"She survived the pteroplasty, and she's been nothing short of a hassle since."

Her boots clacked against the tiles, the sound fading as the door swung shut behind her.

Zokya remained frozen in place, fury bristling beneath her skin.

How dare she treat me like an insolent fledgling! And for what? One mistake?

She understood that she had failed, but the punishment felt excessive. Still, she counted herself fortunate that the agony was only a cruel illusion, a product of the Master's twisted mind control. Now, all she could do was obey, silently hoping that, someday, Cecilia would forgive her transgression.

I can't wait to find out how she punished Craven.

⚹   ⚹   ⚹

Meandering through the narrow halls of the castle, Zokya descended to the dungeons where the Master kept her prisoners, each destined for some new, grotesque experiment. The Ravens had been adding to the collection for moons, their haul growing with every failure the Master endured in her work.

Climbing down the final staircase, the temperature dropped sharply; Zokya saw her breath. Gripping the handle of the iron-plated door, the stitches in her shoulder protested, tugging at the skin.

Slinking through the door, she trudged down the bare hallway, the stone floor cracked and uneven. A sparse growth of tough weeds broke up the otherwise barren path. A single torch flickered on the far wall, its weak light casting long, eerie shadows over the cells that lined either side.

Passing the first cell, Zokya locked eyes with a Dove man huddled in the corner, his face etched with fear.

A voice suddenly pierced the air, echoing down the corridor. "She needs help! Please, help her!"

Zokya paused, narrowing her eyes. She followed the desperate cry, moving further down the hall until she reached one of the cells where a Hawk boy, barely older than herself, pressed himself against the bars.

"Listen, you have to get her out of here." His voice trembled as he pointed across the hall to another cell, his finger shaking with urgency.

Zokya turned and locked eyes with the Hawk girl slumped against the wall. Her limp hand dangled just inches from the floor, her breathing shallow and ragged. For a moment, Zokya's gaze lingered, but she quickly turned her attention back to the boy. She gave him a cold, silent stare, wondering what drove his desperation. Did he love her? Or was it simply loyalty to his tribe? Either way, it didn't matter. If the girl didn't die in the dungeon, she'd likely meet her end on the Master's table. Zokya turned away, heading back to the center of the hall where a grate sat embedded in the floor.

The Hawk's screams followed her, pleading for help, but Zokya ignored them. He slung a battery of swears and slurs, but she tuned him out, her focus on the dark pit below. She crouched by the grate, peering through the metal bars, searching for the Finch boy in the shadows.

"What do you want?" he squawked from somewhere unseen in the pit.

"It's not what I want." Zokya scoffed. "The Master sent me to fetch you."

"Oh yeah?" The faint glow of his red eyes appeared in the dark, accompanied by the crunch of glass beneath his feet.

Zokya tilted her head. "What's wrong?" she asked, her tone mocking. "Can't get out on your own? You're..."

She trailed off, suddenly aware of the boy's dangerous potential. Like Rocque, the Finch had undergone the change. He had taken quite well to it. He was strong. If he hadn't yet figured out what he was capable of, she was better off staying quiet. The last thing she needed was for him to unleash that power on her.

If he even could before I hypnotized him.

"What was that?" The boy asked.

"Nothing." Zokya fiddled with the mechanism of the grate, and with a sharp screech, the stone circle gave way, releasing the metal bars. She glanced at him, the faintest smirk touching her lips. "Cas, wasn't it?"

The Finch didn't move. His gaze was unwavering, burning into her. Zokya rolled her eyes, but the motion tugged at the irritated skin where the blue-feathered boy had caught her. Wincing, she quickly rubbed the tender spot before returning her focus to the cell, but Cas was gone. She leaned further into the opening, scanning the darkness.

Suddenly, she was yanked from the floor, a powerful hand wrapped about the back of her neck. Before she could react, the Finch's fingers tightened around her throat, slamming her against the wall. Panic surged through her as she struggled for air, flapping her wings with all the force she could muster, but he pinned her effortlessly with one arm.

Choking, Zokya's vision blurred, her mind overwhelmed by the fire in Cas's eyes. The red glow of his irises burned like coals, a sneer twisted his face. Desperation clawed at her as she scratched at his arm, but his grip remained unyielding. In that fleeting moment, a surge of clarity struck her. There was only one thing she could do.

Drawing on the power she had relied on so many times before, Zokya focused. Her vision darkened to a deep purple, her mind reaching out to find him, to take control. But as she pushed against the resistance, it felt like trying to break through a wall of solid stone. She gasped for air, her vision dimming, but she didn't stop.

She couldn't.

With one final, desperate push, Zokya felt the wall crack. Cas's grip slackened, and she inhaled deeply, the air filling her lungs like a fresh breath of life. Slowly, she slid down the wall, her boots scraping against the stone floor.

Rage coursed through her. A hundred violent fantasies flashed through her mind: snapping his neck, shoving him back into the hole headfirst, letting him pay for this moment of weakness. But she forced the thoughts aside, knowing that any harm she caused the boy would only fuel the Master's retribution.

She took a labored breath and commanded, "Go, she's waiting for you." Cas didn't reply, merely turning toward the doorway. With swift strides, he passed through the threshold and disappeared up the stairs. As his footsteps faded into the distance, Zokya shook off the tremor in her hands. Her nerves began to settle, but her mouth and throat were still dry. She inhaled deeply through her nose, holding the air in her lungs as long as she could before slowly exhaling, letting the tension drain from her shoulders.

Turning back toward the flickering torchlight, Zokya made her way to the last cell on the right, blocking out the taunts of the Hawk boy. When she stopped before the cell, an overwhelming sense of hopelessness swept over her—more suffocating than when her life had been squeezed from her throat moments ago. Her eyes scanned the dim interior. A pile of straw and two buckets—one for water, one for waste—was all the cell contained. But something was wrong.

The prisoner was gone.

"She's supposed to be in this cell." Zokya's voice was tight with disbelief as she glanced up and down the hallway. Panic started to creep in. The Master had made it clear that the Sapien girl was Zokya's responsibility. The first survivor of the Master's pteroplasty, the only success in more than a dozen failed surgeries. Watching over her was Zokya's one shot at redemption after her earlier failure. But now, the girl was gone.

"Well, shit."

Chapter Twenty-Two
GIDEON

To the north, the Scandiacus Mountains rose in jagged splendor, their snowcaps glistening even beneath the summer sun.

"Are you alright?" Socorra's hand rested lightly on Gideon's shoulder.

"Yeah." The Finch sniffled, brushing away a tear. "It's gonna sound silly, but I never thought I'd get to see snow. I've read about it in my books, but it's…" His voice faltered, words failing him. He gave a small shrug instead.

A gentle smile touched Socorra's lips. Beside her, Gideon felt strangely anchored. "Come on." She tipped her head northward. "We must be close."

They pressed on, soaring over the desolate boglands. The summer tundra stretched below in dull, unbroken bleakness, a stark contrast to the mountains' brilliance. Gideon imagined it must be breathtaking in winter, but now, the endless marshlands sprawled beneath them, offering nothing but mud and murk. Pelanor had flown ahead to prepare the Owls, but suddenly, Gideon wished the Owl had stayed with them. He still didn't trust him, but in this vast and featureless land, Gideon felt utterly adrift. There was no sign of what they were searching for, only an expanse that stretched forever.

"Do you see that?" Socorra pointed toward a patch of jagged rock where the mountainside met the rolling grass, her voice nearly lost in the howling wind. Without waiting for an answer, she descended. Gideon followed close behind.

Scanning the landscape, Gideon's gaze caught something strange. His stomach tightened. "That can't be it…"

As they neared, the shape became clearer—an ancient metallic monolith jutted from the mountainside. Its surface was veined with iridescent glass, refracting the sunlight in shards. Time had tarnished the metal, weathering it under the tundra's relentless storms. It looked impossibly out of place, yet eerily at home. Gideon gauged its width, narrow, barely wide enough for two people to pass side by side. And yet, there was no visible way in.

Then came a deep, grinding groan of shifting gears.

Gideon tensed. From fifty feet away, he watched as a slab of metal peeled away from the front of the structure, lowering to the stony ground like a drawbridge. A dark passage yawned beyond.

He turned to Socorra, hoping for reassurance, but her face had gone pale, her hands trembling. A wave of panic tore through his chest. Tightening his grip on the hilt of his sword, Gideon braced himself.

"What's happening?" He searched for an unseen enemy. "Are we under attack?"

Socorra didn't answer, her gaze locked on the platform. With a resounding squeal of gears, the gangway came to rest at the peat's edge. From the dark passage, a small legion of Owls emerged, their movements disciplined yet weighty with purpose. They wore robes reminiscent of the Owl Scholars, but layered over simple leather armor. Many carried massive war axes, some nearly twice Gideon's height, the heavy blades swaying precariously as they marched.

"Is that…" Gideon craned his neck, squinting at the figures in the lead. Then, he spotted a familiar face. "I can't believe it!" He elbowed Socorra. "I'm not sure what you'll make of Rune, but–"

Before he could finish, Socorra seized his wrist in an iron grip.

"Socorra," he grunted, trying to twist free. "You're hurting me."

She didn't respond. When he looked up, he found tears streaming down her face, her eyes glassy and red. The sight struck him silent. He stopped struggling, standing there stiffly, unsure what to do, his wrist aching under her unrelenting hold.

Without warning, she flung his arm aside unceremoniously. Before he could react, she was sprinting forward, wings flaring behind her as she lifted into the air, cutting toward the monolith.

On the other end, Rune took off as well, his wings beating hard as he shot toward her.

They collided midair.

Rune caught her in a crushing embrace, and together, they tumbled back to the ground. Sobs broke through the field, raw and unrestrained, before Rune pulled her into a long, desperate kiss.

Gideon blinked. "What is happening right now?"

"Though lovers be lost…"

Gideon nearly jumped out of his skin at the voice behind him. "Where did you come from?" He clutched his chest, trying to steady his pounding heart.

Pelanor, unfazed, continued. ". .love shall not; and death shall have no dominion."

The words rolled around in Gideon's head, striking a chord of familiarity. He could picture the book on his mother's shelf, the author's name hovering just out of reach, but he couldn't quite grasp it. Not that it mattered; he was never much for poetry. And even if he had been, he still couldn't see the connection between Pelanor's verse and what was unfolding before him.

Socorra had made it painfully clear that her mate's name was Kyte. That Kyte was dead. Yet here she was, feverishly kissing Rune.

"I have to say, I'm a bit shocked you're not putting this together." Pelanor grimaced, shaking his head. "Not much for romance novels, are you?"

Gideon cocked his head.

"If you were, this shouldn't come as a shock. Regardless, our dear Rune is none other than Kyte, Socorra's lost mate."

Gideon's stomach flipped. "But…" His mind did somersaults trying to piece it together. "I thought Kyte died when Craven attacked him?"

"That's what we let the Hawks believe." Pelanor motioned for Gideon to walk with him, his tone carrying a smug air. "It was easier to let the tribe think Kyte and Socorra vanished in a hunting accident rather than cause a panic. Not that it did us much good after the Hawks started getting captured anyway." He rolled his eyes. "We staged Kyte's death so he could help smuggle you to the Desertlands without drawing attention."

"Then why the name change?" Gideon pressed.

Pelanor gave him a sideways glance, his voice thick with accusation. "First and foremost, to keep you from slipping the information to Socorra."

"Hey!" Gideon squawked. "I can keep a secret!"

"My dear, sweet, naive Gideon." Pelanor raised an eyebrow. "You spend an inordinate amount of time talking to yourself. I don't even think *you* know what's going to come out of your mouth half the time."

Gideon's shoulders slumped, his face burning red.

Pelanor continued, unfazed. "The name change also allowed Kyte to operate without raising suspicion among the Hawks. He arranged the ship's passage, secured our stay at the inn, even handled your travel gear. If the Elder Council knew Kyte was alive, they would have summoned him immediately, throwing our entire plan into disarray."

"So, you've been planning this from the start?"

"I always am." The Owl flashed a wry grin. "I was on my way to Zarpa when a peculiar storm rolled in. Rumors linked these storms to the disappearances, so I decided to investigate. As quickly as it came, the storm dissipated…and that's when I found Kyte. He was bruised, had a nasty bump on the head, but was otherwise intact. He was safe to travel within a day."

Gideon's mind raced. "So that letter you gave to Hepha…"

"From Rune—Kyte," Pelanor corrected, crossing his eyes. "He explained everything and begged Hepha to help you while keeping our secret."

"And you didn't think to tell Socorra?"

"Of course I thought about it, I'm not heartless. I simply decided against it." Pelanor shrugged. "To be fair, I didn't tell Kyte we'd found her either. I thought it would be a nice surprise. Besides, I needed someone to teach you how to use that sword. If Socorra knew Kyte was alive, she would've flown straight here. Instead, she stuck with us, giving you time to train under her. Now they're reunited, and you're not entirely useless in a fight. Everything worked out."

Gideon was still irritated, but he couldn't argue with the Owl's logic. "You know she's going to kill you when she finds out, right?"

"Probably." Pelanor's voice remained steady as they climbed the ramp into the antechamber. The moment they crossed the threshold, the flickering glow of strange, flameless torches against metal walls cast deep shadows across the unadorned space. At the far end of the chamber, a narrow staircase spiraled downward into darkness.

"Shouldn't we get Rune–"

"Kyte," Pelanor corrected.

"Right," Gideon muttered, unsure if he'd ever get used to that. "Shouldn't we get Kyte and Socorra?" He turned to glance back, but they were gone. Only the group of Owls trailed behind, filtering into the entrance. Beyond them, the tundra stretched empty.

"Don't worry about them," Pelanor said. "I'm sure they've gone off for some privacy."

"Privacy? For wha–oh…" Heat rushed to Gideon's face.

Pelanor shook his head but smirked. "Come on, I'll show you to the main chamber."

Gideon fell into step beside him. "You seem like you're in a good mood."

"Just grateful to be home." The sigh in Pelanor's voice betrayed his words. "Unfortunately, I have some things to clear up with the Parliament."

Gideon gathered that was the Owl's version of an elder council. "That sounds...unpleasant."

"It will be," Pelanor admitted, "but let's not dwell on such things."

"Home?" There was a strain in Gideon's voice. "I thought you lived at the Noktern."

"I do." Pelanor took the lead down the narrow stairwell, Gideon following close behind. "Where do you think we are?"

"Oh, I–" Gideon stammered. "I don't know."

"You seem disappointed," Pelanor said over the rhythmic clunk of their boots on metal steps. "Does the Noktern not meet your expectations?"

"Well..." He was unsure how to respond without sounding rude. "I always imagined the Noktern would be something more grand. Maybe a castle, with sturdy walls and towering spires that withstood the Great End. This is just...not what I expected," he admitted with a sigh.

"I see." Pelanor didn't seem fazed. "Perhaps the interior will better serve your fantasies. Don't let the surface fool you."

Gideon mulled over those words as they descended in silence. The stairwell seemed endless, spiraling deeper and deeper beneath the earth. Somewhere in the rock, he heard the distant rush of water. The deeper they went, the louder it became, a rumbling current echoing through the stone.

"Several rivers run beneath the mountains," Pelanor said, his voice carrying easily over the noise. "They flow directly into the Noktern, where we've harnessed them to feed underground crops."

"You grow food all the way down here?" Gideon asked, incredulous.

"Of course. The land above isn't suited for farming, so we cultivate crops in the nutrient-rich soil below."

At last, the stairwell opened into an immense antechamber carved into the belly of the mountain. Stalactites dangled precariously from the ceiling, mirroring jagged stone spires that jutted from the cavern floor like the gaping maw of some ancient beast. The damp rock shimmered like crystal, catching an eerie blue light that flickered off the walls.

Gideon turned in place, searching for the light's source, but found none. A chill crawled down his spine.

"Before the Great End, this place was used by the Sapiens to store seeds," Pelanor said, his tone somber. "It was one of several vaults built by an ancient kingdom, meant to safeguard the world's flora in the event of a mass extinction. Based on what we know of Sapien culture, though, I doubt they ever truly believed they'd need to use it."

His voice lightened. "Fortunately, this facility allowed our civilization to survive, and even flourish, in a barren world. The first Owls cultivated the seeds and distributed them across Avis, Bengala, and Aligaida. Some even say they sought to restore the lost continents."

"Lost continents?" Gideon's curiosity flared. He had never heard of such a thing and leaned in, eager for more.

"Maybe another time," Pelanor said dismissively, much to Gideon's dismay. "Don't look at me like that. There will be time enough for history lessons once the Ravens are purged from Avis."

"If I survive, you mean."

Gideon hadn't meant to say it aloud, but the words slipped out before he could stop them. He bit his lip and fell a few steps behind, waiting for Pelanor's response, but none came. The Owl simply continued forward, his pace steady, until they reached the far wall. Embedded in the stone was a lone metal panel.

Gideon watched anxiously as Pelanor pressed a button with one of his bony fingers. At first, nothing happened.

"Name."

The disembodied, static-laced voice crackled through the chamber. Gideon jumped, eyes darting around for the speaker, but the cavern was empty save for them.

"Pelanor," the Owl answered, pressing another button and speaking into the panel. "And guest," he added, barely sparing Gideon a glance.

Silence stretched between them. Gideon shifted uncomfortably, trying to make sense of what was happening. Pelanor was clearly communicating with someone, but how? Was there an Owl hidden behind the wall? If so, how thin could it possibly be?

"What is that?" Gideon asked, pointing at the panel.

"It's an intercom."

Before Gideon could press for more details, the voice returned.

"Do you play croquet with the Queen today?"

Gideon blinked. The question made no sense. Yet, something about the words scratched at the edges of his memory, familiar and just out of reach.

"I should like it very much," Pelanor replied smoothly. "But I haven't been invited yet."

"The Cheshire Cat," Gideon whispered with a bemused smile.

"Indeed." Pelanor lifted his chin ever so slightly.

"Access granted," the woman on the other end called, her tone utterly disinterested. "Please state the name of your guest and the reason for their visit today."

"Gideon Thrush," Pelanor said flatly. "Reason for visit–"

"Hold."

The sharp interruption sent a metallic screech through the intercom, making Gideon wince.

"Confirm. Did you say, *Gideon Thrush*?"

The question rang in Gideon's head; a shiver ran through him like an ice flow. Even Pelanor hesitated—a rare misstep—before answering with a curt, "Yes."

A sharp click cut off the connection.

Gideon swallowed hard, his knees suddenly unsteady. He cast a glance at Pelanor, searching for any sign of reassurance, but the Owl remained unreadable, his expression locked in stony patience. The silence dragged on, thick and suffocating. A bead of sweat slid down the back of Gideon's neck, freezing instantly in the frigid air.

Finally, after what felt like an eternity, a rustling came through the intercom. "Please stay put," the woman's voice returned, this time tinged with urgency. "Hermanor will come and collect you."

Pelanor let out an audible sigh, his shoulders slumping ever so slightly.

"I heard that!" another voice screeched over the intercom. A scuffle followed, punctuated by a loud *thunk* as if something had been smacked against the receiver.

Gideon shot Pelanor a wary glance. "What's the problem with Hermanor?"

The Owl rubbed his temples, exhaling slowly. "He's just…" He trailed off, shaking his head. "Well, you'll see."

The ground trembled beneath Gideon's feet. He staggered, bracing himself against a stalagmite as the vibrations deepened. His gaze darted around, searching for the source of the disturbance. Then, with a grinding roar, a seam of light burst through the rock wall. The stone itself seemed to crumble as a massive door slid open, revealing a tiled hallway beyond.

At the center of the threshold stood an older Owl, his arms flung wide in an exaggerated greeting.

"Pelanor!" The Owl's voice rang out, dripping with forced enthusiasm.

Pelanor's eyes flicked away. "It's good to see you, Hermanor."

Hermanor wrinkled his nose. "I'd say the same, but we both know that'd be a lie."

Gideon stepped forward to join Pelanor, and Hermanor's gaze landed on him, eyes widening with interest.

"Well, well, well," he mused, sidling closer. "And who is this tall drink of water?"

"Oh, I'm not really that tall," Gideon answered unwittingly.

Hermanor blinked at him, incredulous.

The Owl barely reached his chest. Suddenly aware of their height difference, Gideon wondered if he had somehow offended Hermanor. He opened his mouth to apologize, but Pelanor swiftly cut him off.

"You know full well who he is," Pelanor said flatly. "You wouldn't have been sent to collect him otherwise."

"Just making conversation." Hermanor waved a dismissive hand, his gaze still fixed on Gideon. "It's an art, Pelanor. You might consider taking it up one day."

"At least explain why you were sent instead of letting me take him to the Parliament myself." Pelanor's voice was clipped, his patience wearing thin.

"Ohhhh!" Hermanor squealed, clasping his hands together. "So, you're the champion, too? You must be if Pelanor is hauling you off to that dreadful brood." He scoffed, looking Gideon up and down. "How interesting. I was expecting someone taller…more muscly." With a single finger, he traced a slow line down Gideon's arm.

Gideon recoiled, shuddering. "What do you mean by 'you're the champion, too'? You must've been expecting me."

But his words were ignored as Pelanor and Hermanor continued their conversation over him.

"Did Kyte not deliver the message?" Pelanor's attempt at composure was betrayed by the twitch in his eyelid.

"You mean that devilishly handsome Hawk?" Hermanor purred. "He might have. But you know how little I care for the Parliament and their endless droning."

"You mean how little the Parliament concerns itself with you?" Pelanor shot back.

"Harsh." Hermanor seemed unfazed. "But you might want to watch yourself, Pelanor. Now that Valanor is dead, you have no one in the Parliament on your side."

"Who's Valanor?" Gideon blurted out, but immediately regretted it. The pain that flickered through Pelanor's eyes sent a wave of guilt crashing over him. From the Owl's reaction, Gideon realized Valanor must have been the elder he'd met the right of Goldfinch's dinner party. In fact, he even recalled Goldfinch addressing him by name.

Pelanor took a slow breath, visibly reining himself in. "Hermanor, if you weren't sent to collect Gideon as the champion, then why are you here?"

"Well, I'm glad you asked." Hermanor lifted his nose slightly, as if savoring the moment. "Someone's been looking for you, Gideon. A young Crow girl."

Gideon felt the blood drain from his face. "Zokya," he whispered, his eyes instinctively training at Pelanor. The Owl's brow furrowed, but he remained silent.

"No, that wasn't it," Hermanor mused, stroking his chin. "What was her name again? Farrah? Fantine?"

"Fatima?" Gideon blurted out, his pulse quickening. He wrenched himself free from Hermanor's loose grip, staring at him in disbelief.

"Ah, yes, that was it. Fatima. She's in the med wing."

"But Fatima isn't a Crow," Gideon insisted, irritation rising in his voice. "She's a Sapien. She doesn't even have wings."

Hermanor clasped his hands together, resting his fingers under his chin in a mockery of thoughtfulness. "Dear boy, I think I know a Crow when I see one. But I'll humor you. This girl couldn't have been older than twelve. Spunky personality, might kill you if you looked at her the wrong way. Sound familiar?"

Gideon hesitated, then nodded.

"Well, that girl has a pair of big black wings. So if that's not a Crow, then call me an Aligaidan honey badger."

Gideon's mind reeled. He tried to form a question, to make sense of it, but all that came out were broken, stammered syllables.

"Don't hurt yourself, sweetie," Hermanor patted the boy's shoulder, his hand lingering longer than Gideon would have liked. "I'm here to bring you to her."

"But why?" Pelanor interjected, his sharp gaze locked on the older Owl. "How would you know to bring Gideon to her?"

"Because she's been yelling in her sleep—*warn Gideon, warn Gideon*. Girl's been droning on for days. Hopefully now she can shut her trap."

The words settled like lead in Gideon's stomach.

With a dramatic sweep of his arm, Hermanor looped it through Gideon's. "Now then," he crooned, nudging him forward, "tell me about yourself, Gideon Thrush."

Chapter Twenty-Three
GIDEON

The double doors hissed open, a roar of rushing water filled Gideon's ears. Stepping onto the raised platform, he was immediately enveloped in a cool mist as twin waterfalls cascaded over the edges on either side. Ignoring the damp, he edged forward until he reached the railing.

"Books." Awe swelled in his chest. "So many books."

Below him stretched a vast library, thousands, maybe tens of thousands of books stacked on towering shelves, arranged in three concentric circles. Pathways broke the racks at intervals, allowing Owls to pass through. Some hovered along the upper levels, wings lazily fanning the air as they scanned the titles, while others hunched over desks between the stacks, absorbed in their reading. Beside them, small lanterns cast a steady glow, lights without a flicker, which struck Gideon as odd.

"The knowledge that must be here," he murmured.

"Darlin'," Hermanor tsked. "You're drooling like an animal. Pull yourself together before someone sees."

Snapping his mouth shut, Gideon shook himself from his reverie and wiped his chin against the sleeve of the parka Hermanor had given him. The fabric was oddly glossy, unlike anything he'd worn before. *Polyester*, Hermanor had called it, whatever that meant.

Forcing his gaze from the books, Gideon turned toward the waterfalls, tracking their descent into twin rivers that cut through the chamber's tiled floor. The streams split around the central bookshelves, encircling them before continuing beyond sight. Four iron bridges spanned the waters, linking the heart of the library to its outer sections. He followed the river's path and his eyes widened.

"Crops!?"

Lush rows of plants: fruit trees, vines heavy with produce, stalks bursting from soil-filled beds all lined the stone walls. Irrigation channels wove between them in a careful network. Pelanor had mentioned the Owls grew their own food, but Gideon had never imagined a thriving farm nearly a mile beneath the mountains.

"You never did tell me…how do you make sunlight down here?" he asked, still scanning the chamber, certain there were more secrets waiting to be uncovered.

Pelanor leaned in, his voice low beneath the roar of the falls. "Look closely at the outer wall, you'll see a purple glow. Those are ultraviolet lamps that mimic sunlight."

Gideon nodded along, his eyes full of wonder even though he didn't understand.

"Alright, enough gawking." Hermanor's sharp voice cut through the mist, making Gideon flinch as the petite Owl seized his hand and tugged him toward a set of steps. "Let's get you to the med wing, and then–" he flashed a lascivious smirk "–I'll show you around. The grand tour. Maybe even get you into a nice, hot shower."

"A what?" Gideon asked, glancing back at Pelanor for help.

Hermanor let out a high-pitched whine. "You people don't even have showers? How do you survive out there in that wasteland?"

"Hermanor," Pelanor's voice carried a warning edge, "you know the Innocence forbids us from sharing our secrets with the outside world."

"Don't lecture me about the Innocence," Hermanor huffed, planting his hands on his hips. "But really? No showers? This boy might as well be a Sapien, rolling around in that filthy desert."

Gideon felt lost, questions milling about his head, but he couldn't grasp a single one fast enough to speak.

"And yet they make due." With a brusque flick of his wings, Pelanor lifted into the air, feet skimming the railing before he descended to the floor below.

Scrunching his face, Hermanor mocked him in a nasally tone. "*And yet they make due.*" Rolling his eyes, he followed, his wings spreading as he took off. Half a flap later, Gideon took off after them, landing lightly on the tiled ground.

They wove through the maze of pathways, Gideon trying to pick up his pace to close the gap between him and Pelanor. But before he could get far, Hermanor latched onto his arm.

"No need to rush off," he purred. "We'll get there soon enough. Besides—" he winked, his grip tightening "—you'll prefer my company, I promise."

Gideon's stomach churned. He tried to tug his arm free, but Hermanor held firm.

Crossing over one of the iron bridges into the inner circle, Gideon craned his neck, awestruck by the towering bookshelves. Each was at least two dozen shelves high, packed with tomes of every size and color. The air was thick with the scent of aged parchment and worn leather, mingling with the damp earthiness of fresh soil. The aroma wrapped around him like a familiar embrace, grounding him in a place that felt more like home than anywhere he had ever known. Not the smog-choked streets of the Finch cities, but somewhere peaceful. Somewhere he was always meant to be.

The feeling was fleeting. Hermanor yanked him forward, dragging him across another bridge and back toward the outer wall. The path curved into a rounded hallway that branched off from the grand chamber, its ceiling lined with strange, flickering tubes that pulsed like captured sunlight.

"Have you heard a word I've said?" Hermanor snapped, forcing Gideon to pull up short before stumbling into him.

"Uh, yes?" Gideon lied, hoping the Owl would drop it and keep walking.

Hermanor narrowed his eyes. "Hmm. You're a terrible liar."

Gideon blushed and they resumed walking.

"I was asking how you know the Crow girl," Hermanor pressed.

"She's not–" Gideon stopped himself. There was no point arguing. He still didn't understand why Hermanor was convinced she had wings, and right now, it wasn't worth the debate. "I met her in the Desertlands. Rune–" He shook his head. "Kyte had her steal my mother's book to lure me here."

"That's it?" Hermanor scoffed. "How dull. I was expecting something scandalous."

"We're here," Pelanor called from up ahead, turning around to face them.

With Pelanor's audience, Hermanor tore himself off Gideon's arm with exaggerated nonchalance, smoothing out his sleeves as though he hadn't been clinging to him moments before. Gideon exhaled, rolling his shoulders to shake off the tension.

"Ready?" Pelanor asked, one hand on the swinging door.

Hesitantly, the Finch nodded. He wasn't ready, not really, to see Fatima in whatever state she was in. But there was no turning back now.

As the door swung open, a wall of hot air rushed past him, thick and stifling. For a brief second, he was back in the Desertlands, the heat wrapping around him like an old memory.

"How is it so hot in here?" He fumbled with the zipper of the parka, struggling to peel it off as he stepped inside.

"The offshoot rooms and crop beds are heated by the boiler system," Pelanor explained. "The main chamber stays cold to preserve the books."

Gideon only half listened as he shrugged off the heavy coat. His eyes swept the circular room, scanning past rows of beds sectioned off by curtains dangling from sleek metal tracks. The partitions formed makeshift tents, offering privacy to each patient. Amid the sea of blue fabric, he spotted her.

"Fatima…" Her name was a whisper on his lips. A tangle of relief and dread tightened in his chest. He'd found her, but she looked so pale, buried under a heap of blankets, sweat glistening on her fevered skin.

The coat slipped from his hands, forgotten, pooling at his feet as he rushed to her side.

"Were you raised in a barn?" Hermanor huffed, but Gideon barely registered the remark.

Carefully, he folded his wings in tight, adjusting them to fit within the cramped space of the bed's enclosure. His gaze flickered to her arm, where wires and tubes connected her to machines that beeped and flashed cryptic lines and numbers. Then he saw them. He hadn't believed Hermanor, dismissing the claim outright. But there they were. A pair of charcoal wings spilled over the edges of the bed, their dark plumage stark against the white sheets. Coppery feathers wove through the black, catching the dim light. Something about them was familiar, but the memory lay just out of reach.

"Well, hello there."

The raspy greeting startled Gideon, making him suck in a sharp breath. He stumbled backward into the mobile curtain; thankfully, it didn't topple, but his cheeks burned all the same.

"So sorry, my boy, I didn't mean to startle you." The frail Owl spoke with a slow, rich cadence, his voice carrying an air of quiet wisdom. He extended a trembling hand, and when Gideon hesitantly took it, the Owl gave a feeble shake before withdrawing, steadying himself against an ornate cane, the shaft elegantly wrapped in living ivy, with patches of red flowers blooming along its length. The handle, carved from marble, took the form of outstretched wings.

On Ravens & Riddles

"Ah, Pelanor!" The rickety Owl beamed, patting Pelanor's arm with familiarity. "So glad to see you back, my boy. I'm terribly sorry to hear about Valanor. I know the two of you were close. He thought of you like a son."

"Thank you, Ordranor." Though Pelanor's expression remained reserved, his gratitude seemed genuine. "That means a lot."

"Ordranor…" Hermanor let the name cling in the air as he scooped up Gideon's abandoned jacket.

A thought that had been scratching at Gideon's mind for some time finally pushed its way out. "Does every Owl's name end in 'anor'?"

Ordranor's face lit up. "Indeed, they do! At least the Owl scholars. When we come to the Noktern and begin our training, we shed our old names and take on a new one, befitting the scholar's station. The word 'anor' comes from an ancient Sapien language, referring to the ancestry of Noktern scholars dating back to the…"

"Ugh, you've already got him talking," Hermanor muttered, rolling his eyes as Ordranor launched into his explanation. Folding Gideon's coat over his arm, he turned on his heel and sauntered toward the door. "I can hardly stand it. I'll be outside if you need me."

"Thank goodness," Gideon whispered under his breath. Fortunately, Hermanor didn't seem to hear.

"I'm afraid I have to leave you as well," Pelanor whispered softly in his ear.

"Oh." Gideon stammered, caught off guard. "Where are you going?"

"I have business with the Parliament."

"I'm sure Forranor will be thrilled to see you." Hermanor, already halfway to the door, turned back with a smirk. "In case you hadn't heard, he's the Grand Owl now."

"What?" The word was no more than a whisper on the Owl's lips, but the animosity behind it sent a shiver through Gideon.

"You had to have known it was coming the moment Valanor, well…" Hermanor dragged a finger across his throat. "With that sack of dusty old feathers gone, Forranor was the obvious choice. He's only been after Valanor's seat for twenty years."

Pelanor closed his eyes and drew in a deep breath, releasing it in a slow, controlled exhale. Without another word, he spun around and stormed out of the med-bay, his wings tense. Hermanor followed smugly, the door swinging shut behind them.

Silence settled for a beat. Then, Gideon realized the low drone of Ordranor's voice had never stopped.

"…and so, the First Owl called himself Primanor, and the tradition has continued even after the Great End."

Gideon blinked, scrambling to appear attentive. "Oh, erm…very interesting." He cleared his throat, then flicked his head toward Fatima. "And what about her?"

"Ah, the poor dear." Ordranor shook his head solemnly, his ivory beard swaying at his knees. "She's been like this for days now. Some of our scouts found her washed up on the eastern shore of Dzumel. Half-drowned and frozen, the poor thing. She should be fine, just needs to rest for now."

Gideon swallowed, his pulse quickening. "And… the wings?"

"What of them?"

"How did they get there?"

Ordranor squinted at him, deep wrinkles tightening at the corner of his eyes. "I'm not following, my boy."

Gideon hesitated, unsure how to phrase it. Finally, he decided to start at the beginning—the moment he met Fatima, the chase through the Palerock Mountains, and Jamal's return to the oasis without his owner.

"Fascinating." Ordranor stroked his long beard. He turned to Fatima, studying her as if searching for something beyond what was visible, then looked back at Gideon. "Stay here for a moment, won't you?" Without waiting for a response, Ordranor shuffled away, vanishing behind one of the other curtains. The rhythmic tap of his cane against the tiled floor echoed through the chamber, each beat stretching the silence.

Gideon's gaze darted from the curtain to Fatima, then back again, his stomach twisting with unease as the minutes drew on.

Letting out a slow breath, he tried to push away the rising tension. He turned to Fatima, and the nervous energy in his chest gave way to something heavier. Sorrow.

He should have been relieved to find her. Instead, the sight of the once-vibrant Sapien lying motionless beneath heavy blankets, her face ghostly pale, was gut-wrenching. A part of him wished he hadn't found her here, that he didn't have to see her this way.

Whatever happened to you must have been horrific.

"Fatima…"

The girl was a stranger to him yet he cared for her like a sister. She was nothing more than a fledgling, and he couldn't help feeling responsible for whatever happened to her. He couldn't shake the guilt gnawing at his ribs, the feeling that he should have protected her somehow. That he had failed her.

He reached out, resting a hand on her shoulder. Her skin was ice-cold, despite the heat that filled the chamber.

"Well, I spoke to the resident doctor."

Gideon jerked upright, Ordranor's sudden return startling him so that he had to grip the bedside rail to steady himself.

"Apologies, my boy." Ordranor chuckled lightly as he shuffled back into view. "I seem to have a habit of sneaking up on you."

Gideon forced a strained smile, still catching his breath. As unnerving as the old Owl's sudden appearances were, he was grateful not to be alone with his thoughts.

"Anyway," Ordranor continued, "the doctor mentioned something rather…unsettling. She found stitches on the fledgling's wings."

Gideon frowned. "Okay…but what does that mean, exactly?"

Ordranor's expression darkened, his bushy brows knitting together. "I'm afraid it means something rather sinister."

Gideon inhaled sharply, waiting for him to elaborate, but Ordranor only shook his head and stared down at Fatima in silence. The tension stretched between them, thick and suffocating, until finally, the Owl spoke again.

"Tell me, my boy," he said, voice almost casual, "are you aware of how we came to be? Avians, I mean."

"N–no." Gideon cocked his head, his thoughts scrambling for footing. "But what does that have to do with–"

"In time," Ordranor interjected, his voice as calm as ever. "It's an interesting story, really," the Owl continued. "Why don't you get comfortable?"

With a flick of his cane, Ordranor reached behind him, hooking the leg of a metallic stool and dragging it toward Gideon. Still dazed by the bizarre turn in the conversation, he took a seat, propping one wing over Fatima's legs while the other brushed the floor behind him.

Ordranor settled himself, folding his hands over the carved wings of his cane. "At the peak of Sapien civilization, there were six great nations, each claiming dominion over a different continent. For centuries, they waged brutal wars against one another, each determined to remake the world in their image. The fighting was ceaseless, the destruction unimaginable."

I love history…but what the heck does this have to do with Fatima?

Still, he waited patiently for Ordranor to reach his point.

"The Sapiens of what is now Bengala sought an advantage," the Owl went on. "Something that would tip the scales and bring their enemies to their knees. And so, their leaders turned to science." He leaned in slightly. "They began experimenting on their own soldiers, altering them. They tampered with their genetic structure, weaving animal traits directly into their DNA."

Gideon stiffened. "You mean…they *created* the Bengalan cats?"

Ordranor bobbed his head, slowly, deliberately. "Yes. They kept some Sapien aspects, but they became something new. Something powerful. The first true hybrids."

Gideon shuddered. "So, all of us are…"

"Indeed. We are the living ancestors of those that survived the first hybridization process."

Gideon swallowed hard.

Survived.

The word lingered like a shadow.

"Oh yes, my boy." Ordranor's voice was eerily jovial despite the weight of the implications.

"Even with their dazzling array of technologies, thousands of Sapien men and women were sacrificed to perfect the process. The records are scarce, but the few our scholars recovered paint a horrific picture.

"Their bodies were not just transformed, they were *torn apart.* The procedure shattered their bones, shredded their muscles, reassembled them piece by piece. They endured weeks of agony, their very being rewritten. It was a wicked, vile process…yet one to which we owe our very existence."

Ordranor fell silent, lost in thought.

Gideon cleared his throat. "Erm…Ordranor?"

"Hm? Oh! Quite right, quite right. Got lost for a moment there." He blinked, then continued as if nothing had happened. "Once the other nations caught wind of Bengala's experiments, they launched their own hybrid programs: sharp teeth, claws, scales, fins, and–"

"Wings," Gideon finished, his voice a hoarse whisper.

Ordranor nodded deeply, his beard dipping toward the floor. "It wasn't long before hybrids were everywhere. Once the process was perfected, Sapiens *volunteered* for what they saw as a privilege. And soon, the hybrids began to procreate. Their fledglings inherited the changes, already predisposed to the genetic mutations of their parents.

"Within thirty years, hybrids were no longer just soldiers…they were civilians, leaders, entire populations. Records from the nation of Homo-Avians—what we now call Avis—show that at least a quarter of their people were hybridized before the war reached its end."

Gideon's mind reeled. It all sounded crazy, like the science fiction and fantasy in his stories.

"The Great End came with the whispers of even darker advancements," Ordranor continued, his voice taking on a grave tone. "The records speak of anomalies that allowed some Avians to control the weather, bend the mind, even glimpse the future. Most of it is utter dribble." He waved a hand dismissively. "But then again…the First Owl was…"

Gideon barely heard him. His thoughts raced, puzzle pieces clicking together in his mind. "That explains why Zokya can…"

Not hearing the Finch's musing, Ordranor continued, speaking over the boy.

"In response, the Lupine nation, now lost to us across the Azure Deep, unleashed a weapon the likes of which we can scarcely imagine. In retaliation, the others followed suit, unleashing their own hellstorm. The devastation was swift and absolute. Many perished in the days that followed—Sapiens and hybrids alike.

On Ravens & Riddles

"For centuries thereafter, the survivors struggled, clinging to life as the world slowly healed from their ancestors' folly. But while the Sapiens dwindled, our ancestors thrived. Hybridization made us stronger, allowed us to flourish in a world turned against its makers. Whether you see it as a blessing or a curse…" Ordranor sighed, absently running his fingernails along the carved wings of his cane, "it is the reason we are here."

"Ordranor, this is all very fascinating." There was sincerity in Gideon's voice despite his exasperation. "But you still haven't explained what any of this has to do with Fatima."

The Owl hesitated, his fingers pausing against the cane's handle. Then, with a heavy breath, he met Gideon's gaze.

"Unfortunately…" The Owl heaved a deep sigh, gently scraping at the winged handle of his cane with his fingernails. "I'm afraid that your young friend is a new conception of the hybridization process."

Gideon stiffened. "So, you're saying…" The words caught in his throat, doubt clawing at his reason.

Ordranor met his stare. The glassy sheen in his ancient eyes betrayed his fear.

"Whoever did this to her," his voice dropped to a whisper, "is trying to recreate the technology that destroyed the Sapien world."

A sickening weight crashed over Gideon's shoulders, pressing against his ribs like an iron vice. His stomach twisted, his breath turned shallow. His vision wavered as the horror of Ordranor's words sank in.

Then the world went dark.

For a heartbeat, Gideon thought he'd blacked out. But then the lights flickered back, this time bathing the room in an ominous red glow. A siren wailed, splitting through the air like a jagged knife.

Gideon barely had time to process it before something clamped down on his forearm, the skin ice cold. A violent shudder shot through his spine. His eyes snapped downward.

Fatima was awake.

Her eyes, wild as a cornered animal's, bored into his own. Her lips moved frantically, screaming something. But the siren drowned out her voice, deafening, relentless.

Gideon leaned in, desperate to make out her words.

"She's here for you."

Chapter Twenty-Four

Socorra

"I'll kill him!" Socorra snarled. "He knew this whole time and he couldn't be bothered to say anything? The void take that cursed Owl when I get my hands on him!"

"I'm sure he had a good reason." Kyte shrugged. "He usually does."

Socorra rolled her eyes. "Don't defend him!" But even as she scowled, her gaze drifted to his face: hooked nose, thin lips, bushy brows, and those sharp, piercing eyes. She wanted to stay angry, to cling to the righteous fury that had fueled her for days, but the sight of him disarmed her. A smile betrayed her before she could stop it. She was just happy to be in his arms again.

As she nestled her head against his shoulder, Kyte let out a sharp gasp. She shot upright. "I'm so sorry!" Her heart slammed against her ribs, terrified she'd hurt him.

"Don't be." He chuckled through the pain, rubbing at his shoulder. "Hurt a hell of a lot less than the bullet."

She bit her lip, guilt gnawing at her, but a laugh escaped, unbidden and sweet.

She had missed this. His dry humor, breathy chuckle, the way he looked at her like she was the only thing in the world that mattered.

Kyte caught her staring. A smirk tugged at his lips as he reached up, rough palm cupping her cheek, and drew her into a kiss.

Then, a deep, blaring note echoed through the forest.

Socorra tore herself from his arms and sprang to her feet, eyes scanning the tree line. The sound chilled her to the bone. She turned to Kyte. Their eyes locked.

The Noktern's in danger.

They launched into flight, wings slicing through the canopy of massive pine. The air was thick with tension, storm clouds rolling in from the east. Thunder cracked between the long blasts of the warning horn.

Her feathers bristled. The hairs on her neck stood on end. This wasn't an ordinary storm; it was an omen.

Craven is coming

A snarl curled her lips. Just the thought of that grinning bastard was enough to ignite her blood. But Kyte was beside her, and that made all the difference. They were flying straight into danger, but that had never stopped them before.

I'm going to wipe that smirk off his face... permanently.

They touched down at the tree line, where forest gave way to tundra. Socorra moved to sprint, her adrenaline surging, but Kyte caught her wrist.

Before she could protest, he tugged her back into a tight embrace.

His lips brushed her hairline, his rough hands running along her shoulders in slow, calming sweeps that sent chills through her.

She nestled into his tunic, breathing him in. But when she looked up to meet his gaze, he wasn't looking at her. His gaze was distant, miles away.

A tear drizzled down his cheek.

The air left her lungs. "What's wrong?" she whispered, heart pounding.

Kyte held her fingers delicately between his, head bowed. Slowly, his eyes lifted to meet hers, deep umber and shining in sunlight of the afternoon.

"Your breath smells horrible."

She gaped at him, then growled, shoving him hard. "Asshole! I'm serious!"

But she was already laughing. And so was he.

As quickly as their laughter had come on, it was swept away by the somber shadow that loomed on his face.

"Nothing's wrong," he said, but his voice wavered. "It's just that…Pelanor–" He stopped himself, swallowing thickly. "I just need you to know how much I love you."

"Kyte…"

She wanted to ask why he was saying this now, to demand the rest of that sentence. But she didn't get the chance.

A deafening clang echoed through the clearing as the Noktern's gangway slammed to the ground.

Socorra turned instinctively at the sound. And in that heartbeat of distraction, Kyte slipped from her arms. By the time she looked back, the softness was gone. The warrior had returned, his mask in place, fire in his eyes. Without another word, he strode toward the stronghold.

She hesitated, rooted in place, a hollowness creeping into her chest. But she choked it down, swallowing the uncertainty like poison.

Crossing the field in minutes, the Hawks moved in silence, their focus razor-sharp.

A group of Owl guards waited near the center of the marshy plain. One of them stepped forward, calling out, "Hail!" He held out a small collection of armor.

They selected a few pieces: leather breastplates, bracers, but kept their armor minimal. Against Craven's speed, they'd need every ounce of agility to stand a chance.

Tightening the laces of her wrist guard, Socorra ran her fingers along the shaft of her family's spear. The wood was smooth, worn from years of battle. She held the heirloom up, admiring its simple beauty—runes carved into the serrated iron tip, embedded in a shaved oak handle.

She thought she might never see it again, but Kyte had returned it to her; she felt whole.

"What's the plan?" she asked.

One of the older guardsmen stepped forward. "We hold the plains and defend the Noktern. With the storm coming from the southeast, there's no point in fighting them in the air."

Socorra blinked. "That's it?" There was a sharp bite in her voice. "We're just standing here? Shouldn't we take cover? Find a defensive position? Literally anything?"

"Young lady," the guard scoffed.

Socorra's shoulders tensed; she ground her teeth, but remained silent.

"Where exactly do you propose we go? The forest is too dense for a coordinated strike, and the mountains won't help us. This is the best ground we've got."

"Are there at least more guards coming?"

"No."

"Why the void not?" A numb tingling spread through her wrists.

The man laughed dryly. "Because the Noktern is an impenetrable underground fortress. It has stood for thousands of years, never once sieged. There's no point wasting resources defending what doesn't need defending."

Frustration burned hot in her chest, but she forced herself to breathe through it, keeping her gaze locked on the Noktern's entrance.

At last, Gideon emerged. He trudged down the ramp, dressed in a leather helm, bracers, and a heavy vest made of some strange material. It looked light, but it clearly weighed the small Finch down.

He was pale as a ghost, trembling.

"Hello." Socorra spoke softly and bowed her head.

Kyte dipped his head in solemn acknowledgment. "Ready?"

Gideon nodded silently. He was trying to be strong, but Socorra saw the fear in his eyes, the way his legs wobbled beneath him.

Kyte laid a hand on the Finch's shoulder, his other arm wrapping firmly around Socorra's waist. "We won't let anything happen to you."

A flicker of relief crossed Gideon's face. His shoulders relaxed, some of the color returning to his cheeks.

Kyte pulled a small metal container from his waist pouch. "Before those bastards get here, you're gonna want some of this." Socorra recognized it instantly, the last of the preen oil his father had given them before his passing. The waxy substance would keep them airborne, even in the worst of the storm.

Dipping his fingers liberally into the canister, Kyte smoothed the oil over Gideon's trembling wings. Socorra did the same for herself, working quickly as the wind picked up, howling through the trees like a dying beast.

As Kyte sealed the empty container and stowed it away, the storm roared in full force. The treetops writhed in the squeal of the wind, lightning slashing through the darkening sky. A wall of rain charged across the tundra, swallowing the plains in an unrelenting downpour.

Within seconds, Socorra's clothes were soaked through; her hair clung to the back of her neck like a frigid hand. The icy chill shot her back to that night when she thought she lost Kyte. The night she thought Craven had ripped everything from her.

This time, she wasn't afraid; she wanted him to come. She wanted to see his face when he learned she was alive and that Tama had set her free.

A bolt of lightning struck at the plains' edge, leaving a charred crater in the cotton weed. Smoke curled toward the heavens. Socorra followed its ascent, then stopped. Two dark shapes, slicing through the storm like loosed arrows.

The Owl Guards snapped to attention. Their huddled ranks broke as they rushed to form a defensive line in front of Gideon, Socorra, and Kyte. Through the shifting wall of bodies, Socorra caught a glimpse of the figures.

Rocque. His hulking frame was unmistakable, a towering mass of muscle even against the chaos of the storm.

But the second shape was too broad, too solid.

Is that…

"Cas!"

Gideon's voice cracked, ragged with disbelief.

Socorra gripped his arm. A silent reminder that he wasn't alone.

Her gaze locked onto Cas. Back at the farmhouse, it had been too dark to truly see him. She had only glimpsed fiery wings, the telltale ember of what he had once been. Now, they were black as pitch. Corrupted. Branded by Craven and his heathen band of Ravens.

A sharp pang.

That could've been me.

Before she could even swallow, one of the Owl guards crumpled, clutching a gushing wound in his neck. Blood splattered across the wet grass, dark as ink under the storm's fury.

Panic erupted.

Socorra wrenched her focus back. Pressing against Kyte's back, she yanked Gideon closer, forming a tight defensive cluster. Another guard collapsed. Then another…as if they were cut down by a ghost.

"It's Craven!" Socorra squawked over the storm. "Keep your eyes peeled!"

The Owls recovered, forming a rough circle around the trio.

Socorra lifted her spear, blade poised, scanning the sky. Gripping the shaft tighter, her knuckles burned, but she didn't dare let go.

An arrow whistled through the rain and another Owl fell, a boy barely older than Gideon.

Before Socorra could raise her eyes, another guard collapsed on the other side of her, their battleaxe falling into the mud at her feet.

"Stand your ground!" Socorra felt Gideon's legs tremble beside her. "Keep your sword up!"

She tried to sound strong, but doubt slithered in, tightening around her throat as the Owl ranks dwindled.

A quick glance over her shoulder; Rocque and Cas had stopped. Just standing there. Watching.

They're toying with us.

She wanted to ask Kyte if he saw it too, but she feared what it might do to Gideon.

Then, a single word rang out:

"Retreat!"

The Owls didn't hesitate. Bows and axes hit the ground as they bolted, desperate to reach the safety of the Noktern.

Socorra wanted to be angry, wanted to curse them for running, but she couldn't blame them.

How do you fight something too fast to see?

One by one, Socorra could only watch as the fleeing Owls were cut down, their screams swallowed by the storm. The fire in her chest flickered, sputtering against the brutal tide of reality.

Then a cackle erupted, high, shrill, carving through the storm like a rusted blade.

Socorra's stomach plummeted as she looked up.

Craven.

He swept overhead in a slow, deliberate arc. Not too fast, just enough to taunt her, always beyond reach.

Kyte moved first, breaking from the group, his presence vanishing like a gust of wind. Socorra followed, her damp tunic clinging to her skin, the cold biting deep. They formed a line, squaring off against Rocque and Cas.

Above, Craven's wings beat in time with the thunder. Each downstroke rattled her bones until, at last, he dropped to the ground, joining the other Ravens.

Through the veil of rain, Socorra locked onto his gaze, two beady pupils, stark against the whites of his eyes, fixed solely on her.

"Lovely to see you again, songbird." Craven sneered, his lips twisted in a cruel, sadistic smile. His gaze flicked to Kyte. "And you, sir, have we had the pleasure?"

Kyte clenched his jaw, but remained silent.

"Oh, of course!" Craven's face contorting into a scowl, depravity glimmering in his eyes. "You were with the songbird that day." His tone darkened. "I knocked you from the sky. You should've died."

"You'll have to try harder to kill me," Kyte seethed, his voice acrid.

"So it would seem," Craven hissed. "But neither of you will make it out of this alive." He flexed his talons, sharp and eager. "Ah, and Gideon, I presume?"

The Finch stiffened.

"Charmed." Craven bowed dramatically, his hand resting over his chest. "I am Cra–"

"Cas!" Gideon's shout cut through the air, jolting Socorra. "What did they do to you?"

Socorra's gaze drifted to Cas, but the boy didn't speak. The longer the silence stretched, the more uneasy she grew. Cas stood tall, unwavering, his eyes burning with an intensity that pierced right through Gideon. He didn't blink.

"You'll have to forgive our young Cassin Jay." Craven feigned a sigh. "He's forgotten his manners. He's undergone the change…become a Raven, like us." He leaned in closer, eyes glinting with malice. "Now, you can come with us willingly. Maybe your friends will survive long enough to go through the same. Or, we can drag you to Raven Rock after we slaughter them." His lips thinned. "Your choice, Gideon Thrush."

The wind howled through the field, the only sound the relentless beat of rain on the earth. The standoff held, and for a moment, no one spoke.

Kyte broke the silence, his voice firm. "Don't be afraid." He placed a hand on Gideon's shoulder, meeting his gaze with steely resolve. "I'll fight for you, champion." He winked.

"As will I." She took Gideon's arm in her hand, trying to project confidence even though hers waned. She had no idea how they were going to fight Craven; she'd hoped to come up with a plan, some weakness to exploit.

A warmth radiated up her arm, Kyte's fingers brushing her skin.

"Are you ready?" There was a fierceness in his eyes.

Socorra's doubt faded.

"I'm ready."

Craven's laughter cut through the moment. "Too bad, really." He smirked, eyes narrowing. "I thought you both would have done well with the change. Strong, willful. Shame you'll die instead."

With a flare of his talons, Craven lunged into the air, preparing to strike.

A blood-curdling wail tore through the storm.

Craven howled in rage. He thrashed about, expletives erupting from his maw.

Socorra stared on, bewildered, trying to make sense of what she saw. Something—someone had leapt onto the Raven's back, ripping out clumps of feathers. He howled in rage, thrashing, but the attacker clung tight. It took Socorra a moment to make out the small, wiry figure. A Crow, no more than a fledgling.

"Fatima!" Gideon cried.

The Finch lunged forward, but Socorra caught his arm, holding him back. Before he could take another step, Kyte had already taken to the air, streaking toward the struggle.

From the corner of her eye, Socorra caught movement among the Ravens. As Kyte closed in, Rocque finally stirred. With a sudden lurch, he threw himself into Kyte's path. The Hawk veered upward at the last second, narrowly avoiding the ambush. Rocque hesitated only for a moment before launching into the sky in pursuit.

With Kyte and Rocque locked in their own battle, Socorra turned her focus back to the ground. Craven fought to tear the girl off as Cas stood eerily still, eyes fixed on Gideon. Socorra didn't know who Fatima was, but she wasn't about to waste the opportunity.

Spear in hand, she launched herself into the air, wings battering against the storm as she shot toward Craven.

"Enough!" Craven roared, seizing the fledgling's arm in a crushing grip. With a vicious twist, he flung her halfway across the field. She hit the ground hard, rolling through the dirt before coming to a stop.

Socorra pushed forward, aiming straight for Craven's heart. But he turned at the last second. Her spear cut high across his shoulder instead of striking true.

His claws lashed out.

White-hot pain exploded along her jaw as the impact knocked her sideways. Her spear wrenched from her grip, spiraling into the storm. Tumbling through the air, she fought to right herself, but the force sent her crashing to the ground. The impact rattled through her chest and legs, pain splintering through her ribs. She tried to rise, but her muscles locked, forcing her forward onto her hands and knees. Gritting her teeth, she lifted her head, searching for Craven.

He hadn't moved.

The Raven stood hunched, claws bared, his body rigid with pain. His glare burned through her as he thrust an accusatory claw in her direction.

"You think you stand a chance here, songbird?" he seethed. "You are nothing."

Slowly, Socorra pushed to her feet, reaching for the hunting knife strapped to her boot. She felt naked without her spear, but she didn't dare take her eyes off him to search for it.

Planting her feet firmly in the peat, she let her gaze scroll over the Raven's shoulder, assessing the damage Fatima inflicted. There was a jagged tear in his jacket, and a patch of raw skin where feathers had been stripped away. But more importantly—

His wing's broken.

Her pulse hammered. The arc of his wing drooped unnaturally behind him, the muscles spasming in short, erratic tremors.

There's hope.

Behind Craven's shoulder, Kyte darted toward the mountains, Rocque close on his tail. Socorra's eyes flicked toward them for only a second, just long enough for Craven to close the gap.

Even with a broken wing, he was still deadly, propelling himself forward with raw power.

Socorra barely had time to react. She threw herself sideways, narrowly dodging the slash of his talons. Craven twisted, trying to correct his trajectory, but his injured wing faltered. He tumbled to the ground.

The Hawk scrambled to her feet, heart pounding. She had only seconds before he was up again. Frantically, she scanned the area for Gideon, for Kyte, maybe even the glint of her spear in the grass.

But there was nothing.

Craven was already rising.

No time.

With a running leap, Socorra hurled herself into the howling wind, wings thrashing against the icy rain as she climbed higher. She couldn't fight Craven head-on, not with only a hunting knife. She needed an advantage.

A hundred feet up, she hovered near the peaks of the tallest pines, the storm lashing around her. Below, Craven fumbled, slowed but still relentless. A flash of lightning split the sky, illuminating the mountains and two figures locked in battle. Kyte was still fighting.

Relief flickered through her, but only for a moment.

She folded her wings and dove.

The pines rose to meet her, their bristling branches closing in like grasping hands. She tucked in tight, letting gravity pull her into the dense canopy. Needles raked against her arms, sap clung to her feathers, and jagged branches tore at her clothes like razors.

She hit the ground hard, the darkness swallowing her whole. The shock sent her tumbling, her shoulder slamming into the mud. Pine needles and damp earth clung to her skin. The hunting knife wrenched from her grip, vanishing into the underbrush.

She barely had time to process the pain radiating through her legs before she was scrambling forward, swiping frantically at the ground. Her fingers met only damp leaves and dirt.

Above her, the night split with a singsong voice. "Oh, songbird…where are you?"

Her breath hitched—no time to search, no time to think.

Swallowing a curse, Socorra pressed her back to the earth and crawled toward the nearest tree, disappearing under the skirt of thick branches. She hugged the trunk, her pulse hammering against her ribs. The darkness was thick, suffocating.

Craven's feet hit the ground with a dull *thump*.

Socorra's fingers combed over the ground, searching for something: a rock, a broken branch, anything she could use as a weapon. But there was nothing. All she could do was wait.

"Why don't you come out, songbird?" Craven howled, his voice cutting through the trees. His footsteps grew louder, each step slow, deliberate, taunting. "Let's end this little game."

Socorra curled in on herself, wrapping her wings tight, pressing into the damp earth. Through the pine needles, she could just make out his lanky silhouette drifting toward her, yellow eyes glowing like a predator's in the gloom. Her heart pounded so hard she was certain he could hear it. A few more steps, and he'd be upon her.

Then came a whistle, sharp and piercing. The sound cut through the dense forest, threading through the branches like a blade. Socorra didn't dare move, but she felt it in her bones. Craven halted, his head snapping toward the source. His eyes flickered, searching.

There was movement in the canopy. A small, winged silhouette flitting through the boughs.

Fatima.

Then, something fell through the trees. At first, Socorra thought it was just a broken branch, snapped under Fatima's weight. But as it tumbled closer, her breath caught.

My spear!

It landed with a solid *thud* just inches from her outstretched hand. Awe surged through her chest.

Craven squawked. "There you are, you little wretch!" With a snarl, he lunged, slashing through the pine needles, talons bared.

Socorra seized the spear.

Craven crashed through the brush, his jaundiced eyes wild, his mouth twisted in a grotesque grin. He was close, his claws just a hair's breadth from her throat.

She struck, driving the spear forward with both hands laced around the handle. Steel tore into his chest. He froze, breath hitching, a wet, choking gasp. His eyes stretched wide, disbelief flickering into terror, his head tilting downward as if struggling to comprehend the shaft now lodged deep within him.

Teeth clenched, Socorra twisted the weapon. A raw, garbled shriek wrenched from his lips. She wrenched the spear free, the motion violent, desperate. Blood sprayed, hot and sharp, spattering across her face as her elbows slammed into the ground.

"No, no, no…" His voice was barely a whisper now, breath rattling in his throat. He staggered, knees buckling. His gaze found hers, and in the darkness, she saw it.

Fear. True, desperate fear.

Then, something strange. The black of his wings bled away, thick sludge dripping from his feathers, revealing brown plumage beneath, like ink washed from a page.

"You…" Craven wheezed, blood bubbling at his lips. "You may have bested me, songbird, but the Master…" His body trembled violently. "She's more powerful than you can ever know. You'll never stop her."

His voice wavered. Was that disappointment? Regret?

Slumping face-first to the ground, his body convulsed, wings spasming, twitching against the earth until, finally, he stilled.

Dead. Craven was gone.

Socorra crawled from the tangle of branches, carefully skirting the pool of blood. Rising to unsteady feet, she gripped her spear and nudged the corpse with its butt. No response. No movement.

Socorra felt like she could breathe again. She inhaled deeply, the petrichor filling her lungs, damp and clean. Rain trickled down her face, washing away the grime and blood.

She looked down at him one last time.

"That's for Tama."

Chapter Twenty-Five
GIDEON

"How's it feel to be abandoned by your friends, Gid?" Cas's voice was sharp, cutting through the storm like a blade. His garnet eyes locked onto Gideon from across the field, burning with something raw. "Hurts, don't it…"

Gideon's brow furrowed. "What're you talking about, Cas?"

"Don't play dumb, Gid." Cas drew a quick, scornful breath. "You left me behind at Goldfinch's."

Gideon flinched. "Cas, that's ridiculous. I didn't–" He took a step forward, but his words faltered. His mind reeled back, flashes of that night searing into his memory. Rune—Kyte. Leaning out the window, fists pounding on the door.

"You didn't, what?" His voice was bitter, cutting. "You didn't hide upstairs? You didn't fly away while innocent Avians were slaughtered?" His next words dropped to a whisper, but they struck like a hammer. "You didn't run like the coward you are?"

The words stabbed at Gideon.

"Craven told me all about that night," Cas continued. "He stayed in that dungeon for hours, taunting me." He beat at his temples with his fists. "He told me how you abandoned me to go play hero, that you couldn't be bothered to even look back once you were gone."

"Cas, that's not true, I–"

"I've been alone for weeks." Cas spat, his face twisted in a furious glare. "Nothing but silence and horrible thoughts." His fingers wove through his hickory hair, pulling at the strands as if trying to rip the memories free.

"I've played it through my head so many times." His voice cracked. "The sound of the fire. The squeal of your chair. The screams." He sniffled, eyes glassy with something dark, something broken. "It all echoes in there."

Guilt ripped into Gideon. "Cas," he pleaded, his sword and shield sagging in his grip. "I didn't mean to… everything happened so fast and I…" The words stuck in his throat.

How do you justify leaving your best friend?

"I just want to help you now, like you helped me when we were fledglings."

Cas lifted his head, fingers still tangled at his hair. "Help?" His eyes searched Gideon's face.

"Yes, Cas," Gideon beamed, hopeful. "Help."

For a heartbeat, he swore he saw something flicker across Cas's face, a hint of the boy he used to know. Shivers of hope ran through Gideon, fragile but there.

Cas tsked in a derisive tone. "Gid, Gid, Gid…" His voice dripped with mockery. "You wanna help me?" He pulled his hands away from his head, a mocking smile on his face. "You and your little friends can't even help yourselves."

A void opened in Gideon's chest, swallowing that sliver of hope whole. "And what does that mean?"

Cas waved his hand dismissively. "Just look around you."

Gideon scanned the battlefield. Socorra plunged into the forest, swallowed by the imposing trees. Kyte still wove through the storm-choked peaks, Rocque gaining on him.

"See it now?"

Gideon clenched his jaw, shaking away the creeping doubt. "See what?"

"C'mon, Gid. You're no idiot." Cas's voice turned taunting. "You're s'posed to be the champion, right? That's what the Owls called you. And yet here you are, hiding behind Hawks while they fight your battles."

Gideon felt the weight of Cas's words settle in his chest like a stone.

"That's not fair."

Cas's wings snapped open, mist flying from his soaked feathers as his voice thundered through the rain.

"Not fair!? Not FAIR!?"

Cas launched himself forward in a blur of fury.

Gideon barely had time to lift his shield before Cas's fist crashed into the metal, sending shockwaves of pain through his arm. The impact knocked him clean off his feet, the breath ripped from his lungs as he slammed onto his back.

"Get up." Cas's voice was sharp, commanding.

Dazed, Gideon didn't move. Rain pelted his face, mixing with the ache thrumming through his body.

"I said, *GET UP*!"

A rough kick to his ribs jolted him, forcing a gasp from his throat. He tried to rise, but pain screamed through his arm, radiating from his shoulder down to his chest. His body betrayed him, and he collapsed with a strangled groan.

Before he could hit the ground again, Cas's hand shot out, gripping his tunic. Gideon barely had time to register what was happening before Cas yanked him up, his face inches away, eyes burning.

With a hard shove, Cas flung him backward. Gideon staggered but managed to stay on his feet, chest heaving, pain lancing through his arm.

"Go ahead," Cas dared. "Take a swing. Let's see what you can do with that sword."

It took Gideon a moment to process what Cas had said. Shaking his head, Gideon chased away his stupor, but the words were hollow, meaningless.

None of this makes sense.

Hurt and confused, he searched his friend's face.

"Cas," he pleaded shakily. "Talk to me."

A long silence stretched between them. Even the rain seemed to quiet, as if the storm held its breath for what came next.

Cas broke the silence, his voice devoid of any emotion. "Sword up."

Gideon stiffened, chest tight.

"I won't kill you," Cas continued. "She wants you alive. But I'm gonna make sure you bleed for what you did to me. Everything you see here, what they did to me, it's all your fault. And you're gonna pay."

Gideon's mind reeled.

Who wants me alive?

Zokya? The Master?

Why?

Lightning split the sky, illuminating Cas's face for a brief moment. And Gideon saw the truth. The questions melted away, his mind gone cold. The only thing he could feel was a cold, sinking numbness.

That's not Cas.

Whoever—whatever stood before him was nothing more than a hollow shell.

My best friend is gone.

"No."

The word escaped.

Cas narrowed his eyes. "No?"

"You're still in there somewhere." Gideon swallowed hard. "You have to be."

Cas ignored the plea. "I won't say it again. Sword up. Show me what the Owls' champion can do."

Gideon met his stare and slowly, deliberately, let his arms fall to his sides. The sword's tip plunged into the damp earth, his shield dangling from his fingertips.

"I won't fight you." His voice was calm, despite the terror clawing inside him.

For the first time, Cas hesitated.

Gideon glanced down at the shield: at the dents, the warped steel where Cas's fist had struck. He exhaled slowly, forcing down the lump in his throat. "What happened to you, Cas?"

Cas scoffed. "This is your problem, Gid. All talk, no action."

All talk. No action.

Like the sound of the clock tower back in Moda, the sentence echoed over and over, chiming relentlessly in his head. He wanted to feel hurt. He wanted to deny it.

"You're right," Gideon shrugged.

Cas cocked his head, eyes squinting. "What're you playing at, Gid?"

"Nothing." Gideon hung his shoulders in resignation. "Just do what you have to. I understand."

"Pathetic."

The word struck deeper than any blow.

"I'd say it's been nice, Gid," Cas began with mock sympathy. "But after what you did, we both know that's a lie."

Gideon remained motionless, swallowing the guilt that burned in his throat.

Cas reeled his arm back and launched his fist at Gideon's face.

Fear clawed at Gideon, but he held his ground. He could feel the force of Cas's fist hurtling toward him. At the last second, he hoisted his shield with every ounce of strength. With a sickening crunch, Cas's wrist caught the edge of the shield.

Cas recoiled with a hiss of pain.

Gideon didn't hesitate. He tightened his grip on the leather strap, twisted his body in a nimble pirouette, and swung the shield around with ferocious momentum.

This time, it smashed into Cas's face.

With a strangled howl, Cas crumpled to his knees, clutching a broken wrist and a welted jaw.

Gideon blinked, momentarily stunned. "I can't believe that worked."

He glanced down at his battered shield, pride flickering for a brief second. Until Cas stirred.

"I'm sorry!" Gideon yelped as he dashed for his sword, still half-buried in the sodden earth. His mind scrambled for a plan. He needed to put distance between them, just until he could think of something.

He thrust his wings back, pushing off the ground–

A hand clamped around his ankle.

"Don't even think about it," Cas hissed through clenched teeth. Still on his knees, his fingers curled tightly around Gideon's leg, locking him in place.

"Let go of me!" Gideon thrashed, wings beating frantically. "Cas, this isn't you!" He twisted himself in every direction; no matter how hard he struggled, Gideon couldn't break free.

A deafening roar crashed over the plains, a plume of dust and shattered rock erupting from the mountains.

Terror paralyzed Gideon midair; his wings locked.

No, no, no, no!

The ground rushed up to meet him; Cas's grip didn't waver. They both hit the earth in a tangled heap.

The impact knocked the wind from Gideon's lungs. Stars burst behind his eyes as he lay gasping, trying to force air back into his chest.

There was another tug at his leg. Cas was there, stomach to the ground, dragging himself forward, hand over hand. His fingers clawed at Gideon's breeches, slithering up his pant leg, desperate to overtake him.

Scrambling, Gideon dug his elbows into the mud, his legs kicking wildly. The wet grass slickened beneath him as he writhed, trying to tear himself free, but Cas's grip held firm. "Get off!" Gideon's frustration peaked. Firming his grip on the sword hilt, he swung backward. He meant to strike Cas with the flat of the blade, but in the chaos, the sword's edge bit deep into Cas's shoulder.

Gideon's stomach turned as a fresh wave of crimson bloomed across Cas's tunic. A guttural roar tore from Cas's throat as his fingers clamped around the blade. He ripped it free, yanking it from Gideon's grip, blood streaming from the gash.

Gideon recoiled, horror-stricken.

I didn't mean...

But there was no time for apologies.

Gideon twisted, throwing himself toward the ground to scramble away. Free from Cas's reach, he staggered to his feet, wings flaring wide. With a running start, he launched himself into the air.

"I don't think so!" Cas was already up, brandishing Gideon's own sword. His eyes burned, lips curled in a vicious sneer. "I don't care what she wants. You're dead!"

With a violent thrust of his wings, Cas rocketed toward him.

Panic gripped Gideon.

There's no way I can outfly him.

Spinning midair, he turned to face Cas just as his friend bore down on him, sword raised high.

Brace yourself.

Gideon lifted his shield, gripping the straps tight. The metal was already battered, dented, barely holding shape. One more hit might shatter it.

But it was all he had.

Even with Cas barreling down on him, Gideon couldn't help but notice the shift on the plains.

The shadows seemed to recoil.

That can't be good.

A strange glow pulsed through the sky, flickering like firelight against the storm. At the base of the churning clouds, a luminous disc unfurled, expanding outward, swallowing the darkness.

He barely had a second to take it in before searing pain shot through his eyes.

Focus. Cas.

Gritting his teeth, Gideon forced his eyes open. His vision blurred, swimming with ghostly imprints of light, but he could still make out Cas's dark shape hurtling toward him.

Then, from the corner of his eye, a shadow streaked across the plains.

Kyte.

Flying low, knife in hand, Kyte shot toward Cas like an arrow. Above them, the disc crackled, building with a terrible, humming static.

A bolt of lightning tore from the sky.

"Kyte, NO!" Gideon screamed, but it was too late.

Just as Kyte crashed into Cas, a pillar of light exploded from the heavens, swallowing them whole. A deafening crack split the air. The shockwave hit like a hammer, hurling Gideon backward.

The heat lashed at him, scorching his skin, singing his hair and feathers. The leather straps of his shield snapped; it spun away, lost to the wind.

Gideon slammed into the earth, tumbling through the grass before skidding to a stop on his stomach. Pain flared through every nerve, the acrid scent of burned hair clogging his nose.

Shakily, he raised his head, struggling onto his elbows.

"Cas?" Gideon coughed, the name barely a whisper in his throat. His ears rang, the world around him muffled and distorted as he pushed himself off the ground. A smoldering crater stretched wide before him, steam curling from its depths, deep enough to swallow his father's shop. At the forest's edge, trees had been snapped like twigs, their trunks reduced to splintered ruins.

On the far side, Gideon could just make out Cas's limp form lying in the grass.

"Cas!"

He lurched forward, but his legs gave out beneath him, dropping him to his knees. Gritting his teeth, he flared his wings, propelling himself in a half-stumbling, half-drifting gait along the crater's edge. Each step was agony, his body battered and weak, but he forced himself onward.

With a final burst of strength, Gideon threw himself forward, landing beside Cas in the damp, charred grass.

"Cas." His voice trembled as he reached out, shaking Cas's shoulders. No response. "Cas, wake up!"

Cas's chest barely stirred with breath, faint and uneven.

"You're going to be okay. You have to be. I came all this way to find you. I can't lose you like this."

Gideon's hands trembled as he pulled back, fingers slick with something warm and sticky. Blood. The wound he'd dealt was still bleeding. Without thinking, Gideon ripped off his tunic, the wet fabric peeling from his skin.

"Don't worry." He tied the cloth tightly around Cas's arm, hands fumbling but firm. "I'll get help."

Forcing himself upright, Gideon swayed, barely keeping his balance as the dizziness threatened to pull him back down.

"Socorra! Kyte!"

As Kyte's name left his lips, a flash of memory struck him—the lightning, Kyte diving toward Cas, the blinding eruption that followed.

His breath quickened.

Gideon's frantic gaze swept the battlefield, but there was no sign of him.

"Oh no."

The Hawk's lifeless form sat amid the charred rock and scorched earth. His wings smoldered, embers flickering as the rain pelted his feathers.

Gideon staggered forward.

He reached the edge of the crater when a violent gust roared across the plain, slamming into him like a wall of force. The wind whistled and howled, clawing at his wings, dragging at his body.

Shielding his face with his arms, Gideon fought to stay upright, bracing against the unnatural gale. He squinted into the storm, searching for the source of the onslaught.

The clouds churned, spiraling inward, parting in a slow and ominous unraveling. Beyond the storm, the sky was clear.

Before long, the familiar purple haze bled into his vision.

Then he saw them, wings of marbled black and blue.

Gideon's pulse thundered in his ears. "The Master."

Her movements were hypnotic, from her wind-whipped hair to her blood-red dress that billowed regally as she descended from the clouds.

Gideon scanned the plains for his sword, hoping the lightning hadn't flung it too far. Fortunately, it was still in Cas's hands. Teetering to where his friend lay, Gideon bent over to snatch his weapon when Cas's hand clamped around his wrist.

A cold jolt shot through him.

Cas's eyes barely opened. "Gid?" The word was fragile, as if it might break apart in the wind.

Gideon dropped to his knees. "I'm here, Cas." His voice trembled as he laced his fingers around his friend's arm. "I've got you." He cradled Cas's head, holding him like a fledgling.

Cas's head lilted back, his breath shuddering. "Gid, I'm sorry."

"It's ok, Cas," Gideon's voice broke. He waited for his friend to say something else, but no words came.

"Cas? Cas!?" Gideon shook him, but there was no answer. "C'mon, Cas. Don't do this to me now. I know you're in there. I can still get you back."

Hot tears blurred his vision, cascading down his cheeks. Gingerly, he removed his hand from the back of Cas's neck, letting his head come back to rest on the ground.

Untangling their fingers, Gideon gripped the hilt of his sword in both hands and rose from the ground, every muscle tightening.

"Don't worry, Cas. This'll be over soon."

He turned to face the Master.

With every slow, deliberate beat of her wings, the storm clouds peeled away, rain fading into a mist that fled to the edges of the plain.

Gideon's legs threatened to buckle beneath him, but he held his ground. "I won't let you hurt anyone else!"

The purple haze crept in, unfurling from the trees, swallowing the tundra in rolling fog. It pressed toward him, suffocating, consuming.

Gideon closed his eyes. Lifting the sword above his head, he struck out blindly.

Steel sliced empty air.

"Don't be afraid, Gideon."

Her voice, soft as satin, curled around his ear.

Without hesitation, Gideon twisted and swung. Again, nothing.

"You have no reason to fear me."

The words gave him pause. There was a comfort there, a memory that was just out of reach.

"You're safe now."

She stood in front of him now, not a whisper, but corporeal. He brought the sword above his head, but he hesitated. An irresistible urge gnawed at him.

Who is she?

He opened his eyes; his grip on the sword faltered, his fingers numb around the hilt.

She stood there, smiling.

"Mother?"

"Yes, my love." Her voice was as sweet as he remembered.

Gideon's throat tightened. "But…" He shook his head, struggling to form the words. "But how?"

She tilted her head, smiling. "Does it matter?" She swept a hand behind her back, hiding her talons. "What's important is that I have my boy back."

Gideon stared, his mind a churning storm. His mother stood before him, real. Alive. Whole.

For years, he had dreamed of this moment, pleaded for it. He had imagined her return a thousand different ways. Bursting through the door, a weary traveler come home, sweeping him into her arms and spinning grand tales of peril and adventure. They would go to Wydah's bakery, just like they used to, and he would sit across from her, eating his slice of tart, hanging onto her every word.

Gideon's hands trembled. He should have been elated. He wanted to drop his sword, run to her, hold her, never let go.

But he couldn't.

"What am I supposed to do here?" His voice was barely a whisper.

Her brow creased. "What do you—"

"I wasn't talking to you."

Her sneer was quick, a flash of irritation beneath her composed mask. A vein pulsed at her temple.

"I'm sorry," Gideon said, voice raw. "But this is a lot to process."

"My boy." A gentle coo, but there was a sharp edge beneath it. "I'm sure you have a thousand questions. Why don't we—"

But Gideon wasn't listening. His thoughts raced, tangled and frantic. This should have been everything he ever wanted. Instead, his chest ached.

The words tore from him before he could stop them.

"How could you?"

Cecilia pursed her lips, aggravation in her stare. "You'll have to be more specific."

"How much more specific do you need me to be?" Gideon snapped, his frustration boiling over. "I thought you disappeared. I assumed something terrible had happened. I thought you were dead." His voice caught, raw with emotion. "But here you are…this…I don't even know what you are now."

Cecilia's expression remained infuriatingly serene. "I'm your mother," she said, chiding, as if scolding a petulant fledgling. "And everything I've done has been for you."

"For me?" Gideon let out a bitter laugh. "How has any of this been for me? You left me to be raised by a man who doesn't have an emotional feather on his wings. Then you stole my best friend…the only person who could make me laugh after you disappeared." His eyes flicked to Cas. He was still unconscious, his chest barely rising. "You almost killed him." His throat tightened, but he pushed forward. "He was the only person who understood me when you left. The only thing keeping me alive these past years." His voice cracked. "He was the nicest, most genuine person I've ever known. And you turned him into a monster." The word tasted like poison.

Cecilia parted her lips to speak, but Gideon didn't let her.

"And I'm not the only person you've hurt." His mind flashed to Kyte, his body crumpled in the scorched earth, his feathers still smoldering. Socorra had just gotten him back, and now the agony she would have to endure if he–

No.

He refused to finish the thought.

"How many people have suffered? How many are dead? How many tortured?" His voice was hoarse with fury. "And you want to claim that this trail of despair was all for me?"

His hands curled into fists.

"My own mother…the Master." He spat the words like they burned his tongue.

"You have no idea what you're talking about, boy."

"For once, mother, I do." His voice was resolute.

Raising his sword, Gideon took a hesitant swing. Cecilia pulled back, her wings unfurling with a gust that sent ripples through the grass.

She cackled. "And what do you think you're doing? You don't really think you have the gall to hurt me?"

"You don't know anything about me anymore." His grip tightened, his confidence hardening. He swung again. "You don't just get to show up here and pretend like everything is fine."

Cecilia continued to drift back, the grimace on her face deepening with each strike.

"You're a monster."

With a burst of fury, Gideon flared his wings and lunged, blade arcing toward her–

"Enough!" Cecilia's talons shot out, catching the sword mid-swing.

Gideon gasped as the tension vibrated through the steel. With an effortless squeeze, the blade cracked. Shards of metal splintered apart, glinting as they rained to the ground.

His breath hitched. "That's not–" He stared at the ruined hilt in his hands. "That's not how this was supposed to happen."

Cecilia sighed, shaking her head. "What did you think, Gideon? That you'd have your happy ending? That you could play hero and save your little friends?"

A smirk curled her lips. "This isn't a story book."

A hollow ache spread through Gideon's chest.

"I didn't want to do this," she tsked. "But you've left me no choice."

Her eyes gleamed.

Agony tore through Gideon's skull. He staggered, clutching his head as fire seared through his mind, scorching his thoughts, drowning his will. He tried to resist, to push back against the smothering weight pressing down on him, but the fight was fleeting, slipping through his fingers like sand.

Don't let her…

But the haze coiled tighter and tighter.

From his periphery, Gideon watched as Cas stood, moving, alive.

Relief hit him like a blow, knocking the air from his lungs.

Everything faded; the haze took hold.

Cecilia's voice was warm again, gentle, welcoming. "Now, my dear…are you ready to join me?"

Something in him still struggled, a whisper, a distant pull, urging him to fight. But it was too far, too weak.

"Yes, mother."

Chapter Twenty-Six
Pelanor

"Do you have any idea how irresponsible this is!?" Pelanor's voice cracked through the chamber, his words echoing off the stone walls. "Valanor would never have entertained such a–"

"That's enough!" Forranor snapped, his voice edged with disdain. "Pelanor, I'm sure I needn't remind you that Valanor is dead." The wiry Owl shot up from his leather-clad chair, the wooden legs screeching against the tiled floor. "As the new leader of the Parliament, it falls to me to decide how best to protect the Innocence."

A murmur rippled through the semi-circular table as the other members exchanged glances and whispered to their neighbors.

Pelanor clenched his jaw, drawing in a slow breath to steady himself. He had never been well-liked among the Parliament, but with Valanor gone, it was glaringly clear he had no supporters left. If he wanted to sway them, he couldn't afford to let frustration cloud his judgment. Diplomacy was all he had left.

"Forranor, I meant no disrespect." He lowered his gaze, selling the lie with practiced ease. "But I have serious concerns about how this Parliament is handling the situation."

Forranor arched a thin eyebrow, brushing strands of oily, slate-colored hair from his face. "And those would be?"

Another wave of indistinct whispers passed through the council.

Pelanor bit his tongue, forcing himself to weigh his words carefully. He wanted to demand answers, to rail against their cowardice. How could they abandon the search for the champion? How could they justify igniting a war between the Hawks and the Crows? More than anything, he wanted to shout, to shake them from their complacency.

But that wouldn't get him anywhere.

"Forranor," Pelanor began, keeping his tone level. "I understand that the Innocence is your primary objective. The Noktern has long worked to maintain harmony in Avis, to ensure our world never suffers the fate of the Sapiens. But to stoke the fires of war between the Hawks and the Crows?" He masked his rage, but a short growl slipped through. "How can this body justify such a provocation, especially under false pretenses?"

Forranor leaned back, a smirk curling at his lips. "Oh, Pelanor, I'm disappointed in your lack of vision." He sighed, shaking his head. "The Innocence is the foundation of our order. We keep the peace, yes, but more importantly, we keep the people of Avis safe from themselves. The reality is, Pelanor, our continent suffers from many plagues—not just the darkness."

"Enlighten me." Pelanor's jaw tightened, teeth grinding.

"Overpopulation. Industrialization." Each syllable was punctuated like a swear. "The very diseases that led to the fall of the human empire."

Pelanor stiffened. *Human.* He had never heard the word uttered so freely in the Owlands, so casually. The power of his station had clearly gone to Forranor's head—to feel bold enough to speak it here, in the Parliament, without so much as a whisper of protest. But the others didn't even flinch.

Forranor pressed on. "Our world may have healed from the Great End, but our resources remain finite. We cannot sustain unchecked population growth across all the tribes."

His voice rose, his anger bubbling over. "And then there are the Finches. Greedy capitalists who poison our skies with their factories! The Noktern should have intervened long ago, but Valanor insisted the scale was not enough to warrant interference." He slammed his fists against the wooden arms of his chair. "I say enough!"

Pelanor shook his head. "Do you even hear yourself?" He fought to keep his tone measured. "Overpopulation is hardly an immediate concern. Our cities are still young, more than capable of sustaining themselves without destroying their environments. And as for the Finches–" He met Forranor's gaze, letting the word settle. "Their production benefits Avis as a whole. Their technology isn't even close to what the *Sapiens* had." He stressed the word. "Even if it were, how exactly would a war between the Hawks and Crows slow their progress?"

"That's the beauty of it." Forranor's grin stretched, wicked and knowing. "The Finches can never resist meddling where there's coin to be made. With a little persuasion, the traders of Moda and Duport will funnel their efforts into weapons, selling to both the Hawks and the Crows. A few well-placed whispers, a nudge in the right direction, and before long, the Finches will find themselves enemies of both."

Pelanor's stomach twisted.

This is madness.

The conversation had spiraled far beyond reason, slipping through his grasp like sand in a storm. Forranor was beyond logic, and none of the other Parliament members looked inclined to challenge him. He needed another angle.

"And what of the darkness…these Ravens?" Pelanor pressed. "How do you plan to face that while sending thousands of innocent Avians to slaughter one another?"

Silence gripped the room, thick and electric. Across the semi-circle, the council members stiffened, their wings rigid, eyes sharp, awaiting Forranor's response.

The Owl sneered, lowering himself deliberately into his high-backed chair. The brass claws of its legs screeched against the tiled floor. "Well, Pelanor, I must say I'm confused." His tone dripped with mock sympathy. "Surely, with the fabled champion at your side, our victory is all but assured? Or…" He leaned forward, smirking. "Are you beginning to doubt the ravings of an ancient lunatic?"

A ripple of nervous laughter skittered around the table.

"It isn't that simple." Pelanor forced his voice to steady, swallowing his frustration.

Forranor scoffed. "Oh, come now." His arrogance rang through the chamber. "Before we convened, Hermanor was all too eager to tell us about your little pet project. Gabriel, was it? A fledgling. A lost soul plucked from that filthy Finch city." He shook his head, feigning pity. "You've done him no favors, and he'll do none for us. You filled his head with nonsense, dreams of grandeur, all because he happened to know the answer to some ridiculous riddle in a book from a thousand years ago?"

Pelanor watched in silent frustration as most of the council nodded in agreement. Only a handful showed any sign of unease. He had long known that Forranor was a skeptic of the prophecy and the power of the First Owl, but he hadn't expected so many others to align with him. Then again, perhaps he should have.

Before becoming a Noktern scholar, Pelanor himself had doubted the First Owl's supposed foresight. Ten years ago, he would have scoffed at the idea that ancient Sapiens possessed technology capable of granting clairvoyance.

But then his own visions began.

At first, they were just dreams—banal, everyday moments that felt like déjà vu when they played out in real life. Then they became more specific. Conversations unfolded word for word, lectures repeated themselves exactly as he had dreamed them. Eventually, the visions came when he was awake. It wasn't perfect, but sometimes, just at the edge of his perception, he saw things before they happened, as if the world just beyond his sight was moments ahead of reality.

He had only ever told Valanor. The former head Owl had been like a father to him, and as the premonitions grew more frequent, he had needed someone to confide in. Valanor had tried to help him harness the ability, but Pelanor never mastered it. His foresight came and went, often striking when he least expected it.

Pelanor exhaled slowly. "You're wrong about him."

Forranor's expression darkened. "Excuse me?"

"You don't know Gideon." Awe crept into Pelanor's voice. "He may not seem like much, but there's more to him than meets the eye."

Forranor scoffed. "Is that so?"

"Yes, that's so." Pelanor's certainty made Forranor recoil slightly. "Gideon may not be the warrior we expected, but he's incredibly bright and intuitive. He deciphered parts of the prophecy that took our scholars decades to piece together." He couldn't contain a smile. "But what truly makes Gideon the champion is his imagination."

Forranor let out a sharp laugh and threw up a hand. "Tut, tut. Need I remind you that imagination is precisely what led to the downfall of the humans? They lusted for power, sought ever more efficient ways to destroy one another. It was their innovation and invention that collapsed their entire society! And now you believe that qualifies your so-called champion?"

"I do."

Forranor blinked at the conviction in Pelanor's voice.

"Gideon is nothing like them. His imagination doesn't stem from ambition or greed. It comes from innocence. From curiosity." Pelanor's gaze swept over the Parliament. "He spent his life immersed in stories, feeding his mind with ideas and creativity. He sees solutions where others see only problems."

Forranor leaned forward, his beady eyes glinting. "And what good will any of that do against the darkness?"

Before Pelanor could answer, Forranor sneered. "If Ordranor's report on the Crow girl is anything to go by…"

"Sapien girl," Pelanor corrected under his breath.

"…holds any merit, then this organization has potentially recreated the hybridization process."

Forranor leaned forward, planting his hands on the table, his sharp gaze drilling into Pelanor. "If they can do that, what else do you suppose they're capable of? Do you truly believe your half-pint champion can stand against them?"

Pelanor lowered his eyes to the floor, letting the weight of the moment settle over him. He knew that standing by Gideon meant alienating the Parliament, a body he had long aspired to join. Valanor had been grooming him for leadership. One day, he had imagined himself as head Owl, guiding the Noktern with wisdom and foresight.

Was he truly willing to throw all of that away?

"You're right," Pelanor murmured.

Gasps rippled through the chamber as stunned faces turned toward him.

Forranor's eyes narrowed. "Go on."

Pelanor exhaled slowly, then met Forranor's gaze. "Ordranor's revelation does raise serious concerns, the likes of which the Noktern never anticipated. The truth is, the champion we envisioned may very well be powerless against this new threat. We don't fully understand what we're dealing with."

Forranor's smug grin spread wider. With a slow clap, he basked in his apparent victory. "At last! I'm glad you're finally coming to your senses, Pelanor. Perhaps there's hope for you yet." He rocked back in his chair before rising to his feet, waving a hand to signal the others to stand. "Now, I think we should all retire for the evening before–"

"But Gideon isn't the champion we envisioned."

Pelanor's words clung in the air, a strangled silence settling over the chamber. Forranor froze mid-step, all eyes locked on Pelanor.

"Pelanor," Forranor snarled, his patience fraying. "I have tolerated your insolence long enough." He leaned forward, his knuckles pressing into the table, arms rigid, back curved like a predator poised to strike.

But whatever he said next was lost.

The words reached Pelanor's ears as little more than a muffled hum, drowned beneath the sudden pressure building in his skull. A familiar tickle crept into his throat. His vision blurred at the edges, pulling back, unfocusing.

Something shifted at the edge of his perception.

He turned just in time to see the doors of the chamber burst open.

A rush of armed guards flooded inside, their faces tight with worry. A voice, muffled but urgent, called his name over the growing din.

"Pelanor…"

He barely turned his head toward the sound. His attention locked on Captain Aldanor, the weight of her words pressing down on him before she even spoke. He clung to every syllable, his pulse quickening. And then–

"Gideon…"

The name barely left his lips, nothing more than a breath of air. His fingers curled against the table as a shiver ran down his spine.

This wasn't right.

The battle had played out in his mind a hundred times, every possible outcome considered, every scenario accounted for. But never had he foreseen Gideon leaving with the enemy.

"Pelanor!"

Forranor's knobby fists slammed against the lacquered oak, his voice like a whip.

Pelanor gasped, snapping back to the present, the vision shattered.

Forranor's glare burned into him, his nostrils flaring. "Who in the name of Mim are you talking to?"

Pelanor forced himself to steady his breathing as he scanned the faces around the chamber. Two dozen eyes bore into him, some laced with concern, others cold with suspicion, and a few twisted in outright disgust.

"I…" He faltered, rubbing his eyes as the world came back into focus. With a slight shake of his head, he pulled himself together. "No one. My apologies. I'm not sure what came over me."

Forranor's gaze lingered, piercing and distrustful. He studied Pelanor for a long moment before he finally spoke.

"As I was saying, if you ever intend to sit on this council, you would do well to keep your criticisms to yourself."

"Understood." Pelanor's reply was sharp, clipped. A ripple of shock passed through the Parliament.

Forranor's brow arched in suspicion. "What was that?" He had expected resistance, a fight, something more than this cold compliance.

"You're right." Pelanor dipped his head curtly. It wasn't what he wanted to say, but there was no point in pressing further. Not now. Not when every second wasted here was another second Gideon slipped further from his grasp.

Forranor blinked, thrown off by the unexpected surrender. "Well…good!" he blustered, his usual arrogance laced with awkward uncertainty. Silence hung in the air, thick and stifling, until Pelanor finally spoke again.

"If it pleases the Parliament, I ask permission to dismiss myself."

It stung to concede, but the battle was already lost. Without Gideon, there was no chance of shifting the Parliament's course.

Maybe I'm not meant to.

Forranor waved him off with an impatient flick of his hand. "Yes, yes, of course."

Pelanor didn't wait to be told twice. He turned abruptly, striding toward the door, but kept his pace slow as he crossed the threshold, his ears trained on the conversation behind him.

"Assuming there are no further objections, we will proceed as planned. Airutanor, prepare an envoy to head to Zarpa."

Pelanor barely breathed.

"Ensure the Hawks still intend to engage the Crows. If they seem hesitant, be sure to–"

Forranor stopped abruptly, the silence thickening.

"Can I help you, Pelanor?" Forranor's voice cut through the quiet, cool and dripping with condescension.

Thinking quickly, Pelanor thrust a hand into his sleeve, fumbling deliberately. "Aha!" His fingers brushed against a sleek piece of metal, and he pulled it free with practiced ease. "Found it." He turned to face the Parliament, brandishing the keycard as if it had any real significance. "My apologies, I thought I'd lost my key."

The silence in the room was suffocating. Dozens of unreadable eyes bore into him, unblinking. He wasn't fooling anyone.

Forranor's thin lips twisted into something sinister. "Have a pleasant evening, Pelanor." His voice curled around the words, each syllable deliberate, weighted. "I'm glad you've finally come to see things my way."

Pelanor dipped his head in an awkward genuflect, refusing to break eye contact. Forranor's gaze was razor-sharp, cutting through any pretense. It sent a shiver down Pelanor's spine, but he stood firm, unwilling to let the Parliament see a crack in his resolve.

He scanned the tables one last time—not a single sympathetic face, not one ally.

He swallowed the bitterness rising in his throat, scraping his tongue over his teeth as he weighed his next move. Then, without another word, he bowed his head and strode toward the door, his steps echoing through the chamber.

As he walked the chilly corridors, a gnawing thought took root in his mind.

Gideon wouldn't have gone willingly.

But it couldn't have been Zokya who took him. The captain's description in the vision didn't match the Crow who had attacked them in the Kestrel Desert.

It must have been the Master.

Pelanor's jaw clenched.

"But Gideon resisted before." He murmured the thought aloud, remembering how Gideon had used his shield to avoid hypnosis in the desert. "He's too canny to have just been swept away."

Shaking his head, Pelanor shoved the speculation aside. Worry wouldn't bring Gideon back. His first priority was clear: put as much distance as possible between himself and Forranor.

Chapter Twenty-Seven
Pelanor

A low rumble shuddered through the stone walls, the floor quaking beneath Pelanor's feet. Dust trembled in the air. Then, just as suddenly as it began, the fluorescent bulbs flickered back to full brightness, the final tremors fading into silence.

What was that?

Pelanor shook his head, pushing the thought aside. He turned off the small desk lamp and stepped into the doorway, his hand resting firmly on the handle. One last look at the tiny hovel he had called home for so long, uncertain if he would ever return.

"Good evening, Pelanor."

Pelanor tensed, spinning toward the voice.

"Ordranor," he exhaled, still catching his breath. "You startled me."

The ancient Owl chuckled softly. "I seem to be making a habit of that today." His tone was light, but his eyes gleamed with something unreadable. He tapped the butt of his cane against Pelanor's satchel. "Going somewhere?"

Pelanor hesitated, measuring the older Owl's expression. "I…no, just returning some books to the main hall," he lied smoothly. "Tecanor's going to give me an earful for keeping them for so long."

Ordranor didn't respond immediately. His glassy eyes lingered on Pelanor, unblinking, assessing. Pelanor shifted under the scrutiny, enough to wake Ordranor from whatever trance he was in.

Finally, the old Owl's lips curled into a small, knowing smile. "You're probably right," he mused. "Tecanor does tend to take his librarian duties very seriously." He paused, then gave a slight bow. "Go on, then. I won't keep you."

Without another word, he turned and shuffled down the corridor toward the med wing, the sharp clack of his cane reverberating against the concrete walls.

Pelanor watched Ordranor disappear beyond the swinging doors, his presence lingering like a shadow.

"Strange."

Shaking off the interaction, Pelanor turned and strode in the opposite direction. Within moments, he reached the landing overlooking the main hall. From down the narrow passage leading to the front gate, the rich, familiar scent of freshly brewed coffee wafted toward him. He inhaled deeply. It had been too long since his last cup—the Noktern imports from Aligaida were a luxury not found in most of Avis. He would give almost anything to sit down and savor one, but he had no time to spare.

Stepping through the metallic doorway, Pelanor squared his shoulders and addressed the lone security staff.

"Hermanor," he said flatly, the name tasting bitter on his tongue.

The tiny Owl dragged out his name with an unsettling drawl. "Why, Pelanor…I thought I might see you again this evening. To what do I owe the pleasure?"

"If you expected me, then you know why I'm here."

Hermanor gave a theatrical sigh. "Far be it from me to strike up conversation," he mused, an extra layer of smugness coating his words. "But I gather you're looking to head to the surface?"

"Indeed."

The older Owl's beady eyes slid over Pelanor, his grin widening. Pelanor couldn't tell what he was playing at, but he didn't trust it.

"Of course," Hermanor gave an approving flourish of his hand.

Pelanor let out a quiet breath of relief and took a step toward the security door–

"But before you go," Hermanor added, his tone laced with false regret, "I'm going to need to see your travel visa."

Pelanor stopped short. "My what?"

"Your travel visa." Hermanor's stare was unwavering, his satisfaction barely concealed. "Forranor has instituted a travel ban. No one leaves the Noktern without written permission, strictly for Noktern business."

"I know what a travel visa is," Pelanor snapped, heat flaring behind his eyes. "But what authority does Forranor have to–" He cut himself off with a sharp slap to his forehead. "Never mind. Just tell me how to get one."

Hermanor gave an exaggerated shrug. "Unfortunately, you can only get one from Forranor directly." His smirk widened. "I gather that'll be difficult for you, considering your little outburst in Parliament."

Pelanor's jaw tightened. Hermanor had always excelled at gathering gossip, particularly anything scandalous, but for news to have spread this fast…

Before he could respond, a motion-sensor beeped, and one of the security monitors flickered to life. A grainy figure moved outside the Noktern's entrance. A burst of static crackled through the speakers. Then came a voice, barely audible over frantic banging against metal.

"Help!"

Hermanor's smirk faltered. He swiveled in his chair, rolling to the control panel. With a few keystrokes, the exterior camera feed sharpened.

Pelanor sucked in a breath. "Socorra." His wings stiffened.

"Please, we need help!" Her voice rang clear through the security room.

Hermanor pressed a button, lips brushing against the microphone. "Name?"

Pelanor snapped. "For Mim's sake! She's with me. Open the door!"

The older Owl tsked, his smugness returning. "We have rules down here, in case you've forgotten. I need to know why she's here."

"She's the sword! What other reason does she need?"

Hermanor arched his brow. "The sword? As in, the one from the prophecy? That sword?"

Pelanor's patience shattered. "Yes, that sword! Now open the damn door!"

Hermanor eyed him for a long moment, then sighed dramatically. "Oh, alright." He leaned into the intercom. "Stand back. I'm lowering the gangway."

Before he could press the release, Socorra's voice crackled in again, desperate. "Please! Kyte's injured. He needs help! I can't get him here on my own!"

Pelanor's heart slammed against his ribs.

He's alive?

Taking his finger off the mic, Hermanor lifted a skeptical brow. "Kyte? The debonair Hawk?"

Pelanor heaved an exasperated sigh. "Sure. Now open the door, I'm going up there to help."

Hermanor smirked. "I'm sorry, but have you magically obtained a travel visa in the last two minutes?"

Pelanor's patience snapped. "You're seriously going to make me get a visa to help a fallen warrior? The shield, I might add! And before you have to ask…yes, the one from the prophecy."

Hermanor leaned back in his chair, unimpressed. "He could be the Bengalan Queen for all I care. No visa, no surface access."

"Hello?" Socorra's voice crackled through the intercom, followed by another desperate bang on the gangway.

With a grumble, Hermanor slammed his palm onto the console. "I'll send a med party. Stay put! Help is on the way." He flicked a series of switches and pressed the intercom again. "Med team to surface. I repeat, med team to surface, stat."

Swiveling back to Pelanor, he sneered. "There. Happy? Medical will handle it. Meanwhile, why don't you head to the med wing and wait for your little friends?"

It wasn't a suggestion.

Before Pelanor could fire back, a feeble voice spoke behind him.

"Good evening."

A shudder ran down his spine. He didn't need to turn around to know who it was.

Ordranor.

The ancient Owl stood at his back, bushy brows drawn in a look of exaggerated worry. "Terribly sorry to interrupt." He tapped his vined cane against the floor. "Forranor sent me to fetch you. He wants you in the med wing. Immediately."

Pelanor's chest loosened with a silent sigh of relief.

Hermanor's eyes narrowed, his lips pursed. "If Forranor wants to see me, why send you?"

Ordranor shrugged. "Oh, I just happened to be near the med wing when you called for a team to the surface. Next thing I knew, Forranor came barreling in, screaming bloody murder that no one was to go anywhere. Something about new surface visa requirements and incompetent security personnel."

"What!?" Hermanor squawked, throwing his hands up. "That's ridiculous! He never told me anything about that."

"I won't pretend to know," Ordranor responded coolly. "But he seemed furious. Said the scholar on security needed to report to the med wing immediately to…how did he put it? 'Get this potential breach under control.' Or something like that."

Hermanor's hands trembled. His eyes darted to the control panel, then back to Ordranor. Pelanor fought to keep his expression neutral, but inwardly, he relished watching the pint-sized Owl squirm.

Ordranor let the silence stretch before tilting his head. "But if you'd like, I can tell Forranor you're too busy to–"

"I'll be right back!" Hermanor snapped, practically leaping from his chair. He wagged a finger at Pelanor. "Don't touch anything."

Shoving past them, he stormed out the door, muttering under his breath as his footsteps faded down the hall.

Pelanor stayed still, hoping that Ordranor would leave too. But the old Owl didn't move. A quiet unease settled over him. He had no real reason not to trust Ordranor, but something about the ancient scholar set his feathers on edge. Still, with Hermanor gone, this might be his only shot at escaping the Noktern.

Keeping his expression aloof, he stretched his arms, subtly shifting his stance to get a better view of the control panel. If he could just figure out how to open the front gate.

"Big blue button to the left and the middle lever."

Pelanor cocked his head, but Ordranor's face was unreadable. "What?" The word came out more aggressive than he'd intended.

With a patient smirk, Ordranor repeated, "That big blue button will open the gate." He pointed with a wrinkled finger. "And the center lever above the panel will lower the gangway."

Pelanor hesitated, torn between thanking the old man and demanding answers. "How do you know?"

Ordranor shrugged. "When you've been here as long as I have, you learn a thing or two."

Pelanor tried to make sense of it, but a sudden rush of dizziness hit him. His vision blurred, a familiar fuzziness creeping into his eyes. The pounding of rushing footsteps filled his mind, the foggy apparitions of the med team appearing in the doorway, a stretcher carried between them as they hustled past without so much as a glance.

Not far behind, furious wingbeats tore through the vision, followed by a shrill voice.

"Ordranor, you have some explaining to do!" The outline of Hermanor appeared at the corner, his head snapping into view "Who!? Who opened the gate?" His face twisted in a grimace before he reeled back and screamed–

"Pelanor!"

"Oh my," Ordranor marveled, pulling Pelanor out of the vision. "That was…an experience."

Pelanor blinked hard, his head still reeling. "What are you talking about?"

"I've known for a long time that you had the gift, just like Primanor before you, but it's really something else to experience it." Ordranor shook his head in awe. "It's humbling, really."

Pelanor barely had the words. "You mean…?"

"Yes," the old Owl affirmed, eyes twinkling. "I can read minds. Or, well, hear thoughts is probably more accurate." His grin turned cheeky.

Pelanor stared. "Why haven't you told anyone?"

"I could ask you the same question." Ordranor stepped past him toward the control panel. "But we don't have time for that. My guess? You've got about five minutes before Hermanor realizes I lied and comes barreling back."

Pelanor watched as the ancient Owl worked the controls. With a few swift motions, a hiss of air rushed through the chamber.

The gate was open.

"At least tell me why you're helping me." Pelanor's eyes narrowed. "Hermanor might be a pain, but he is the head of security. Lying to him is a serious offense. If you get caught, it won't end well."

Ordranor met his gaze with a hard stare. "Because there are still those of us at the Noktern who believe in the champion and the prophecy. You are not alone."

A rush of hope fluttered through Pelanor, his sense of purpose reaffirmed.

"And that young man you found has a remarkable mind. I would know." Ordranor winked. "If anyone can save Avis, it's him. As for getting caught–" he waved a dismissive hand– "Forranor and his band of misfits have written me off as a senile old man. Don't worry about me. I've gotten out of worse."

From somewhere deep in the Noktern, the muffled stirrings of a commotion reached the security room.

Ordranor sighed. "That'll be the med team. Looks like we're out of time." With a haggard *thud*, Ordranor lowered himself into the swivel chair. "Be off with you, or you'll miss your chance."

Cinching his satchel over his shoulder, Pelanor strode through the door. At the threshold, he glanced back one last time. "Thank you."

Ordranor simply dipped his head.

Turning forward, Pelanor pressed into the narrow corridor, his focus locked on what lay ahead.

The cavernous vestibule of the stronghold loomed before him, its towering walls slick with condensation. As he stepped forward, icy daggers shot up his leg and into his spine. His foot had plunged into an ankle-deep pool of water. He groaned, the sound echoing through the chamber as he yanked his foot back in a precarious dance. His cloth shoes were soaked through.

That storm…

Captain Aldanor had mentioned torrential rain, but the vestibule had never flooded before, not even after the massive winter snowfalls. Something had compromised the gangway. Maybe the same thing that caused those tremors.

By the time he reached the staircase, he could barely feel his feet, pins and needles shooting up to his hips. Gritting his teeth, he gripped the metal handrails and dragged himself upward, his breath coming in short bursts.

As the pain ebbed and his steps evened, his thoughts shifted to the surface. What kind of condition would Kyte be in? He had assumed the Hawk would die in the battle.

He still might…And Socorra…Oh Mim, what am I going to say to her?

He wouldn't have much time. If the med team reached them before he left, they'd surely try to intervene in his escape. He had to keep it short. But there was so much she needed to know.

Reaching the final steps, Pelanor squinted as the last slivers of twilight pierced through the entrance of the Noktern. His eyes adjusted to the darkening landscape, and he caught sight of a lone Avian standing on the plain.

A Raven.

The figure was petite. It must've been Zokya, but she was smaller than he remembered. But it had to be her. A fire ignited in his stomach. Without thinking, Pelanor broke into a run, wings unfurling as he shot down the gangway. The wind caught in his feathers as he lifted off the ground, scanning the area below. His breath caught.

An immense crater scarred the earth at the edge of the woods.

His chest tightened, but he didn't stop. He pressed harder, instincts screaming that those black wings could only mean danger—for Kyte, for Socorra.

"Pelanor!"

The voice rang out, high and excited. The Raven jumped, waving their arms almost gleefully.

Pelanor squinted, trying to make out their features against the dark forest beyond.

Fatima…?

He recalled Hermanor's mention of her transformation, but seeing it with his own eyes was another thing entirely. The spunky, young Sapien, now with a mammoth set of wings.

Landing a few yards away, he approached her cautiously, his mind still struggling to process what he saw. "You look…different."

Fatima smirked, flicking her head toward the Noktern. "They gave me a haircut down there. Thanks for noticing."

Pelanor couldn't help but let out a hardy chuckle, but the pained smile on Fatima's face did little to ease the churn in his stomach. Without speaking, the two of them turned their gaze down into the smoldering crater. At the center, Kyte's lifeless form lay face down in the mud, while Socorra knelt over him like a sentry, guarding him.

Sliding knee-deep into the muck, Pelanor strode across the sodden earth, his heart heavy with each step. He knelt beside Kyte, his eyes scanning the Hawk's battered body. The stench of charred feathers assaulted his senses. One wing was in worse shape than the other, the lacerations exposing sinewy connective tissue where the limb met his body. His back was a mess. burnt, singed skin stretched over his shoulders, lightning-shaped wounds carving jagged lines in every direction. Yet, despite the dirt, blood, and scorched flesh, Kyte was still breathing, each exhale a haggard rasp.

If he lives, he'll lose that wing.

The thought sunk like lead in his chest.

Lifting his eyes, Pelanor met Socorra's gaze. Her eyes were alight with a mixture of sadness and rage, her cheeks streaked with tears.

"The med team will be here soon." Pelanor's voice was flat, carrying an air of certainty he didn't quite feel. "The Noktern has the best medical practice in Avis, maybe the whole world. If anyone can save him, they can." He tried to be reassuring, though he wasn't sure he believed the words himself.

"What about Gideon?" he asked, quickly moving on. "Did you see what happened to him?"

Socorra blinked at him, taken aback by the question. "No," she answered hoarsely, wiping her eyes. Clearing her throat, she went on. "I was trying to make it out of the woods when I saw this explosion of light through the trees." She shook her head, as if the memory hurt. "I ran as fast as I could, but when I got here, Gideon was already flying off with her."

"How did he seem?"

"I…I don't know," Socorra said, her voice trembling. "I called out to him, but I don't think he heard me."

Pelanor dipped his head, trying to make sense of the chaos. "And the Ravens?"

"Craven's dead." A dark snarl crossed Socorra's face. "I killed him myself."

Finally, some good news.

Pelanor allowed himself a small breath of relief.

"And Cas flew off with Gideon and the Master. As for Rocque, I have no idea, but I haven't seen him, so—"

"He's dead," Fatima called down to them, her voice heavy. "While I was climbing through the trees, I saw Kyte lead him straight to the mountain. Kyte dove right for the stone, but pulled up at the last second. I don't think the giant could stop. He crashed headfirst."

"That must've caused the earthquake I felt earlier." Pelanor shook his head.

Rocque's death could work against my plans to get Gideon back.

Socorra opened her mouth to respond, but Fatima cut her off. "Socorra, it's the med team!"

"Shit." Pelanor's voice cracked with panic as he jerked his head toward the distant sounds of rushing footsteps. Socorra looked confused, hurt even, but Pelanor couldn't explain everything to her now. "Sorry," he muttered, his voice tight with urgency.

"Listen to me, Socorra. I don't have much time. Whatever happens, stay here and serve the Noktern. Follow whatever Parliament says, but no matter what…" He took a step closer, his gaze fierce. "Do not trust Forranor. Just keep Fatima and Kyte safe." The words felt like a weight sinking deep in his chest. "I'm leaving. And I'm not coming back." The reality of it stung. "I'm going to help Gideon."

Without waiting for her response, Pelanor threw himself into the air, wings beating powerfully as he rose from the crater. Hanging high over the forest, Pelanor glanced back at the Noktern's entrance. With a curt nod, he said a silent goodbye to the only home he had ever known. He didn't know when, or if he'd ever return.

He twisted in the air, aiming southeast. The journey would take hours over the open seas, but at least he could rest in Tartarus for a few days before things became even more complicated.

"I'm coming for you, Gideon," Pelanor muttered aloud to the wind. He shook his head, a smirk tugging at his lips.

Mim, I'm talking to myself. Gideon really must've rubbed off on me.

"It's a long shot, but with the right allies and a bit of luck, I'm going to get you back."

Epilogue

The eve of the Litha Moon

Ama Hepha,

Please forgive the brevity of this message, but I am short on time and paper. I doubt youll receive this until after Ive left the relative safety of the Noktern. It has taken some convincing, but the Owls have finally agreed to my departure. In a few days, I will head off to Raven Rock to find Gideon, the young Finch you might recall from your forge.

There is so much more I wish I could tell you, but Kyte will fill you in on the missing details. The Owls have agreed that in his condition, its best if he returns home. I worry about his return to Zarpa. As good as they are, you know how cruel our people can be. They will look at his missing wing and..Ama, please look out for him. I just got him back and I feel Im going to lose him again.

With courage and honor,
Socorra

<u>Acknowledgments</u>

When I was ten years old, I picked up one of those old video game manuals and stumbled upon an advertisement that featured winged humans. There was a dove, a hawk, and a crow, each drawn in a beautifully campy anime style. I wish I could find it today so others could see my inspiration, but sadly, I haven't been able to track it down. Even still, something about that image sparked my imagination, and in that moment, an incredible world began to take shape in my mind. For years, I held onto that world, never believing I had the agency to bring it to life. I was convinced that someone else—some other writer—would tell its story.

Then, during the pandemic, locked away in my apartment and separated from my students, I decided to try. Writing became a refuge, a way to create something meaningful in uncertain times. And now, that long-held story has finally taken flight.

This book would not exist without the incredible support of so many people.

To my dear friend and personal editor, Emily, thank you for the countless hours you poured into helping me shape this story. From our endless phone calls dissecting every who, what, where, when, why, and how, to your major edits that refined my early drafts, this book carries your fingerprints in so many ways. Several characters may not have existed without your input, and for that, my readers and I can never truly repay you for all you've given me over the years.

To my mom, thank you for reading along, chapter

by chapter, and for offering your insights with the keen eye of an avid reader. You are the reason I love reading. Much like Gideon inherited in the story, you gifted me the power of imagination through hours of reading together. You put on silly voices and helped bring books to life. Your encouragement throughout the years has helped me deepen this world in ways I never could have alone.

To my friend, Steve, thank you for listening to me talk about this book nonstop, for sitting at the computer with me after every sentence, and for helping me refine its structure and story. Your patience and enthusiasm kept me going even when I doubted myself.

To my friend, Keith, despite not being much of a reader, you took the time to sit with me, read through the book in its various iterations, and offer insights that helped to further develop these characters. While we've weathered many hardships over the years, through it all, you've been one of my best friends and biggest supporters. Thank you for being a part of my life.

To my friend, Christina, thank you for providing me with enough wine and common sense to get me through the last couple of years while writing. Your deep talks have always meant so much to me, even if I didn't always listen to your advice. I've always looked forward to our 'Moaning Mondays,' and here's to many more! *Clink.* I am grateful for the educator, writer, and person that I have become for having you in my life.

To my brother and sisters, thank you for bravely tackling the roughest early version of this book and providing honest feedback that helped shape it into something stronger.

To all those readers who lent their time and perspectives—my colleague, Daniella; my friend, Mike;

and many more, who helped me polish this book into the best version it could be—thank you for your thoughtful feedback and encouragement.

To my wonderful artist, Alexandre, I cannot express the depth of my gratitude. When I received even the draft of the cover, I couldn't hold back tears. It was a moment I'll never forget, finally seeing my vision explode into being. The art is beautiful, and I look forward to working together on future projects.

And last, but certainly not least, to my students, both past and present. You have been with me every step of this journey, cheering me on, reading sample chapters, offering marketing and social media advice, and reminding me why storytelling matters. You have embraced my whacky style with open hearts, and I am forever grateful for you.

This book is not just mine, it belongs to all of you who believed in me. Thank you, from the bottom of my heart.

With courage and honor,

Monsieur Sean W. Bagan

www.ingramcontent.com/pod-product-compliance
Lightning Source LLC
Chambersburg PA
CBHW050508110726

47899CB00005B/1371